BIG CITY JACKS

Nick Oldham

This first world edition published in Great Britain 2005 by
SEVERN HOUSE PUBLISHERS LTD of
9–15 High Street, Sutton, Surrey SM1 1DF.
This first world edition published in the USA 2005 by
SEVERN HOUSE PUBLISHERS INC of
595 Madison Avenue, ⋯ ⋯ ⋯ 10022

Copyright © 2005 by N

British Library Catalog

Oldham, Nick, 1956
   Big city jacks
   1.   Christie, Hen
   2.   Police - Eng
   3.   Detective and
   I.   Title
   823.9'14 [F]

ISBN 0-7278-6159-X

Except where actual historical events and characters are being
described for the storyline of this novel, all situations in this
publication are fictitious and any resemblance to living persons
is purely coincidental.

Typeset by Palimpsest Book Production Ltd.,
Polmont, Stirlingshire, Scotland.
Printed and bound in Great Britain by
MPG Books Ltd., Bodmin, Cornwall.

BIG CITY JACKS

Recent Titles by Nick Oldham from Severn House

Inspector Henry Christie Mysteries

BACKLASH

SUBSTANTIAL THREAT

DEAD HEAT

Jack (sl); Detective; money – *Oxford Modern English Dictionary*

For Belinda

One

Keith Snell was on the run.

In the grand scheme of things, the £25K in wads of cocaine-tainted notes stuffed untidily into the cheap blue sports bag by the side of the bed was insignificant. But it was enough for someone to want him dead. It did not take a mastermind to work that one out. He had been given the chance, pretended to heed the warning, made all the right conciliatory noises, then blown it when faced with the cash. He could not bear to let go of it because he was greedy, poor and wanted it for himself.

As he lay there in the dank guest-house bedroom, he was sweating profusely, even though he was on top of the wire-framed bed, legs splayed, dressed only in grubby, once-white Y-fronts. The transom window was slightly open, allowing a chilly early morning breeze to waft through the curtains over his skin, but it did not help cool him down.

He laid the ice-cold barrel of the sawn-off shotgun across his chest. This made him shiver, but not from cold – from fear.

It was a side-by-side double-barrelled 12-bore, loaded, safety off. He kept his forefinger away from the triggers knowing they were extra-sensitive. He'd done the work on the trigger spring himself and did not want any accidents. He had taken the gun on the last two armed robberies he'd pulled, neither of which had gone to plan. From one he'd had to leg it empty-handed – bad planning – and from the other he'd got just short of four hundred quid (bad planning again: his information had been there was four grand for the taking) and had almost blown his foot off into the bargain.

He had not been a good armed robber, nor a particularly competent thief, not really having the necessary psychological make-up for either. That was why he hung up the shotgun and went into drugs. The robbery and thieving only paid for his habit anyway. His short-sighted strategy had been to offer his services to a dealer – which, he reckoned, would be a nice, easy way to keep close to the scene, get paid for being a gofer, and feed his addiction without putting himself in constant danger of being arrested seven days a week for being such a useless crim.

What he had not bargained for was his own greed.

He had started to come into regular contact with lots of cash and drugs.

At first he fought his inner demons, but it was a losing battle. In truth he should never have allowed himself to look into the packages he was entrusted to deliver. But he had.

It was the last one that had been his downfall.

Twenty-five thousand pounds. More money than he had ever seen or handled in his life. An amount that could change his life, he believed. Mere pocket money to the parasites he was working for, but to him it was a lottery win. The difference between living hand to mouth and the good life.

What he should have done with the package then was deliver it. Easy. If only he had not looked. If only he had not unzipped the bag, stuck his hand in like it was a tombola and drawn out a handful of cash prizes. But he had done, and then he was hooked by the sight, feel and rustle of bundles of notes. And instead of putting them back in and forgetting what he had seen, and going on to his destination, he had landed back at his flat – almost in a trance – and counted it. When his girlfriend came in, he recounted it in front of her.

Twenty-five thousand pounds. Exactly. Maybe drugs debts, maybe purchase money, he didn't have a clue. All he knew was that it was untraceable and it was in his possession.

Grace was his girlfriend's name. He loved her and she was his world. She was thin and bony, with self-inflicted tattoos on her knuckles and suicide scars on her wrists. She was as much of an addict as him. They shot up together regularly, sharing the warmth and tranquillity of a heroin trip between themselves. Yes, he loved Grace. She was his soul mate and normally he went along with her.

Not this time.

'Yeah, luvverly,' she said worriedly in her rasping, smoke-roughened voice, clearly unimpressed by the sight of the cash. Even though she was an addict and a thief – a very slick shoplifter – she could see the glaring error of her boyfriend's intentions. 'And now you've counted it, go and take it, every last note of it, to who it belongs to.'

'What?' he said in disbelief.

'You cannot even think about keeping it, Keith. No way. You know that, don't you?'

He stared blankly at her while she expertly did a roll-up and lit the thin stick of tobacco. She flicked her flaky hair off her forehead.

'Yeah, yeah, guess you're right.' He sighed wistfully.

'Keith,' she said firmly, not taken in by his response, 'you don't take that money where it belongs, they'll kill you.' She was scarily matter of fact. 'Or worse,' she added.

He re-zipped the sports bag with a heavy heart, thinking, 'One hundred quid, a ton, that's all I'll end up with.' He said nothing more to Grace and left the flat as though he had heeded her eminently sensible instructions.

Back on the street, his face turned into an angry snarl at the thought of the unfairness of it all.

The money, he decided, was now his.

Two days later, they found him and grabbed him. Obviously the word was out and everyone was looking for him. Fortunately he had stashed the cash safe and sound round at a mate's house.

When he came in front of them, they were remarkably reasonable about things. They did not attempt to break anything of his, such as his legs or head. Instead they cocked a listening and sympathetic ear to Keith's tale of woe and weakness and gave him the chance to go and retrieve the money, although they did warn him in no uncertain terms of the consequences of not having it all back to them within eight hours.

Foolishly, Keith perceived this as a failing on their part.

When they let him go in one piece he could not believe his luck. He had no intention of returning the money. Empty threats, he thought. They have no bottle this lot, he thought. All bark, no bite.

It was the condition in which he discovered Grace ten hours later that made him change his mind and plans.

She was in the council flat, lying on the kitchen floor in a pool of spreading blood. Her left forearm was twisted out at an obscene angle, the splintered and jagged end of a broken bone jutting out through the skin. She had been hammered remorselessly with baseball bats or iron sticks and when she had gone down, succumbed to the blows, they had kicked her and stomped on her, making a terrible mess of her frail body. She was conscious when Keith found her, blood-filled eyes fluttering but vacant. She rallied briefly and was able to whisper Keith's name and look sadly at him before closing her eyes and exhaling as though it was her final breath.

As much as Keith adored her in his own way, he wasn't going to hang around. It looked as though her attackers had only just gone, and could be back at any time. Keith was intelligent enough to make the connection to himself and he had no intention of again coming face to face with the people he had ripped off. He knew that he would not be so lucky as to walk away again. He had to run . . . and he had the money to do it with.

After collecting a hidden stash of heroin, he left the flat and sneaked nervously down shadow-laden stairwells, crept along needle-littered balconies and emerged unscathed on to the streets below.

Keith had never been so utterly terrified in his life before. He had gone a mile on foot before stopping at a piss-filled phone box and dialling treble nine for an ambulance for Grace. He refused the kind request to leave his name and contact number. At the end of the call, he hung up with a heavy feeling in the gut: he doubted that even the best paramedic in the world would be of much use to Grace now. At least he had tried, which was the main thing. He knew she would understand, wherever she was. He wiped a tear away and turned his mind to more pressing matters.

The retrieval of the money and some form of protection were the next priorities. Then he needed to get some breathing space so he could have time to work out exactly what he was going to do with his life and his newly acquired wealth. The only thing he knew for sure was he had to leave the city and never return. The streets of Manchester would never be a safe refuge for him again.

His friend, Colin the Commando, with whom he had stashed the cash, lived on a housing estate about three miles away.

The big, burning questions for Keith at that point were – how much did they know about him? Did they know of Colin, his mate? What, if anything, had Grace blabbed?

He was under no illusions. They would have tortured the poor cow. So Keith knew he had to work fast and put some real distance between him and them, keep a step ahead and get the hell out of the city.

Three miles on the hoof would take too long. He needed transport.

Keeping to the dark spaces, Keith spent several valuable minutes in search of a suitable motor.

He found an 'F' registered Ford Escort Fresco that fitted the bill nicely. It was the sort of car that could have been started with a spoon, but Keith used the screwdriver he always carried with him and jammed it into the ignition. Within a minute he was on the road, threading his way through the streets towards Colin's pad.

It was a nightmare journey for him, constantly believing he was being tailed. But he arrived intact and pulled up down the road from Colin's house, which was in a cul-de-sac. He remained in the car for a while, eyes peeled and watchful, his thin-walled heart pounding – for a change – a self-induced drug, adrenaline, through his veins. He pulled out the screwdriver and the engine died. Then he sat there a while longer in the darkened car, watching, waiting. Everything seemed fine. Colin's house looked normal, in as much as a house with a US army tank and a British army Land Rover parked in the front garden could be.

Eventually Keith climbed slowly out of the car, senses pinging with tension, and walked to the front door of the house. He knocked gently, head hunched down between his shoulders. From inside he could hear the sound of a battle raging. He knocked louder and tried the handle, but the door was locked. Annoyance got the better of him then and he hammered on the door until, suddenly, the sound of warfare stopped, the door was unlocked and opened.

In full World War Two battledress, the chubby yet diminutive figure of Keith's best friend, Colin the Commando, stared at him from under the rim of a tin hat.

'No need to knock so bloody loud!'

'Let me in.' Keith shoved past.

'I'm just watching *Saving Private Ryan*.' Colin locked the front door.

'Fancy that,' Keith said sarcastically. 'That sports bag I left you to look after? I need it.'

'Summat up?' Colin sensed his friend's tension.

'You could say that. Where is it?'

'You OK, pal? You look shell-shocked.'

Keith caught his breath with a stutter, momentarily realizing just how bad things were. 'I need the bag, man . . . OK?'

'OK, OK.' Colin saluted, then removed his helmet, revealing his totally bald head. 'Under the sink.' He led Keith through. 'So what's going on? You look like you've shat yourself.'

'You don't need to know, OK?'

'Whatever,' Colin shrugged. He placed his helmet down in a space between ration tins on the draining board, opened the cupboard below and pulled out the sports bag.

'You haven't looked in it, have you?'

Colin the tubby commando shifted uncomfortably. 'You told me not to, so I didn't,' he tried to blag it.

'Good.'

'What's in it?'

Keith opened his mouth, but his proposed little speech about what was and wasn't good for Colin to know was terminated before it began by a pounding on the front door. 'Shit,' he breathed. 'You expecting anyone other than Germans?'

Colin looked towards the front door, then at the ash-grey face of his friend from school days. 'No, I'm not . . . but you're in deep shit, aren't you?' he said perceptively.

'Yeah, look pal,' Keith said urgently, 'stall the bastards for me, will ya?'

'Colin? Colin Carruthers?' a harsh voice demanded through the letterbox. 'We need a word, matey.'

'You go out back and leg it . . . I'll sort these people out . . . go on, shoo, fuck off!' He urged Keith towards the back door.

6

'Thanks – you're a mate.'

'No sweat.' Colin saluted him again, then said grimly, 'I just hope that twenty-five big uns is worth it.'

The two friends exchanged knowing looks.

'Cunt – you peeked.'

'Yeah, now go,' Colin ordered him with a push, 'and thanks for bringing the heavies to my house.'

'No probs.' As Keith turned towards the back door, a chill of deep fear spread through him faster than Ebola as the voice through the letterbox shouted, 'Colin, we know you're in there. We can hear voices. Open up or we'll kick the fucking door down.' He yanked open the back door and ran into the obstacle course of discarded, rusting army machinery that littered Colin's garden.

Inside, Colin donned his tin hat again and went to the understairs cupboard. He pulled out a Thompson sub-machine gun, strapped the weapon over a shoulder and turned menacingly to the front door, which was now being kicked violently.

'OK, OK,' he shouted and flung open the door, stepping back into a threatening combat stance, Tommy gun at the hip, trained and ready to fire ... except it was empty. 'Right, you mothers,' he screamed, 'what the chuffin' hell do you want?'

There were two men there, hard-looking and eager – but when they saw the gun in Colin's hands, they stopped dead. Their own hands shot up and they backed off warily.

'Whoa ... hold it, pal,' the best-dressed one of the two said. 'Take a chill pill.'

'Why the fuck you tryina knock my door down?' snarled Colin.

Keith jumped and stumbled through Colin's garden, climbed through the broken fence into next door's less cluttered one, and started to run hard. He was not thinking now, just responding to the stimulus, getting as far away from danger as possible. And then his small brain kicked in and directed him back to the stolen Ford Escort parked down the road from Colin's pad. If he could just get back to it, sneak into it, get it going again ... that could put real distance between him and his pursuers.

He fell spectacularly through a hedge and found himself back on the cul-de-sac, only metres away from the car.

7

Ducking low, he crept round the back of it, down the side and slid into the driver's seat. He kept his head down at the level of the dashboard, one eye on the road, whilst he started to fiddle with the screwdriver. He jammed it back into the ignition and rived it round.

The engine whirred over, died.

Keith cursed desperately.

Down at the gate leading to Colin's house, he saw the dark figure of a man appear and stare in his direction. Keith's head bobbed down out of sight as he fiddled with the screwdriver again.

Once more the engine turned reluctantly. And died.

The man at the gate was peering with more interest towards him.

'Come on, come on,' Keith muttered.

There was a shout. The man at the gate took a few strides in Keith's direction.

He twisted the screwdriver desperately. This time the car started with a backfire and a plume of blue smoke. Ahead, the man stepped into the road and shouted again. He was joined by a second man who vaulted Colin's garden wall. Both then began to hurry towards the car.

Keith rammed it into gear and the old banger lurched.

In the glow of the fluorescent street light, Keith saw both men reach underneath their jackets. At first, his intention had been to mow them down, but as their hands came out with guns, he had an immediate change of heart and courage. He literally stood on the brake and found reverse gear. Within a second the Escort was slewing backwards, picking up speed, the engine and the gearbox screaming in unison as speed increased.

Keith's head swivelled backwards and forwards as he tried to keep an eye on his own rearwards progress and that of the two armed men who were now on their toes.

He saw one raise his gun. There was a crack and a hole appeared in the windscreen, then a whizz as the bullet almost creased his arm and embedded itself somewhere in the back of the car. They were firing at him!

Keith yanked the wheel down and the front of the car spun, tyres squealing. The back tyres smacked on the kerb. He heaved on the steering wheel, wishing he had stolen a car with power steering.

They were closing on him and he was presenting them with a nice wide target. Ducking low again, he forced the gear stick down into first and revved the nuts off the engine as the clutch connected it to the gearbox and, once more, the car did a good impression of a marsupial – bouncing like mad – until he regained control and, then – miraculously without stalling the beast – he raced away.

Behind him, both men came to a standstill, watching him disappear, their guns held down by their sides.

Keith watched them in the rear-view mirror.

'Bastards,' he said. He punched the air victoriously. Then he saw the bullet hole in the windscreen and his guts churned with a loud, slurping noise.

'What do we do?'

The men were panting, but not breathless. They slid their guns back into their waistband holsters and stood side by side in the middle of the road, watching their prey escape.

It was the older of the two who had asked the question.

The younger man glanced furtively up and down the street, noticing they were quickly becoming the centre of attention as one or two people emerged from their houses, drawn by the sound of gunfire and the screaming engine.

'We get out of here and we find him and we sort him – that's what we do.'

He was called Lynch. He was young and out to make an impression. He spun on his heels in the street, muttering, 'Even some of these low lifes might call the cops,' referring to the nosy householders, 'so we'd better get gone.'

Followed by the older man, whose name was Bignall, the two disappeared into the night like spectres.

'We nearly had him,' Bignall said as they got into their car parked three streets away. It was a dull-looking Rover 214, nothing special or memorable, just the right kind of transport for the city. The sort of vehicle that fitted in with any back-ground and could be left anywhere and probably not get stolen because it was such a boring car.

'Yeah, nearly,' agreed Lynch. He sat in the front passenger seat, next to Bignall who would be driving. His mind was working fast, going over the few snippets of gen that Colin the Commando had divulged in their very short, but fruitful and violent meeting. Lynch looked at his fist and winced at the grazed knuckles, where he had slightly mis-punched and caught Colin's tin hat instead of his face. It had hurt . . . but it had hurt Colin more.

Lynch sucked his knuckles thoughtfully. Bignall started the car and began to drive.

'Where to?'

Lynch checked his watch. 'You're due to start work soon, aren't you?'

'Yep – but I could call in sick.'

Lynch shook his head. 'No need for that. You drive round to your place and I'll keep the car. It's always better to go to work.'

Bignall squinted cautiously at Lynch. 'How about some dosh? I've been doing this most of the day with you.'

Lynch nodded and pulled out a fat roll of banknotes. He peeled five twenties off and dropped them into Bignall's greedy paw. As an afterthought he dropped him an extra twenty. 'Bonus for being so helpful.'

'Cheers . . . you're a real mate.' Bignall grinned widely at the unexpected windfall. This game was pretty worthwhile after all.

Lynch ran his hands over his short-cropped hair and smoothed down his sharp jacket, breathing out, getting comfortable, whilst he thought about the problem of Keith Snell. In some ways he was responsible for letting Snell off the hook in the first place and now he was charged with the responsibility of dealing with the issue. It was a task that meant a lot to Lynch, his make-or-break time. If he was successful it would do him no end of good, but if he ballsed it up he could say bye-bye to a lot of wealth and status. Dealing with Snell and retrieving the money was a route to the inner sanctum, to the lucrative lifestyle offered by the invincibles. But only if he got the money back.

They arrived at Bignall's flat. Lynch slid awkwardly across into the driving seat as Bignall got out. Bignall leaned back into the car.

'Want me to deal with the shooters?'

Lynch considered the question for a moment, chewing his bottom lip. It was unlikely he would need a gun again that evening, so it would be better not to have it with him. He handed the weapon over to Bignall and said, 'You know what to do?'

'I know.' Bignall slid the gun into his jacket pocket and slammed shut the car door, turned to walk away to his house.

Lynch wound his window down. 'Did you get the car number?' he called to Bignall's retreating back.

'Yeah . . . I'll sort it and let you know what the score is.'

Lynch drove away and headed towards Manchester city centre, his grazed knuckles throbbing painfully. 'Not good,' he said to himself, 'not good at all.'

Keith drove the old car hard, clouds of black and blue fumes pouring from the exhaust as he gunned the engine against its natural desire to rest. His watery eyes kept returning to the bullet hole in the windscreen. Shit, he thought, as it dawned on him for the first time that he had made a very serious error of judgement. He shivered involuntarily at what might have been had the bullet smacked him in the head. But never once did he consider returning the money. Now it was his and he refused to sacrifice the prospect of the new life he had set his heart on.

He drove recklessly across the city, constantly checking his mirrors to see if he was being tailed, finding himself descending the slip road on to the M60 Manchester ring road at Prestwich. How he had arrived there, he did not know. He was beginning to sweat and shake slightly . . . the first signs of a requirement for what he knew would be a heavy hit.

Only when he was on the motorway proper did his brain clear slightly and he realized where he was. He had been navigating on autopilot, no particular plan in mind, but as he gathered his senses he had an idea. He veered off the M60 and joined the M61, heading west.

'Blackpool!' he thought with a blinding flash of clarity, 'is the place for me.' It was the resort to which all runaways went and hid. He knew people there who might hide him, would give him some protection; it was a place he could catch his breath and make some real plans.

11

Cheered by the thought of the bright lights – he could have some fun there, too, and definitely score – he pushed the accelerator to the floor, noting for the first time he could actually see the road surface through a hole in the footwell.

'Bleedin' kids, joyridin' bastards,' snarled the owner of the car. 'I've had it nicked a few times, but it always turns up eventually. No doubt it'll get torched sometime.' His anger turned to resignation, the sad attitude of a repeat crime victim past caring. He was a big, unshaven man with a massive beer gut hanging over the waistband of his tracksuit bottoms, wearing a grubby vest and zip-up slippers. 'Bloody thing's droppin' t' pieces anyway.'

'How much is it worth?' the police officer taking the report inquired.

'Coupla 'undred, maybe less,' the man pouted thoughtfully. 'No great loss, just means I'm walkin' t' work tomorrow.'

'OK,' the officer said, 'let's get this right . . .' He checked his notes. 'Blue Ford Escort Fresco, registered number . . .' He reeled off the details to verify them, then said, 'OK, I'll get it circulated right away.'

'Whatever,' the owner shrugged.

The officer returned to his patrol car and settled in next to his shift partner who had not bothered to get out for such a mundane job. He radioed the details in and a communications operator took them down, circulated them locally, then forcewide across Manchester, then entered them on the Police National Computer. Having done this, the operator stood up, stretched and mouthed, 'Going for a pee,' to his colleague on the adjacent console.

He made his way to an empty office and picked up a phone.

'It's me.'

'Any news?'

'The car has just been reported stolen.'

'It is a legit report?'

'Yes.'

'Did you sort out the you-know-whats?'

'I did – they're safe and sound.'

'Good . . . keep me informed of any developments.'

*   *   *

12

By the time Keith Snell drove into Blackpool ninety minutes later, he was shivering and sweating and beginning to hallucinate. He needed something desperately – and he knew where he was going to get it. He came off the M55 at Marton Circle and drove down Blackpool's back roads on to Shoreside Estate.

After a couple of fruitless drive-arounds, he found the house he was searching for and pulled up outside. He heaved the money bag on to his shoulder and stumbled down the short pathway to the front door, smacking it loudly with the palm of his hand.

Inside he could hear the TV blaring out loudly, and voices.

Eventually the door opened. A teenage girl stood there in a skimpy T-shirt exposing a diamond-studded belly button and tight shorts. She was chewing and sneered at Keith. 'Yeah?'

'Troy? Is Troy here?' he gasped.

'Who wants to know?'

'I'm Keith Snell . . . he's a mate. I need to speak to him . . .'

A figure appeared behind the girl and barked, 'Fuck off out the way!'

'Troy . . . mate,' Keith wheezed as the man shouldered the young girl out of the way.

'What the hell are you doin' here?' There was suspicion in the voice.

'Man . . .' Keith extended his arms, palms outward. 'I need somewhere to doss, man, somewhere I can get my head together . . . and I really, really, need some shit.' The sports bag rolled off his shoulder and crashed to the ground, the zip bursting and revealing the shotgun resting on wads of cash.

It hit the spot with alacrity and immediately Keith started to feel mellow and warm, like he was sitting in front of a gas fire. It also pleased him he had not had to break into his own stash. He exhaled and relaxed for the first time in hours. His head lolled back and his mouth opened. 'Jesus . . . fuck . . .' he said slowly, then, 'Ahhh . . . this is good shit, man, real good.' Gently he extracted the hypodermic needle from the well-accessed vein at his elbow.

Troy Costain stood at the end of the bed and watched Keith shoot up, then experience the drug which Troy knew to be – as Keith had indeed verified – very good quality indeed.

'Nice one, man,' Keith said coolly, rolling back on to the bed and closing his eyes dreamily.

Troy had bundled Keith away from his house and into his own car after instructing one of his cousins to dump the stolen car in which his friend had turned up. Troy had driven the increasingly nervous, almost delirious man down to North Shore in Blackpool where he knew he could find some accommodation. Troy knew exactly where to go and within twenty minutes had escorted his friend into a very dubious bed-and-breakfast establishment not far from the back of the Imperial Hotel on the promenade.

He had provided Keith with another free sample, remaining with him whilst he mainlined it.

Troy knew this would loosen Keith's tongue. He was intrigued by the contents of the sports bag, particularly the money. It looked a substantial amount and his antenna had extended with interest.

He perched on the end of the bed as Keith continued to make orgasmic sounds whilst the drug permeated all points of his system. He watched with a sneer of disgust on his face. Troy dealt drugs, having recently gravitated from ecstasy to much more potent substances, but he did not use them himself. He was in the trade for profit, not for pain.

'How's it going?'

'Good . . . yeah,' breathed Keith. 'Like it.'

'Do you want to talk?' Costain suggested slyly.

'About what?'

'Why you're in sin city, why you called on me, and why I'm helping you.'

'No, no, it's right.'

'No it's not, Keith. You need to be speaking to me because I think you're going to need me, aren't you? I can put two and two together.' Troy's voice was soothing and cajoling at the same time.

The Costain family lived and operated from a large semi-detached council house on the Shoreside Estate in Blackpool.

They were numerous and claimed descendency from the Romanies and also had a stranglehold on the estate via their intimidatory tactics, burglary, thieving and now, through Troy, drug dealing. The youngsters in the family ran wild on the estate and two of them, Roy and Renata Costain, sixteen-year-old twin cousins of Troy, were being hounded by the cops, desperate to make the two little rascals subjects of Antisocial Behaviour Orders. It was to Roy that Troy had entrusted the dumping of the stolen Ford Escort.

Troy had given him specific instructions. 'Just get it off the estate, dump it, fire it, and nothing else, OK? Do not fuck around, just do what I say, OK?'

Roy could hardly keep a smile off his face. 'How much?'

'Tenner.'

'Oh – OK.' Roy extended his greedy, grubby paw.

When Troy disappeared with his spaced-out junkie friend, Keith, Roy got into the car and twisted the screwdriver. He drove away with glee and cruised the estate until he found Renata hanging out with a group of like-minded girls on a street corner. 'Get in,' he shouted. Without a moment's hesitation or one question, she was in the front passenger seat. Renata was the girl who had answered the door to Keith earlier.

'Spin time,' he said.

'Yes!' she responded, clenching her fists.

He stepped on the accelerator and skidded away from the kerb. 'Bit of a shit heap,' he observed, 'but it'll do.' He veered back across the kerb, mounted the footpath and gunned the decrepit vehicle half-on/half-off the footpath.

Renata screamed with hysterical laughter.

When Troy Costain left Keith, his friend had slipped into a deep slumber. Troy had waited until he was certain Keith was well gone before peeking into the sports bag and inspecting the contents. His heart skipped a beat or two at the sight of all that money and the deadly looking firearm.

Troy, however, touched nothing – despite his urge to gather all the dosh into his hands and disappear with it.

Instead, troubled by what he had seen and what Keith had told him, he backed quietly out of the room, wondering if he

15

could profit in any way from the knowledge he possessed. He walked slowly down the dingy, mouldy corridor of the guest house, his mind in turmoil, his loyalties being tested to the limit.

At four minutes past midnight Blackpool was buzzing with crowds of punters moving from pub to club, all watched over by the cynical eyes of a few pairs of patrolling police officers. One such pair found themselves parked on the promenade in the wide open space between the colourful entrance to Central pier and the tram tracks which ran north–south down the promenade.

For Blackpool it had been a fairly quiet evening, even though at the last count there were forty-two jobs outstanding on the log in the communications room. Most could wait, some needed attention, but even so, this duo of officers had told comms a lie (that they were busy) and had decided to chill out for a few minutes (by watching the ladies of the night tootle by).

Neither officer had been particularly motivated by their work that evening. Most of it had been boringly mundane and they were hoping that something interesting – and fun – might happen. A good fight, maybe; perhaps a sudden death or a good car crash. What they didn't realize was that they were about to get a combination of the latter two.

They had sat in silence watching the crazy world called Blackpool speed past their windscreen as they faced the traffic lights at the junction of the prom and New Bonny Street, quite close to the central police station.

Then both officers shot bolt upright in their seats as they simultaneously clocked the blue Ford Escort which had stopped at the red lights, then kangarooed through, heading north, when they changed to green.

Even from a distance of twenty-five metres and with the road lit only by street lights and the windows of the car reflecting the bright glare of Blackpool's myriad coloured lights, both men recognized the driver and passenger.

'The cocky little shits!' one said.

Their blue lights flicked on and the police car slotted in behind the Escort which, as expected, accelerated.

That 'something interesting' they had wished and hoped for was about to happen.

'Yes!' Triumphantly Roy Costain punched the air, looking over his shoulder, his eyes a-gleam with excitement. 'The plods are with us . . . hold on,' he warned Renata, who had a grim smile on her face, heart pounding with the rush of adrenaline. The chase was on and both of them loved it to bits.

Her right hand slid across to Roy's thigh and she jammed the edge of it up into his crotch.

Roy dragged the gear lever down into second and slammed his foot down on the gas pedal. The old car responded quite well, actually.

Behind them, the police siren came on in accompaniment to the blue lights.

'Stolen earlier tonight from the Greater Manchester area,' the comms operator informed the two officers on the tail of the Ford Escort in response to their PNC enquiry.

'Bingo!' the driver blurted.

'Doncha just lurv it when a plan comes together?' his mate said, rubbing his hands together. Into his radio he said calmly, 'We are behind this vehicle now, heading north along the prom, just gone past Talbot Square. It looks like he doesn't want to stop.'

'Roger that,' the operator said.

'We're taking up a following position,' the officer doing the radio said, very aware of the force pursuit policy.

The comms operator started to direct other patrols to the area.

Traffic was light on the promenade and it was easy for Roy to put his foot down in the battered Escort as there was nothing to get in his way. He was going to enjoy himself and then get into a position where he could ditch the car and leg it with Renata. He knew there was a good chance he would get locked up for it at some stage but that did not bother him unduly. In fact he rather liked getting arrested. It was great being obnoxious to the cops and there being nothing they could do about it. They even had to feed him!

17

He checked his rear-view mirror. The cop car was still behind, keeping his distance. Roy tutted with frustration. He also knew the force policy on chases and that he could lead them on a merry dance all over town without them even trying to ram him or stop him or box him in if he didn't look likely to endanger life. If he drove really recklessly they would back off and let him go, or maybe just follow him with the helicopter if it ever appeared.

'C'mon, put your foot down,' Renata encouraged him. She squeezed his thigh. 'If we outrun 'em, I'll give you a blow job,' she promised him.

That made him press even harder.

His plan was to do a scoot around the highways and byways of North Shore, then head back to Shoreside Estate, or nearby, and dump the car, then run.

'C'mon, c'mon!' she urged, tightening her grip.

'I'm doin' the best I can,' Roy rasped. 'It's bloody clapped-out, this thing.'

'So?'

The Escort hurtled along the promenade. Another police car swerved out of a side road and slotted in behind the first one.

'Seventy miles per hour now,' the officer riding shotgun in the first police car commented down his radio. 'No other traffic to worry about, though,' he added.

'Roger,' the comms operator acknowledged. 'Be careful. Oscar-November ninety-nine has been scrambled,' he said, meaning that the force helicopter had been turned out from its base at nearby Warton. 'Be with you in a few minutes.'

'Thanks for that.'

When they shot past the Imperial Hotel on North Shore, the speedo in the Escort was hovering somewhere in the region of 75mph. He knew that some very sharp braking and cute manoeuvring would be required for the roundabout at Gynn Square. In his mind's eye he was working out where he would position the car, how he would brake, which gears he would use. It must be said, though, that because of Renata's hand working excitedly away on the outside of his trousers, his brain was not 100 per cent focused on the driving.

Roy almost lost it on the roundabout, the car skittering sideways and the back end slewing wildly. Gripping the steering wheel for grim death, he managed to keep control, accelerated right around the hazard and back down Dickson Road, the two police cars on his tail.

Renata screamed delightedly.

By going along Dickson Road, Roy had changed his plan, as this road ran almost parallel to the promenade and back into Blackpool town centre. He had now decided to ditch the car in town, where he knew he and Renata would have a better chance of disappearing into the alleyways of the night.

There were actually more cars and pedestrians using Dickson Road than the promenade, all serving to slow down Roy's progress.

He weaved the car in and out and overtook a slow-moving taxi as he passed the rear of the Imperial Hotel and then shot right across the two mini-roundabouts and plunged down the slight gradient before hitting the town centre again.

The cop cars were still with him. He wondered if they had managed to get any other cops up ahead to roadblock him, but he doubted it. This chase was only really seconds old and he knew the cops wouldn't have yet been able to deploy too many officers to it.

Ahead of him was the old cinema now converted into Funny Girls, one of the country's leading nightclubs. The road here split into a one-way system. Roy squeezed the Escort between parked vehicles on his left and oncoming traffic, but he was going far too fast to make the almost 90-degree left-hand turn into Springfield Road, which was the one-way street looping round the nightclub.

'Christ!' he muttered and slammed on the brakes, wrenching the wheel down to the left.

Nothing happened. The car did not slow down. There was no pressure on the brake pedal.

'What?' cried Renata.

Roy held on grimly, pumping the pedal repeatedly.

Still nothing.

'Fuck!'

The Escort swerved and the back end came round. Roy found himself travelling broadside into the path of an oncoming black cab.

Renata screamed, realizing the car was totally out of control. It was not a scream of delight anymore.

Roy knew there was nothing he could do. He braced himself for the coming impact.

'Ooops, he's lost it,' one of the officers in the following police car stated coolly.

Both cops saw the Escort being driven at high speed towards the left-hand bend, realized it wasn't slowing down, saw the brake lights come on, saw it still wasn't slowing down, saw the car twist mid-road and start to skid sideways into the unsuspecting cab.

The taxi driver tried to veer away, but there was nowhere for him to go, nowhere to manoeuvre and in the end he just slammed on and held on for dear life.

The area of the stolen car which smashed into the front of the taxi was around the offside back door and rear wheel arch. Both cars became a tangle of scrunching metal. The Escort came off worst. It was old, rusty and past it; it disintegrated like a vampire being hit by a shaft of daylight.

The impact threw Roy hard against the driver's door, but somehow he managed to avoid banging his head against the window. He was stunned for a moment and was surprised to be still sitting on the driver's seat, hands holding the wheel. Next he was astounded he could open his door – which actually just dropped off its hinges and clattered to the ground – and he climbed out.

'Come on, let's fuck off!' he yelled.

It was only when he stopped to glance back at Renata that he saw she had not been quite so lucky.

Roy's shock at her bloody and smashed appearance was over in an instant when his self-preservation gene kicked in. Without a further backward glance, he ran, leaving her in the car.

He had a pretty good idea she was dead.

Two

Lynch leaned over the snooker table, lined up his cue and slammed the white ball into the pack of reds to break off the game. One red dropped luckily into a pocket and the white ball rolled into a potting position behind the blue. He sniggered at his good fortune and his opponent shook his head disparagingly.

As he lined up his next shot, his mobile phone rang. He cursed but answered it and listened intently before ending the call with a terse 'Been chased and dumped in Blackpool? Interesting.'

He stood up and bounced the thick end of his cue thoughtfully on the floor. 'Bloody Blackpool,' he muttered thoughtfully.

'Eh?' his opponent enquired.

'Nowt.' He dropped into position over the snooker table again, but once more his phone rang out. 'Shit . . . yeah?' he answered.

He walked across to the window and gazed down on to the street below the private club, a quiet Manchester street, close to the town centre.

'You're sure he's there? Right . . . right . . .' As he spoke and listened he became more and more agitated and excited. 'Leave it with me. He pressed the 'end call' button and re-dialled immediately. 'C'mon, c'mon,' he muttered. 'Biggars? It's me again . . . got a location this time . . . yeah, a grass . . . how are you fixed? Can you finish? Can you provide the necessary tools and equipment? Yeah, yeah . . . good, half an hour . . . I'll be there . . . you'll need a shooter, too, just in case . . . yeah, nice trip to the seaside . . . see ya.'

Lynch picked up his cue and walked back to the snooker

table, potted the blue, then a red, then laid the cue down across the green baize. 'Got to go.'

It was 3.32 a.m. when they found the guest house and parked the car in the street outside. Bignall had been driving. He killed the lights and engine and the two of them sat in the dark of the car, watching the front of the premises.

Nothing moved. The street was dead. Few lights were on in the buildings and in the one they were watching there was a dim light at one window on the top floor.

'He's in there,' Lynch said quietly.

Bignall nodded nervously.

'We do this right, it does us a lot of good.'

'I know.' Bignall's voice rasped dryly in his throat.

'You up for it?'

'Yeah.' Still rasping.

Lynch reached into the footwell and pulled up the sawn-off shotgun and revolver, handing the latter to his companion. The shotgun was double-barrelled. He snapped it open and loaded two cartridges in with sure, steady fingers, then clicked it shut, flicking the safety on. He knew how sensitive the trigger was. He rested the weapon across his lap and pulled on the stocking mask.

Bignall did the same.

It wasn't as though they were worried about Snell recognizing them, it was a defence against other witnesses. Just in case.

Keith Snell was awake. The mainlining of heroin had helped him to sleep deeply for a couple of blissful hours, but now he was very much eyes wide open, splayed out on the ropey bed, scratching and sweating, twitching nervously, the cold shotgun across his chest.

The chill breeze from the slightly open window made his skin goosebump.

From outside in the street below he heard a click, then another click.

Keith's heart lurched. He froze on the bed, his whole being tensing up, his senses razor-sharp. He did not really know why. There had been lots of noises outside. Blackpool rarely

22

slept. But somehow and for some reason, his gut instinct told him this was different.

He spun his legs off the bed and sat up, a puzzled, worried expression on his face. What made those noises so different? Two clicks . . . car doors closing quietly. Why hadn't they been closed noisily, with a bang? People in Blackpool did not close car doors softly, they didn't care about waking other people. It wasn't that sort of town.

Switching the low-wattage bedside light off, he gripped the shotgun and took two strides across to the bedroom window, flattening himself against the wall. Using the muzzle of the shotgun, he moved the curtain just wide enough to peek through the gap, down into the street.

Two dark figures moving silently and quickly down the pavement confirmed Snell's worst fears.

He was on the run and they had found him.

Vomit rising in his throat, he thought about how his supposedly good friend had betrayed him.

'Fuck you, Troy Costain,' he said under his breath.

The front door of the guest house was open. They went straight in, down the short hallway, then up the stairs on to the first floor, twisted back along the landing, then up the next set of stairs, which took them up to the top floor. They knew where they had been going, had been well briefed.

They came low on to the landing, now extremely cautious, knowing that Snell was armed.

Lynch put a finger to his lips.

Bignall nodded.

Both men took a couple of seconds to control their breathing. Then, wordlessly, Lynch mouthed a slow, 'One . . . two . . . three,' and they began to progress slowly along the landing, taking careful steps, attempting complete silence.

They knew which door opened into Snell's squalid room. They paused a couple of metres short of it. Lynch signalled for Bignall to go past the door – which he did with long strides and a shuffle – then both men were in position either side, their backs tight against the wall, weapons ready in their hands, Lynch with the shotgun held vertically and Bignall with the revolver in a two-handed grip, pointing it skywards.

The door was unlocked. They were told it would be.

Lynch reached for the handle, which he turned with agonizing slowness. Then, with a surge, he leapt into the room, brandishing the shotgun, legs spread, body hunched, and he accompanied his grand entrance with the scream of a banshee.

The scream died in his throat as he realized the room was empty. He uttered a stream of swear words and went to the wire-framed bed, heaving the soiled mattress off with his left hand, making certain that Snell wasn't hiding underneath.

He spun to Bignall. 'Bastard's legged it!'

Bignall actually looked relieved. His shoulders sagged and he breathed out.

'Musta seen us coming,' Lynch said. 'He won't be far away, c'mon. Here,' – he handed Bignall the shotgun and took the revolver off him, then pushed past his partner back into the dingy hallway at the exact same moment that a terrified Snell burst out from the cover of an alcove near to the top of the stairs.

Snell's courage to remain in that deep, dark recess had deserted him. He made a manic dash for freedom and loosed off one of the barrels of the shotgun in the general direction of his two hunters.

Both ducked instinctively, but Bignall emitted a loud howl of pain and staggered backwards, then dropped on to his backside.

Snell hit the stairs running.

Lynch lurched into a forward roll, the sound of the shotgun blast in the confines of the narrow hallway echoing disorientatingly in his ears. As he came up on to his feet, the revolver cocked and ready, Snell was halfway down to the next floor.

'I've been fuckin' hit!' screamed Bignall, his hand coming away from his shoulder dripping with blood.

Lynch didn't pause to see. His mind was concentrated on his quarry. He slammed his body against the wall at the top of the stairs, weapon held steady in both hands ready to fire, but Snell dived out of sight, raced along the landing and hurtled down the next set of stairs to take him down to ground level.

With a snort, Lynch hurled himself in pursuit, taking the stairs six at a time, steadying himself with the bannister as he landed hard and unsteadily. Using his lack of balance to aid momentum, he ran on and spun towards the next stairway just in time to see the fleeing figure of Snell heading towards the front door.

His face a hard mask of anger, Lynch threw himself down these stairs, aware that if Snell made it out through the front door and on to the street, he might as well say 'Adios' to him and the money. Lynch knew from experience that scrawny little thieves-cum-druggies could run like a hurricane when they had to. It was only when they knew they'd escaped did they stop and cough up their lungs. They could be very slippery bastards when necessary.

As Lynch landed in the ground-floor hallway, Snell had just snaked out through the front door.

For a nanosecond Lynch thought about taking a shot at him . . . but he held back. He was too far away to guarantee a hit.

Lynch ran, determined that Snell would not be going far.

In his time as a low-level crim, Keith Snell had been forced to outrun the law on many occasions and, more often than not, he had been successful. This was because he had learned one thing about being chased: never, ever hesitate. The trick was to keep going and hope for the best, because it didn't matter where you ran, it's just that you needed to keep on doing it.

Having said all that, he had never before been hunted down by someone with a gun and a grudge.

As he landed on the footpath outside the guest house, he gyrated on his heels and sprinted down the street, then cut out between a couple of parked cars to put some sort of barrier between himself and Lynch, then turned on the speed.

Each pound of a foot on the ground was matched by a similar one in his cranium, in his ears and behind his eyes. His whole head seemed to be loose.

He glanced over his shoulder. No one was there. He was approaching the end of the street. No pause. He ran across the junction, dimly aware of blue lights and police activity down the main road to his left, near the town centre. He pushed on in the direction of the sea, the blue sports bag on his back, bouncing and banging against his spine, his arms threaded through the straps, the shotgun in his right hand.

Another glance. Still clear.

Snell was finding it harder to catch his breath now, but he knew he had to keep going. He urged himself on, motivated by two men with guns, keeping to the darkness of the building line until he broke cover on the promenade, where he stopped . . . and almost toppled over.

But there was no time to think.

He veered right, heading north, now keenly aware that he was under the bright street lights of the sea-front. An easy target. He needed to return to the safety of darkness. He spun next right, back inland, now suffering, hardly able to keep going. At the first alleyway on the right he turned in and slumped down in the recess of a doorway. His breath came in painful rasps.

Had he done enough to save himself again?

Snell took a minute to calm down, easing his arms out of the straps on the sports bag, placing the shotgun carefully on the ground.

Eventually his body returned to almost normal. He stood up and stepped out of the doorway, bag in one hand, shotgun in the other.

Time to steal another car.

'Keith . . . Keith Snell!' Lynch's voice came ominously from behind.

Snell felt his whole body contract on those words.

'Drop the gun.'

It clattered from his fingers.

'And the bag.'

It landed with a dull thud.

Snell began to rotate slowly.

'No need to move, Keith my boy.'

'I'm sorry,' Snell gasped. 'I've been a fool.'

'Trouble is,' said Lynch, 'when you realize that, it's just too late. Well anyway, it's all over now. No more need to run.'

The way in which Lynch raised the revolver in his right hand, supported it in the palm of his left, and double-tapped two bullets into Keith Snell's back was almost casual.

Three

There was nothing special or remarkable about the murder, other than the fact that all murders are special and remarkable to those affected by them. A man and wife. A silly drunken row about nothing which escalated into violence and then a brutal stabbing. Just another something that happened every day that was impossible to prevent but easy to detect. In police terms, a 'one for one'.

The only thing about it was that tonight it happened in the sleepy backwater town of Bacup in the Rossendale Valley, tucked away high on the hills in the very eastern corner of the county of Lancashire. God's country, some say; others would be less enthusiastic about it.

Following the procedures laid down for such occurrences, the duty police inspector ensured that the scene of the crime was dealt with professionally, as well as the arrest of the offender, then informed the on-call Senior Investigating Officer (SIO), who, at the moment of the phone call, was playing a game of late-night chess with his eldest daughter, Jenny, whilst the rest of the family, mother and daughter number two, were tucked up in bed.

Instinctively, and before picking up the phone, the SIO – Henry Christie – checked the time and made a mental note of it. Times could end up being crucial to an investigation and several investigations that he knew of had rocked because of disputes over them.

Henry knew the call would be for him and a frisson of excitement tremored through his whole being. He cleared his throat, announced his name, then, 'Can I help?'

'Henry, sorry to bother you. This is John Catlow over in Pennine Division.'

'Hello, John.' Henry knew Catlow and also knew that he was the uniformed night duty inspector in the huge division which covered Bacup, but stretched from the Greater Manchester boundary in the east, right up to abut with North Yorkshire in the north. It was a big, sprawling area, one which used to be covered by an inspector in each of the towns therein. Now it was down to one poor soul. How times had changed. As night-call SIO, Henry had made it his business to know who was on duty throughout the force of Lancashire. 'What can I do for you?'

'We've got a domestic murder in Bacup . . . big drunken row, big falling out, wife stabs pissed-up husband to death . . . twelve times at least. It's pretty much sewn-up. She called the ambulance, they called us, we went and she gave herself up. Cut and dried, so to speak.'

'Is your on-call DI aware?'

'Yeah. He's turning out.'

'Where did it happen?'

'Moorside Terrace.'

Henry knew it. Visualized it. 'Is everything done that needs to be done?'

'Yes. Body's still in situ, scene sealed, CSI en-route, police doctor pronounced life extinct. Home Office pathologist informed and on the way. . .' It was as though the inspector was counting things off with his fingers. 'Offender banged up, clothing seized, forensic issues addressed – no cross-contamination anywhere . . . yep, all done.'

Even so, Henry made him go through it in more depth and when he was satisfied said, 'Right, I should be across there within the hour. I'll make to the scene and meet the DI there. Can you ensure he meets me, John?' The Inspector told Henry that the DI was actually at Burnley police station, where the offender had been taken. Henry accepted this and said he would see him there after the scene visit instead.

They hung up. Henry looked at his daughter. She tilted her pretty head and squinted quizzically at him.

'Dad?' she said. 'Don't you think it's a bit odd?'

'What's that, my dear?'

'Y'know – sitting around, waiting for people to pop their clogs?'

Henry pouted thoughtfully. 'Never really considered it in those terms.'

'Anyway,' she said, her expression changing to one of glee as she moved her Queen regally across the chessboard, dramatically wiping out Henry's remaining Bishop with a flourish. She announced, 'Checkmate!' very smugly.

Father and daughter faced each other over the board for a few silent moments.

'You've been toying with me,' Henry accused her.

'Yep – out-thought and outmanoeuvred,' she admitted, stood up and said, 'Bed for me.' As she walked past him, she patted him patronizingly on the head.

In terms of the county of Lancashire, Bacup and Blackpool – where Henry lived – could not be much further apart, but he arrived within the environs of the small Rossendale town in about fifty minutes without breaking the speed limit too many times.

Henry knew the area well, having spent a large proportion of his early police service in the east of the county. He had been on the Task Force prior to its abandonment in the early 1980s and in that time – those 'hallowed times' Henry called them – he had regularly worked the 'Crime Car' as it had been known, in that neck of the woods. He was very comfortable about finding his way around, ably assisted by a detailed street map.

Whilst driving across the county from the flatness of the Fylde coast up into the hilly region of the east, Henry reminisced a little about those days. A time when coppering had been a simple fun job, when a guy in uniform could do almost anything – and get away with it.

In some ways he missed it, but some of his memories made him cringe and wonder how the hell he'd survived some of the things he'd done.

Society had been very different then. The Toxteth riots and subsequent public enquiries had changed the face of policing forever.

But one thing that could never be changed was the popular music of that era, and on his late-night journey Henry allowed himself to wallow in some nostalgic rock of the time by sliding one of his 'sad old git' compilation tapes in and turning it up. He arrived in Bacup accompanied by Queen.

He found Moorside Terrace easily, parked up some distance away and got out of the car.

The cold hit him hard and immediately. A cold he had not felt for years. Half-past midnight in Bacup on a braw windy night was no place for the faint-hearted. He wrapped his coat tightly around him, pinned his ID to his chest and trudged towards the crime scene, hoping that most of the scientific work had been carried out by now. The house was slap-bang in the middle of a terraced row on a steep cobbled street which seemed to be holding on to the hillside by its fingertips.

The street was a buzz of activity. Staring, nosy people, and cops.

Every available officer in the division seemed to be hovering around. Probably all been to have a sneak peek at the body. A job like this was a magnet for the curious and it was often surprising how many cops turned up out of the woodwork. Henry prayed that the night-duty inspector had been telling the truth about scene preservation. Nothing fucked-up a crime scene better than a bunch of wanna-see bobbies in size elevens.

As it happened, the scene was well preserved. The only people who had trudged through it were the ones who'd had no choice: the paramedics, the first officers on scene, the CSIs and the Home Office pathologist who, as Henry poked his head around the kitchen door to have a look at the carnage, was just rising to his feet having examined the body which was still in situ.

The room was swathed in blood and the body itself lay pretty much in the centre of the floor, skewed at an awkward angle, limbs splayed to all points of the compass. Theatrically, Henry thought, the murder weapon was still sticking in the man's chest. It was a very big kitchen knife. Henry winced.

Backing off carefully, placing his feet with caution, the pathologist turned away from the body to be greeted by Henry's beaming smile.

'Hallo, H,' he said pleasantly, easing his hands out of his latex gloves.

'Dr Baines, I presume,' Henry responded. The two men

had known each other for many years and had established a friendly rapport which, on occasion, spilled beyond the professional and into drinking establishments. Baines was as thin as a post, with ears like car doors, but Henry knew his ability to imbibe was second to none. All the beer, Henry guessed, went straight to his legs. 'You're a bit off your patch, aren't you?' Henry asked. Baines covered the west of the county usually. 'Filling in for a colleague out collecting dead bodies, or something?'

'Something like that,' Baines replied as though hurt.

'OK, pleasantries over – what's the prognosis?'

Baines and Henry both turned their heads down and looked at the body on the kitchen floor. 'Not good. Not likely to recover. He's been stabbed to death, probably over a dozen times. The knife is in the heart at the moment, but any one of six other wounds could have been the fatal one. I'll know for sure when I carry out the PM.'

There was a blinding flash as a CSI moved in with his SLR to record the scene.

'As far as I'm concerned you can move the body to the public mortuary. I'll do the PM now and get it over with. No point trailing all the way home only to have to come back in the morning.'

'Good idea.'

He and Henry withdrew from the scene. After ensuring continuity of evidence regarding movement of the body – an officer had to accompany it to the morgue – Henry took his leave of Baines and headed back towards his car, thence on to Burnley custody office to take a look at the perpetrator of the foul deed.

It took about fifteen minutes to get there, travelling over the wild moors at Deerplay between the two towns and dropping down into Burnley. Henry spoke to the on-call DI on the way.

Burnley's custody office had been recently refurbished and this is where Henry met up with the local detective inspector. His name was Carradine, one of the old school who had adapted pretty well to the new ways of doing things. Henry had known him for many years. They had been together at the Police Training Centre at Bruche near Warrington, having joined the job at the same time. Carradine had originally been a member of Merseyside Police, but had transferred quite a few years before to Lancashire. The two had never been close friends, but were comfortable enough with each other. At least Henry thought they were.

'Hello, Barry.'

'Henry,' Carradine nodded curtly.

Henry picked up a strange tension in the DI's manner which he had not locked into during the phone call.

'Everything OK?'

'Yeah – shouldn't it be?'

'Er, yes,' Henry shrugged uncertainly.

'Wanna see the prisoner?'

'Yeah . . . yeah.'

'This way.' He beckoned Henry, calling out to the custody sergeant, 'Bernie, me and the temporary DCI are going down to the female side to have a glance at our murderess. Make a note on the custody record, please.'

'Whatever,' groaned the old-lag sergeant.

Henry and the DI walked down the corridor.

'She's drunk out of her skull,' Carradine explained. 'We've done a preliminary interview in the presence of a duty solicitor – authorized by the on-call super,' Carradine qualified; it was a very big no-no to interview drunken suspects unless particular circumstances prevailed and then it had to be signed off as necessary by a superintendent or higher rank. 'We didn't get much from her, to be honest. She got stripped and swabbed and banged up for a good sleep. It'll be the morning detectives who'll be sorting it.'

'Fine,' said Henry.

'Have I done all right?' Carradine asked sycophantically.

'Beg pardon?'

'I just want to know if I've done OK – sir.'

Henry stopped in his tracks and held Carradine back with a touch of his hand. 'What's eating you?'

Carradine eyed Henry through slitted lids. 'Nowt,' he lied very obviously and carried on walking. 'She's in here.'

Mmm, Henry thought, guessing that the earlier dig to the custody sergeant – the 'temporary DCI' business – could be the key to Carradine's less than enthusiastic welcome. Henry wondered if his continuing temporary promotion had ruffled feathers across the world of Lancashire detectives.

As per force standing orders, the cell door was open and the occupant, the murder suspect, was inside, now deep asleep; outside the cell a uniformed constable sat on an uncomfortable plastic chair, reading a magazine and – hopefully – keeping an eye on the prisoner. It was referred to as 'suicide watch' and was applied to all people arrested on suspicion of murder in Lancashire, people who often had their minds unhinged and were capable of doing themselves in. The officer engaged in this task – a policewoman – looked glazed with boredom.

'How's she doing?' Carradine asked her.

'Fine – flat out – no problems yet.'

The DI nodded. He and Henry glanced through the door into the poorly illuminated cell. The prisoner was stretched out on the concrete bench/bed, lying face up, mouth open, snoring. Her own clothes, taken for forensic examination, had been replaced by a paper suit about ten times too big for her. She looked a slight woman in her late twenties, hardly capable of brandishing and using the size of knife Henry had seen embedded in her husband's chest. However, he also knew what strength rage could bless on a person.

To the policewoman, Carradine said, 'OK, keep vigilant. Never trust anyone accused of murder.'

'Sure, boss,' she responded with surly lack of interest, settled back with her magazine and started to flick through the pages.

'Shall we talk it through?' Henry suggested to the DI.

Carradine nodded and led Henry back through the cell complex, out through the custody office and up into his own cubbyhole of an office on the first floor of the building. There was freshly filtered coffee on the side, smelling wonderful. Carradine poured out two mugs of the steaming black gold.

Easing himself into a chair, Henry took a sip, then, over the rim of the mug, got straight to the point. 'What's gnawing away at your bones, Barry?'

'What do you mean?' he replied innocently.

Henry's mouth twisted sardonically. He said nothing.

Carradine shrugged and kept up the pretence.

'I think you know – the attitude.'

33

Carradine manoeuvred himself to his desk chair and sat down on it. He swivelled slowly around, stopping at 360 degrees and considering Henry. 'All right,' he relented. 'You have severely pissed off a large number of detectives in this force by coming back from suspension and being given your sweet job back – and keeping your temporary promotion to boot! Quite a few people I know were chasing a job on the SIO team.'

'You being one of them?'

Carradine's narrow eyes seemed to hood over. 'I'd been made a promise.'

'By whom?'

'Can't say, but all I can tell you is that a lot of people think you've been given preferential treatment. Everyone knows you're right up the chief's arse. Pity there isn't a competence in brown-nosing.'

Henry bridled, feeling his whole body shimmer. He reddened angrily and shifted on the chair. It took a lot of self-control to keep himself from banging the mug down and rising both physically and metaphorically to the bait. Instead, he tried to remain unaffected and calm – except for the redness, which he could do nothing about.

'All I did was return to the job I left,' he explained.

Carradine shook his head slowly, in disbelief. 'Many, many people are not impressed,' he insisted, sticking to his guns.

Henry cracked a little then and blurted, 'In that case, a lot of people can go and fuck themselves.' He winced inwardly as soon as he'd said it; not a turn of phrase designed to get 'a lot of people' on his side. Huffily, he said, 'Shall we talk about the case in hand?'

Henry stumbled out of Burnley police station into the chill Pennine night. The briefing about the domestic murder had gone well, if a little coldly, after his and Carradine's exchange of views about Henry's predicament. As he slid back in the car, Henry grated his teeth and grimaced as he reviewed what the DI had said.

Henry had known that his return to work would be difficult. He had envisaged it many times in his mind. He knew that the detective fraternity was a close-knit but intensely competitive bunch of individuals who would have been eyeing his post up like salivating dogs – or a pack of hyenas – the stimulus being the SIO job and their response being their tawdry elbowing and kneeing to jockey themselves into position. Henry almost chuckled as he imagined the insistent lobbying and kow-towing that would have been going on whilst he was suspended.

Being a member of the SIO team was one of the plum detective jobs.

And Carradine had the audacity to accuse Henry of being up the chief constable's backside.

However, it was only to be expected. Henry had been suspended for allegations of disobeying a lawful order and displaying judgement that was, to say the least, suspect. The resulting disciplinary action had been dropped and Henry exonerated, but he was intelligent enough to know one thing about cops: when mud got slung, some of it always stuck, usually in big clods.

He now had the difficult task of proving that the allegations that had been made against him were unfounded, not to a disciplinary panel but to his peers. Far more difficult.

In some respects it would have been better to have returned to a less prominent role, somewhere out in the sticks, but he was actually glad to be doing what he was doing. He felt very suited to the SIO role. Only thing was, there would be many out there only too ready to take a pop at him, not least the detective chief superintendent in charge of the SIO team, who simply did not want Henry on the squad.

Henry knew he would have to be meticulous in his approach. He would have to work to the book and yet get results – quick. He had a very tattered reputation to repair and it would not be easy pulling the threads together.

This was his sixth week back at work and it was still early days. He had dealt with two other domestic murders successfully and had been given a fifteen-year-old cold case to review. A fair proportion of his time had been spent working on the job he had foolishly got himself involved with whilst on suspension – one of the reasons why the detective super did not want Henry back on the team, because he suspected Henry of telling lies. That case was ongoing and still generating more questions than answers. It would be a long, drawn-out process before the horrible mess was anything like sorted.

In the six weeks he had also drawn the short straw in terms of night cover, having had to cover three weeks in that time. Henry saw this as a less than subtle message from the boss: don't think for one moment you're going to have an easy ride of it.

Yes, Henry had no illusions. He would be up against it for a long time. In the past this could easily have fazed him, but now, being physically and mentally balanced, he was up for the challenge. He felt so confident he believed he could take on the world.

Before setting off home, he spent a few moments ticking off a mental checklist to ensure he had done everything necessary; then, positive he had hit all the buttons, he started the car.

The first call came on his mobile just as he accelerated down the slip road on to the M65. Using his recently acquired 'hands-free' kit, he kept both hands on the wheel and complied with the law. 'Henry Christie.'

'Dave Anger.'

'Hello, boss.' Henry had been expecting the call. The Detective Superintendent checking up on him. Yes, he was expecting it, but on the other hand he wondered who had informed Anger that he had turned out to a job. No doubt Anger had secretly briefed the control room inspector to call him if Henry was mobilized. Anger would be eager to keep a close eye on the disliked new boy . . . or was it that Henry was being paranoid?

Henry shrugged. Just because you are paranoid it doesn't mean that people aren't out to get you.

Anger skipped the pleasantries. 'What's the job?'

'As if you don't know,' Henry wanted to say – but didn't. 'Domestic murder.'

'Why haven't I been informed?'

'You obviously have been, otherwise you wouldn't be calling me,' Henry said, too sharply. 'Or are you just calling on spec?'

'Don't push it, Henry. You might well be up FB's shitter, but that doesn't mean to say you're untouchable,' Anger responded with a dangerous undertone. 'You haven't informed me, that's the point I'm making.'

'Only because it's a straight-up, no complications murder. All angles covered. One body, one offender – who is too drunk to be properly interviewed now. You don't need to be told. The morning would suffice.'

'Judgement call, eh?' Anger sneered. 'We all know about your judgement calls, don't we?'

'Procedural call, actually,' Henry corrected him.

'I like to be kept up to date.'

'OK, fair do's,' Henry acceded, seeing no mileage in annoying Anger any further. He'd made his point. 'I'll tell you in future.' He did not have the willpower to carry on an argument at that moment in time.

'So it's sorted?'

'Yes . . . I'll go back across in the morning. We'll have the offender in court by the afternoon.'

'OK, fine.' Anger hung up.

'Twat,' Henry uttered, feeling himself flush red. He took a deep breath and put his foot down. The motorway was quiet and, just to be awkward, he moved out to the fast lane and stayed there.

The second call he received on his mobile was totally unexpected. He received it as he looped round on to the M6 northbound. The display on the phone told him that the person calling had withheld their number. He assumed it would be control room contacting him with another death, perhaps, as all calls from police numbers were automatically withheld.

'Henry Christie.'

At first all he could hear was a hollow, metallic emptiness. He repeated his name.

'Hello . . . hello . . . Henry?' came the female voice he recognized instantly.

'Tara?'

'Henry – hi.'

He did a double-check of the time on the dashboard clock. 'Tara – hello.'

The connection seemed to break and then re-establish itself. He knew why it was a poor line. She was calling from Lanzarote.

Her name was Tara Wickson and it was because of a request from her that Henry had become involved in something whilst

37

suspended from duty. A little something, a favour that had ended up in a complex and murderous investigation into Mafia activity and connections across the world. Henry had foolishly become embroiled because he had been bored witless whilst on suspension, then the whole kit and caboodle had got completely out of hand. He could trace his involvement back to the fact that Tara was a very attractive and sexy woman, appealing full-on to Henry's main weakness in life: the female of the species.

After it was over, Tara and her daughter had gone away to help them recover from the trauma they had undergone.

'What's up?' Henry asked.

'I'm sorry to call. I half-expected your phone to be off . . . I was just wondering how things were going,' she said weakly.

Why at this time of day, Henry wondered. 'Oh, slowly,' he said. 'It's all very complicated. Another of my colleagues is actually dealing with it. I'm involved, obviously, but it's not my job, if you know what I mean?'

'Yeah, yeah.' She sounded distant. More than just in a geographical way.

'What's the matter, Tara? How are you?'

'OK – ish. Physically battered, as you know; mentally fucked up, feeling guilty.'

'Don't,' Henry counselled her quickly, firmly. 'There's a lot to get over, a lot to come to terms with, but you can do it. I have total faith in you.'

Once again, the line seemed to go dead. Then Tara's voice came back. 'No one has ever said they have faith in me,' she said tearfully.

This time it was Henry who hit the pause button. He gulped. 'How's Charlotte?'

'Bearing in mind what she went through, pretty good.'

'Nice to hear that.'

'Henry?' Tara's voice faltered. 'I'm really sorry to bother you . . . it's just that I can't stop thinking about you . . . and what you did for me.'

'Don't . . . it's OK,' he insisted.

'But I can't stop thinking about you . . . you put yourself out for me and you did something that has deeply affected

38

me . . . shit!' The line then did go dead, leaving Henry open-mouthed, hurtling along at ninety miles per hour, his mind not on the driving, and he almost missed the Blackpool exit off the M6. He could easily have landed in Lancaster, but he veered left just in time and gunned the car west towards the coast, wondering what the hell Tara had meant.

Was it that she had fallen for him?

Or was it that she'd been thinking about what Henry had actually done for her and she was now having mega problems in coming to terms with it?

The former thought was reasonably pleasant; the latter made him shudder, because if Tara bottled out, Henry would be finished for good. He could say 'ta-ra' to his pension and possibly 'g'day' to a prison cell.

The third call on his mobile was the one that kept him from hysteria. It was another job, this time much closer to home.

In some ways, Henry was relieved. This, too, looked as though it would be pretty straightforward to solve: stolen car, pursued by police, driver crashes and legs it, one dead passenger in the car. They knew who the felon was – local toe-rag, prolific offender – the only problem being tracking him down. Only a little problem, because people like Roy Costain are creatures of habit and sooner, rather than later, he would be caught. This would be an easy one to bottom, Henry thought as he surveyed the wreckage. The hard part here would be dealing with the media uproar that would be caused. Another fatality caused by a reckless police chase. Henry could visualize the headlines now.

Bugger, he thought.

He walked round the stolen Ford Escort, now mashed sideways on to the front end of a black cab. Stopping at the front passenger side window, Henry bent down and looked at the young girl, the body not yet having been removed from the scene.

Henry knew Renata, just as he knew Roy and the rest of the Costain family, which had a notorious and fearful reputation in Blackpool. He had encountered Renata a couple of times. Young though she was, she dallied on the periphery of the main activities of the Costains; bit of a shoplifter, bit of an assaulter on other girls, bit of an old-lady mugger. Her

future was pretty much mapped out: crime, unwanted preg-
nancies, abuse . . . probably. Who was Henry to say? Maybe
she would have turned her back on it all, become respectable.

Whatever, her death was a tragic waste. Henry hated it when
young people died.

Standing upright, he turned. Looking north up Dickson
Road he saw the figure of a man hurtle across the road as
though his life depended on it.

'Mr Christie?'

Henry's puzzlement about what he had seen was curtailed
by the appearance of the local road policing sergeant. But
before he could respond to the officer, another figure raced
across the road, as though in pursuit of the first one.

'Boss?'

Henry's attention twisted to the sergeant. 'Yep?'

'Can we get the body moved now?'

'I think so, yeah . . . I need to speak to the officers in the
vehicle which chased this one as soon as; but before that I'll
need to contact your divisional commander and my super.
Both will want to have a handle on this,' he said, ever so
slightly troubled by the image of the dark shapes running
across the road. Why he was affected, he could not really say.
Blackpool is Blackpool, he thought wryly, one of the weirdest
places on planet earth. He shrugged. Bollocks to it. He had
more on his plate to think about than two idiots running around
town in the early hours.

Renata's dead, but wide-open eyes seemed to catch his,
sending a shiver down his spine.

'We'll catch him, lass,' Henry said under his breath, 'but
you shouldn't have been here in the first place.'

As he walked back round the Escort, something in the glint
of the streetlights reflecting on the front windscreen made him
stop. He stopped, puzzled, eyebrows meshing together.

The sergeant, who had been standing next to him, saw the
hesitation.

'Summat up, boss?'

Henry tilted his head, peering at the windscreen. Above the
domed bulge made by the impact of Renata's head in the glass,
just on the edge of the screen, he had spotted something
unusual. 'What is that?' He pointed.

40

The sergeant followed the line of the pointed finger, then his own eyes widened. He stepped in for closer inspection.

'Well,' he drawled without too much commitment, 'I wouldn't stake my reputation on it, but I'd say it was a bullet hole.'

The close proximity of cops just down the road made Lynch uncomfortable. Justifiably so. After all, he had blasted someone to death in an alleyway not very far away from a dozen boys in blue.

After shooting Snell, he had dragged his body to one side, to lie in shadow, then returned to the guest house.

The police were very busy, dealing with what looked like a nasty accident. Blue lights, ambulances, the works. But Lynch, though uneasy, smirked: not half as nasty as the 'accident' in the dark alley behind the prom, prom, prom.

As he crossed back over Dickson Road, he was tense, but exhilarated.

He made it unscathed.

At the guest house, Bignall was lying in Snell's recently vacated room, bleeding from the wound to the upper arm inflicted by the fleeing thief. He had ripped a dirty bedsheet into strips, then bound the injury with it, afterwards slumping weakly on to the metal-framed bed, pale, dithering. Blood seeped through the grubby material like spilled ink on blotting paper. He attempted to sit up when Lynch returned, but did not have the strength.

'Not good,' the wounded man rasped. 'Not good at all.'

'You'll be right,' Lynch breezed without concern. 'Bloody body armour didn't do you much good, did it? Anyway – look! Success!' He held the blue sports bag aloft triumphantly. 'Got the dosh back.'

'Great.' Bignall winced with pain. 'I need a quack. I think I'm bleeding to death.'

'Rubbish,' sneered Lynch. 'I'll get you to one when we get back, OK?'

'Did you shoot him?'

'Right between the shoulder blades,' Lynch nodded. 'Went down like a sack of spuds.'

Bignall shuddered. He knew he was involved in a deadly game now, but just how ruthless and nasty it was, was only

41

just dawning on him as he lay there feeling strength ebb out of him. It had just spiralled out of control and suddenly he felt very foolish and vulnerable. Shit, shit, shit, his mind whirred. Get me out of this now.

'We need to get him back to Manchester.'

'Who?'

'Snell.'

'Why?'

Lynch looked despairingly at his wounded partner in crime. 'Control . . . it needs to be controlled and we can only do that if his body turns up within the environs of the city . . . yeah?'

'Fuck!' Bignall muttered. A searing pain radiated out from his arm. 'Hell!' he grimaced, gritting his teeth.

'And there's no way on God's earth that you can see a doctor around here, mate. That needs controlling, too. Fancy getting bloody shot!'

'Yeah, fancy. Just what I wanted. How the hell am I going to explain this away?'

'We'll think of something.' Lynch's nostrils flared as his mind cogitated. 'Let's get Snell-boy sorted first.'

Henry took a great deal of wicked pleasure in telephoning Detective Superintendent Dave Anger. He left it until the last possible moment when he thought he could get away with it . . . then rang him.

It was five thirty a.m.

He had waited at the scene of the accident after Renata's dead body had been removed to the mortuary and then until the local rota garage had turned up to remove both cars. He watched the vehicles being pulled apart with an ugly-sounding tearing of metal, then winched into place on the back of the recovery truck. He knew the garage had a secure compound in which the cars would be stored. He instructed the recovery driver to ensure that no one, other than himself and crime scene investigators, had access to the cars. Henry wanted to see if a bullet could be dug out of the stolen Escort.

He phoned Anger as the fully loaded recovery vehicle was driving away. It was a very satisfying moment to hear the sleep-jumbled voice at the other end of the line.

Just following orders.

Well in that case, Mr Anger, I'll follow them to the letter, Henry thought.

His smile was warped as the conversation ended and Henry folded up his mobile phone.

'Right,' he then said to himself, suddenly feeling a chill from the Irish Sea. 'Let's go and knock on a door.'

Lynch and Bignall drove across the breadth of Lancashire and back into the Greater Manchester area without incident. Both men were at cracking point on the journey, not surprising as the dead body of Keith Snell, low-level low life, was folded up neatly inside the boot of their motor, covered by an oily blanket. One pull by a curious cop, one pull by a cop who wasn't impressed by their credentials, would have ended the game for them there and then. Such a cop would have found a murder victim, the best part of £25,000, an injured passenger, a revolver and a shotgun. It would have made the cop's career.

But their journey was uninterrupted and no cops were even spotted.

Lynch, at the wheel, mumbled angrily to himself for much of the way. He was annoyed at having to heave Snell's body into the boot of the car with no assistance from his partner, who claimed that his injury prevented him from doing anything other than sitting there like a spare part, or as Lynch said, 'Spare prat.'

As spindly and light as Snell might have been, he still seemed to weigh a dead ton. Manoeuvring, dragging and heaving him into the car required a lot of effort and more time than Lynch would have liked to spend on the job.

He was sweaty and panting when he finished and did not let up on reminding Bignall that he was a 'soft, lazy, mardy-arsed twat' for most of the journey.

Wounded, hurting badly, pain increasing all the time, Bignall did not care. All he wanted was a doctor and some drugs.

Lynch drove the full length of the M55, turned south on to the M6, then bore left towards Manchester on the M61. At the first junction he left that motorway and headed down to the M65, making Bignall stir from his torpor.

'Where we going?'

'We need to dispose of our chum in the back, don't we? We're not gonna take him home with us, are we?'

Bignall groaned. 'OK, OK.'

'I know just the place,' Lynch declared.

'But you're driving into Lancashire,' Bignall said, protesting mildly.

'Yeah, but I'm gonna drive into Manchester another way . . . to somewhere quiet where we can dump him and then set fire to the fucker . . . I know just the place . . . Deeply Vale . . . peace guaranteed . . . which reminds me . . . need to get some petrol . . .'

Bignall slumped down, now in agony. It was as though electrodes were being applied to him with shots of a million volts. He swore, felt weak . . . and passed out.

Lynch shook his head with annoyance. Bignall was turning into a liability now. He sped quickly down the M65, exited at junction 8 and headed across the moors to the Rossendale Valley along the A56, a good fast dual carriageway taking him high above the old mill town of Accrington and towards Bury, which was back in Greater Manchester. Rain began lashing down as the car descended into Rossendale, driving as hard as the car, and also annoying Lynch.

Before the A56 merged to become the M66 – a motorway which speared into the heart of Manchester – Lynch came off and drove towards Bury.

He was back on home turf. Disposing of the body and dealing with the aftermath would now be a simple matter.

Lynch relaxed. Control had reverted to him.

Four

Henry Christie knew a large number of criminals. He had been a cop over twenty-five years and had worked right across the county of Lancashire, east, west, north and south, though the majority of his latter service had been on the Fylde coast around Blackpool or at headquarters in various departments. Over that time he had come to know and deal with petty thieves and drug barons, drunks and murderers. He had put many of them away, never having tired of the process, nor the feeling of elation to see a bad guy get his come-uppance.

He had known the Costain family who lived on the Shoreside Estate in Blackpool for many years. They had been a thorn in the side of the police ever since they had landed from God knew where in the sixties and taken up residence. They were born troublemakers and law breakers and had established themselves as burglars, handlers of stolen property, loan sharks and protection racketeers, and, as Henry knew, more recently as drug dealers.

They were never an easy family to deal with. He did not know of one occasion when the police hadn't been given a rough ride by them – even when one of the Costain brothers had been murdered and Henry had solved the case. They still hated Henry with a vengeance because they were unable to make themselves see the police as anything other than the enemy.

Not that Henry gave a stuff. A jousting match with the Costain clan was always a bit of a wheeze . . . and he always had an ace up his sleeve when dealing with them.

Driving on to the Shoreside Estate brought back myriad memories for Henry, some minor, some major – such as the racially fuelled riot (caused by the Costains) he had once quelled; he drove on past a row of derelict shops, all now burnt out and dilapidated, never to be resurrected. The local hooligans had systematically destroyed them and all the shop-keepers had been driven off the estate, ensuring that law-abiding residents no longer had local services. It was now a car or bus journey to the local supermarket, though even the bus service to the estate had been severely curtailed. Too many drivers had been attacked and injured, too many buses had been trashed.

Some people on the estate seemed intent on making it even more depraved than ever. Its future, Henry thought, was bleak.

Even cops had to tread carefully. It wasn't quite a no-go zone, but it wasn't far off.

45

If the millions of tourists who poured annually into the resort only knew about the crime-ridden, poverty-stricken hinterland just behind the tacky, money-driven seafront, Henry thought . . . then smirked . . . they wouldn't give a monkey's.

He drove slowly along a debris-strewn avenue, no street-lights working (all smashed), and pulled to a halt behind another car. The occupant of this one climbed out and walked back to Henry, who lowered his window. It was the on-call detective sergeant, Rik Dean.

'Hi, boss,' said the tired-looking sergeant, groggy from recent sleep.

'Rik,' Henry acknowledged him. He knew Dean well, had been instrumental in getting him on to CID in the first place. Dean was a good thief-taker, had an instinct second to none. 'You know the score, pal?'

Dean nodded. 'How are we going to handle it?'

Henry rubbed his fatigued face. It felt leathery and harsh. 'Well, the Costains are never easy. How the hell they're going to react to the knowledge that Renata's dead and Roy killed her, I dunno.'

'Blame the cops?' Dean suggested.

'Mmm, quite possibly.' Henry's mouth turned down at the corners. 'Always a good option.'

'Shall we go in one car?'

Henry shook his head. 'Take both. If we leave one here it's more than likely to be a wheel-less shell when we get back.' Henry's personal radio squawked into life. He answered it. 'Yeah – receiving, go ahead.'

'Van in position, four on board.' It was the voice of the uniformed police sergeant who had been at the crash scene with him earlier.

Henry 'rogered' that and smiled slyly at Rik Dean. 'Bit of insurance, just in case the family from hell kick off.'

The two detectives got back into their cars and drove around the corner up to the Costain household, passing a big police van on the way, parked up out of sight and as discreetly as possible – bearing in mind it was big, blue and in your face.

Several lights burned at the house. It was a twenty-four-hour dwelling. The only time there was much of a lull in the activity was around breakfast time, as the Costains tended to sleep in when most other people were getting up. A bit like shift workers.

It is fairly true to say that most crimes committed in a town are done by a small minority of people, the repeat offenders, the skilled burglars, the car thieves. Henry thought that if the government gave the go ahead for a crim-culling process across the country, by eliminating a couple of thousand felons, the crime figures would probably be reduced by about two-thirds. He knew that if this cull was applied to selected members of the Costain family, the crime rate in the resort of Blackpool would plummet to around zero.

Wishful thinking.

He and Rik Dean walked up to the front door and knocked. Henry speculated as to which combination of Costains was presently residing herein. The family had a tendency to be fluid about living arrangements, but he knew this was their main house, the one presided over by old man and old woman Costain, the house through which most of the extended family passed or stayed at one time or another. Henry was fairly certain that Roy and Renata lived here at the moment.

Music and speech could be heard through the door – a hi-fi and TV on in different parts of the house.

Henry rapped on the door again. The music level reduced a couple of decibels. Someone was coming to the door. Henry braced himself, ID at the ready, foot prepared to jam down into the opening and wedge the door if necessary.

A smile spread wide across Henry's face when he saw that the person opening up was Troy Costain. The smile was only fleeting and morphed into Henry's best funereal and serious expression.

'What?' Troy asked cautiously. He knew Henry very well and did not trust him. He was forking Pot Noodle into his mouth from a tub in his hand. It smelled awful, looked awful and sounded awful.

Henry sensed Troy's tension. It made him feel good. He liked to keep these people on the back foot.

'Troy, mate, I need to come in and speak.'

'I don't think so,' Troy sneered. 'Cops don't walk into this house without warrants.'

Henry stifled a chortle. He was always amused by the wide-

47

spread misconception held by most members of the criminal fraternity, even the ones who purported to know the law, that the police only had the power to enter premises brandishing a warrant. Henry could rhyme off at least a dozen powers under which a cop could lawfully bundle into someone's house and cause havoc.

'Troy,' Henry began patiently. 'Mate, let me and my fellow officer in. You are not in trouble, but you and your mum and dad need to know something, something about Roy and Renata.'

Troy seemed to relax slightly. 'Mum and Dad are in Spain.'

'Who's in charge, then?' Henry asked, aware that no one was ever really in charge of this house. Theirs was a world of anarchy.

'Me,' Troy boasted.

'The family's in safe hands, then,' Henry guffawed. 'Let me in, then, Mr Responsible Adult. This is serious stuff.'

Troy and Henry had a little eyeball-to-eyeball competition then, just for a few moments until Troy relented and looked away.

'OK, what have the little shits been up to . . . ?' Troy's words stopped suddenly. He and Henry had a lot of history between them, as well as a lot of up-to-date dealings, so Troy knew Henry's status in the police. 'You still an SIO?' he asked Henry, who nodded. Troy gulped. 'So what *have* they been up to?'

'Let me come in and I'll explain.'

Keith Snell took a long time to catch fire. Lynch doused him thoroughly with petrol from a plastic can he had just bought from a twenty-four-hour service station. He flicked a lighted match on the dead body he'd had to drag out of the boot. The trousers ignited quite well, but for some reason the upper part of the body did not get going. The two extra matches he threw down extinguished themselves before they even touched the body.

'Fucking weather,' Lynch cursed and added more fuel.. He almost set himself alight as he splashed more and more petrol around.

Even then, Keith Snell did not burn well.

'Too fucking riddled with drugs,' Lynch muttered, flinging match after match at the body which refused to burn. 'Come on you wiry bastard.'

Flames flickered uncertainly, then there was a restrained whoosh and they began to lick Snell: lick, burn and take hold.

'Thank fuck for that.' Lynch turned and trudged back to the car in which Bignall was ensconced, the agony of the gunshot wound increasing incessantly as he faded in and out of consciousness.

The knock on the door had roused various members of the clan from all points of the household and several faces showed themselves, none friendly. Henry's ears caught a few under-the-breath obscenities. He decided to ignore them. Troy led the two detectives into the living room, adorned gypsy fashion with horse brasses, intricate ornaments, figurines and a lot of sepia photographs of distant relatives. The Costains claimed a line back to Romany gypsies, but Henry had to be convinced. He thought it was just a clever ploy to use when they got discriminated against, which was quite often.

In the lounge, a teenage girl was splayed out on the deep, black leather settee, dressed in a micro-nightie and nothing else. She left the room unwillingly when Troy jerked his thumb at her. She flounced out, offended, displaying what Henry could only describe as a 'pert little bottom'.

'Sit,' Troy said generously with an open wave of his hand.

'You too, Troy,' Henry said, easing down into an armchair.

'OK – fire away,' yawned Troy, scratching his head with his fork, then plunging it back into the Pot Noodle. Rik Dean's disgusted face said it all. 'What've they done? Murdered somebody?'

'No . . . they were in a stolen car, a Ford Escort, nicked earlier from Manchester,' Henry explained, seeing Troy tighten up ever so slightly. Henry had built a career on responding to body language and he immediately knew that Troy was not surprised by this news. He had interacted with Troy many times over the years and felt he particularly knew Troy's non-verbals. He could tell that he knew something about the stolen car. He paused.

'And . . . ?' said Troy.

'There was a chase and an accident, I'm afraid.' Troy's face drained to the grey colour of the noodles he was devouring. 'We think Roy is OK. He legged it from the scene.' Again, Henry paused. Delivering a death message was never easy, even when there was no real sympathy. He had been doing it since the age of nineteen and it never got easier. 'I'm afraid Renata did not make it. She was killed in the collision. She is dead.' Henry said the words forcefully because he had learned that people had to be told that a person was dead. Not passed away. Not lost. Not gone to a better place. Not couched in any other term but dead. Otherwise the recipients often hung on to this in the hope that they were being told something different. They had to be told it unambiguously.

'In a collision with a cop car?'

'No – a taxi.'

'So the cops were chasing them and now Renata's dead!'

'They were in a stolen car,' Rik Dean interjected quickly, bristling.

'And the cops killed her,' Troy said fiercely, brandishing his tub of Pot Noodle.

'This is a mess.' The mahogany-coloured Nigerian doctor examined the wound in Bignall's upper arm. 'He needs surgery.'

Pacing up and down behind him, Lynch spun ferociously. 'I didn't bring him here for you to tell me that. You're on the payroll, get him fixed the best you can.'

Bignall, in a haze of disorientation, was in no position to make any sort of contribution to the debate. He did not know where he was, what was going on, who the hell these people were . . . nothing. All he knew was pain and sickness. He wanted to die.

'He needs blood . . . he's lost a lot . . . he needs to be on an operating table . . . I think he could be bleeding internally,' the doctor said. 'I can give him something for the pain. I can bandage it up, but he needs a surgeon to look at this.'

'You do it.'

'What with – a knife and fork? I have no facilities, don't you see?' he pleaded.

'Sort him,' Lynch said brutally. 'Patch him up, drug him

up . . .' He relented a little. 'Then let's think about getting him operated on.'

The doctor paused thoughtfully, then, in a caring way which transgressed his hypocritical oath by 100 per cent, he said, 'It'll cost a grand.'

'Then you'd better do a bloody good job, hadn't you?'

Henry had been in this position before. Right in the middle of a grieving Costain family, with lots of wailing, moaning, shouting, cursing and gnashing.

On hearing the news about Renata, even more family members seemed to appear out of the woodwork. Where they had all been previously secreted mystified Henry. He had once been on safari in Kenya with Kate in the pre-child days (following a massive paycheck during the 1984 miners' strike) and their tour bus had got stuck in mud in the middle of nowhere. There had not been a soul in sight, just vast plains of emptiness and wild animals. But within minutes the bus was surrounded by kids and adults, all eager to assist for a small consideration. Henry had been astounded and it was rather like that with the Costains. They just appeared from nowhere. He could only guess at what the sleeping arrangements were.

Eight people of varying age ranges were now in the brass-adorned living room.

And they were moving en masse to an ugly mood.

Henry knew it was time to beat a hasty retreat, otherwise there would be trouble. But even there and then, his mind was thinking of the future. The Costains were past masters at whipping up frenzied mobs on the estate and he could already envisage anti-police problems arising unless some pretty swift action was taken with the press and the community.

The community beat bobbies were going to have their work cut out for a few days, he guessed.

But in the here and now, he and Rik Dean needed to get out, preferably with Troy in tow, because they needed him to formally identify Renata's body.

Henry was attempting to get through to him. The Pot Noodle had been smashed angrily against a wall, the contents slithering down it. Troy was doing some classic ranting and raving, which did not actually quite ring true with Henry. There was something slightly suspect about the whole display.

'Troy . . . *Troy!*' Henry shouted above the collective din. 'You have to come with us, OK, pal?' Henry played the sympathetic cop. Hand on shoulder. Sad expression. 'We need you, pal . . . c'mon, we have to do this.'

Troy slumped into an armchair, head dropping into hands, sobbing, 'I know, I know . . . I loved the girl, she was fantastic . . .'

'Yeah, I know she was. Look, I'm really sorry, but we have to get this thing done. You know that.'

'I know!' he bawled, wiping his eyes. He rose to his feet unsteadily, trying to regain control of himself, his chest heaving.

'Good man.'

Troy shoved past Henry. 'I need a coat.'

Henry and Rik Dean stood in the middle of the living room, surrounded by other members of the family. The detectives eyed each other uncertainly, wishing they were out of there. They were encircled by hostility which could easily flip over into violence.

'Bastard cops,' one hissed: a six- or seven-year-old lad in raggy pyjamas.

'Twats,' said an older one.

The scantily clad female teenager sent from the room earlier was with them, still so dressed. She looked coyly at Henry and raised the hem of her nightie.

To Henry's relief, the temporary head of the household reappeared. 'I'm ready,' he sniffed. Henry eased past him out of the room and took the opportunity to whisper, 'Keep it up,' into his ear.

Blood seeped through the bandages, blossoming like some sort of flower. Bignall struggled to maintain consciousness and compos mentis.

Lynch knew this could be big trouble and he was in two minds about what he should do for the best.

He had a horrible feeling that Bignall would die if he was returned home, so he decided to do the decent thing. He drove through to the A&E unit at North Manchester General Hospital in Crumpsall, leaned across to open the passenger door and rolled Bignall out.

'Best o' luck, pal,' he muttered and drove away quickly.

Five

Phil Whitlock's journey had taken him across the breadth of Europe and back again. As far as Greece, then returning through Italy, France and finally up into Belgium to the port of Zeebrugge prior to the trip across the water and back home via Hull. All in all it had been a smooth passage with the usual and expected red tape and bureaucracy which Whitlock was accustomed to. He accepted it with equanimity, an inconvenient facet to his job as a long-distance lorry driver.

The company which employed him, based in the north-west of England, were respected international hauliers with a sound, profitable business. No part of Whitlock's journey had been undertaken without a container load of goods. From the UK he had delivered his first container – washing-machine parts – to a warehouse on the outskirts of Paris. At another depot he picked up a load of bonded cigarettes (millions of the fuckers, he thought – the cancer express) and delivered them to Milan. From there, with a load of hardware-type goods, he had driven down to Athens, dumped them, then virtually retraced his journey. He had dropped off a final consignment of medical sundries in Brussels and, very unusually, had nothing further to pick up. He contacted his firm who instructed him to return home empty, but could he be ready for a further trip in three days?

Yesiree. He loved the job. He was proud to be a knight of the road. He enjoyed meeting people, passing through different cultures. It was wonderful. He had been doing it for twenty years. It's what kept his marriage together, he often joked.

The weather on the Belgian coast was horrific, gales and

high seas preventing sailings across to England. All crossings were cancelled and rescheduled and Whitlock was informed by the port authorities that the soonest he could expect to get across would be eleven a.m. next day.

It was six p.m. He had a night and a morning to kill.

Best take full advantage of it, he thought.

Whitlock had spent a lot of time in Zeebrugge over the years. He knew it well, where to eat and drink, where to find a clean prostitute, where to be entertained and where to get his head down, other than in his cab. Although he would rather have been on the ferry, he was content to while away the time in bars and finally a club where he knew he could get laid.

He'd had too much to drink, the excellent Belgian lager slipping down nicely, followed by an Italian meal, then more beer. He was slumped in a club by eleven p.m., wondering whether he was capable of sexual intercourse at all. The beer was making him belch.

The dark figure at the bar beside him was only a hazy spectre really. Whitlock was in his own world, one with few cares. The man was sitting on a bar stool, his back to the bar, elbows propping him up as he watched a lurid floorshow.

He turned back to the bar, shaking his head, smiling, catching Whitlock's very watery, bloodshot ones.

'I would not have thought that possible,' he said to Whitlock whilst sipping what looked suspiciously like a glass of water.

'Wha—?' Whitlock slobbered.

'Her – that girl.' The man indicated the raised stage on which a naked female was dancing.

'Yeah, whatever.' Whitlock turned to watch the show for a few moments.

'You're a driver, aren't you?'

'Yep,' Whitlock said. It never crossed his mind to ask how the man knew this.

'Bad weather, eh?'

'Shockin' . . . can't get over.'

The man looked him square on. 'How would you like to make some extra money? A nice, fat bonus?'

Part of Whitlock's bonus included a three-in-a-bed romp with two of the most attractive prostitutes he had ever seen. They were experienced girls (though later, when he reflected, he would describe them as 'slappers') and gave him the full works, which, had he not been so inebriated, he would have appreciated more.

They left him after an hour's work.

He fell straight to sleep, snoring loudly in the tiny room above the club.

The man he had met at the bar, the one who had offered him a bonus, walked into the room and surveyed the naked driver. He shook his head, then lifted the camera and finished off the roll of film. The flash did not have any effect on Whitlock at all and he did not stir.

'I don't think I want to do this,' Whitlock said. His head seemed to be a raging furnace and every time he moved, even slightly, pain creased the back of his eyeballs. It was a bad hangover, maybe the worst he'd ever experienced. Now regret was setting in, big style. He was back at the truck stop where his lorry had been parked overnight, having been driven there by the man who had approached him in the bar. Whitlock and the man were standing next to the lorry's tractor unit and Whitlock was beginning to feel fear.

The man, who said his name was Ramon, sneered and shook his dark-skinned head. 'You have no choice, my friend. The deal is done and you will be travelling across with five hundred pounds in your pocket, a few extra guests for company, and something else to deliver.'

'No – I don't think so,' Whitlock said in an attempt to assert himself.

Without warning, Ramon spun and punched Whitlock hard in the stomach. Years of HGV driving had given Whitlock a substantial paunch, but not one big enough to withstand such a well-delivered blow from a man well used to handing out physical punishment. Whitlock's breath steamed out of him and with a gasp like a geyser he doubled over, clutching his guts in agony. Ramon grabbed the driver's collar, heaved him upright and ran him back against the lorry. He whispered in Whitlock's ear. 'There is no going back. A deal is a deal. If you say no, two things will happen. Firstly, your body will be found floating in the shitty harbour waters, and secondly, your wife will receive photographs of last night's love-in.' Ramon slammed him against the lorry again, then released him.

Whitlock tried to catch his breath, hands on his knees, his head spinning. 'OK, OK,' he spat, saliva dribbling from the corners of his mouth. 'What do I have to do?'

Ramon consulted his watch. It was eight a.m. 'Get into your truck and follow me.'

'I don't want to miss the crossing,' Whitlock whined.

'You won't.'

He followed Ramon's car to the perimeter of Zeebrugge, to an industrialized section of the port full of low-rise factory units and grime, into a huge yard containing what looked like a million scrap cars piled high and dangerous, as though on supermarket shelves, and a vast number of container units for as far as the eye could see. Thousands of them.

There was plenty of room for Whitlock to manoeuvre his lorry.

Ramon stopped and jumped out of the battered Citroën he was driving and signalled for Whitlock to do the same.

Almost immediately the yard came to life. Several men appeared from the inside of a static caravan. One jumped into Whitlock's lorry, whilst others made their way towards a huge crane, the jib of which hung over a container. Two of the men attached thick chains around the container on the back of Whitlock's lorry. The crane came to life and swung over the container. The men attached the chain to the hook and the crane rose, lifting the container off the back of the lorry and depositing it amongst the other containers. Another container was then attached to the crane, this was then dropped expertly on the back of Whitlock's trailer and secured quickly in place.

Whitlock watched the change with growing trepidation, his guts churning from the recent blow to them, and worry, because he knew why the change was being made. The replacement container was fitted with a unit which looked like one for chilling the air inside it, but was actually one which fed fresh air into it and sucked out stale air – air which would keep his new cargo alive. He wanted to be sick. The only thing he had ever smuggled back into the UK was some jewellery for his wife. The only thing! Once! Of course he knew all about the problems with illegal immigration and so far he had managed to steer clear of the problem, but now his own stupidity had caught up with him, his own weakness.

He was going to smuggle people.

Ramon approached him with a big smile on his face. 'See – simple. Now all we do is collect the goods.'

'Fuck you,' blurted the lorry driver.

'You do not need to worry, my friend. You will not be caught, if that is what is bothering you.'

Whitlock was not assured by the words. All he wanted to do – still – was vomit. He nodded numbly, watching as the new container was finally fixed and the jib of the crane was raised away.

A car drove into the yard, but it was nothing like Ramon's beaten-up old banger. This was a smooth-looking black Mercedes, two men on board. It stopped near to the static caravan and both men climbed out. They were expensively dressed and a little incongruous against the background of scrap-heap cars and containers.

Ramon hurried across to them, like a puppy.

Whitlock thought, 'Boss men.' He climbed quickly into the cab of his lorry, feeling safer in the confines of his comfort zone, but kept watching the men, unable to stop his face contorting with an expression of contempt, and a feeling of looming disaster in the pit of his stomach. He swore continuously under his breath, hoping the repetition of that single, obscene word would somehow ease his burden.

It was interesting to watch Ramon's body language towards the new arrivals, as though he was a serf and they were lords of the manor.

No doubt they were.

The three men had an intense conversation. Ramon turned and pointed to Whitlock's lorry, obviously explaining something. Instinctively Whitlock shuddered and ducked as the two new arrivals looked across at him. He averted his eyes, still swearing.

When he looked again, they were back in huddled conference. One of the men walked round to the back of the Mercedes and opened the boot. He heaved out three heavily packed holdalls and dropped them on to the floor. They were big bags, obviously weighty. Ramon and the other man gathered around them and Ramon listened as they spoke to him, nodding.

The men then got back into their luxury car and set off with a scrunch of tyres, leaving a cloud of rising dust as they accelerated out of the gates and disappeared in the direction of Zeebrugge.

Ramon watched them go. The tension which had been visible in his body was replaced by relaxation and the resumption of his role as boss. He barked a couple of things at the men who had fitted the container. They picked up the holdalls and put them into Ramon's car, whilst he strode across to Whitlock, who lowered his window.

'Follow me.'

It was only a short journey. Two or three minutes at most, and once again Ramon led Whitlock into another industrial park, driving to a detached factory unit in its own grounds, surrounded by a high, chain-link fence. Ramon drove around the perimeter of the building, Whitlock following in his artic, coming right back around the front where they started from.

Immediately shutter doors began to rise, revealing the inside of the building, nothing more than a concrete-floored warehouse.

Whitlock caught his breath.

The whole place seemed to be packed with people, levered in there like sardines in a tin. At least a hundred of them, possibly more. All blinking as the daylight hit them, all tired, all beaten. It was, literally, a transit camp, although it reminded Whitlock of the old photographs he had seen of people bedding down in the London Underground during the Blitz. People were laid out on military-style camp beds, others were standing huddled around free-standing gas heaters, warming themselves. Some were sat at trestle tables scattered throughout the floorspace. Their faces looked pale and uncertain, hopeless yet hopeful at the same time.

Whitlock was staggered by the sight.

Ramon got out of his car and entered the building, emerging moments later with two more heavies who opened the container door on the back of Whitlock's trailer.

Some of the people inside the warehouse moved forward expectantly. Ramon barked a warning. A gun appeared in his hand. They hesitated and retreated. In his other hand he had a list from which he began to call names.

From the cab, using the wing mirror, Whitlock counted the number of people being herded into the container. Twenty poor souls climbed in, all men, he noticed. His heart pounded and he thought it was going to explode, that he was going to have a heart attack.

As the last person scrambled inside, the door was secured. The cargo was on board and ready for transportation.

Ramon swung up to the driver's door window. 'OK?'

'Great.'

'Just pretend they're chunks of meat,' Ramon said with a sneer. 'And don't worry about them. The ventilation system will work for about forty-eight hours, there's a chemical toilet in there and plenty of food and drink. All you have to do is follow the instructions on this piece of paper.' He pushed the said paper into Whitlock's hands. 'Simple.'

The passenger-side door of the cab opened. Whitlock watched as the three tightly packed holdalls which Ramon had been given by the two boss men at the container depot were dropped into the footwell.

'What the fuck's this?' the driver demanded.

'Just something extra . . . don't worry about it, and don't worry about getting caught. The law of averages is on your side. Here . . .' He dropped an envelope on to Whitlock's lap. 'Pounds sterling,' he said with a wink.

Whitlock sneered, engaged first gear and Ramon jumped down off the lorry as it began to move. Once again, the obscene word under Whitlock's breath was repeated continually. But it did not make him feel any better, because whatever, he had just become a human trafficker.

Six

The identification of the body of Renata Costain had gone as well as it could have done, given the circumstances.

59

Henry and Rik Dean drove Troy Costain to the mortuary at Blackpool Victoria Hospital and the dirty deed was carried out in the identification suite. Once away from the confines of his family, Troy had chilled considerably and been pretty indifferent to the point of apathy at the sight of his dead cousin, whom he had loved so deeply less than twenty minutes earlier. He merely blinked, nodded and said, 'Yeah, that's her,' with a shrug of his shoulders. The whole of that family-induced emotion seemed to have evaporated in the early-morning sunshine.

Back outside the mortuary Henry said, 'Sit in the car,' to Troy.

'No, it's right, Henry – I'll be on my way.' He made to walk off, but the detective clamped a heavy hand on his shoulder. A very worried expression smacked on to Troy's face.

'Uh-uh, no chance, pal,' Henry said. 'Let me rephrase that – sit in the fucking car – got that?'

Troy wilted visibly under Henry's hard hand and slunk to the car. If he'd had a tail, it would have been tucked between the cheeks of his backside.

Rik Dean watched the interaction, puzzled, his dark eyebrows in a deep furrow over the top of his nose, trying to get the measure of the relationship between the two men. It was plainly obvious they knew each other quite well. Henry smiled corruptly at Dean, noticing his expression. 'Old friends,' he said, which in no way explained a damned thing to Dean.

When Troy was seated in the car, out of earshot, Dean said, 'What's the plan, boss?'

'Strategy, you mean?' Henry corrected him. 'Plans go wrong, strategies get tweaked.'

Dean shrugged. 'And the strategy is . . . ?'

'OK – the big issue here is that someone has died in a road accident after being pursued by the cops, yeah? The fact that it was a stolen car and they were joyriding doesn't hold much sway anymore, and neither does the fact that it wasn't much of a chase. The added complication is that the girl who dies and the offender who killed her and then legged it are members of the same shit-house family, a family who happen to be one of the biggest trouble-making clans in Blackpool.

'They will blame the cops for everything, and therefore we need to handle this carefully with the media. We know we're not to blame, but we're never that good at proactively defending ourselves . . . so, as soon as we can, we get our heads together with your divisional commander and our media people and put a strategy together before facing the media out there. Are you with it so far?'

Dean nodded.

'So that's the PR, public bullshit side of it – that and the community reassurance and hi-viz patrols on Shoreside to quell any disturbances that the Costains might like to ignite.' Henry took a breath. His brain was feeling slightly woozy, having now been on the go for twenty-four hours. 'The real policing side is to get good, strong statements from the officers who chased the stolen car and any witnesses in our favour; then we need to trace our chum Roy Costain and nail the little bastard to the wall. Still with me?'

'Yep.'

'And I need to speak to Troy here.' Henry nodded at the cowed Costain in the back of the car. 'Because I think I might have some influence on him.'

Following the introduction of the Human Rights Act and the Regulation of Investigatory Powers Act (also known as RIPA), the handling of informants by the police – now termed Covert Human Intelligence Sources (CHIS) – is tightly regulated. The days of informal 'snouts' are, by and large, long gone. Informants are now formally registered and dealt with by handlers who have day-to-day responsibility for dealing with the 'source', and by the controller who has general oversight of the source. All information or intelligence from these sources is then sanitized and forwarded to local intelligence departments who then forward it for operational action. It is a system commonly referred to as the 'firewall' or the 'sanitized corridor'.

However, some informants slip through the loop. And one of them was called Troy Costain. He had been Henry Christie's only unregistered informant for about fourteen years. Henry was acutely aware of the disciplinary tightrope he was walking with Troy, but he was loath to register him because he would lose him.

He had first met Troy when he had arrested him for an assault, when Troy was a mere teenager. Troy's subsequent introduction to the inside of a police cell had sent the young-ster almost insane as he suffered from severe claustrophobia. Seizing gleefully on the condition, Henry had seen an oppor-tunity. Troy was a member of the Costains, one of the most feared criminal clans in town, and Henry realized that an informant in their midst would be a godsend. So, with ruth-less efficiency and calculated threats, Henry gave young Troy an option: get banged up and go mental or get talking and go free.

A desperate Troy chose the latter option and Henry had exploited him ever after. Troy had provided Henry with masses of information about low-level crimes and criminals over the years, and some higher-level stuff too. At times, when it looked as though Troy was about to stray from the path of right-eousness, Henry had administered an appropriate short sharp shock to keep him in line.

The downside of the relationship was that Troy had moved into drug dealing. Though it was common for cops to protect and turn a blind eye to the activities of their snouts, Troy had gravitated into territory which Henry disapproved of and Henry knew that there could be problems if Troy's activities got out of hand. It was a question of proportionality. Was it worth letting him carry on, weighed against the quality of information he could give? Henry had not yet decided Troy's future.

Henry slid into the front passenger seat of the car. He twisted round and scowled at Troy, whose eyes dropped.

'I'm sorry about Renata.'

'Yeah, sure you are,' sneered Troy. 'You're making a habit of getting me in to ID my dead relatives, aren't you?' He was referring to a couple of years earlier when his younger brother had been murdered and Henry had got Troy to identify the corpse. 'I think you get a kick from it.'

Henry arched his eyebrows.

Troy knew that what he was saying was pure bollocks. He spat a 'Tch!' and his mouth twisted down at the corners.

'How's the drug dealing going?'

Troy's face became bland and expressionless. He chose not to be baited. Henry sighed, recalling how not very long ago he had confiscated a revolver and a bag of drugs from Troy, which he had subsequently, and illegally, disposed of. Henry said, 'Next time I find you with dope in your hands, I won't be so lenient. You understand that, don't you Troy?'

Troy merely looked bored, feigned a yawn.

'So now we come to our present predicament.'

'You bastards will suffer for this,' Troy said gleefully.

It was Henry's turn to look indifferent. He sighed. 'OK, battle lines drawn . . . what can you tell me about Roy? Such as where can I find him, for a start?'

'Dunno.' Troy's thin shoulders rose and fell.

'OK . . . how come he was in a stolen car from Manchester?'

Troy squirmed ever so slightly and fourteen years of harassing him suddenly seemed to come good for Henry as he knew he could read Troy's body language like a large-print book. Henry smiled slightly. 'Is there something you'd like to tell me, Troy?'

'Nope.'

'Did Roy go to Manchester last night and come back in a stolen motor?'

'How the bleedin' hell should I know? I'm not his keeper.'

'But that's exactly what you are, Troy. At the moment you are head of the Costain household. You said so yourself.'

'Look,' Troy said, beginning to get uncomfortable. 'I don't know what he's been up to, all right? He comes 'n' he goes as he pleases. He's bloody fourteen for fuck's sake.'

'When did you last see him?'

'Erm . . . tryina think . . . em . . .' Troy's mind was whirring now as he tried urgently not to drop himself in anything smelly. 'Probably about six last night . . . tea time . . . yeah, that was it.'

'Hm, interesting.'

'Why?' Troy asked worriedly.

'If you saw him at six, the car was only stolen at seven in Manchester – he made bloody good time to the city.'

'Didn't he just . . . well, maybe someone else stole it and—' Troy began, but stopped himself on a sixpence.

'Good theory. Go on,' Henry urged him.

'No, nothing,' he said with a wild back-pedal.

'OK – so where do I find him, Troy? You know we have to talk to him sooner rather than later, don't you?'

'Henry, if I knew where he was, I'd tell you.'

'Not a terribly good answer.'

The wind screamed into the port of Hull from the River Humber and beyond from the North Sea, carrying with it stinging particles of sleet. It was bitter cold and driving hard, making Karl Donaldson burrow down even more deeply into his thick reefer jacket, tug up his collar and wish he'd had the foresight to put on a further couple of layers. The sea was running high as the weather deteriorated and Donaldson felt as though his recently acquired tan was being stripped from his face. It had been difficult to hear the voice down the mobile phone, but eventually Donaldson confirmed everything twice, then hung up. A slight change of plan, but not drastic.

He squinted out across the murky sea, but could see nothing other than low cloud and high waves. His ship had yet to come in, though he knew it was not far away.

With a judder, Donaldson turned his back to the wind and made his way to the permanently sited Portakabin on the quay-side adjacent to the customs channel through which all vehicles rolling off the ferries must pass. There was some warmth in the hut provided by the meagre portable gas fire, but this was having to be shared around the six people inside, all attempting to get a few therms for themselves.

Donaldson nodded at a few of the raised pairs of eyes, but none returned the greeting. They were all miserable – and Karl Donaldson was responsible for their plight.

He edged over to the kettle, flicked it on and selected a coffee from the mouth-watering selection of freeze-dried drinks on offer. As he poured steaming water into it, he saw there were no spoons so he stirred it with a pen, then took a sip. It tasted dreadful, but at least it was hot.

He took a few moments to look around the 'building'. There was a real cocktail of people therein, a genuine multi-agency approach, and yes, he was the one who had brought them all together to the salubrious Port of Hull.

There was a pair of surly individuals from the Immigration Service, a customs officer, a cop (a rather deliciously attractive female, Donaldson noted innocently), a social worker and some low-ranking bod from the Home Office who had come close to being punched by Donaldson on two separate, but recent, occasions. Nearby and on call was a customs search team with dogs and all manner of specialized equipment. They were housed in the main customs building where there was real heat and coffee to be had.

And they were all there because of him.

Donaldson, an American, worked for the FBI's Legal Attaché Department at the American Embassy in London. Much of his time was spent in liaison with law-enforcement agencies in the UK and Europe and it was acting upon information he had personally sourced that this pleasant bunch of people had been mustered. The information was that a particular lorry would be landing in Hull and would contain a number of illegal immigrants and a large stash of drugs. It had taken Donaldson a lot of cajoling to bring them together because these days there was a fair degree of apathy in response to such information. Illegal immigrants? So what? Hundreds came across every day. It was easier to let them in. Drugs? Not sure if we have the resources. Get in the queue, our priorities are not your priorities. These were the types of responses he'd had to field. Eventually he'd shamed the other agencies into pooling their resources in this ragbag team who probably wouldn't scare the skin off a rice pudding. They had been sent along merely as a sop to the Feds.

It didn't help matters that the boat carrying the expected illicit cargo did not land the previous day when expected due to extremely rough seas. At the last moment the team were all forced to find accommodation in Hull for the night. It wasn't the most sociable of evenings and Donaldson, exasperated, had retired early for a restless night.

Donaldson stood awkwardly in one corner of the hut, concentrating on his coffee and thinking through why he had engineered this operation. The hope was, of course, that illegal immigrants would be prevented from entering the country and that a haul of drugs would be seized and there would be some arrests too. But even as he stood there, he concluded that was not enough for his purposes. It would not go deep enough into the organization he was looking to destroy. It would be a minor blip for them, nothing more, but it might just open up some alleyway into their structure that he could then begin to widen into a six-lane highway . . . his thoughts were interrupted by the woman detective who stood up and sidled across the room to him, rubbing her chilly hands together.

Donaldson gave her a weak smile. She returned it with a warmer one.

'Not long now,' she said hopefully.

'No.'

She dropped her voice conspiratorially. 'You went to bed early. I didn't get a chance to talk to you.'

'Needed the shut-eye.'

'Hm . . . what's it like working for the FBI? Dead exciting, I bet.'

'I'm mainly office-bound, to be honest. I used to be a field agent – over in Florida – but I'm too old for that now, on a regular basis, that is.'

'What made you come over here?'

'Love and marriage.'

The detective seemed to be taken aback by this remark. She was about to say something, but the cabin door opened and a high-viz-jacketed customs official stuck his head in and announced, 'Your ferry is due in ten minutes.'

There wasn't quite a groan from the assembled team . . . but almost.

'Hold on,' Donaldson said before any of them moved, 'the target has changed . . . I've just had some up-to-date information . . .' He reeled off the new gen to them and they listened as though they were having needles stuck into their eyes.

When he had finished, Donaldson tossed his plastic cup into the bin, excused himself and eased past the female detective who, he thought, purposely did not make his passage easy. He wanted to watch the ferry dock.

Donning a hi-viz jacket himself, he walked out to the quayside of King George Dock and waited, peering into the low cloud.

Suddenly a ro-ro ferry, the *Nordic Pride*, emerged like a bull elephant out of a thicket, huge and impressive, the dark shape looming larger and larger as she approached port.

From that point on it took only minutes of well-rehearsed manoeuvring before she was moored, the ramp lowered and the vehicles starting to spew out on to dry land. It was a very smooth operation.

'You definitely know which one you're going to pull,' one of the pair of sulky immigration officials said into Donaldson's ear. 'Only I wouldn't like to think I've wasted my time. I'm very busy, y'know. I'm working on the cockling disaster.'

Donaldson nearly snapped something back, but held his tongue.

'They're out of control – immigrants. Bugger all we can do about them, if truth be known. They outnumber us by the thousand. I'll bet when we stop your lorry and there's, say, twenty on board, another hundred'll get through just from this landing. Happenin' all over the country,' the official moaned. 'Hundreds of the fuckers every day.'

'I know,' Donaldson sighed. 'Bit of a problem.'

'A bit!' he blurted, flabbergasted. 'It's a major social and political scandal, compounded by the ineptitude of a weak-kneed government which cannot get its own bloomin' house in order . . .'

Donaldson held up a hand with a very sharp gesture. 'Enough,' he said. 'We have work to do here.'

Open-mouthed, the officer watched the American muscle past and make his way towards the ferry. 'Twat,' he said quietly.

The heavy lorries had just started to roll off.

Henry Christie worked out that he had been on his toes for about thirty hours and that he was no longer a fully functioning human being. The morning had been spent in a whirl of hastily arranged meetings and briefings both to deal with the inevitable media onslaught and to get the bones of the investigation set up. He had even given two press interviews, one for local radio, one for TV, and he cringed when he thought about how he must have come across. Like some half-brained dimwit, he imagined. At least they were done and out of the way.

Attempts were in hand to trace Roy Costain, who had gone well to ground, and to encourage the Costains to hand the little bugger over. Troy had been unshakeable in his unhelpfulness towards Henry, who felt that whacking him might not be the best approach under the circumstances. But Henry was not impressed by his informant and could tell he was lying to his back teeth. As a result of Henry's frustration, he had let Troy walk back from the hospital.

At one p.m. Henry decided he had had enough.

He called Dave Anger to let him know where he was up to.

'Henry, we're just talking about you,' Anger said on hearing his voice.

'I thought my ears were burning.'

'They should be,' Anger said darkly.

'Anyway,' Henry said, clearing his throat, 'I'm calling it a day. I'm off home to bed for a few hours, but I'll be ready for on-call at six. If that's OK with you.'

'Yeah . . . you've done a pretty good job actually,' Anger said reluctantly. 'Oh, Jane Roscoe's here. Do you want to say hello?'

'I'll pass,' Henry said, feeling his stomach grind over. 'I'll be back on at six.' He ended the call and stood there thoughtfully, his nostrils flaring. Jane Roscoe, not really a name he wished to be associated with any more, particularly as it seemed she and Anger were gunning for him.

What worried him most, though, was that they had a smoking gun and lots of ammo for it.

The crossing on the *Nordic Pride* had been rough and unpleasant. Whitlock, the lorry driver, was surprised they had been allowed to sail – but perhaps it was more that he would rather not have sailed with his current cargo.

As the ferry docked at Hull, Whitlock dragged himself reluctantly back to his vehicle in the belly of the ship and clambered into the driver's cab, aware that for the first time in his life he did not want to get in.

He loved driving. He loved his lorry. But not today.

He wondered how the people stuffed into the container were doing as he turned on the ignition and started the engine.

The massive doors which formed the bows of the ferry opened with painful slowness, revealing the Port of Hull, a place Whitlock had passed through on hundreds of occasions.

With trepidation he wondered if he would actually pass through it today.

Seven

The problem with a trial of such magnitude was that you never could tell when you were going to be ambushed.

It seemed to be going well, had been for six weeks now, but there was always the possibility that something unexpected could come up – or, even worse, something that had been buried could rise from its grave like a zombie and screw the whole thing up.

Detective Superintendent Carl Easton gazed around the magnificent Shire Hall courtroom at Lancaster Crown Court within Lancaster Castle, an absolutely splendid setting for such a major trial. It was rarely used as a court venue these days because of the new Crown Court built in Preston and there were good facilities in other locations, too. However, a logjam of cases coupled with a desire to hear these proceedings as far away from Manchester as possible – but yet remain within a reasonable distance for witnesses – had made the powers that be plump for Lancaster.

Easton folded his arms as he squinted at the huge, ornate room, taking in the unique display of heraldic shields adorning the walls, whilst his mind wondered if that 'something' he was dreading would pop up.

So far, so smooth and in a couple of days all the witnesses would have been through the mill, prosecution and defence, then it would be time for the final address, the summing up, the deliberation by the jury, then the verdict.

Guilty. He crossed his fingers.

'All rise in court,' an usher shouted as the spectacularly robed judge regally entered the court and sat down at the high bench. It was Her Honour Mrs Ellison, approaching eighty years old, but definitely still with it, ruling the proceedings before her with a rod of iron, allowing nothing to get past her. Behind the pince-nez, her little grey eyes sparkled with cunning and intellect.

She sat as the prisoner was led into the dock from the holding cell underneath the courtroom. He was book-ended by two towering security guards from one of the private companies now contracted to perform prisoner-escort duties. In terms of sheer presence, though, the guards were completely overshadowed by the man between them, even though he was much smaller in stature. His eyes flickered quickly around the courtroom, resting fleetingly, but obviously, on Easton. The prisoner allowed himself a knowing smirk, bowed graciously to the bench then sat on his seat in the dock, waiting for the jury to be wheeled in.

His name was Rufus Sweetman. He was thirty-three years old. He was dressed smartly and expensively, oozing wealth but restraint. As an individual he looked mild-mannered but at the same time exuded an aura of confidence that made him very special and a little scary. A lot scary, actually, especially to people who got on the wrong side of him.

He was in court charged with murder.

The usher announced that the Crown Court was now in session.

Detective Superintendent Easton settled himself down and waited for proceedings to commence.

He was feeling pretty confident in the way that things had gone. A life sentence for Sweetman would be just the ticket he needed career-wise, both inside and outside the job. Getting rid of Sweetman from under his feet would be very good all round.

Easton had expected the prosecuting council to rise to his feet and was puzzled slightly when the defence QC stood up instead. The judge looked slightly perplexed too. She pulled her glasses down her nose.

'Your Honour, if I may . . . ?' the QC said politely. His name was Sharp and his way of operating reflected this. He was good and costly. The judge nodded at him. 'As of this morning we are in receipt of new information concerning these proceedings. Could I please approach the bench . . . together with my learned colleague, that is?' He nodded sourly in the general direction of the prosecution.

Both berobed, bewigged men made their way across no-man's-land to the high bench.

Easton leaned forward, straining to catch any snippets of the hushed conversation. He glanced at Sweetman, who was sitting comfortably cross-legged, his fingers tightly inter-twined, thumbs circling, looking extremely smug.

Easton's attention returned to the conflab at the bench. Suddenly he had a very queasy feeling in his stomach.

The sweat and pounding in his heart made Whitlock think he was about to have a cardiac arrest. His breathing was shallow and stuttering, his vision swimming, unfocused.

There was some hold-up ahead. He had only reached the lip of the ferry's ramp where he was now poised in the queue down to the quayside. A lot of activity was going on, lots of people in yellow jackets strutting about. More than usual, he thought.

'Oh God,' he murmured. 'I am fucking dead.'

The thought of dropping out of his cab, doing a runner and leaving his lorry behind entered his head.

The two counsels backed respectfully away from the bench and retreated to their respective tables, a smug expression on the countenance of the defence QC, who also managed to catch Detective Superintendent Easton's eye.

'What's happening here, boss?' the detective sergeant sitting next to Easton in court whispered harshly.

'Don't know, but I don't like it,' Easton said through the corner of his mouth. His eyes twitched. He looked across at Rufus Sweetman in the dock, who deliberately remained firmly focused ahead, although there was a wicked glint in his eyes and the glimmer of a grin on his face.

The prosecuting counsel sat, grim, unhappy. Defence remained on his feet, rearranging and straightening his papers on the table in front of him. He cleared his throat in

71

preparation for an address to the court. Easton thought, *Bombshell coming.*

'If it may please your honour,' he began formally, 'I would like to recall a witness to the box.' The judge nodded her assent. The lawyer turned slightly in Easton's direction. 'Detective Superintendent Easton please.'

An usher repeated the summons.

'Fuck!' Easton muttered under his breath as he stood up and crossed the courtroom. His legs felt as though lead weights were attached to them as he stepped into the witness box, all eyes on him, all curious and excited by this new development. The press box seemed particularly energized.

'Officer,' the defence QC smiled. He was a fantastically experienced defence QC, the one the wealthy villains always chose to represent them, his fees running into thousands even for short trials. But he was worth it. His track record was phenomenal. He went on, 'May I remind you that you are still under oath?'

Easton spoke to the judge. 'Yes, Your Honour, I understand that.'

Then it began and the gates of hell opened for Easton.

Henry Christie was almost home when he received the call. With a groan he u-turned the car and drove to the garage premises to which the stolen and very mangled Ford Escort had been towed for safe keeping. He knew the firm well, respectable and reliable, and through twenty-four-hour call-outs and the rota garage system, the police had put a lot of business their way over the years. This garage in particular was one which would always turn out, any time of day, and had never yet let the cops down.

Henry pulled up outside and strolled into the office, staffed by a single female – Joyce – the wife of the proprietor. Henry had known her for a long time, had lost count of the number of cars he had sent her way.

'Oh my God, Henry Christie!' Joyce rose from the swivel chair behind her desk and Henry tried to disguise the fact that his male antennae had registered the voluptuous and curvaceous lines of her well-stacked body. She was approaching fifty – not necessarily a bad thing, Henry thought, as he too wasn't that far away from that landmark – and was built like a racing yacht, all the curves in all the right places. She pulled down her tight figure-hugging woollen sweater, accentuating everything even more perfectly. It was no secret that she had been trying to bed Henry for a long time now. For himself, he was terrified of being devoured.

'Hi, Joyce.'

'Haven't seen you for quite a while.'

'I'm too important now,' he laughed.

She literally batted her heavily mascara'd eyelashes. 'I'll bet you are.'

'I've come to see the car involved in last night's accident.'

'Out back, darling. One of your crime scene guys is with it.'

'Thanks, Joyce.' Henry paused, unable to prevent his eyes giving her a critical once-over. 'You're looking well, by the way.'

'You do know I'm ripe for an affair right now, don't you?' She looked demurely at him. 'Particularly one based purely on sex . . . very dirty sex.' Her voice had the timbre of a gravel driveway.

'Joyce!' a man's voice called from the office behind. 'Leave him alone, you'll scare the poor bugger to death.'

Her lipsticked mouth turned down with disappointment as her husband, Lee, emerged from the office.

'Morning, Lee,' Henry nodded.

'Henry . . . keep your hands off her, she's mine, all mine,' Lee said dramatically and grabbed her from behind, his arms encircling her. She melted her ass into him and Henry beat a hasty retreat. He moved quickly through the reception area into a yard at the back of the premises. Beyond this was a security-fenced area, inside of which was a variety of vehicles. Henry went through the open gate and found the smashed-up Escort, next to which stood an individual Henry recognized as one of the crime scene investigators based at Blackpool. Dressed in a white paper suit pulled up over his clothes, he was bespectacled, rather short and a bit ugly, the complete antithesis of his American counterparts portrayed in the slick TV series, CSI.

'Hello, sir,' he said.

'Hello, Tom. You got something of interest?' Henry stifled a yawn.

'Am I boring you?'

'Just been on the go a long time.'

The CSI reached into his bag of tricks and pulled out a clear plastic bag, about four by four inches, with a strip-seal across the top. Resting in the bottom corner of it was a misshapen blob of metal, not much bigger than a thumbnail.

'Bullet,' the CSI announced. Henry had already recognized it as such. 'Found embedded in the back seat of the car, having entered same through the front windscreen.'

Henry peered at it. 'Any idea of calibre?'

The CSI shrugged. 'Maybe a thirty-eight.'

'Well found,' Henry congratulated him. 'Do what you have to do with it, will you?'

'Yes, I know my job.'

'And for that we're all thankful.' He bade farewell and headed back to the main garage building, entering reception as Joyce emerged from her husband's office looking rather flushed and ruffled. She gave Henry a wry smile as she straightened her jumper. Despite himself, Henry could not prevent his investigatory instincts from noting that when he had first seen her she was definitely wearing a bra; this had now disappeared.

She sat down at her desk and said, 'Could've been you, Henry.'

He was out of the door real sharpish.

'Your Honour, ladies and gentlemen of the jury, may I be so bold as to refresh your memories?' Sharp smiled at Easton. 'You were the senior investigating officer in charge of the inquiry into the murder of Jackson Hazell. Is that correct?'

'That is correct,' Easton responded guardedly.

'So,' the QC said, his brow furrowed, 'you were the person who was responsible for the policy log . . . the log, that is, which decides the route and key decisions made in the investigation?'

'With others,' Easton said, a little too hurriedly, 'but yes.'

Sharp screwed up his face, looked pained – all for effect, obviously. 'But you made the final decision?'

Easton sniffed and shuffled his feet. 'Yes, but all decisions are outlined and backed up with sound arguments based on facts, information, intelligence and good practice. As you know, the policy log has been scrutinized on several occasions during this trial.'

Sharp nodded sagely. The policy log had stood up well to the rigours of the scrutiny.

'So, basically, though, as SIO, you decide the direction of the investigation?'

'I think we have ascertained that,' the judge interceded, a slightly impatient note in her voice.

'Quite, Your Honour,' he conceded. He faced Easton again and smiled humourlessly. 'As investigations proceed, numerous calls are received from members of the public. Is that correct?'

'Thousands, sometimes,' Easton agreed, then closed his mouth. The rule was that you should never offer an answer to a question that hasn't been asked.

'How many phone calls were received from members of the public in this investigation, Superintendent?'

'I don't know the exact number.'

'Ballpark figure.'

'Nine hundred, a thousand.'

'Every call logged?'

'As far as I know.'

'Every one passed to the major incident room – that is, say, those calls received at other police stations?'

'Procedure says that should happen.'

'So if someone made a call to a police station other than to the one where your major incident room was situated, that call, or the details of it, would be passed to your murder team?'

'That should be the case.' A bead of sweat rolled down Easton's spine, between his shoulder blades. He was trying to remain calm, resisting the burgeoning urge to shout, 'What the fuck are you getting at here, you bastard?' Only thing was, he had a feeling he knew what was coming. Sharp was smiling again.

'Are all the messages received acted upon?'

'Not necessarily.'

'What do you mean by that, Superintendent?'

'They are all scrutinized and assessed by experienced detectives and a decision is then made as to the value of the message. Sometimes no action is taken and messages are simply filed.

Sometimes immediate action is taken ... basically the response to them is graded.'

'I see,' Sharp said thoughtfully.

'It would be impractical to deploy an officer for every message received, so therefore decisions have to be made.'

'But every call received is assessed in some way? Is that correct?'

Easton nodded. 'Yes.'

'So, for example, if you received a telephone call from a member of the public saying that such-and-such had committed the murder you were investigating, and that named person was different from the one you suspected, or had arrested, how much credence would you give that call, Superintendent? How would you assess that call?'

Easton swallowed something which felt like a huge, rough stone, and reached for the glass of water next to him.

The hold-up seemed to go on forever. Whitlock, sitting high in the cab of his vehicle, perched on the lip of the ramp off the ferry, with a view of the line of cars and trucks ahead of him, had moved on internally from mere heart attack and breathlessness. He was shaking uncontrollably now, his whole body dithering and weak. His left foot quivered visibly whilst resting on the clutch and he wondered how the hell he was going to press the bloody thing in.

The delay had been almost half an hour.

Nightmare.

Then the line started to edge slowly forwards.

With great will-power, Whitlock pushed the clutch in and engaged the gears, started to move down the ramp, just as something deep in Whitlock's mind clicked and he felt something was very wrong. Other than the fact he was carrying twenty illegal immigrants and three holdalls containing something he didn't even want to think about. There was a difference in the feel of the truck, just a subtle one, and he could not decipher what it was. Something was missing and his brain could not quite pin it down.

On the quayside, Karl Donaldson and his mix 'n' match team were overjoyed to see the vehicles start to roll again off the ferry. There had been a three-vehicle shunt which had stopped everything in its tracks. Soon their target would be in their grasp and they would all be able to go home – when the paperwork was done.

In fact they could see it now, rolling slowly down the ramp.

Sharp paused patiently as Easton replaced the glass on the ledge in front of him, then ran a set of shaking fingers through his thick hair. Then he embarked on a slightly different tack. 'How many suspects did you have in this case, Superintendent?'

'Only the one,' he croaked.

'And that is my client?'

'Yes.'

'No more suspects at all?'

'No.'

'That's not true, is it?'

'It is absolutely true.'

The QC consulted a sheet of paper in front of him. 'No, it is not true, because there were at least two other suspects, weren't there?'

'No.' It was almost a whisper.

'In fact, you received several telephone calls from the public naming two other people who could have committed this horrible crime.'

'Not so.'

'In fact the man who was murdered – a man who lived in the criminal underworld – was someone who had many enemies, wasn't he? He owed a lot of money to a lot of people. He had upset many people in many ways and I find it very odd that there was only one suspect in this case.'

'Rufus Sweetman was the only suspect,' Easton insisted.

'I'm afraid not, and I have the documentary proof in front of me showing that at least two other men were strong suspects.'

There was an aura of triumph about Sharp as he stood facing Easton and steepled his fingers together in front of his chest while he surveyed the officer over the rim of his glasses. The unsaid word, *Gotcha!*, hung in the air.

The team moved in, signalling for the driver of the heavy-goods vehicle to pull out of the line and into a specially erected marquee which would protect everyone from the elements as a search took place.

Donaldson watched as the customs officer swung up to the cab and spoke to the extremely worried-looking driver. Some questions were asked and answered as both the officer and driver climbed down then approached Donaldson.

'This is bollocks,' the driver was saying. 'Total bollocks.'

Donaldson shrugged. 'If that's the case, you've nothing to worry about, have you?'

'What's a bloody Yank doing here?' the driver demanded to know.

Donaldson gave him a slit-eyed stare which shut him up. 'Have you got anyone or anything in your vehicle you shouldn't have?'

The driver hesitated. 'No.'

'Look-see time, I think,' said Donaldson.

Whitlock had been certain that he would be pulled. When he was waved almost regally through and the hi-viz-jacketed officials went to the lorry behind him instead, he almost died of relief.

He had made it through.

Five hundred pounds richer and with twenty illegals on board, plus a shag that was pretty hazy in his memory, but so what?

And it had actually turned out to be painless. There had been no need to worry, as the man had said. There were probably a hundred other illegals secreted on the ferry anyway and maybe the authorities had caught some in the lorry behind him. But they hadn't caught him.

Jesus, he'd done it!

He slammed his fist on the steering wheel and as he accelerated towards the motorway network, he gave his horn a blast for good measure.

Whitlock was feeling good.

The one, cowering, terrified, illegal immigrant in the back of the lorry was not what Karl Donaldson wanted to see. An old man, badly hidden between boxes of Spanish tomatoes, was not what should have been there.

The team ripped the vehicle apart, found nothing else.

'I didn't know he was there, I swear on my daughter's life,' the driver insisted passionately, as both he and the stowaway were led away to be processed. 'The bastard hid there.'

'I know, I know . . . let's just get the paperwork sorted,' one of the immigration officials said, taking the driver's arm and shooting a glance at Donaldson which said it all – and more.

'And who's gonna repack my lorry?' the driver whined, his voice getting less audible the further he got out of earshot. Donaldson was glad to get shut of him because he was dangerously close to laying one on him.

He strutted angrily to the quayside, hands thrust deep inside his pockets, kicking an imaginary stone into the murky water. Fuming did not come close to describing his mental state. He raised his face to the sky, nostrils flaring, wishing to scream.

'Ah well,' a voice said behind him. 'It's always hit and miss.'

He turned and looked through a pair of very pissed-off eyes at the woman detective from the local force who had been assigned to the job. 'It's always a hit with me,' he growled dangerously. 'I don't do misses.'

She smiled coyly. 'Does that apply to women too?'

Donaldson blinked and the devil in him replied, 'Oh, yes.'

'You going back to London now?'

'Not necessarily.'

She remained silent, brushed the windswept hair back from her face, raised a well-made-up profile to the grey sky and then dropped her chin and looked up seductively at the American through two wide-spaced, elliptical eyes that shone with promise.

'How about a coffee somewhere?'

Eight

By the time Henry Christie eventually arrived home, his brain was definitely the consistency of porridge oats. He felt jet-lagged and not a little weak. He needed to sleep and hoped that the night ahead would be lacking in dead bodies.

It was three p.m. when he walked in through the door, which he knew gave him about an hour uninterrupted before his youngest daughter arrived home and a couple before Kate landed. He did a quick phone call to Burnley to see what stage the domestic-murder inquiry was at. He was told that the offender, the knife-wielding drunken wife, had been interviewed once she had sobered up, but that it was unlikely she would be put before court for the morning; she had admitted the offence, apparently, claiming she had been a victim of domestic violence for over four years. Henry could see her walking free at the end of proceedings. He also spoke to Rik Dean at Blackpool, but was told that Roy Costain had not yet been found.

The work done, Henry did not hesitate further. He took the stairs two at a time and almost ran into the bedroom, divesting himself of his clothes as he went. The bed, a king-size, looked totally fantastic and it was all his! Within seconds he was naked and underneath the cool duvet, drawing it up over his head, which was resting on his soft, favourite pillow.

Moments later he was flat out and snoring gently.

Outside the Crown Court it was chaos as Rufus Sweetman emerged a free man, all charges against him having been dismissed. He nodded, waved, and smiled enigmatically at the banks of press cameramen, turning as his name was called and posing for photos.

His girlfriend, the stunningly attractive Ginny Jensen, clung tightly to his arm, and she too responded professionally to the cameras, her radiant – but fixed – smile and catwalk looks and figure being captured for posterity.

Flanking Sweetman on the other side was his solicitor, Bradley Grant, smooth and smart.

'Mr Sweetman, do you have any comments to make?' one journalist yelled, pushing a tiny microphone into his face.

'What do you think of the police?' screamed another.

'Are you actually guilty or not?' ventured another one.

'Please, please,' his solicitor intervened placatingly. 'Can we have some decorum here?'

Cameras flashed. Sweetman and Ginny posed. Even more flashes.

In the background the armed cops who had been providing protection for the proceedings were being withdrawn from their positions.

Grant shushed everyone. 'I have a short, prepared statement to make and there will be nothing more said today from Mr Sweetman . . . if you please, gentlemen, ladies.' The solicitor, revelling in the attention, surveyed the assembled media until some sort of quiet came about. Then he started to read from a sheet of paper. 'I have always maintained my innocence in this matter and also that I was unfairly charged with the offence of a murder I did not commit. May I just say that my condolences go out to the family of Jackson Hazell.' Grant paused for effect. 'The police have shown that they are out to get me at whatever cost and I have now shown that their procedures are flawed and very suspect. All I can say is that justice has been done and my absolute faith in the legal system of this fine country remains unshakeable. I will be consulting my legal advisor about how to progress this matter further and, rest assured, it will be progressed.' Grant folded up the hastily prepared statement with finality. 'Now, ladies and gentlemen, if you would be so kind. Mr Sweetman has been in custody for almost nine months now. He wishes to bring some normality back to his life by returning home to his loved ones and friends so that he can pick up the threads of his shattered life, so cruelly overturned by the vindictiveness of certain police officers.'

Sweetman and his lady friend moved forwards. The journalists and photographers surged towards them, more flashlights popping, more questions being barked. One newspaperman pushed to the front of the throng and stuck a mike under Sweetman's nose. It was the same one who had posed the question about Sweetman's guilt.

'Mr Sweetman, is it true that the question of your guilt still remains?' he probed. 'The police procedure may well be flawed here, but that doesn't actually mean you are not guilty, does it?'

Sweetman caught the man's eye and stopped abruptly, dragging his girlfriend to a ragged halt. 'You saying I'm guilty? I was fitted up.'

'I'm saying the question of your guilt still remains.'

Sweetman's solicitor laid a restraining hand on his client's bicep.

'My client is not guilty . . . that is our final word on the subject . . . Come on, let us through.'

Sweetman allowed himself to be urged through the melee, though he kept staring angrily at the journalist who had been so unwise as to ask him that question.

A large stretch limousine was waiting in the car park, hastily rented for the occasion. Sweetman and Ginny dropped into the back seats, whilst Grant jumped into the front passenger seat. The driver, one of Sweetman's men, accelerated away.

Sweetman leaned back, closing the partition, exhaling an extended sigh as the overlong car whisked him through the streets of Lancaster. 'Now,' he said, draping an arm around his girlfriend's shoulders, 'there's a few people I'll be wanting to slap.'

Detective Superintendent Carl Easton and the DS who had been sat with him at court, a guy called Hamlet, were sitting low in their car, watching the exit and flashy drive-off of Sweetman from the Crown Court.

'The implications are worrying,' Easton said. 'I thought we had him stitched . . . Fuck!'

'Yeah,' Hamlet said quietly.

'There'll be an investigation, probably some other force.'

'Yeah.'

'Fuck!'

'Yeah.'

'We need to think about how we're going to sort him out, we need to find out who let the defence know about these alleged other suspects. That's an internal thing, got to be.' Easton was counting out the things that needed doing on his fingers, but stopped when Hamlet sniggered. 'What's so funny?' Easton was not laughing. He was enraged.

'Just thinking about "other suspects",' he said.

'What other suspects?'

'Exactly,' Hamlet said firmly. 'What other suspects?'

Easton sighed a long and very exaggerated sigh, then glowered sideways at Hamlet. 'There were no other suspects.'

'I know that, you know that, but nobody else knows it.'

Easton huffed through his nostrils. 'We should've taken the time to cover that one,' he said bitterly. 'It's bloody obvious that Sweetman got people to call in about the other suspects. I mean, we knew that at the time, but we should've gone through the process of eliminating them properly, blowing them out of the water. But we got complacent and thought we could bury it, but I should've known the defence would uncover the phone calls. I shouldn't be surprised.' He shook his head. 'I mean, the thing is, we know exactly who was guilty of the murder, don't we?'

Hamlet shrunk back into his seat. 'Yes we do,' he muttered uncomfortably.

'And it wasn't our friend Mr Sweetman, was it, even though we did our best to prove it was.'

The articulated lorry thundered down the M62 motorway towards Leeds, Whitlock at the wheel. He was trying to put as much distance between himself and the Port of Hull as possible. Something told him that if he stopped or slowed down, the authorities would catch him up.

What he did not know was that it would have been much better for him to have been caught by the authorities.

The M62 was horrendously busy on the stretch between the east coast and Leeds, and no doubt would be all the way from Leeds to Manchester. It was one of the most congested and turgid motorways in the country and Karl Donaldson held out no hope for a speedy journey, even in the 4x4 Jeep he was driving. He went as fast as possible from tailback to tailback, happy to be passing the slow-moving heavies in the first lane. At least it would be comfortable and the musical accompaniment was first rate – a selection which included the country of Dwight Yoakam, the edge of the Stones and the melody of McFly, who were his eldest daughter's favourite of the moment.

Donaldson had thought about travelling back to London

that same day, but decided against it. Instead he was going to nip across the breadth of the country (although he soon realized that no one 'nipped' anywhere by way of the M62) to see an old friend on spec. He phoned his wife, Karen, and told her he would be home the following day. The tone of his voice made her say, 'It didn't go well, did it?'

'You know me so well.'

'So you're hoping for a shoulder to cry on and a beer to alleviate the symptoms,' she laughed.

'You know me so well.'

Donaldson's mind strayed briefly to the woman detective back in Hull, as he drove. Hm . . . he had taken her up on her offer of coffee, knowing full well where it could have led, or at least where she wanted it to lead, but he'd done a runner even before the cappuccino, much to her dismay. Since taking his marriage vows he had remained faithful to Karen and had no plans to ever stray from that worthy path.

The lengthy roadworks on the motorway between Leeds and Manchester slowed traffic down even more, with three lanes being filtered into one for a four-mile stretch near to Rochdale. Huge, creeping and often stationary queues were formed in both directions.

Whitlock needed a stress break. He was still tense and his middle-aged heart was smashing hard against his chest wall, even now, two hours west of Hull. If it continued he thought he would explode internally and it would be a gory mess.

He tried to purge his mind of the poor souls in the container. He hoped they were OK and was desperate to release them out into the world. His instructions had been to drive to a business address in Rossendale where he would be met by an 'agent' who would take control of the illegals.

That moment could not come too soon . . . but . . . he still needed a break. Ten minutes just to cool down, to chill. He had travelled far enough now, he guessed.

Normally Whitlock, a driver proud of his road skills, spent a lot of his driving time using his mirrors. It was imperative that a lorry driver be totally aware of everything going on around, but on this particular journey, he had hardly looked in them, his mind so preoccupied with his predicament.

That was why he did not clock the black Citroën van which had been sitting behind him for most of his journey along the M62.

The frustration of the stop-start, but mainly stop, journey made Karl Donaldson switch off his CD player and fume. He was getting annoyed now, an annoyance on top of what he was feeling with regards to the cock-up at Hull, and was beginning to think that maybe he should have gone due south – and home. If the M1 had been clear, he could have almost been there by now.

Instead he was sitting in virtually motionless traffic somewhere on the bleak moors above Rochdale. One of the signposts he saw pointed to Saddleworth Moors and he realized he was quite near the spot where in the 1960s Myra Hindley and her murderous lover Ian Brady buried the bodies of the children they had abused and killed, crimes so appalling they were internationally known. Donaldson looked at the bare, brown moorland and shivered at the thought that there were still bodies out there unrecovered. 'Bastards!' he said under his breath.

He shrugged and brought himself back to the present.

Suddenly his whole body tensed.

The traffic had started to move again where the roadworks came to an end, fanning out across three lanes. But it was the van in front of him which held his attention rigidly. It was a black Citroën van, similar to a Ford Transit. From his elevated viewpoint in the Jeep he had a good position from which to look inside the van through the windows in the rear doors.

There was a driver and a passenger and a couple of huddled shapes in the back, four guys in total.

Not that that in itself was significant. It could have been a group of men on their way back from, or going to, some labouring job or other.

What grabbed his attention was what he thought he had seen.

He could not be 100 per cent, but his gut instinct told him he was right. One of the men in the back had passed something to the man in the front passenger seat. Donaldson had excellent vision which had not diminished with age. If anything it was even better and he was pretty sure that what had been passed forwards was a sawn-off shotgun.

OK, it was just a glimpse. An impression more than anything. But everything that the American knew, all his points of reference, told him he was correct.

The Citroën accelerated lumpily away from the roadworks ahead of him.

Donaldson hung back slightly, curious, alert, as the van drew alongside a heavy goods vehicle also speeding up after the roadworks. There was a container on the back of the HGV and as Donaldson saw it and his brain dealt with this information, he emitted a groan.

He had seen the heavy before. He had watched it rolling off the ferry at Hull, one vehicle ahead of the one his uninspired team had pulled over.

The Citroën drew parallel with the lorry and Donaldson made out the passenger 'me-mawing' to the driver of the HGV.

Donaldson dropped back. The passenger's left arm was out of the window, gesticulating to the driver.

Then both arms came out, holding the shotgun briefly, then it was gone.

The passenger continued to gesticulate, pointing and, Donaldson assumed, shouting. He was telling the driver to pull off the motorway at the next service area, which was fast approaching.

Donaldson had stumbled on a robbery about to take place, he believed.

Suddenly he felt naked. He had no gun because he wasn't allowed to carry one as a matter of course in the UK, and just occasionally he would have liked to have touched the coldness of a weapon for reassurance. Like now.

Instead he reached for the next best thing . . . his mobile phone. Dialled treble-nine.

The three hundred metre marker for the exit on to Birch Services came into view. The HVG signalled the intention to pull off. The Citroën dropped in behind into the heavy's slipstream. Donaldson eased even further back off the gas. A man's face pressed up to one of the windows in the back of the Citroën and glared through the glass. Donaldson rammed his foot down on the gas pedal and surged out into the middle lane of the motorway, accelerating past the Citroën, pretending to pay it no heed. He sped past the HGV too, and with little room to manoeuvre, he managed to tuck the Jeep in front and swerve on to the exit lane leading up to the service area, angling across the chevrons in the road and churning up dirt as he did. He hoped that the occupants of the Citroën were taking no notice of him.

He drove far too quickly up the lane, one hand on the wheel, the other holding the phone to his ear, steering the big 4x4 recklessly into the designated area for car parking, close to the entrance to the shops and cafés. He veered into a tight parking spot and sank down into his seat, craning round to watch the HGV enter the service area and drive toward the appropriate parking area. The Citroën was behind it.

No one had yet answered his treble-nine.

Donaldson cursed, ended the call, redialled, all the while his eyes fixed on the progress of the two vehicles which were stopping on the far side of the service area, as far away as possible from prying eyes.

'Can you give me your name and telephone number, please?' the operator said when, at last, the call was answered. Despite wanting to yell at the individual, Donaldson kept his calm and gave the required details, then asked to be connected to the police. The connection was answered immediately. Quickly and succinctly Donaldson relayed his position and what he thought might be happening, always watching the HGV and the Citroën.

The HGV had looped around the far perimeter of the lorry park and pulled up at such an angle that the container on the back obscured a decent view of the front cab. The Citroën looped around, too, almost out of sight on the other side of the HGV. Donaldson saw four men leap out.

Sometimes, Karl Donaldson hated himself.

In his bones he knew exactly what was going down here. A robbery. An armed one at that. The knowledge and experience of his time as a first-class FBI field agent screamed at him. But what was worse, what really annoyed him, was that he was powerless . . . powerless, that is, to stop himself getting out of his car and making his way across and intervening. Even though he knew it was the most stupid, foolhardy thing

87

he could do. He should stop right where he was, stay safe, and wait for the police to arrive. Be Mr Sensible.

Naah . . . not his style.

He jumped out of the Jeep, fighting the urge all the time, but letting his will-power collapse under the desire for action.

He dropped low between a line of parked cars and began a bent, loping jog towards the situation. There was a wide area of no-man's-land between the car park and the point where the HGV had stopped. He wanted to get into a position from where he could approach unseen from a blind spot. When he reached it, he ran hard and low across the tarmac, feeling as exposed as a soldier storming a machine-gun emplacement. It was at least one hundred metres before he slammed up against the rear nearside corner of the container, where once again his foolishness overwhelmed him. It would have been an easy option, maybe the right option, to run back to the Jeep and keep his head down.

Naah . . . especially as he had seen a police Range Rover tearing up from the motorway, blue lights flashing, tyres squealing. He held himself back from leaping up and down and waving like a windmill. Instead he tried to attract the attention of the cops with urgent, but more restrained, hand signals.

The Range Rover raced towards him, full blast, no subtlety whatsoever, which in the circumstances was probably OK.

Donaldson pointed in the direction it should go.

They went that way, screeched round the side of the HGV and skidded to a dramatic halt. The whole car rocked dangerously on its soft suspension and the two uniformed officers leapt out at a run. Donaldson twisted around the back corner of the lorry and wished immediately that things had not happened so fast.

Four men in clown masks surrounded the lorry driver, who stood on the tarmac, his hands held high, terror stuck on his face. In the hands of one of the masked men were three heavy, well-packed holdalls. The three others brandished guns of different varieties. One sawn-off shotgun, one pistol, and one H&K MP5 machine pistol. They were seriously well armed.

All five men in this tableau turned in the direction of the police car and its occupants.

'Get down on the fucking ground, you black twats!' screamed the robber holding the shotgun. He waved it at them, his stance dangerous, menacing, the gun ready to be discharged. From that distance it would not take any aiming.

'Now come on,' one of the officers started reasonably.

'I am not fucking about here . . . you get down on the ground or I'll blow your cuntin' head off . . .' As he shouted this, his eyes – visible through slits in his black mask – caught the figure of Donaldson, who had seen what was going on but had been unable to melt himself away quickly enough. 'Shit!' the felon groaned. 'Get that fucker, too!' he bawled at one of his mates.

The one with the MP5 ran to Donaldson and snarled, 'Get over there, shit face.'

Only in his mind did Donaldson hesitate. He did as requested, allowing himself to be manhandled. He could feel the tension in these guys. They were on the edge. The adrenaline rush, probably enhanced by speed, meant they were dangerous and unpredictable, very likely to shoot.

He was pushed next to the driver, the two cops roughly ushered likewise, so now four men faced four.

'Now – all down! Face down on the floor! Do it! Do it!' screamed the first robber.

Donaldson and the three others sank to their knees.

'All the fucking way!'

Donaldson eased himself on to the cold hard ground, his cheek against the tarmac. Suddenly the shotgun was rammed hard into the side of his face, jarring his jaw. 'Get yer fuckin' face down.'

The inside of his cheek split on his teeth. He tasted blood immediately on his tongue. He complied, resting his forehead on the ground.

'None of you fucking move,' they were ordered.

Donaldson stared at the black ground at the end of his nose, angry with himself that things had turned out this way. It had been a rushed, thoughtless approach and now he was paying the price for such hastiness. He gritted his teeth, tried to imagine what was going on around him.

Two shotgun blasts sounded. Donaldson jumped and his heart sank as he wondered what had happened, who had been shot . . . Christ! A door slammed, an engine revved, tyres squealed and skidded . . . Donaldson knew they were gone. He raised his head, exhaled, unaware that he had even been holding his breath.

He saw the back of the Citroën van speeding across the garage forecourt of the service area, towards the motorway. The policemen rose to their feet, brushing themselves down. The driver who had been ambushed lay unmoving. Fleetingly Donaldson assumed he had been murdered, but then he moved and the American understood why the shotgun had been discharged: two tyres on the Range Rover had been blasted out and the vehicle stood there as if with a limp, unable to be used for any immediate pursuit.

The lorry driver remained face down. Donaldson got to his feet, gave the two cops a withering look, and stood over him. 'It's safe to get up now,' he drawled.

'I think I'd rather stay here,' he whimpered pathetically.

'Shit – that should never have happened,' the Citroën driver screamed as he pulled off his mask and powered the van on to the motorway.

'Such is life,' one of the others in the back said philosophically. This was the man leading the gang. The driver was right, of course, cock-ups should not happen, but if they do they have to be dealt with appropriately. 'It's not rocket science, this. There's always imponderables. Sometimes do-gooders get in the way, but at least no one died,' the leader went on to say as he too tugged off his mask and shook his head. He tossed the mask into the black bin liner that was being passed around. 'We'll be OK. We've done good. No worries at all.'

He leaned back against the inner wall of the van, the strength draining out of him. He needed to rest, to sleep, to recuperate. The last forty-eight hours had been a real tester, but he had shown he was up to it. A grim smile of satisfaction creased his mouth. He was now very definitely a player, which is what he wanted to achieve. He looked at the big holdalls in the back of the van. He was getting good at taking holdalls from people. But these holdalls were not full of cash.

90

He reached across for one, eased back the zipper and peeked inside. It was tightly packed with hundreds of vacuum-sealed plastic bags, stuffed with cocaine, packaged in a Spanish factory. He did a few calculations, his eyes jumping between each holdall. Street value, maybe four or five million – a guesstimate on the low side.

Lynch closed his eyes and his smile widened.

A good day's work, to say the least. Five million pounds worth of drugs seized and twenty-five grand's worth of bank notes recovered, one man wasted.

Very definitely he was now a player.

Whitlock, the poor victim, was assisted into the rear seat of the Range Rover by one of the uniformed motorway cops. The manager of the café on the service area had been tasked with getting some brews and Whitlock was sipping one of them, his hands hardly able to hold the cup. Other police patrols, including the CID, were expected on the scene imminently.

Karl Donaldson established his credentials with the motorway officers. They were suitably impressed by the mention of the FBI and the sight of his badge, but they clearly did not see the American as adding any value to the investigation of the robbery, other than as a normal witness. He was immune to this reaction by British cops. As a whole, their mindset was that they knew best and no one, not even the world's most effective law-enforcement agency, could tell them anything.

Donaldson sauntered across to Whitlock, who looked fearful and very apprehensive. Maybe his experience justified some of this, but not all. Donaldson opened the door on the lopsided Range Rover.

'How're you feelin', buddy?'

'Oh – OK,' he squeaked.

'I'm Karl Donaldson.' He reached in and offered a hand, which the driver shook hesitantly. 'FBI, London.'

'Phil Whitlock – driver, Accrington.'

'Nasty business.'

'Uh-uh.' He sipped his tea, now lukewarm. 'Thanks for trying to help out. I appreciate it.'

One of the constables walked across to them, speaking into his shoulder-mounted personal radio.

'We've circulated details and descriptions of the bastards,' he said to Whitlock as Donaldson stepped aside. 'Just need to know what they stole from you, mate.' He paused, waiting expectantly for the answer to be filled in.

Whitlock licked his lips and swallowed. After a few moments' thought he shrugged and said, 'Dunno,' weakly.

Initially the cop did not register what he had said. Then his brow furrowed deeply. 'Come again?'

Blinking rapidly, the driver said, 'I don't know.'

'You don't know. What do you mean, you don't know?'

'What I say. I don't know.'

'You've been robbed by four armed men, but you don't know what was taken from you?'

Whitlock nodded. Donaldson was riveted.

'Why don't you know?' the officer asked, his cop hackles rising as he sensed there was more to this than met the eye.

'They weren't my bags.'

'Whose bags were they?'

Whitlock shrugged again – pathetically – and Donaldson thought he was going to cry. 'Dunno,' he said once more. Then, more forcefully, Whitlock said, 'Excuse me.' He placed his cup down on the floor of the Range Rover, pushed the cop out of the way and staggered round the back of it, where, leaning with both hands against the vehicle, his head between his arms, he was violently sick. Donaldson heard the splatter of vomit as it cascaded on to the ground.

Donaldson said to the officer, 'Can I give you a clue?'

'Surprise me.'

'This vehicle has just come into the country from Holland.'

'Ahh.' The officer grasped the scenario instantly.

'And I think it'll be worth having a look in the back.' He pointed to the container. He stepped to one side and gobbed out some blood from the cut inside his mouth.

Rufus Sweetman and Ginny, his girlfriend, lounged in the plush back seat of the stretch limo as it sped south down the M6, the driver occasionally touching eighty, but never more. Next to the driver sat Grant, Sweetman's solicitor and, less well known, the number two man in Sweetman's whole organization. Both men were trying to ignore what was happening behind the partition.

Almost as soon as they had pulled away from Lancaster Crown Court, Sweetman and his girl fell into each other's arms, drooling, devouring each other with wet, passionate kisses, trying to make up as quickly as possible for nine months of separation.

After this necessary release, Sweetman opened the well-stocked in-car bar and helped himself to a Glenfiddich on ice.

'God, it's good to be out,' he sighed. He opened the partition and said to Grant, 'We need to sort the cops now, though, get 'em off my back for good.'

'I agree.'

'Legally and illegally.'

'Sure, Rufus.'

'I want them to think they're gonna get stuffed through the courts . . . I want them to know that, actually . . . and I want them worrying about me all the time, I want them looking over their shoulders, wonderin' when they're gonna get it next. I want 'em shittin' 'emselves in all directions, the bastards. I want every innocent cop on the beat to think he might be the next target. I want them all to be afraid, Bradley.'

'Sure, Rufus.'

'And I want my business back.'

'It's happening, even as we speak.'

'Good . . . and another thing . . .'

Grant looked over his shoulder. 'You don't want much, do you?'

'I haven't even started,' Sweetman snarled. 'I want to find out who actually killed Jacko Hazell.'

Grant was still looking back over his shoulder, trying to avert his eyes from the half-dressed Ginny. He killed the image and raised his eyes to Sweetman's smirking face, avoiding the look of dare which he knew was on Ginny's face. 'The business is due some good news today, boss.'

Sweetman brightened up. 'Today, is it?'

'Yeah . . . thought I'd keep it until the moment was right. Yeah, it's due in today . . . five mill worth of product . . . the foundations to take the business forwards.' His eyes looked beyond Sweetman and for a moment the expression on Grant's face changed, darkened. He was watching something through the back window. A car was moving out for an overtake. The look made Sweetman turn and follow the line of sight. The car drew level and held that position.

Sweetman opened his smoked-glass window.

His eyes locked with the front-seat passenger in the car.

'Ignore,' Grant instructed.

But Sweetman could not stop looking across the gap from car to car, looking into the eyes of Detective Superintendent Carl Easton. The man who had gone to the extreme and set him up for a murder both knew he had not committed. Easton had been like a zealot in his pursuit and Sweetman did not fully understand why the cop had gone to such lengths. Sure, Sweetman was a big operator, probably the biggest and most organized in Manchester at the moment, and had been a thorn in the side of Greater Manchester Police for years. He had managed to evade justice time and again . . . but yet Easton had been obsessive and gone on to try and prove something with which Sweetman had no involvement. Why? Sweetman needed that answer, maybe would get it in the near future. He knew he was fair game for the cops, it was the nature of the way he lived; but the ruthless way in which Easton had pursued him actually frightened him a little . . . which is why those phone calls had been made, firmly putting suspicion on other people. Sweetman had been so worried that he might get convicted that it had been necessary to do that, but yet Easton had obviously tried to bury the information.

Easton brought a mobile phone up to his ear. Grant's phone rang out.

The cars stayed parallel with each other, eighty mph.

'It's for you.' Grant handed the phone to Sweetman.

Both men were still eye to eye, maybe six feet apart, eighty mph.

'Don't think this is over,' Easton said. His mouth moved soundlessly, but Sweetman heard the words.

'Nor you,' Sweetman said.

'I'll always be after you.'

'Go and fuck yourself.'

'Real clever words, them.'

The line went dead. Easton broke the locked gaze and sat forwards in his seat. His car surged ahead of the limo.

Sweetman tossed the mobile back to Grant and sat back. Anticipation coursed through his veins at the prospect of what lay ahead.

'Before we open up, is there anything there that should not be in there?' Karl Donaldson asked Whitlock as they stood next to the container. The driver looked more than ill now. He looked as though he should be on his death bed, or maybe being transferred into a coffin. He made no reply. 'Better open it then,' Donaldson said to one of the traffic cops.

The latches were pulled down, forced sideways on their heavy springs, the door heaved open.

Several seconds passed before everyone registered what exactly they were seeing.

'That was what was wrong,' Whitlock said to himself, agonized as he recalled his feeling that something was amiss with the lorry. Now he knew. The noise made by the air-circulation unit had stopped.

Donaldson's stomach churned emptily. The breath in his lungs hissed out and his lips popped open.

Nine

Henry Christie rubbed his tired eyes and focused them on his friend. The two men were sitting in a public house within walking distance of Henry's home, a hostelry called The Tram and Tower in deference to a couple of the main attractions of the resort of Blackpool. Of course, Henry was not drinking alcohol. He was still on-call and was sipping a pint of lemon and lime, with ice. His friend was on something stronger, having just downed his second Jack Daniel's double, a third sitting conveniently in front of him, ready for consumption.

Henry's friend was Karl Donaldson. They had met several years earlier – their paths had crossed when Donaldson, then an FBI field agent, had been investigating American mob activity in the north of England. Since then their paths had continued to intercut and at the same time their friendship had grown, even though Henry hated Donaldson's guts for being such a good-looking bastard. Donaldson had been posted to the US embassy in London for a number of years and had married a high-ranking British policewoman he'd met on that first investigation.

Donaldson looked more drawn out than Henry, and definitely more emotional. It was usually the other way round. In fact Henry had never seen the normally cool, laid-back Yank so stressed and uptight.

There was good reason for his condition.

'Unbelievable,' Donaldson was saying, shaking his head despondently. 'God, if only I'd pulled the right truck . . . maybe they could've been saved.'

'They could have been dead for a long time, Karl,' Henry said softly. 'You shouldn't punish yourself.' He could see Donaldson was going through that cop-type thing – blaming yourself for something that was impossible to prevent.

'I know, I know, but it's so hard not to.' He could clearly envision the opening of the rear of the container, could not eradicate it from his mind. 'It was awful . . . I've seen a lot of bad things in my life, H, but this is up there in the top five. Twenty dead bodies, suffocated because of an electrical failure . . . just imagine their suffering.' He took a mouthful of the JD. Henry noticed Donaldson's right hand was quivering ever so slightly. He was in a bad way, Henry thought.

'What has the driver to say about it?'

Donaldson blew out his cheeks. 'Nothing – yet. He's terrified and probably with good cause, because I have a damned good idea what was in the bag which was stolen from him.'

'Drugs?'

'Millions of pounds worth.'

'So he failed on both counts . . . didn't deliver the human cargo, nor his other package. Do you think he knows much?'

The American shook his head. 'Doubtful. Just a mule, a fool . . . or maybe a man who didn't have a choice.' He shrugged. 'Who knows?'

'Will he talk?'

'Maybe, but my guess is he'll say nothing.'

Henry poured some of his cold, sweet drink into his mouth, wishing it was Stella Artois. It was approaching ten p.m. and so far his evening had been quiet. Roy Costain was still on the loose and the husband-murderer from the night before was tucked up in bed, ready for court next day. He hoped it would stay like this, because he needed a full night of beauty sleep.

'Hope you didn't mind me turning up out of the blue,' Donaldson said glumly. 'Been a bad day in more ways than one.'

'Not at all. You can crash out in Jenny's bed if you want. She's out for the night at a pal's.'

'Appreciated . . . I was gonna go to a Travelodge . . . you saved me that agony at least.' He tipped his head back and downed his third JD.

'So what drove you to Hull in the first place?' Henry asked.

'Same old, same old.'

'Ahh,' said Henry knowledgeably, tilting his head and looking down his nose at Donaldson. 'If I'm not mistaken, your friend and mine . . .'

'Mendoza,' they said in unison.

'Can I get you a refill for that?' Donaldson said, pointing at Henry's light-green drink.

Detective Superintendent Carl Easton had convened an emergency meeting of his team at a pub not two miles away from the Greater Manchester Police Training Centre at Sedgeley Park. Easton knew the landlord and he was allowed to use the upstairs function room. Easton arrived first, together with DS Hamlet. They quickly set out a few chairs to accommodate the others who would be arriving soon.

Easton and Hamlet reflected on the day. One that had gone very badly. They were worried men.

'I know I keep saying it,' Easton pondered, 'but it is not good, not good at all.'

Hamlet took a deep swig of his pint of Boddington's Bitter,

wiped his mouth and agreed. 'Puts us in a very delicate position.'

Two men wandered in through the double doors, pints in hand – two members of Easton's close-knit team. They acknowledged each other and, sombre-faced, seated themselves. Within minutes, four more arrived, all equally worried-looking, then a woman, then finally the last member of the team, who ensured that the doors were closed properly.

'OK, thanks for coming at such short notice, everyone,' Easton began. 'By now you all know what's happened at Lancaster Crown Court today . . . it's across all the papers and on TV.' They all nodded or murmured. 'Sweetman is back out on the streets again, a free man.' He let the words sink in and tried to catch everyone's eye. 'This is a very bad thing.' He inhaled deeply. A couple of the team lit cigarettes. Smoke rose languidly in the still air. 'It affects us on two fronts . . . firstly because Sweetman is back out there, it means we have to be very careful about how we operate. I don't want anyone to think they're safe, because they're not. Sweetman will want his revenge and so will his backers . . . and I was called in to see the chief constable this afternoon. To say he was pissed off is an understatement. I argued that any inquiry into this matter at court should be kept internal . . . but he wouldn't have it.'

'Shit!' was one reaction.

'Bollocks!' was another.

'Another force will be coming in to investigate us,' Easton announced.

A collective groan filled the air.

'Who?' someone asked.

'Our Chief has asked the Chief Constable of Lancashire Constabulary. He had already done that before I saw him, so it was a done deal. He's taken this measure because it was such a high-profile case and he needs to be seen to be doing things right. I can appreciate this point of view.'

'So we're going to be investigated by a bunch of fuckin' country bumpkins,' one of the detectives ventured. He laughed. 'We'll run rings round the fuckers.'

'No doubt we will,' Easton said cautiously, 'but we have to be seen to be cooperating as much as possible, and that means we have to get the house in order as of now. We need to have answers ready for the questions we're going to be asked. And not only that, we need to ensure that every door that needs to be closed is closed, that every report is sanitized . . . outside detectives sniffing around in our dirty washing makes us very vulnerable indeed.' He looked knowingly at his team. 'And not just because of what might be uncovered in relation to the way Sweetman was investigated.'

It must have been the time on remand that did it. That was all Rufus Sweetman could put it down to, but he was finding that as he probed and thrusted himself into Ginny's willing body, he could not come.

'Fuckin' prison,' he blasted, sitting up on the edge of the bed. 'Screws your mind, does your head in . . . my mind's all over the place.' He stood up and crossed to the en suite, where he relieved himself and stepped into the shower. Just too many things going on in his head, competing, making him feel disconnected and slightly spaced out. He knew he needed to make an effort to calm down and think normally again, if there was such a thing as normal in the world of Rufus Sweetman.

So immersed was he in his thoughts that Ginny had to knock hard on the shower door to attract his attention. It did not help that the power shower was pulsing hot jets of water into his tensed-up shoulders and back muscles. He switched it off and opened the door. She held out a mobile phone.

'Grant,' she said distastefully.

'Thanks.' Sweetman reached for a towel and skim-dried himself before taking the phone from her. 'It's me.'

'How's it going?'

'So-so.' He glanced at Ginny. She was sitting naked on the edge of the bed, filing her nails.

'Got news for you . . . in fact, have you seen the news on TV?'

'No, been a bit tied up, if you know what I mean?'

Ginny looked up and giggled.

'Yeah, sure.'

'What's the news?' Sweetman asked.

'The consignment's gone.'

'What do you mean, gone?'

Sweetman started to look round the bedroom, finding the TV remote and aiming it at the portable.

'It's been taken, is what I mean.'

Sweetman perched on the corner of the bed, his breathing shallow. 'Tell me,' he said quietly, the undertone dangerous.

'The lorry got robbed on Birch Services. The goods were stolen . . . and that's not all . . . the cargo is no longer alive . . . all dead. It's very big news.'

'Murdered?'

'Suffocated.'

'Christ! And the shit's all gone, has it?'

'Yeah . . . look, it's all over the TV . . . watch News 24 . . . it's massive . . . well, the deaths of the immigrants is . . . there's no mention of anything else, obviously.'

'But it's gone for sure?'

'Yeah.'

Sweetman flopped back across the bed. 'Who did it?'

'No idea.'

'We need to meet . . . usual place . . . one hour . . . I want Theodore and Tony there . . . we're going to find out who's responsible and crush the bastard.' He paused. 'Does the big man know about this?'

'I haven't told him . . . but he may know something.'

'He needs to be informed . . . and he needs to be told that I'm back on the case, not fucking running things from a cell, for shit's sake.' He hung up and looked at Ginny. 'Has Grant been coming on to you?'

Donaldson returned to the table and placed the drinks down. Henry looked enviously at his friend's and wished he wasn't on call. It was tempting to have just a wee one, but Henry knew it would be a mistake. Even after a pint he tended to drive as though he was Michael Schumacher and he could tell his judgement was impaired even from such a small amount of alcohol. He knew that fine judgement was an essential for an on-call SIO and did not want to take any chances. His own judgement and decision-making had been savagely questioned in the not-too-distant past and he was sharply aware that while several people in the organization were out to knee-cap him he had to be cleaner than clean at all times.

The wide American sat down and glanced around the pub. Henry clocked the sly looks he was attracting from most of the women, the good-looking bastard. Secretly Henry hated him for being such a handsome twat and also because he was such a goody-two-shoes; Karl would never have considered cheating on his wife, whereas Henry, despite his commitment to being such a changed man, remained weak and vulnerable around a pretty face.

'How's work?' Donaldson asked.

'Fraught,' Henry admitted after some consideration. 'Always being watched, always being tested, always being treated with suspicion.'

Donaldson nodded, knowing what Henry was referring to. 'I thought FB said you'd be working to him? Anything come of that?'

'Six weeks in and I haven't had two words from the guy. He's been too busy being a chief constable, I suppose. Still, he let me get back on the SIO team, so I can't complain too much, though I do detect an undercurrent of resentment across the force in my direction.'

'Like you've been given some sort of favouritism?'

Henry nodded.

'Don't let it get you down . . . you're a good detective.'

'With a history . . . and everyone's just waiting to see me fall off my pedestal again.'

'You won't,' Donaldson said confidently.

'We'll see.' Henry sipped his lemon and lime, wiped his mouth, raised his eyebrows. 'You were saying . . .'

'Oh, yeah, developments on the Spanish front . . . mm, let me see . . . none really after today.'

'What about your informant?' Henry probed, aware that the American was playing footsie with a guy very high up in Mendoza's organization. As a seasoned – some would say 'long in the tooth' – detective, Henry knew how fraught informant handling could be, but this was the way in which the FBI had chosen to get to Mendoza, coupled with hi-tech approaches. Other ways had proved disastrous. Two under-cover agents had been compromised and then ruthlessly murdered by Mendoza, which was why Donaldson was so focused on the target: Donaldson had personally managed the second u/c operative and when the man – codenamed Zeke – had been discovered and killed, Donaldson had taken it badly, personally. He now wanted Mendoza's blood and it was becoming an obsession with him, one that Henry hoped would not destroy his friend in the process.

'Ahh, my informant.' Donaldson had bought himself a pint of San Miguel lager – a special promotion at the bar – which he raised cynically and toasted.

Whitlock was being held at Rochdale police station, the one with the jurisdiction over that section of the motorway on which the robbery and subsequent discovery of the bodies had occurred. He was only too glad to be sitting alone in a cell, his hands holding his head as his predicament whirled around in his mind like a sandstorm. How had it all happened? How had he been sucked in and duped? How had he got into a position from which it was impossible to extract himself?

He thumped his forehead into the base of his hands, but found this was not doing the trick. He stood up and on trembling legs he walked to the cell wall and began to smack his head against it.

Once Rufus Sweetman had realized he was going to be released from court, the quick plan of the day sketched in his head had been to spend time screwing Ginny – which he had done, though not as successfully as he would have liked; then he planned for them both to go into the city for a meal in Chinatown, then on to one of the clubs in which he held an interest to begin networking again, plan how the new stash would be distributed, then get totally and utterly smashed out of his head.

But suddenly, the goalposts moved.

The loss of the consignment was a major blow. It was a situation that demanded urgent attention.

Following the phone call from Grant, Sweetman dressed quickly. He tossed a couple of hundred pounds at Ginny and told her to go and meet some friends, have a good time, and catch up with him later. Naked, still, she eagerly grabbed the cash and ran giggling into the dressing room.

Sweetman's face was hard as he pulled on his leather jacket, paused by the mirror and considered his reflection. He had lost a lot of weight whilst inside the joint, but this had given him a razor-sharp edge to his features. His close-cropped hair gave him the appearance of being haunted and desperate. His piercing green eyes stared sunkenly back and he quite liked what he saw. But he wasn't standing there just to preen himself. He reached out to the edge of the mirror and touched a hidden catch. The mirror swung away from the wall on concealed hinges revealing the front of a push-button safe fitted flush with the wall. He prodded the four-digit number and the safe door opened silently to reveal its innards.

Stashed in there were bundles of tightly packed banknotes, a mix of sterling and euros, sitting on which was a small revolver and two speed loaders. Sweetman pulled out the gun and flicked out the cylinder. It was fully loaded with soft-nosed .38s. A good gun, easy to conceal. He slid it into his waistband at the small of his back, the speed loaders into his pockets, then relocked the safe, pushing the mirror back into place.

Then he ran his hand over his hair and gave himself the final once-over. 'Definitely back in business,' he said.

Karl Donaldson could have reeled off every known fact about the Spaniard: that he was believed to be one of Europe's most successful criminals, that his wealth could be counted in millions and that most of his money had come from human suffering, be it drugs, illegal immigration, gambling, whoring or guns. That he was fluent in Italian and English. Donaldson could even tell you the Spaniard's current mobile-phone number from memory. He knew that Mendoza's tightly run organization dealt in everything on a big scale. He was known to have close links with the Sicilian Mafia and their American brethren. It had been those connections which had brought Mendoza to the attention of the FBI and caused two agents to be infiltrated into the organization – which ended up with those two agents dead. Donaldson was confident that the contract killer who had actually pulled the trigger had been dealt with, but that still left Mendoza, the man at the top, the man who drove it all. Mendoza was also suspected of ordering the assassination of a gangster from the north-west of

England, a young man called Marty Cragg, who had welched on debts to Mendoza. He had been murdered at the same time and place as the second of the undercover FBI agents, and this double murder was still an ongoing investigation being handled by Lancashire police. However, because of its lack of success, it was being scaled down . . . something else which made Donaldson even more determined to nail Mendoza.

There was no way in which another undercover officer would ever be put into Mendoza's organization again, so other methods were being used against him, one of which was to cultivate informants who could provide damning evidence against him . . . hopefully.

'The information I had,' Donaldson explained, 'was precise. It detailed the lorry, everything.'

'And yet it was duff gen?'

'Duff gen?'

'Y'know – bollocks.'

'Bollocks? Jeez, you English crease me up.' He paused, a smile playing on his face. He loved English phrases and slang and whenever possible used the vernacular himself. 'Yeah,' he admitted eventually, 'it was wrong.'

Henry knew some peripheral things about Donaldson's source and had previously been able to adduce from the American that the informant was high up in Mendoza's food chain, that he was empowered to order hits and, not least, he possibly knew where the bodies of two Greater Manchester detectives might be buried. Henry had promised himself that he would pursue this with Donaldson, but had not really had the chance since returning to work. They had been two young surveillance officers who had been unfortunate enough to stumble on Mendoza's hitman burying the body of a drug dealer who had just been culled on the order of Donaldson's informant.

It was all complicated, delicate stuff, but made no less easy by Donaldson's personal desire to nail Mendoza and the fact that informants are very easily lost. Donaldson knew he had a gem and was loath to jeopardize the relationship by pumping him for information he did not want to give . . . such as information that would incriminate himself.

The only good thing was that Henry knew that the man

who had murdered the detectives was the same one who had killed the undercover officers, and Henry knew how sticky and fiery his death had been. He also suspected that Donaldson knew a lot more about the demise of the killer than he cared to divulge. Secretly Henry suspected that Donaldson had some part in the death, but he could not be sure of this . . . and part of him did not want to know, if truth be told.

'So what you gonna do?'

'Meet, see, talk with him.'

'What's his agenda? What's he going to get out of this relationship?'

'That's something I need to ask him, I guess.'

The reasons why people become informants varied. Usually it was for financial reasons or revenge or the thrill of it. Rarely was it for altruistic reasons. Every informant had a personal agenda and it was vital that the officers who managed them knew the reasons, or the whole relationship could easily go shit-shaped.

'You must have some sort of inkling,' Henry said.

Donaldson screwed up his face. 'He's playing a game, but . . .' He bit his lower lip. 'And this is only a feeling . . . I guess he's out to stuff Mendoza. I think he wants the business.'

'And if you act on what he tells you and you bring about Mendoza's downfall, the business might just revert to him. He might just end up stepping into a dead man's shoes, as it were.'

Donaldson nodded. 'And that's not the idea of an informant, is it?'

'No.'

'But yet it doesn't fully explain Hull.'

'Unless he's playing some sort of double game?'

'The trouble with us, Henry, is that we are too suspicious of people, aren't we?'

Henry raised his glass. 'No bad thing.'

Carl Easton's team drifted back into the main bar of the pub, having been thoroughly briefed about what was expected of them when the outside force came in to investigate. In essence it was that they should be as helpful as possible – on the face of it – but actually be as obstructive as possible below the surface. It would be a fine balancing act, but he knew his team was up to it. They had been scrutinized before but had come out of it smelling of roses.

Easton and Hamlet sat alone in the function room, saying nothing to each other, deep in thoughts of strategy and tactics.

'We'll be OK,' Easton said at length. Hamlet nodded. 'It's Sweetman himself that bothers me more than anything. He'll be like a raging tiger now.' His lower jaw rotated. 'We may need to deal with him for good.'

'I was thinking the same.'

'Any ideas who?'

Just then the door opened. One of Easton's team re-entered the room, carrying a refilled pint. He came in and sat opposite the detective superintendent. He looked haggard and drawn, ready to drop from exhaustion. Easton and Hamlet exchanged a quick glance.

'Leave us,' Easton said to Hamlet. He took no offence, collected his drink and left. When they were alone, Easton said, 'You look knackered.'

'Been busy.' He stifled a yawn.

'Got some good news, I hope?'

'Very good news.'

Karl Donaldson had to be eased out of the Tram and Tower and guided into the front passenger seat of Henry's car. It was one of the few times that Henry had ever seen his friend the worse for wear from drink. It was good to see there was some weakness in the Yank's armour after all. On the other hand it made Henry worry slightly because it showed just how much the obsession with Mendoza was getting to him.

Henry jumped in behind the wheel and watched his inebriated mate tugging on his seat belt, making the inertia reel lock repeatedly as he pulled at it. Henry let him struggle just for a while longer before taking the seat belt out of his hand, letting it run back on to the reel, then fastening it for him.

'Thanks, pal,' Donaldson slurred, slumped back in his seat. 'Guess you think I'm an asshole.'

'Not at all.'

Suddenly Donaldson went silent. He was asleep.

Henry emitted a long, weary sigh. As he engaged first gear,

his mobile phone rang. *Shit!* he thought. 'First death of the night coming in.'

The meeting convened by Rufus Sweetman was perhaps less than two miles away from the pub in which Easton was meeting his team. The venue was a shabby hotel near to the motorway junction at Prestwich. It was a place he often used, because he owned it.

Sweetman and Grant, the solicitor, arrived first and together. They walked through the reception area of the hotel, making towards a conference room. Once inside, Sweetman positioned himself at the head of the oval-shaped table and helped himself to a bottle of fizzy water from the tray on the table. The door opened. The other two people Sweetman had ordered to attend sauntered in. Theodore Jackman and Tony Cromer, Sweetman's top negotiators and influencers, as he referred to them.

Solemnly they shook hands with Sweetman, then both men could hide their emotions no more and they hugged their boss with tears in their eyes. Sweetman's cold front evaporated and a lot of weeping and backslapping went on for a long time until Sweetman said, 'Enough, enough, you blabbering idiots. Anyone'd think I'd been banged up for the best part of a year on a trumped up charge.'

'But you have,' Theodore Jackman said, missing it completely.

'Yeah, I have . . . but I'm back out now and there's some wrongs to put right. Are you guys up for that?'

There was no hesitation: both were.

'OK, we need to prioritize here,' Sweetman said when all four men had settled at the table. The first thing we need to do is find out who ripped us off . . . five million quid's worth of coke . . . any ideas? Who's got the connections to deal that amount? Guys?'

Jackman – known as Teddy Bear – and Cromer looked blank. 'It's all been really quiet,' Teddy Bear said, his nickname belying his looks. He was nothing like a Teddy Bear, more an angry, hungry, grizzly bear.

'Well, it's time we were knowing . . . someone's got very cute in a way which could put us out of business. All that dope is on the drip and the man we owe the money to will not be very happy if we don't deliver. I think someone is trying to bring us down . . .' And even as he spoke a thought whacked him like an uppercut. He knew it was an assumption, but he kicked himself for never having thought of it before. His voice trailed off, eyes narrowed. 'Shit . . . I think I've just added up two and two.'

It had been bad enough getting Donaldson into the car in the first place, but extracting him – a guy well over six foot tall and built like a cooling tower – was no joke either. Then guiding him into the house and up the stairs was even less amusing. His legs and feet seemed to have disconnected themselves from his brain and it was as though the steps had come to life at the same time. The big Yank simply could not co-ordinate himself to climb them and it took the joint effort of Henry and Kate to literally drag what was almost a dead weight up and into Jenny's bedroom. They dropped him on to her bed, where he began to snore immediately.

Panting and sweating, Henry and Kate surveyed their handiwork.

'I've never seen him drunk before,' Kate said. She bent down and eased his shoes off.

'I have, but for a different reason.' Henry attempted to get Donaldson's jacket off him, but could not manipulate his arms. Eventually he gave up.

'He'll be OK,' Kate assured him. 'How much has he had?'

'Not too much. He's just not used to it.'

'So what's up with him?'

Henry shrugged. 'I think that to say he's had a bad day is an understatement.' He had no desire to tell Kate exactly what his friend had experienced over the last twenty-four hours. 'I need to go into Blackpool. There's someone come in to see me, says they have some vital information about something.' He raised his eyebrows disbelievingly. 'Not sure how long I'll be. Not long, I hope. I could do with a good night's sleep.'

Kate touched Henry's face with the tips of her fingers, a tender, loving gesture. She tiptoed up and kissed him on the cheek. 'You look tired, sweetheart.'

Henry took hold of her and kissed her hard on the mouth,

letting his lips and tongue linger. She pushed herself into him and their mouths crashed together, but the moment of passion was destroyed irrevocably by one of the loudest and longest and perhaps most perfect farts either of them had ever heard, which emitted from the arse of the sleeping drunk.

'Middle C,' Henry said. In a fit of giggles the pair backed out of the room and closed the door behind them. 'Hope you have a good supply of air freshener,' he added.

Sweetman was standing and pacing the conference room like some executive on a creative roll, banging a fist into the palm of his hand, making points, spinning on his heels as he tested his hypothesis on his workers.

'Just think back – two and a half, three years. What was happening to us?'

'We were establishing ourselves across the city,' Grant ventured. 'We set up the contract with the spic.'

Sweetman pointed, nodded.

'And we had a whole lot of trouble with the niggers in Stockport,' said Teddy Bear Jackman. 'Soon sorted them out, though.'

'Go on,' the boss urged.

'We dealt very firmly with a couple of them.'

Sweetman laughed. 'Yep, we did.'

'We professionalized the organization,' Grant suggested.

'And as a result of that, what happened?'

All three faces remained blank. Sweetman closed his eyes despairingly, opened them and said, 'We got our best ever supplier, yeah, and we built up a business which stretched from here to Birmingham and across the hills to Sheffield . . . yeah?' he finished hopefully.

They all nodded enthusiastically.

'We got the contact, we got the goods, we crapped on the opposition, we forged new links, we set up good structures with firewalls and we made real money . . . yeah?'

More enthusiastic nods.

'So who came into our lives?'

'Mendoza,' blurted Jackman.

Sweetman glared hard at the man. 'No names,' he warned him. 'No names . . . never trust that anywhere could be safe unless you can put your hand on your heart and say it is.' He waved his hands at the conference room. 'It's two years since we've been in here, so you never know . . . OK, who else?'

Blankness returned to their faces.

'How much heat did we start to get from the cops?'

'A lot,' Cromer ventured.

'Too much,' Sweetman corrected him. 'Who's the guy that's been harassing me all the time?' He held up a finger to stop them from replying, even though he was beginning to think that any reply would be good. So far it had been like trying to get blood from millstone grit. 'Do we now know who we're talking about?'

They nodded unsurely, but guessed he was referring to Detective Superintendent Carl Easton.

'So why has he had a vendetta against me for the last two years?'

'Perhaps he doesn't like you.'

'Or perhaps he had another reason? Perhaps it's not personal, perhaps it's business. Y'know, c'mon, let's think outside the box here. I'm put into bat for a crime I definitely did not commit, one you all know I didn't commit, which he knows I didn't commit . . . why? What's his agenda? A cop with a grudge? OK, they exist, but it's going a bit far, don't you think?' Sweetman's eyes narrowed. 'So I ask again – why?'

'Perhaps we should ask him ourselves,' Teddy Bear said. All eyes turned to him. 'I could put the squeeze on him. He'd chat then.'

'That,' said Sweetman, 'could be a bloody good idea.'

'Hang on, hang on,' Grant cut in, dissatisfied with this thinking. 'Is he not just a cop who wants to be the one that catches the big bad wolf? Y'know – career aspirations. You're not suggesting he stole your consignment, are you? That's taking it a bit far, isn't it?'

Sweetman considered this, then relented. 'Yeah, I suppose you could be right.' He sighed, scratched his head. 'He's just a mean bastard prepared to break the rules for a big result, nothing more . . . you're probably spot on there. Maybe my thinking's skewed because I hate the twat so much. It's a bit much to think he's after my business, isn't it?'

*　　*　　*

If he was honest, Henry Christie would say that he could have done without traipsing into Blackpool police station at that ungodly hour on the strength of some half-baked message or other. He would very much have liked to crawl into bed with Kate, clamber all over her for a while, then get some sleep and hope there would be no call-out during the night.

However, he was on-call, no escaping that. Blackpool nick was only a few miles away and he fully intended to fob off the person and head back home ASAP to a warm bed.

It took him less than ten minutes to get to the station. He parked in the basement car park, making his way into the multi-storey building past the entrance to the custody office. There was a lot of noise emanating from there. He took the stairs to the ground floor and went to the back office of the enquiry desk where the front counter clerk was closing down for the night: it was midnight and, like most stations in the county, the enquiry desk closed down at that time.

Henry did not know the woman clerk, so he introduced himself.

'Oh, yeah,' she said to his query, 'I've put her in the waiting room.'

Henry thanked her, sauntered to one of the rooms just off the public foyer and walked in.

His heart literally sank in his chest. He felt it drop to the floor, like a lift hitting the basement. His throat dried instantly and he found it hard to get the words out of his mouth, even though they were only short ones.

'Tara,' he said. 'Hi.'

Ten

The two uniformed constables stared impassively at each other. It was a stand-off, neither of them wanting to give way, rather like Robin Hood and Little John.

There was little to choose between the two officers. They had both been patrol constables all their service and their uniforms were very similar, other than for the insignia they bore. The crest on one of them proclaimed him to be a member of Lancashire Constabulary, whilst the crest on the other identified him as a serving officer of Greater Manchester Police.

Although there was nothing to choose from them in this respect, there was, literally, something between them, and this 'something' was the cause of their disagreement, their bone of contention.

'Definitely not on us,' the GMP officer stated, shaking his head whilst pouting.

'Cannot agree with that,' said the Lancashire officer. 'This,' he gave a sweeping gesture, 'is your patch and whatever happens here is your responsibility.' The Lancashire man folded his arms defiantly.

GMP sighed down his nose. 'I've been working this patch for twelve years and I know where the boundaries are. That,' he pointed to a patch of grass, 'is Greater Manchester, and that,' he pointed a few feet to his right, 'is Lancashire. No question about it.'

Lancashire shook his head. 'Wrong way round. That's yours and this is ours. I'll get a fucking map if I have to.' He was getting, as they say in those parts, 'het up'. 'The boundary line is there.' He drew an imaginary line with his forefinger. 'So that means it's on you.'

GMP's left leg was beginning to do a little impatient jig. 'Not having that.'

Lancashire shrugged. 'That's the way it is.'

Both men now had their arms folded.

They were standing about fifteen feet away from each other, an area of grass between them. Lying on this grass was the object of their disagreement – a dead body, burned, charred, blackened beyond all visual recognition.

'It's on you,' Lancashire said.

'No it isn't,' GMP said petulantly, stressing the last word. 'You have a murder on your patch and you're gonna have to sort it, OK?'

'Not OK.'

And on it went . . .

There was no other call-out during the night, which meant that when Henry eventually got to bed, he had about five hours uninterrupted sleep – or it would have been uninterrupted if he'd been able to actually get to sleep and not toss and turn and sweat and groan all night long.

But whatever, it meant that he was able to get into work for eight that morning.

He drove from home in Blackpool to Lancashire Constabulary HQ at Hutton, to the south of Preston. The journey took about thirty-five minutes. It was a fairly pleasant trek, cutting down across Preston Docks, now a combination of marina, retail park, fast-food outlets, cinema and a variety of apartment-type accommodation.

He drove into the HQ complex, waving at the security man, then driving to the car park near to the recently built major crime unit building, named the Pavilion in memory of the cricket pavilion which had been demolished to pave the way for it. His office was actually situated in what was once a residential block for students attending training courses at the training centre, but it had been snaffled and converted to provide accommodation for the SIO team. They were housed on the middle floor of the block. Henry's office (made from two old bedrooms knocked into one) was halfway down the corridor.

With a filtered and very caffeinated coffee in hand (four-star as opposed to unleaded, he would say), he settled down at his desk to review exactly where he was up to with things. A few phone calls brought him up to date with his most recent cases.

The domestic murder in Bacup was as good as sorted. The wife who had stabbed hubby was due to appear in court. It looked as though a not-guilty plea was being entered, but Henry did not have a problem with that. His job was to ensure the case was as watertight as possible . . . beyond that, anything could, and often did, happen.

At Blackpool, Roy Costain was still at large, evading the cops at every turn. Henry thought that a personal revisit to

113

the Costain household was on the cards. If he got the chance, that's what he would be doing later in the day. 'Look out, Troy Costain,' he mumbled to himself.

He sipped his coffee – from his own filter machine – and savoured its bitter taste. He loved fresh coffee first thing in the morning and the investment in the machine had been worth every penny. He sat back and listened to the signs of the department coming to life.

Despite it being plainly obvious that the detective superintendent who ran the department did not want Henry in the team, Henry loved this job more than any other he had ever done, including the time he had spent on the Regional Crime Squad, as it was then called, which had been exhilarating. He truly believed he had found his vocation, waiting around, as his daughter described it, for people to die.

He just wondered how long he would be able to hold on to it. The pressure of the boss not wanting him, the bad feeling caused by his posting within the rest of the detective community, could be irresistible. That, coupled with the mystical job that the chief constable had promised him, might prove all too much.

In the meantime he was determined to get on and do the best he could. Then he winced at a thought. There was something else preying on his mind too. Tara Wickson. He shuddered when he thought of her.

'Henry!'

Henry jumped out of his reverie, swivelled on his chair. That very detective superintendent – Dave Anger – was leaning into the office.

'Morning.'

'Bob down to my office, will you?'

'Yeah, sure . . . give me a minute, boss.'

'Enjoy your brew. Don't hurry for me.'

He did not hurry. He deliberately savoured his coffee down to the last drops, stood up slowly, stretching a very stiff body. He could feel himself getting out of condition. When he had been suspended from duty he had taken to jogging three miles a day, but since returning to work the long hours he was expected to put in had cut into the exercise regimen. Now, six weeks later, he never ran at all.

He collected some paperwork and strolled casually down the narrow corridor to Dave Anger's office, knocked, entered.

'Take a pew.'

Henry sat.

'Update?' Anger said brusquely.

Henry briefed him about the last two jobs he had attended. Anger listened and asked pertinent questions which Henry was ready for. He seemed to be satisfied that Henry had dealt with the jobs competently, if not spectacularly. Henry wondered if this irked him, the fact that Henry could actually do the job. In some ways, Henry could understand Anger's frustration. He had been recruited from Merseyside Police a few months earlier and was trying to build an effective team around him of people he had chosen. To have someone foisted on him, particularly someone he had suspicions about, did not sit well with him.

When Henry had completed the update, Anger paused.

'How are you?' he finally asked.

'OK.'

'I've spent some time going over your personal record, Henry,' Anger revealed. Henry braced himself. 'Impressive and appalling at the same time.'

'Nice of you to say.'

'You veer between the devil and the deep blue sea, don't you? You are a very brittle character, too. Suffer from nerves, don't you?'

'I don't suffer from nerves,' Henry corrected him. 'Look.' He held up his right hand, flat and steady. 'No dithering there. I've had a nervous breakdown. There is a difference, but I've always done my job, always seen everything through.'

'Hm,' Anger uttered doubtfully. 'Your sickness record is pretty poor.'

'I'd dispute that. I never, ever go off sick with anything minor. I don't let colds or flu keep me off, I don't have a bad back or anything like that. I was off once for a hernia operation, years ago. I think a nervous breakdown is pretty major, don't you?' Henry was starting to prickle and speculate as to where this was leading.

'There's no place for someone with a nervous disposition on the SIO team.'

115

Henry sighed. 'What are you trying, so inelegantly, to say?'

Anger stood up, crossed the room and closed the door quietly. He leaned on the closed door and spoke to the back of Henry's head. 'In case you hadn't already gathered, life for you on the SIO team is going to be very uncomfortable. Heard the phrase "intrusive supervision", Henry? That's what you're going to get and more. I know there are jacks out there more skilled and capable than you and I want them on this team – not you, basically.'

'Who do you have in mind? I'll tell you if they are better than me.'

'The only thing I have in mind is offloading you onto another unsuspecting department. You are a liability and I don't trust your judgement. You will have to go a very long way to impress me.'

'Ahh, judgement . . . that old chestnut.'

'You were suspended for it, then you foolishly got involved in something that ended up with people dying. You should've left well alone, but your judgement let you down again, didn't it?'

Henry suddenly felt exhausted. He scratched his neck and cleared his throat. 'Maybe you need to ask the chief about my involvement with that particular job . . . he might have another tack on it.'

'I'm sure he would,' Anger said cynically. 'You're up his arse, I know . . . but don't use him as your defence, Henry, it's not a pretty thing to do. Actually, by getting you off this team, I'll be doing him a favour, protecting him from some other almighty cock-up with your name on it.'

Fuck you, Henry said – but only to himself.

'Anyway, in the meantime I'll do my best to get you something not too taxing,' Anger promised patronizingly. 'That's if you get out of this department now. Something you can idle your time away with until retirement . . . how long have you left? Three years? How about some nice office job at HQ where you can get a shiny arse, go for fish and chips in the canteen every Friday, work nine to five, ESSO, y'know? Every Saturday and Sunday off. How does that sound?'

Henry rose slowly to his feet. He knew that bright redness

had crept up from below his collar. He stepped across to Anger, who, he saw, cowered slightly.

'Sounds shit, actually.'

It's funny, Henry thought, how different people can have two completely different perspectives. I thought I was completely right for this job, yet my boss thinks I'm a liability. How does that get reconciled?

He slumped back at his desk and stared glumly out of the office window, through the trees towards the tennis courts.

Anger had got it in for him and there seemed no way in which Henry could change this attitude. He shrugged his shoulders and poured himself another coffee which he sipped thoughtfully, wondering how to play the situation.

The only thing he could think was to keep his head down, work hard and get results.

'So, therefore, Detective Superintendent Anger,' he said quietly to himself, 'you'll have to prise me out of here with a lever if you want to get rid of me.' And with that he raised his mug and toasted his boss.

Whitlock was handed a cooked breakfast on a plastic plate with plastic cutlery and a plastic beaker containing hot, strong tea. The cell door remained open as the officer on suicide watch sat down on a chair in the corridor, keeping an eye on the prisoner he'd had to restrain from banging his head on the wall.

Whitlock sat on the bed, looked at his food. He was not hungry, had no desire to touch the breakfast, which was starting to gel obscenely as it cooled. It made him want to retch. He removed the plate from his lap and placed it on the cell floor, holding his tea in both hands, warming himself against the imaginary cold.

He began to shiver.

'Thanks, Kate. I feel much better now.' Karl Donaldson kissed her briefly on each cheek.

'You're not a good drunk.'

'Not used to it.'

They gave each other a friendly hug. Donaldson picked up

his belongings and turned to leave the Christie household, feeling much better after a few slices of warm toast, a cup of black coffee and, of course, two paracetamol tablets.

'I need to get going.'

'Take care and give my love to Karen.'

'I will.'

Five minutes later the FBI legal attaché was on the M55 motorway, heading east away from Blackpool.

'I need a shower, I need a shave, I need a shit in private and I need a solicitor,' Whitlock told the constable in the cell corridor.

'The first two I can sort. You can shit on the bog in the cell. I won't close the cell door, but I promise I won't peek. And I can sort out a brief, no probs.'

The cell complex at Rochdale police station was teeming, prisoners being led into and out of doors, corridors, interview rooms and, of course, cells. Whitlock was guided down towards the washing area, where he stripped off his paper suit and stepped into the curtainless shower cubicle. The water was hot and he stood soaping and shampooing himself for about five minutes, emerging clean and scrubbed. He was handed a clean, but grubby-looking towel to dry himself.

He jiggled back into the creased paper suit and tied it at his waist, his heavy gut hanging over the knot.

'Shave,' he said.

The bobby pointed to a washbasin on which stood a squeeze tube of shaving foam, soap and a disposable safety razor.

'Thanks.'

He took his time over shaving his face, hesitating each time he looked at himself in the polished metal mirror attached to the wall with hidden screws. Finally he finished, wiped and dried his face, stood upright and eased the top half of the paper suit over his flabby shoulders. Turning to face the constable, he announced he had finished his ablutions.

Actually, he did not think he would get away with it.

But he did, assisted by the bored and distracted constable.

As he walked back to his cell, Whitlock had a small smile of triumph on his face.

*   *   *

118

Henry had the telephone to his ear. 'He won't stay out of sight for very long,' he was saying. 'People like him don't . . . yeah, yeah . . . we do need to get him, though . . . I was thinking I'd come across, maybe this afternoon, and put some pressure on the relatives. I mean, after all, it's one of them that's dead . . . yep . . .' Henry became aware of someone standing behind him. He glanced, saw it was Dave Anger holding a piece of paper, flapping it. 'OK . . . probably see you later, Rik, bye.' He hung up, swivelled round to his boss.

'Here.' Anger handed him the paper. 'Body turned up in the east of the county . . . bit of a boundary dispute with it. Could be ours, could be GMP's. Go and have a look . . . and Henry,' he concluded warningly, 'do your best to make sure it's on them.'

Whitlock was informed that the duty solicitor would be with him in about an hour and that detectives would be interviewing him within a couple.

'I'd like to phone my wife.'

The constable nodded. 'Sure.' He unlocked a cupboard in the cell corridor and took out a telephone which he plugged into a socket on the wall. He held out the phone to the prisoner. 'Nine for a line.'

'Thanks.' Whitlock dialled. 'Glenda? Honey? It's me . . . I know, I know . . . I'm sorry. I should've let you know sooner . . . but I'm in big trouble . . . locked up . . . yeah, c'mon, love, it's OK . . . eh? Rochdale. Hm? What have I done? Got involved in something very, very stupid . . . you seen the news? I'll bet it's all over the news . . . bodies, yeah, twenty bodies . . . me . . . yeah, Jesus!' Whitlock had to hold the phone away from his ear as, after he had explained his predicament, his wife screamed and wailed. 'Look, calm down . . . no, I don't want you to come here . . . just sit tight, wait . . . and whatever happens, remember I love you . . . bye,' he finished weakly and hung up.

'OK?' the constable asked.

Whitlock nodded. His eyes were moist, he was close to tears. The PC led him back to his cell and he lay down miserably on the bed, staring up at the graffiti-ridden ceiling, calculating how he was going to make best use of the item he had managed to secrete in his sleeve. He needed the right time and the right place for the best effect.

Henry pointed the remote at the car door, looked over his shoulder and saw the all too familiar figure of Jane Roscoe hurrying towards him. He groaned, his shoulders drooping. What did she want?

Roscoe was the detective inspector tasked with investigating the incident in which Henry had become embroiled which had led to the death of Tara Wickson's husband and others. Henry had spent many hours being skilfully interviewed by her and he knew she was not convinced by his recollection of events and was determined to get to the truth. Unfortunately for Henry, part of the truth was that he had gone to the wire for Tara by covering up for her and now he was beginning to regret his rather hasty, if knightly, decision. He had thought he was doing the right thing, but maybe his judgement was suspect – again. He knew that if the cops got to the real truth, and could prove it, he could easily be prosecuted for perverting the course of justice. And that could mean up to seven years behind bars.

He leaned on the car and waited.

'Hello, Henry,' she panted, slowing up as she reached him. He nodded, now heartily sick of his interactions with her over the last few weeks. It was like having a Jack Russell terrier attached to his trouser leg. Nor did it help the situation that she and Henry had been lovers in the past and both had a bitter aftertaste of the affair in their mouths. 'I've just spoken to Dave Anger.'

'Lucky you.'

'He said you were going on a job down in the Valley.' By 'Valley' she was referring to the Rossendale Valley, but everyone in the Constabulary knew it as the 'Valley'. A posting that often struck fear into most bobbies' hearts.

'He was right.' Henry braced himself, knowing what was coming.

'Said I should tag along with you.'

'That's nice. As a chaperone?'

'No, your assistant.'

Henry's mouth distorted and morphed into a sneer. He shook

his head and opened the driver's door. 'You'd better get in,' he said with resignation, knowing he would be powerless to fight the decision. Under his breath he mouthed the word, 'Fuck' and his lips twisted grotesquely as his face took on the expression which, in Lancashire, would have been described as 'like a bulldog licking the piss off a nettle.'

They drove in silence for the first part of the journey, Henry at the wheel of his Mondeo, acutely aware of Jane Roscoe's presence, trying to concentrate fully on the road, yet desperate to glance at her. He was certain she was eyeing him surreptitiously. The tension between them was almost like a living, breathing thing, could be felt, could be touched. Like a pair of lungs being pumped up, it was almost ready to explode.

In the end it was Henry who broke. He could stand it no longer.

As the car accelerated on to the M65, he blurted, 'OK, so what's the bottom line here?'

There was a beat of silence as Roscoe considered the question, then came back, 'Why Henry, whatever do you mean?'

'I mean – what are you doing here? Why are you here? Why are you accompanying me to this job? Are you harassing me, or what?'

'Henry! Questions, questions, questions,' she tutted, then sniffed. 'Superintendent Anger thought this would be an interesting case for me. He wants me on the SIO team, so he thought I should go and "sit by Nellie" as they say, and watch a master detective at work.'

Henry grunted. 'It might not even be on our patch.'

'But if it is . . .'

'I think we've worked closely enough together in the past, don't you?'

'Yeah, well, this is on a professional basis, not clouded by any personal agenda. As we are no longer "seeing" each other' – here Roscoe tweaked the first and second fingers of each hand to indicate speech marks – 'I'm just happy to learn.' She smiled.

'Mm,' Henry murmured doubtfully. 'How is the investigation going?' he asked, referring to the Tara Wickson debacle. 'You still not happy with my version of events?'

'Not remotely . . . something just doesn't sit right with me.'
She and Henry then did look at each other, eye to eye. Henry
felt a cold chill ripple through his heart and guts as he thought,
*Shit, she might get me here if I'm not careful . . . tenacious
bitch.*

'Still,' Roscoe continued, 'I'll keep digging.'

Henry looked back at the road again, grim-faced. At least
the only living witness to the murder he had covered up was
Tara Wickson. The other people present were now dead and
gone. Henry took a crumb of comfort from that, but not a big
one: Tara was still a wild card and he was not sure which way
she would fall, especially now that the full inquest was
looming.

'You're woofing up the wrong tree,' Henry said, trying to
sound confident. 'You're looking for something that isn't
there.'

'Am I?' Roscoe said. 'Did you know Tara Wickson's back
in the country?'

'Yes . . . no,' Henry said quickly. *Fuck*, he thought again.

Roscoe sniggered. 'Seen her, have you?'

And it was on that question that Henry closed his mouth
and said no more on that subject because he wondered whether
Roscoe was wired up to record the conversation. His mind,
however, returned to the early hours of the morning, when he
had, indeed, seen Tara Wickson.

'He's in with the duty solicitor,' the detective superintendent
said to Karl Donaldson. They were seated in the canteen at
Rochdale police station facing each other over a coffee.
Donaldson was feeling a little better, but not much. His head
still felt hollow and achy. The superintendent's name was
Brooks. He was a member of GMP's SIO team and had been
drafted in to run the inquiry into the deaths of the illegal immigrants. He was looking very stressed about the whole thing.
He shook his head. 'As you can appreciate, this is a mega-
job. The press are all over it, the immigration service – God
love 'em, the useless bastards – Customs and Excise, the Home
Office, the local MP, you and every bugger else and his dog
and I've got to keep them all sweet. The hospital mortuary is
full to bursting with dead bodies, none of which have any ID

on them . . . we think they could be from Albania, but who knows? It's a mess,' he admitted. 'Our chief constable is very twitchy about it, as you would expect. He wants to know everything. Our ACC Ops is running the show, but I'm the one doing the donkey work.' He gave an imitation of a silent scream, shook his head and blew out his cheeks. 'And you, where do you come into all this, Mr Donaldson? Other than being in the wrong place at the wrong time . . . which I'm having trouble buying, by the way.'

Donaldson filled him in with as much as he felt he needed to know, which wasn't much, but when he had finished, Brooks said, 'What's your view on how we progress this?'

The American glanced briefly at the townscape of Rochdale, gathering his thoughts. 'Depends on how deep, long or complicated you want it all to be. The easy thing is to charge the driver with the appropriate offences, try to ID the bodies and pretty much leave it at that. Just another sad tale of illegal immigrants.'

'Or?'

'Or do your job. Go deeper. Spend time and resources on ensuring the bodies get identified – and that will cost a lot of money in man hours – interview relatives, friends, trace their journeys back to source and start identifying the people behind this whole sorry mess . . . whilst at the same time trying to track down the guys who robbed the driver. My guess is that both lines of inquiry will intermesh somewhere along the way.'

Brooks eyed Donaldson. 'What do you think was stolen from the driver?' The two men stared knowingly at each other. 'Drugs?' Brooks ventured.

Donaldson shrugged slowly. 'Who am I to say? But whatever you choose to do, I would like to speak to the driver, if that is possible.'

'Why?'

'Purely from an intelligence point of view,' Donaldson parried.

Brooks nodded sagely. He was a very experienced detective and reading people was his game. 'So you were at the scene purely by accident?' Donaldson nodded. 'An FBI legal attaché on the scene purely by accident – when twenty bodies turn up and a robbery takes place . . . mmm . . . let me think about that one.' He put his chin on his thumb and gazed at the ceiling. 'I don't think so.'

'There always seems to be a doctor or nurse on the scene on a road accident, doesn't there? Same sort of thing.'

'Run it by me again – why do you want to see the driver?'

'Intelligence-gathering . . . the FBI are heavily involved in investigating human trafficking.'

'I'll let you speak to the driver just so long as the interview is fully recorded and a member of my team is present . . . how does that grab you?'

'How about if you are present?'

'OK . . . but remember, I'm only doing this because I'm one of those blokes – and call me old-fashioned if you like – who doesn't believe in coincidence.'

'Henry, hello,' Tara had responded to Henry's words of surprise in the waiting room at Blackpool police station. She stood up and crossed over to him. She looked as good as ever. Slim, blonde, highly attractive if a little too heavy around the jawline to make her stunning. Since Henry had last seen her, she had acquired a golden tan which set off her azure eyes and blonde hair brilliantly. She took hold of Henry's hand, tiptoed into him and kissed him on the cheek. She was wearing a beret tilted at an angle on her head. Henry knew it was covering the injury she had received to her head, the blow from the handle of a gun administered ruthlessly by the man who had gone on to murder her husband. She'd had to have part of her head shaved for the wound to be treated, but six weeks on, it looked as though much of the hair had grown back, at least enough to provide some cover.

Henry recoiled slightly from her lips, even though they felt soft, warm and wonderful, sending a little twelve-volt jolt through him. She gazed with disappointment at him. 'What is it?'

'Nothing, nothing,' he shrugged it off. 'What can I do for you?'

'I need to talk . . . talk things through.' She looked awkwardly around the waiting room. 'Can we go somewhere else? I don't feel at ease here in the police station.'

'Such as where? It's very late.'

'I have a suite down at the Imperial . . . maybe there?' She saw his disinclination to say yes. 'In the bar, I mean.'

He relented. Less than five minutes later he was driving northwards along the promenade, Tara's Mercedes behind him, wondering what the hell he was doing.

The Imperial Hotel is on the sea front at North Shore, Blackpool, a five-star hotel used most famously by visiting politicians during the annual party conferences in the resort. All the great and good had stayed here, some not so good either. Henry knew the hotel well, inside and out, though he was glad to say on that night he did not recognize any of the staff as he sat in the bar being attended by a waiter who brought him a large cappuccino and Tara a black coffee and double brandy.

She took a big mouthful of the spirit and *aahed* as it sank down into her chest and stomach.

Henry waited, sipping his hot frothy coffee.

'The full inquest is in a month,' she said, opening her gambit.

'I'm aware of that.'

'I'm worried about things. About what to say, about being questioned by barristers, about slipping up and telling the truth.' She spoke the last three words in a hush.

Henry rubbed his eyes, scratched his head. 'Just stick to the script and it'll be fine.'

'That's easy for you to say. You're used to being cross-examined, I'm not.' She supped the rest of her brandy, gestured for the waiter to return with a refill.

'It's not like a court of law,' Henry said patiently.

'That's not what I've heard. They're just as hard on you, or they can be, and I feel like I might crack under pressure . . . this isn't easy, you know.'

Henry could feel his heart changing up a gear, whilst his stomach seemed to contract. This was not a reassuring thing to hear. As he massaged his tired face again, his hands shook slightly as though his sugar levels were low.

'If you tell the truth, you'll go to prison for murder,' he said harshly. 'Is that what you want?'

Henry's mind came back to the present. He shivered apprehensively.

125

'You OK?' Jane Roscoe asked.

'Somebody just walked over my grave.' He saw Roscoe smirk.

'How are you and the chief these days?' she asked out of the blue.

He frowned. 'What do you mean?'

'You and FB. Like that, aren't you?' She held up two crossed fingers.

'Oh,' Henry said dubiously, 'haven't seen or spoken to him in weeks.'

'You and he reckon to dislike each other, but actually he looks after you, doesn't he?'

Henry's mouth turned down at the corners. It was true to say that the relationship between him and the chief was a complex one. Henry often thought that Fanshaw-Bayley simply used Henry's skills and abilities callously without any thought to the damage it did to Henry, just so long as a result came about. Having said that, Henry had some things to be grateful to FB for, recently in particular, so there was a two-way exchange, though much of the bias was tilted towards FB. Most lately FB had secured Henry's return to work following suspension, but that in itself was now having repercussions which left Henry feeling a little numb.

'I think we know each other well enough to call a spade a spade, don't you?' Roscoe pummelled on. Obviously she believed she had a right to say anything she wanted to Henry following the acrimonious end to their brief affair. Henry braced himself for something unpleasant. 'Dave Anger wants rid of you from the SIO team.' Henry sighed. So what's new, he thought. 'He's come into the force and been given the job of running the team and he feels hampered by having you in it – someone he first met under very dubious circumstances, someone he suspects is not being quite straight with him. Not a good start, is it? He wants to get people in he knows and can trust.'

'How many people can he know? He's only just come into the force,' said Henry crossly.

'He knows people . . . me, for example. I've shown him how well I work and he wants me on the team. There's others, too. Having people like you dumped on him gives him very little room to manoeuvre.' She paused, then pounced. 'Can I be blunt with you, Henry?'

Henry sighed through his nostrils. 'Would it make any difference if I said no?'

'No.'

He waited nervously.

'This is just between you and me, Henry, and if you repeat any of it, I'll deny it, OK?' Their eyes locked at seventy mph on the M65. Henry had once thought Roscoe beautiful, but now to him her face seemed hard and callous. She had lost a lot of weight and her face had become thinner, chisel-like. 'He's out to get you and so am I . . . but actually all we want is for you to request a move . . . if you don't, life will be very uncomfortable because we'll keep digging and digging into this Wickson thing. We won't let it drop . . . unless you ask for a transfer out.'

Henry, jaw clamped tight, muscles in his face tense, turned his eyes back to the motorway and felt himself begin to waver.

The chance came as Whitlock had planned. He had been wheeled in to see the duty solicitor in an interview room specifically reserved for such private consultations between client and brief. The room was not monitored by either CCTV or audio.

He spent an hour in discussion, told the solicitor everything that had happened to him. In some ways that was good. A cathartic release, but finally the conversation was over.

'Are you ready for the police to interview you now?'

Whitlock nodded. 'There is one thing . . . I don't want to go back into the cell just yet . . . is there any way I could sit here for a while? It's so depressing and claustrophobic, even with the door open. This isn't much better, but at least it's brighter.'

'I'm sure it'll be all right, but I do need to have a chat with the interviewing detectives first. You could be here for a good ten minutes.'

'That's OK . . . just as long as it isn't a cell. It's doing my head in.'

'No probs.' The solicitor pressed the attention button. After a minute the door opened and a civilian gaoler poked his head in.

Karl Donaldson was allowed to listen to Detective Superintendent Brooks's chat with the duty solicitor, together with the two other detectives who would actually be carrying out the interview with Whitlock.

The solicitor did not give much away and the purpose of the interaction was more about setting ground rules than anything else. This was a very big job and everybody wanted to get it right. It took about ten minutes, then they were ready to proceed.

They had been ensconced in one of the interview rooms just off the custody reception area. They emerged like rats out of a tunnel and headed towards the desk.

Brooks said to Donaldson, 'I want to get the initial interview done before I let you loose on the prisoner. We have the facility to watch interviews taking place, so you and me can sit back and watch my detectives talking to this guy for a while.'

It was as good as it was going to get. Donaldson accepted it.

At the custody desk, Brooks spoke to the sergeant. 'We're ready now, Colin.'

The sergeant opened the custody record and made an entry in the log. He turned to the civilian gaoler and asked him to produce Whitlock from his cell.

'He's still in the solicitor's room.'

'What? Why? He should've gone back in a cell.'

'The brief asked if it was OK if he could stay there,' responded the gaoler petulantly.

'And you agreed?' The sergeant stared askance at the duty solicitor, who wilted slightly.

'Er, yeah . . . didn't seem to be a problem. The door is locked.'

'Next time, cell, OK?'

'OK.'

'Go get him.'

Donaldson watched and listened to the exchange with

interest. He knew that there was a move within the British police service to appoint civilian gaolers because they were cheaper to employ than constables. The problem was that, unlike cops, who were steeped in custody procedure and dealing with deceitful baddies, civilian gaolers tended to be rather naïve and trusting.

The gaoler strolled sloppily down the short corridor to the solicitor's room, swinging his keys. He inserted one, unlocked it, pushed.

The door would not open.

He pushed harder, a puzzled expression on his face, which turned worriedly towards the custody desk.

The duty solicitor, Brooks, the interviewing officers and the custody sergeant were huddled in a chat-scrum and were unaware of the gaoler's difficulty. Donaldson, however, had watched him all the way and seen the struggle to open the door. He pushed himself off the custody desk. 'There's something wrong down here.' He hurried down the corridor. 'What is it?'

'Can't get the door open.'

'It is unlocked – yeah?'

'Yeah,' snarled the gaoler.

Donaldson pushed the door. It opened an inch, no more. He looked around the door frame and then stepped back, his foot slipping on something. A moment passed before he realized he had blood on his shoe, blood which was seeping underneath the door.

Without further vacillation he placed his shoulder to the door and pushed hard, his feet slithering in the blood. Slowly the door opened, inch by inch. People gathered behind him. He pushed and the door finally opened wide enough to allow him entry, revealing exactly what Donaldson expected to see: Whitlock's body hanging by the neck from the inner door handle, his wrists slashed up each arm.

Donaldson twisted into the room, bending down to look at Whitlock, whose bloodshot eyes bulged, his tongue hanging thickly out of his mouth. The American knew even before he reached for a pulse that there was nothing that could be done for the long-distance lorry driver.

Eleven

'Superintendent Anger won't be very pleased,' Roscoe pointed out unnecessarily.

'That doesn't surprise me, but the fact of the matter is that this body is lying within our jurisdiction, so it's our murder.'

Henry spoke with an authority that cut Roscoe dead. She clammed up.

Henry knew the area well from many years before when he had served in the Rossendale Valley. The quirk was that to get to Deeply Vale, you had to drive out of Lancashire into Greater Manchester near Bury in order to get back into Lancashire. Deeply Vale thrust out like a peninsula surrounded by the water of a massive Metropolitan area, and if true logic had been applied then the area should probably have been part of that urban sprawl, but it wasn't. Where Henry was now standing was definitely on his patch, which meant he knew exactly where the body was lying.

The reason why Henry knew it so well dated back to the early 1980s when the phenomenon of travelling hippies hit the country. It was a time when such groups of people would, during summer months, descend in droves on various locations, set up camps for weeks on end, and hold impromptu and illegal pop concerts and smoke a lot of hash. Deeply Vale was one of these locations. A peaceful, picturesque area, accessible only via rough farm tracks. Ideal, it might be argued, for such peace-and-love events, but not so great for local residents, councils and cops who had to clear up the mess.

There had been boundary disputes in those days and it was during them that Henry got to know well what was and wasn't in Lancashire.

A couple of Greater Manchester detectives from Bury

huddled near their car, deep in conversation and surrounded by cigarette smoke. Henry walked over to them and explained the situation. They couldn't have left the scene any faster, so relieved were they that a ball-aching murder was not on their area. Henry watched the exit with a shake of the head, then spun round and surveyed the scene.

By virtue of its openness it would be difficult to secure. It also pained him that quite a few pairs of boots and sets of tyres had been across the scene. But there was one thing that Henry knew well and he reminded himself of it at every murder he attended: you didn't get a second chance at a crime scene. He would do all he could to protect it in order to secure and preserve any evidence to be had. That would be his first task.

Time to get the ball rolling.

Time zones meant that the Costa Blanca in Spain was one hour ahead of Britain.

Carlos Mendoza had been up since dawn, having taken his favourite horse Flamenca out for an hour-long hack in the hills behind the winery, both returning hot and sweaty from the exertion. Mendoza handed the horse to a stable boy who led the beast away for food, water and grooming. Mendoza went into the cool house, showered, then made his way to the pool side where he swam thirty hard lengths before pulling himself out and letting his brown, muscled body dry itself in the early sunshine.

Breakfast – black coffee and warm rolls – was brought to him by a maid. He ate alone at table by the pool, looking down at a view he loved.

It was not the fact that from where his winery was situated he could see down across the coastal plain to the port of Torrevieja and beyond that to the shimmer of the Mediterranean. That was OK, yes. Pleasant, picturesque, yes. What really pleased Mendoza was the sight of dozens of huge cranes standing there in the distance, reminding him of the flamingos which could be found feeding in the salt pans further north, near Alicante. But, again, this was not what pleased him. What really made him smile was that cranes meant building sites, building sites meant new houses and new houses meant vast profit to him – eventually. Much of his money was tied

131

up in the recent and unprecedented housing boom on the Costa, where prices had doubled in a year. Mendoza owned six large building sites which would become housing estates. He could not build them fast enough to feed the demand. He had even bought a hotel in Torrevieja in which he lodged prospective clients for high-pressure three-day inspection visits.

Although the money was tied up, it was profit for little effort, like most of his enterprises, although the housing market was perhaps the most legitimate area he dabbled in.

A noise made him glance round. He squinted against the sun as he watched his number two, his business director, emerge from the house flanked by two heavies.

'Hola,' Mendoza called with a little wave.

The man – Lopez – nodded and approached his boss. He wore a wide-brimmed straw trilby which shaded his pale skin and thick pink lips. In his hand he carried a briefcase containing the day's business, which he placed on the table. The two heavies who had accompanied him dropped on to sun loungers on the other side of the pool, out of earshot. One read a newspaper, another played with a GameBoy. 'Another beautiful day,' Lopez commented. He flipped open the case.

'Indeed.'

Lopez extracted some papers which he scanned quickly. 'Legit first,' he said. 'Acquisition of land south of the town . . . some pressure needed to be applied.' He smirked. 'The pressure worked and the contracts were signed . . . and you need to sign, also.'

Mendoza nodded.

'Bulldozers will be clearing the site within three weeks.'

'Good, good.'

'Also the supermarket acquisition is going well . . . the present owner has seen the error of his ways . . .' Lopez continued the briefing of his boss, who, he noticed, seemed only to be half-listening, slightly distracted. He continued, despite this. 'Forty more en route to Zeebrugge,' Lopez said, moving on to criminal matters. 'That should gross four hundred thousand sterling . . . twenty crossed yesterday, together with the other merchandise . . . we haven't heard about that yet . . . but the money should start filtering through soon.'

'That is good . . . how is the cash flow?'

'OK,' Lopez said, but not with gusto.

'You hesitate.'

'There is a lot of money tied up in property. We are still borrowing. We need the drug money to help us out, otherwise certain people will become restless.'

Mendoza held up a weary hand. 'I know . . . but the omens are good, aren't they?'

Lopez nodded. '*Si.*'

The maid brought out coffee and rolls for him and the two other guys.

'I have been thinking,' Mendoza said, 'my mind has been wandering, as it often does . . . I was thinking about Verner again . . . I am still unsettled as to how he met his death . . . have we made any further inroads into that situation?'

Lopez shifted on the pool-side chair and wished he hadn't moved an inch. He cleared his throat, then wished he hadn't done that either. Mendoza had noticed both things, things which betrayed inner tensions.

'No, nothing yet. I have our contacts all over Europe probing and asking, but nothing has come out yet.' Lopez screwed up his face.

'Verner was a good operative,' Mendoza said. He was so good that he had murdered over a dozen people on behalf of Mendoza and had been about to dispose of another – John Lloyd Wickson, an entrepreneur from the north of England who had tried to wriggle out of his obligations – when he himself had been assassinated by someone who remained, as yet, unidentified. 'What concerns me,' Mendoza said thoughtfully, 'is that I do not know who could possibly have known Verner's location on that night . . . it worries me, as you know.'

Lopez felt his throat constrict.

'Only you and I knew – isn't that correct?'

Lopez nodded.

'But clearly someone else did too?'

Lopez emitted a stuttery breath. 'I think he may have got careless. He must have been followed for several weeks . . . one of our rivals, is my guess. I won't rest until I find out who, you can trust me on that.'

Mendoza fixed his second-in-command with a glare laced

with acid. 'When you find them, they must die, do you understand that?'

'*Si.*'

'Good . . . now, where were we?'

With a hand which wobbled slightly, Lopez reached into the briefcase to extract more papers.

Henry tutted as he glanced skywards and saw the clouds beginning to thicken and threaten rain. 'Please don't,' he whispered, knowing that if a downpour came it would destroy evidence. He had already got specialists up to the scene: a team from the divisional operational support unit were already planning how they would get a fingertip search underway, spreading out from the body; CSIs were in attendance looking for tyre tracks and doing their usual stuff with the body; scientific support were there and the Home Office pathologist was en route. Lots of other people were coming too, not least Dave Anger and the detective inspector who had been on night duty regarding the domestic murder in Bacup; the chief constable had also intimated that he would be putting in an appearance at some stage, as well as the ACC Operations. Henry was also negotiating the numbers of detectives for the murder team and also a location from where the investigation could be run.

There were many things to consider and Henry did not want to miss anything, especially as everything he did would be under the microscope.

'I'm impressed,' Jane Roscoe said, 'you've got it all under control.'

Henry regarded her cynically. Before they had embarked on their ill-fated affair, she had thought of him as one of the best detectives she had ever met. Now, it seemed, she thought he was an incompetent idiot. He was about to open his mouth and tell her something he would regret, but he bit his tongue – literally – to stop his mouth from spouting before his brain got into gear. Instead, he decided to spend a few minutes in deep thought. The last hour had been task, task, task, but now he needed to have a bit of cogitation.

He gave Roscoe a wink and turned away from her, strolling back to where the body lay – using the now well-trodden, but carefully chosen and slightly circuitous route that had been decided everyone approaching the scene would use. This led Henry to the taped cordon which actually surrounded the immediate vicinity of the victim. This was an area that no one was allowed into, unless specifically authorized, the most protected area of all. Henry, even though in charge, did not cross this line. The fewer people the better was the best policy until everything forensically and scientifically had been done.

He knew that crime scenes were precious and that at every scene the offender leaves messages behind indicating motivation and drive for the crime and that investigators must try in their minds to reconstruct what has happened. The crime-scene assessment recognizes that when a murder is committed, three elements exist which are coincidental in time – namely, location, victim and offender. Henry knew that the process of concentrating on the relationship between these three elements can be crucial in the development of lines of enquiry.

Henry looked at the unidentified body lying in the grass. Burned to a crisp from the shins upwards, the skin blackened like overgrilled steak, the surrounding land charred. The body was unrecognizable but Henry could tell it was a man, which was a good start. Obviously he had been brought up to this out-of-the-way place and set alight, probably with petrol as the accelerant. Was he dead before being brought here, or had he been murdered here then set alight? The crime-scene examiners would be able to guess at that and the pathologist would confirm it.

And why here? In the middle of nowhere? Yet no attempt had been made to hide the body . . . why here, on the boundary between Lancashire and Greater Manchester? Was that significant?

And who the hell was the poor victim? When the ident was made, that would give one almighty thrust to the inquiry, but Henry knew that whilst the ID was critical, it shouldn't be rushed at the expense of anything else.

In Henry's experience, this type of killing occurred in two areas – not to say they were exclusive – but he knew of several gangland murders in which the victims had been set alight, and also of several Asian family killings where victims had been burned.

Henry hoped it would be neither, but if he had a choice he

would go for the gangland killing any day. This type of killing was usually driven by simple motives – business deals gone wrong, debts unpaid, whatever . . . but Asian murders were far more complex to deal with and were usually related to family matters that could be impenetrable.

If he had been asked to make a guess, he would have said this was probably gang-related and that most of the work he and his team would have to undertake would be in Manchester. Not rocket science by any means.

'Thoughts?'

Henry spun. Roscoe was behind him.

'To quote from the *Murder Investigation Manual*,' Henry said haughtily, '"Why, plus where, plus how, equals who," and the old maxim, "Find out how a person lived and you will find out how they died."'

'Very profound.'

'But also very true.'

It was a very defensive Superintendent Brooks who faced Karl Donaldson at Rochdale police station. 'If somebody wants to kill themselves, are determined and devious enough, then no matter what measures you put in place, they'll do it. They will lie in wait for the opportunity and they'll top themselves.'

Donaldson glared furiously at him, knowing what he was saying was true, but . . . big *but* . . .

'But,' Brooks went on, picking up on Donaldson's thoughts, 'there is no excuse to let it happen to someone in custody, particularly someone who should have been under constant supervision.' His head shook as he considered the enormity of the problem. Yes, bad enough if any prisoner does it, but one responsible for the deaths of so many other people was unthinkable. 'Somehow he managed to secrete a safety razor on him. He removed its blade, then when he got time alone – when we were talking to his solicitor – he stripped off his paper suit, tore it into strips, twisted them like a rope, made a noose and hung himself on the door handle after slitting his wrists.'

'Double whammy.'

'I just wish he'd done it elsewhere, the bastard. We're going to get some real flak for this. Everybody and his dog'll want a piece of us.' Brooks looked beleaguered.

'And not only that, it screws up the investigation. He could have been the direct key to unlocking a whole chain of illegal people smuggling.' Donaldson's temper got the better of him and he slammed his fist on to the desk.

A strange, knowing expression came to Brooks's face. 'Why are you so bothered, Mr Donaldson? If you are to be believed, you were just an innocent passer-by.'

'International crime is my remit.'

'Bollocks! You've been really cagey with me and I think I've had enough of it. If you were the innocent bystander you claim to be, then it's time to say goodbye. I'm sorry you were involved in it, but thanks for making a statement. I can well do without you muddying the waters. However, if your involvement is deeper, then I should be knowing.'

They were in Brooks's office, sitting on opposite sides of the desk, steadily holding each other's gaze.

'I made a few phone calls earlier,' Brooks admitted. He beamed as he revealed, 'You had a multi-agency team at the Port of Hull yesterday, didn't you? Please do not continue to duck and dive, Mr Donaldson. I don't have the time for it. Be straight with me or piss off because I'm up to my neck in shit right now. If you're worried about confidentiality, don't be. I'm as honest and reliable as the day is long, and if you've got something which will help me, I need to know.'

Donaldson exhaled. 'OK, I did pull a team together yesterday, but we hit the wrong vehicle. It *was* a coincidence I was on the motorway when Whitlock got robbed, actually.'

'His vehicle was the one you should have stopped, isn't it?'

Donaldson nodded.

'It's like getting blood out of a stone, talking to you.'

Donaldson smirked.

'Can I hazard a guess at something?'

'Fire away.'

'You investigate organized crime on the continent of Europe that has ties with US organized crime?' Donaldson gave a slight shrug. Brooks pushed on. 'And you were acting on information at Hull, but the information was not quite right, shall we say?' Donaldson raised his eyebrows. 'Am I on the right track?'

'Could be.'

'But you're not going to say any more?'

'Nope.'

'Why not? Inter-agency cooperation and all that?'

Another smirk crossed Donaldson's face, this time a very sardonic one.

'The great myth of modern law enforcement,' Brooks said. 'Inter-agency working . . . only when it suits, but in most cases, knowledge is power.'

The smirk remained on Donaldson's face.

'OK, then.' Brooks laid his hands flat on his desk. 'Just tell me one thing . . . was it definitely drugs as well as bodies in the lorry?'

The smirk evolved into a smile of confirmation. 'Millions of pounds worth of coke.'

Brooks's jaw dropped and his lips opened with a little 'pop'. 'Shit!' he uttered as a scenario dawned on him. 'Stolen by one gang from another . . . gang wars here we come.'

Henry Christie began his policing career in East Lancashire. His first posting as a newly scrubbed bobby off the production line had been to Blackburn – then, as now, the busiest town in the county – closely followed by a move (for manpower reasons he had been told) to the Rossendale Valley, which is where he had really learned to be a cop.

He had attended his first sudden death in Rossendale. It had not been suspicious, just an old lady who had died and not been seen for a few days, nor had she seen her doctor for a few weeks, so there had been the necessity for a post-mortem. This had been carried out in the mortuary situated, appropriately, in the cemetery on Burnley Road, Rawtenstall.

The memories of that first PM were still vivid in his mind, even after all these years. It had been such a big thing: the journey following the hearse from the woman's home to the morgue, assisting the undertakers to heave the very large body from vehicle to gurney to slab, undressing her ready for the examination; then Henry's sergeant – in collusion with the pathologist – closed all the doors and windows and

138

turned the heat up so the stench of death would, hopefully, become unbearable and the young officer – PC Christie – would give them some amusement by lurching out and hurling up.

The tyro cop had taken it in his stride. He hated the smell of death, the way it clung to nasal hairs, grabbed and did not let go of clothing, but he had never once been sick.

Ahh, the good old days, Henry thought. That sort of treatment of police probationers these days would probably end up in an employment tribunal.

And now, suitably masked and gowned, he was back at that mortuary, looking at the remnants of a body that had been burned beyond all recognition. It was a shrivelled, blackened mess, parts of it charred away like paper, other parts burned away completely – such as the face. The skin and muscle tissue had been well and truly razed, leaving a burned-black skull. Henry walked slowly round the mortuary slab, taking his time, taking in everything as it was because soon, except for the still photographs and video footage of the PM, very little would be left of this body once the pathologist got his knife into it.

A slightly woozy Jane Roscoe, also masked and gowned, sat in the corner of the room, swallowing heavily, watching the activity: the CSI recording everything, the pathologist carefully preparing his tools, the mortuary assistant doing everything else . . . and Henry on the prowl. His eyes watching, studying, his brain clicking over, learning.

The odour of burned flesh was overpowering here, despite the windows being opened. Roscoe was feeling quite unwell.

Henry circled and reached the pathologist who, once again, was Dr Baines.

Roscoe also knew Baines, had worked closely with him previously. He was probably the most popular Home Office pathologist on the rota and always worked well with the police, eager to share his knowledge. He and Henry were in a mini-scrum, muttering under their breaths into each other's ears with muffled sounds from behind their surgical masks. Roscoe strained to hear, but could not quite make out a thing. She assumed they were discussing the body.

Wrong.

'I see that bonny, if homely, Mrs Roscoe is here,' Baines noted.

'Uh-huh.'

'You still plating her?'

'What?'

'Y'know – dinner-plating her.'

'Eh?'

'Y'know . . .' Baines pretended to hold a dinner plate between his hands, which he pretended to lick, making a slurping noise. 'Gravy off a plate?'

Henry groaned at the less than subtle reference to cunnilingus. 'Sometimes you make me sick, Doc.'

'So what's new?' giggled the massively educated professional like a schoolkid. He eased on his latex gloves. 'So . . . are you?'

'No.'

'Not surprised. There's a certain tension between you.'

'Tension is an understatement.'

'You should really keep your dick behind the barn doors, H,' the pathologist admonished.

'Doing my best-ish,' Henry said doubtfully.

'And failing miserably, I'll bet.' Baines turned to the body. 'Now, let us begin. Are we recording, please?' he asked the mortuary assistant, who pressed a button which switched on the three wall-mounted video cameras. Baines moved to the slab. 'A terrible, terrible way to die . . . if, indeed, death was this way.' He began to commentate for the benefit of the recording, describing the body and the burns in minute detail, always surprising Henry with his observations. For over ten minutes he talked and did not even once touch the body. Then he reached the stage where he could truly begin the physical examination.

'No chance of fingerprints,' he said, inspecting each blackened digit. 'Now, let's have a look underneath first . . . you never know, there might be a knife in there.'

With the mortuary assistant, Baines gripped the body and rolled it up on to its side. Baines bent double and looked closely, 'Hmm-ing' to himself. 'Well, he wasn't killed where you found him, Henry. He was certainly dead before he was set alight. The back is virtually untouched by the fire, from

140

the shoulders down to the backside, so he was laid out on his back before being set on fire. He was either dead or unconscious at that point, but I would say dead, though I will confirm that of course.' He turned to the mortuary assistant. 'Can we cut off the clothing, please.' He looked across the body at Henry. 'The item of clothing on the upper body is a T-shirt, by the way, not burned at all on the back. Looks like it has some rock-group tour dates on it . . . bit of a line of enquiry for you there, maybe.' Henry nodded. The assistant began to ease up the fabric, revealing the man's skinny back. Henry walked round for a better view without getting in Baines's way.

'Oh,' he said.

'Yes,' said Baines. 'This man has been shot twice in the back.'

Mendoza actually did little business from the winery. Other than occasional briefings from Lopez he did most of his dealings on the hoof, meeting people, phoning people, killing people; sometimes he did it himself, more often he used hired hands, men he knew he could trust.

Verner had been one of those. Originally a Brit, Verner had emigrated with his family to New York and from there had turned to a life of crime. He became a remarkable and ruthless killer for the mob, but when the heat turned up and the Feds started manoeuvring he was moved quickly to Europe, where he came under Mendoza's line management. He carried on working for Mendoza with ruthless efficiency until he came to an ugly end in England, gunned down by an unknown shooter who was still on the loose. Despite all of Mendoza's resources, that killer still remained unidentified, something which rattled the Spaniard.

Surely a name should be surfacing by now, he demanded.

But nothing . . . other than the Cosa Nostra, members of which were starting to ask awkward questions about Mendoza and his lack of control.

Mendoza and Lopez and the two heavies had driven into Torrevieja, where Mendoza owned a few bars and a couple of restaurants, one of which overlooked the harbour. At six p.m. that afternoon, Mendoza was sitting on the terrace of that restaurant, enjoying the heat, the view and the cool drink in front of him. He had ordered prawns in garlic and was waiting with anticipation for its arrival.

Lopez was pacing up and down the quayside, speaking animatedly into his mobile phone. The two guards sat at the far end of the restaurant, dozing; at the table opposite Mendoza sat the manager of the restaurant, going through the accounts.

'Business is not good,' the manager wailed as Mendoza looked at the figures.

'Why not?'

The manager shrugged.

'Two months ago this was the best eating place in town . . . what has happened? Has the food gone off?'

'No, Señor. People have moved on.'

Mendoza scowled at him, thinking that the poorly performing restaurant was just another fly in the ointment. He picked up the accounts and flung them at the manager, who ducked and cowered. Mendoza's voice stayed level. 'Get people back in here,' he said simply. 'Do what you have to. Burn other restaurants down, if necessary. Otherwise, I will have you . . . removed from your post, shall we say? Now get out of my sight, you shit-faced worm.'

The manager dropped to his hands and knees and collected the scattered papers, then scuttled away, terrified.

Lopez finished his phone call. He had been doing a deal with a drug importer in Lisbon. From his body language, Mendoza picked up that the deal had gone through . . . but then the phone rang again.

Mendoza watched Lopez's whole body posture change. He stiffened. His face had a look of shock on it and he immediately shot Mendoza an expression of horror.

Four hours was long enough to be at a post-mortem, especially one like that, but it had to be done. When it was over, Henry gratefully stepped out into the cemetery, where the air was wonderfully fresh, the scent of many flowers hanging in the cool afternoon.

Henry, Roscoe and Baines stood by the door of the

mortuary, enjoying breathing the air into their lungs, until Baines lit up a very smelly cheroot which smelled worse than the dead guy. Both Henry and Roscoe squirmed away from him.

The PM was over, complete, thorough, detailed. Everything that could have been evidence was bagged up and being fast-tracked through forensic submissions. That included the two misshapen slugs that Baines had rooted out of the dead man's heart and the dental X-rays which would go a long way to identifying the body.

After a short debrief and a promise of a quick report followed by a more detailed one, Baines bade the two detectives adios. As he turned away, he pretended to lick an invisible plate.

'What the hell did that mean?' Roscoe asked, puzzled.

'Sick humour . . . don't go there,' Henry said. 'Let's get to the cop shop.' He checked his watch. He had originally scheduled a briefing for four p.m., then put it back when the PM went on longer than anticipated. They jumped into the Mondeo and Henry drove them to Rawtenstall police station, where the incident was to be run from. If it had all gone to plan, twenty detectives, a uniformed support unit (one sergeant, fifteen constables) and various other bods would be waiting for the briefing.

All he had to do now was think of something to say to everyone.

'*Muy mal*,' Lopez said. Very bad.

'Just tell me.'

A waiter appeared with the garlic prawns, sizzling in the skillet. Mendoza waved him away.

Lopez took a breath, steadied himself.

'It is all gone and they are all dead.'

'What is?'

'Everything.'

Then Mendoza knew.

'*Todo?*' he said coldly. 'Everything?'

Lopez nodded numbly.

'Then I am finished,' Mendoza said desperately.

Twelve

For the next fifty-four hours Henry Christie felt as though he hardly took a breath. The time shot by in a spiral of activity and images and it was only at eleven a.m., two days after the initial briefing to his team of detectives, that he found the opportunity to sit down, catch up, review and properly document everything that had transpired.

In days gone by, when Henry had been a pasty-faced rookie, naïve enough to think he could even get away with wearing yellow socks with his uniform, the cops in the Valley had been supervised by a superintendent, a chief inspector and a whole rake of inspectors, one for each town in the Valley and more besides. Now there was one inspector covering the whole lot and it was in this man's office that Henry secreted himself for half an hour to reflect – with a mug of coffee – on the progress, or otherwise, of the investigation.

The inspector was busy up the road in Bacup and Henry knew there was little chance of being interrupted.

Then he began.

The first briefing had gone well. He had revelled in it, despite his nerves, finding himself playing up to the assembled team, which had swelled to include Dave Anger and DI Carradine, the man who saw Henry as a blocker to his career. Even if he said it himself, Henry had performed brilliantly and his gut feeling was that the murder inquiry had got off to a splendid start.

Even the very begrudging Anger commented on Henry's performance with a curt nod and a 'well done'. The atmosphere of feeling good did not last long, though, when Anger announced that both Jane Roscoe and Carradine would be attached to the investigation. Henry accepted the two members of staff with good grace and immediately allocated them the shared role of office manager. Their faces told their own stories. Not happy teddies.

Next up was the media, which had descended in all forms on Rawtenstall police station, clamouring to be fed.

Henry dealt easily with them, feeling more relaxed than ever under the spotlight. He gave them a typical holding statement and promised he would hold press briefings regularly as the investigation continued. He took the opportunity to make a quick appeal for witnesses at that point.

By the time he had finished that first evening it was nearly midnight.

He winced when he remembered he had brought Jane Roscoe with him and that he would have to take her back to headquarters so she could pick up her own car before he could head home. That deflated him somewhat, but when she said that Anger would do the honours instead, Henry nearly jumped for joy. He was home and in bed for one a.m., snuggled up tight to a very hot ex-wife who awoke feeling horny. Their love-making was quick, urgent and fulfilling. Two people who knew each other's bodies, who knew just how to satisfy the other fast or slow. They fell asleep, back pressed to back.

By seven thirty a.m. Henry was forty miles from Blackpool, sitting at Rawtenstall police station a full hour before the second briefing was due.

Everyone was bouncing, ready to rock, motivation and anticipation at a high level.

Early days, Henry thought, knowing that if there was not a significant breakthrough by the end of the next day, spirits would start to flag. At the very least the body needed to be identified, but Henry was confident this would happen sooner rather than later. The nature of the man's death would see to that. No innocent, law-abiding person would get two bullets in the back and then get bonfired; whoever he was, Henry convinced himself, he would have a string of convictions and would have had his DNA taken, which would be on the national database. He would have bet his next pay cheque on that. Even so, it would have been nice to get a breakthrough before that information came through; a good witness, a vehicle type or number, something to really focus the investigation. It was a hell of a shame the dead guy's fingers had been burned off.

Overall, he had a good feeling about it.

That whole next day was hectic and, following the evening debrief at nine p.m., Henry lurched home, knackered, was in bed by ten thirty p.m., only to be up and operating at Rawtenstall by seven thirty a.m. next day. At least the journey was nearly all motorway, so he didn't have to concentrate on driving too much.

He swivelled round in the inspector's desk chair and squinted through the narrow floor-to-ceiling window out to the public car park in front of the police station and beyond to the entrance to the shopping centre.

'Have I covered everything?' he asked himself out loud. 'Have I done as much as I possibly could in the circumstances?'

He thought deeply about the questions, his mind tumbling, revising it all again.

He supped the last of his coffee, now gone cold.

'Yes,' he said firmly. 'I bloody have. Come and scrutinize me, Mr Anger, if you dare.' But he sighed deeply as he got to his feet, collected his paperwork and prepared to leave the office as he had found it. 'A little breakthrough would be nice, though . . .'

Which was very much the thought that Rufus Sweetman was having at that moment in time, as he glared angrily at Tony Cromer and Teddy Bear Jackman. They had spent the last two days heaving their considerable and justified reputations around the city of Manchester in an effort to unearth information which would reveal to them who had stolen the property belonging to their boss.

It had not been a pretty sight.

Blood had been spilled and left in their wake. Snot, vomit too. Shit and piss also, and burnt flesh. They had visited many people, most of whom had been more than willing to divulge what little they knew. Some folks, however, had been truculent and not a little belligerent. Foolish people.

Jackman and Cromer were at the top of their game, a game which they loved and revelled in. One seemed to know what

146

the other was thinking and they acted with the precision, if not the grace, of ballet dancers. And, whenever possible, they took turns, because there was great satisfaction in hearing someone scream when a steam iron, on its hottest setting, was placed on their skin as though they were branding a calf. It was an unworldly sound, but music to their ears.

'Nothing, you say?' Sweetman said.

'Fuck all,' Jackman confirmed to the boss.

Sweetman looked at Cromer, who also confirmed, 'Fuck all.'

'I don't fucking believe it!' roared Sweetman. 'You are telling me that you've been out and about and no one has heard a damn thing? There's millions of quids worth of cocaine been stolen, twenty dagos have snuffed it, and no cunt's heard a thing? No names, sod all?'

'Sorry, boss.'

Sweetman smashed a fist into the wall of his apartment and strutted across to the huge floor-to-ceiling window overlooking the Lowry Museum on Salford Quays. He kicked the window, but it was made of thick, bulletproof glass and did not even tremble.

'Bollocks,' he uttered, spun fiercely on his heels and faced his two rather sheepish men, who both recoiled miserably. As tough and as hard as they were, they still feared the wrath of Sweetman. He left them standing when it came to violence.

'There is a whisper, though.'

Sweetman became very still, waited for Cromer to continue.

'Just a whisper, that's all . . . that a big player is on the streets, someone new, someone untouchable, but no names, nowt.'

'And . . . ?'

'Supposed to be targeting rich kids, university lot, young bankers, accountants, teachers, even . . . no street dealing, just in good class pubs, clubs and offices and on the university campus.'

'And . . . ?' Sweetman insisted again.

'Er . . . that's it,' Cromer said inadequately.

'That's it? You two are a pair of wankers!'

They coloured up wretchedly.

'I wish I was still inside,' Sweetman blasted, shaking his

147

head, his fists clenched. 'Right, right, right . . .' He paced up and down the thick, cream carpet, thinking hard, pounding his head with his fists, trying to get his brain working. 'It's fucked my head up being in the slammer, can't fuckin' think straight, can't get it right.'

He was still pacing when the solicitor, Bradley Grant, entered the room and gingerly took a seat, crossing his legs and raising eyebrows at Teddy Bear and Cromer, gesticulating a question with a shrug of his shoulders: 'What's going on?'

Teddy Bear began to speak. 'We didn't find anything . . .'

'What?' shouted Sweetman, looking up abruptly, stopping in his tiger tracks, his thoughts interrupted. He seemed to notice Grant for the first time. 'Did I say you could speak?' he snarled at Jackman.

Teddy Bear shook his head like an admonished kid.

'No I fucking didn't. I've lost four or five million quid's worth of coke that doesn't belong to me and you make small talk. I'm tryina work out where it's gone, who had the bottle to nick it . . . I wanna get all the players in and I want to hang the twats out to dry until one of them spills his guts . . . like in that film, y'know . . . that one with Bob what's-his-name . . . the gangster thing . . . c'mon, what's it called?' He clicked his fingers rapidly.

'*The Long Good Friday*,' Grant offered.

'Yeah – that one. I think that's what I'll have to do, hang 'em upside down.'

Grant coughed nervously.

'What's that for?' Sweetman demanded savagely.

'Not a good idea, boss. Recriminations afterwards.'

Sweetman was on Grant before he knew what was happening. He spun fast and grabbed the solicitor's face between the fingers of his right hand, squeezing the man's face, digging his nails into the soft skin of his cheeks, puckering his mouth, distorting it and making him whimper fearfully, his eyes almost popping out of his skull.

'Never, ever, question my decisions,' he whispered into Grant's face. He was almost nose to nose with the solicitor, his own eyes glaring and wide. He let go with a flick, stood up and started to pace the room again, trying to control his breathing. Grant rubbed his face, which now bore the deep, half-moon-shaped marks of five fingernails. 'But maybe you're right,' Sweetman conceded. 'It wouldn't do to upset them all at once, would it?' It was a rhetorical question, made even more so by the reluctance of anyone else in the room to answer it.

Having composed himself, Grant spoke hesitantly. 'What about your thoughts on Superintendent Easton?'

Sweetman sneered derisively. 'Hm, been giving it a bit of thought, yeah, but I don't see a detective superintendent dealing a few million quid's worth of coke, do you? Or robbing it in the first place? Naah,' he dismissed the idea. 'He got into my ribs as a coincidence, I reckon. Just got a downer on me.'

'Enough to frame you for a murder you didn't commit?'

'Cops do shite like that. I'm a good target, they want me off the streets, yeah? Nothing else.'

'OK, so who committed the murder you were framed for? That has to be answered, hasn't it?'

'Not my problem,' said Sweetman. 'Don't get me wrong, I haven't finished with Easton yet, I just don't think he's capable of being a drugs dealer, do you? Mr Big? I don't think so.'

Grant shrugged.

'I'm gonna back-shelf him for a while, come back to him later and get this sorted. My first priority is to find out who's got my gear, because it's mine and I want it back and if I don't get it back, I'll be under the hammer.' Sweetman exhaled as though he had just gone ten rounds. He turned back to his two negotiators and influencers. 'Do you think you're up to this, or do I hire people in from the Smoke?'

They looked at each other, their professional pride dented. 'We're up for it,' Cromer assured him. 'Big style.'

'OK,' Sweetman said, accepting this. 'I want to send out a big message, boys. I want to root out the do-badder, here. I want people to come out screaming, "It's him, it's him," because they think they might be the next ones on your list. It's time to stop treating people nicely and time to start cutting bollocks off.'

Henry was back at the scene of the murder. It was still sealed off tight as police officers, CSIs and forensics continued to

149

comb it for clues. Not much of interest had been found, actually. A partial tyre track had been lifted and was now being analysed down at the forensic science lab near Chorley. Little else found seemed to be of much evidential use.

Being a fantastic detective, Henry guessed – not too smartly – that the body had been set on fire by someone dousing the victim with petrol from a can. No great intellectual leap there. Further to that, he speculated that, maybe, the can could well have been bought specifically for that purpose, so he already had detectives visiting petrol stations in the locality to see if any cans had been sold recently. A long shot, maybe, but one worth trying, especially as most garages were equipped with CCTVs and video-recording facilities.

He gazed around almost from the spot on which the body had been discovered.

'Why here?' he asked himself again. He narrowed his eyes into the sunshine as the cogs in his mind whirred and clicked. Deeply Vale was not that well known a place. Whoever brought the body here could not have done so by accident, Henry believed. So what was it that linked the killer to the victim and to this location? That was always the puzzle, those three elements in every murder: killer, victim, location. Always a connection, always a reason.

A support unit personnel carrier, windows darkened, riot grilles tilted back in place on the roof, was parked a hundred metres from where he was standing. It was the vehicle in which the support unit team doing the scene search had arrived. A number of officers in their blue overalls were gathered around the open back doors of the van, sipping tea from the urn they had brought along with them. *Hm*, Henry thought, and sauntered across. They parted as he reached them.

He nodded at a few faces he recognized and said, 'Any chance of a wet?'

'Sure, boss,' a PC responded, grabbing a polystyrene cup and filling it with hot, dark-brown liquid. 'Milk, sugar?'

'Just a drop of milk, thanks.' Henry took the brew and sipped it. The metallic taste evoked many memories for Henry. Days and nights spent at the Toxteth riots on Merseyside in '81, the Messenger dispute in Warrington and, of course, the famous miners' strike in '84. Milestones in Henry's career in terms of massive social and industrial unrest. The tea always tasted the same. You'd throw it away at home, but somehow its appallingness was a comfort in these circumstances.

'Your sergeant about?' Henry asked the PC who had served him.

'In the front seat.'

'Ah, so she is.' Henry spotted the officer sitting alone in the front of the carrier, head down, concentrating on something. Henry walked along the vehicle and tapped on the window. The sergeant looked up, startled. She had been completing the search logs which were spread out on her knees. A large-scale map of the area was on the seat next to her. She put the logs to one side, opened the door and swung her legs out.

'Boss.'

'Hello, Hannah,' Henry said. He knew her reasonably well. She had been originally posted as a PC to Blackpool probably ten years before, promoted after about six years' service. She had spent a short time on CID, which is where Henry knew her from. She preferred the uniform side, though, and as she was a bit of a tomboy, graduated to the rufty-tufty life on support unit, or the 'bish-bash-bosh' squad as they were often called, or even 'Ninjas' because of their skills in defensive tactics. 'How's the search going?'

'OK – but nothing much has come of it.' She sounded apologetic. 'I think we'll have finished later today, to be honest.'

Henry knew the support unit were meticulous in their approach to jobs like this, very proud of their professionalism, so he did not doubt her word . . . but he had been part of search teams in the past and knew how easy it was to miss things. Even objects like knives and guns. 'Will you do me a favour?' he asked, because he hated searches which uncovered nothing. Hannah, the sergeant, nodded. 'Redo the scene, say to a radius of fifty metres?'

She took it in her stride. 'Sure.'

'Thanks, appreciate it.'

The afternoon heat was stifling at Alicante Airport on the Costa Blanca. The asphalt on the roads and the concrete of

151

the multi-storey car park burned to the touch. The hundreds of tourists disgorging from the terminal buildings seemed to put the heat even further up, but inside the structure itself the air conditioning actually made Lopez shiver.

He was standing at the bottom of the dog-leg concourse, down which arrivals walked in order to reach awaiting tour reps, buses, taxis and car-rental firms. He lounged idly behind the array of people who were meeting and greeting – friends, businessmen, reps. His eyes roved continuously, checking and rechecking every face, every movement, because you could never tell when it might come. The arrest or the bullet. He had to keep keen and vigilant.

A mass of bodies had just swarmed through the airport, having alighted a plane from Liverpool. They had been noisy, badly behaved Brits, all displaying the stereotypical lager-lout mentality – or so it seemed to Lopez – though in reality it was probably only a small minority who were chanting football songs.

The plane he was waiting for, from Rotterdam, had just landed. The passengers were due through shortly.

Lopez found himself thinking about Mendoza, his boss, and the predicament he was in at the moment.

Many people wrongly believe that top criminals are rolling in money. Sometimes it was true, but like other businesses in the legitimate arena, even crime has its ups and downs. Sometimes there was solvency, sometimes not. Sometimes there was loads of cash, other times it was tight. Sometimes you could loan, sometimes you needed to borrow. Sometimes business was good and sometimes it was *muy mal*. Feast or famine.

And just at that moment for Carlos Mendoza, life was looking rather grim. He had lent money – other people's money – and failed to get it back. Case in point was the second-rate gangster from the north of England who had borrowed money from Mendoza to initiate criminal activity. The guy had been a loser, a no-hoper – the money never came back and Mendoza had resorted to having him wasted and had transferred the debt to his more successful brother . . . who now languished in prison, unable to pay a bean, even if he had wanted to. The problem would have been manageable had Mendoza not compounded it by then borrowing a huge amount of money himself to purchase cocaine from a Colombian cartel for a deal he had set up in England. That massive consignment had now been stolen and Mendoza found himself in hock in excess of two million pounds sterling without any conceivable way of paying it off, because the majority of his wealth was tied up in building sites and half-built properties around the Costa.

It wasn't as though the debt was with a respectable clearing bank, either. Not the Bank of Santander, not Telebanco.

But the Cosa Nostra. They were his financiers.

Lopez knew that interest payments were already overdue and no one, not even someone of Mendoza's stature, would be allowed to welch.

Mendoza had already received a polite phone call from a 'business partner' in Sicily, enquiring as to how the deal was progressing and looking forward to the first instalment.

It was a call that Mendoza had reacted to with horror, making him recognize that, as big as he was in the world of organized crime, he was nowhere near the players who lounged around in the sun in Palermo. All he was, was another fairly minor cog in their engine and they had the power to change gear whenever they wanted.

The illegal-immigration side of Mendoza's business was going well, but even the profits from that were not as great as the media claimed. So many people were involved in the chain of events who needed paying, that by the time Mendoza received his cut, whilst considerable, it was not as great as people imagined and nowhere near enough to clear his debts to the Mafia.

In short, Mendoza was in a critical condition and if he wanted to save himself, he needed to act swiftly, decisively and ruthlessly.

Which was why Lopez was at the airport.

He chuckled to himself as he stood there

The passengers from the Rotterdam flight filtered peacefully through the airport until there was just a dribble left.

Lopez grinned as the man he was waiting for appeared. They glanced at each other, nodded almost imperceptibly. Lopez turned and walked out ahead of him, stepping into the oppressive heat of the day, crossing the road and making for the multi-storey car park where he had parked the car he had arrived in, an unspectacular-looking Seat. A driver sat in it, waiting patiently. Lopez paused at the car and waited to greet the man who had discreetly followed him.

His face broke into a wide smile as they shook hands, embraced, and indulged in a lot of hearty back-patting. 'Ramon, my friend, it is good to see you. Very good.'

'And you, and you,' Ramon responded ebulliently. '*Como esta?*'

'*Muy bien* . . . come, we need to get out of this heat . . . you sit in the front next to Miguel . . .' He opened the door for Ramon, the guy who headed Mendoza's operations at Zeebrugge. The chill from the air-conditioning system whipped up.

Ramon hesitated, almost stepped backwards. His smile dropped and he eyed Lopez suspiciously. 'What is this?'

Lopez laughed, sensing quickly what Ramon was worried about. 'Ahh, the front seat,' he said knowingly. 'The death seat . . . the bullet in the back of the head seat . . . do not worry, my friend . . . it is nothing like that.'

Ramon was not convinced. He knew of too many people who had been foolish enough to be suckered into climbing into front passenger seats of cars for innocent journeys, only to have their brains blown out or their throats slit, or to be strangled with piano wire.

'Are you sure?'

Lopez smiled, but was irritated. 'Of course. We have urgent business . . . but I have a laptop in the back seat, and papers which I need to work on. Come, my friend, have you heard of anyone being beaten to death by a laptop computer? No, I think not . . . please . . .'

Spinks was the name of the big man operating on the Rochdale side of Manchester. He owned pubs and clubs, controlled all the town-centre drugs trade via his bouncers on the doors. Control the doors, control the drugs. That was the saying. He lived a flash lifestyle with good cars, clothes and good-looking women. He was brazen and open and did not mind who knew just how wealthy he was, which was partly his downfall. The other 'partly' was that he had once called Rufus Sweetman a 'no-good shit' and threatened that one day he would 'take everything he owned away from him'.

In those terms, Spinks was a good starting point for Sweetman.

Teddy Bear Jackman and Tony Cromer did not take long to latch on to Spinks. They cruised the streets of Rochdale for a while, wondering where best to find him, racking their brains for inspiration, when suddenly Jackman blurted, 'Vic and Tom's!'

Cromer smiled wickedly. 'You're bloody right.' He was driving and executed a wild u-turn without warning or signals and accelerated in the direction of the town centre. He abandoned the car on double yellows outside the high-class hair salon known as 'Vic and Tom's' on a crowded side street close to the location of the world's first ever Co-op.

Side by side they muscled into the busy salon, a place frequented by the area's richest and swankiest women, the side of the business run by Victoria. All eyes swivelled and watched the progress of the two heavies across the shop floor and out the other side through Wild-West-type saloon swing doors into Tom's. This was a gent's hair stylist designed to resemble a Victorian barber's shop, all tiles and leather chairs. It was busy in here, too, a customer on every chair, several waiting, reading magazines.

Cromer and Jackman continued their relentless march towards the office at the far end of the salon, until one of the braver members of staff, tiny scissors in hand, stepped in front of them.

'Can I help you gents? It's appointment only, you know?' he challenged nervously, eyes taking in the sheer bulk and animalism of the two men . . . and rather liking what he saw.

'We've come to see Tom,' Cromer said.

The hairdresser shook his head. 'Not in. Sorry. Can I take a message?'

'Fuck off!' Jackman growled.

The scissors wavered in the air. All eyes were now focused on the incident.

'I'm sorry, he's not in, honestly.' His voice sounded weedy.

'I'll just check that out, if you don't mind,' Cromer said,

leaning towards the young man, 'by going in there' – he pointed to the office – 'and having a look.'

'Staff only,' he squeaked.

Cromer's hands closed around the scissors and he eased them gently off the hairdresser's thumb and finger. He held them like a knife. 'Like my friend said – fuck off.'

Meekly the hairdresser stepped aside, slim shoulders drooping, his body deflated. Cromer and Jackman walked past as though nothing had happened. They barged into the office.

Tom looked up in surprise, as did his newest sixteen-year-old male employee, who was kneeling down in front of Tom.

'Jesus Christ, I told you lot to . . .' Tom began, knocking the young man away with a slap and attempting to do up his trousers. 'What the . . . ?' he continued when he saw who was interrupting him, hopping around. 'What do you want?'

'Just a little word,' Cromer smiled cruelly. He clicked the scissors. 'You – out,' he told the young lad, who scuttled out of the office, trying to rise from his knees as he went, leaving his boss to face two very evil-looking men.

The MIR at Rawtenstall police station was quiet when Henry arrived back from the revisit to the murder scene. The only person in was Jane Roscoe, who was deep in a review of actions taken and pending. All other officers were out, just as it should be, Henry thought. Out digging, overturning rocks, annoying the bugs which lived under them. One other person, though, should have been in the office.

Henry strolled across to Roscoe, his eyes taking in everything which had been plastered on the walls. Known details about the victim, the location, speculation about motives, time-lines, photos of the scene and all manner of other items from the intelligence cell Henry had established, including where to buy the best sandwich in town.

Roscoe did not notice Henry's approach. She looked up, startled, to see him hovering next to her.

'Where's my chum, Carradine?'

'Lunch,' Roscoe said shortly. 'Gone with . . .' She checked herself abruptly.

'With who?' Henry asked.

Roscoe looked away, averting her eyes.

'With who?' Henry probed again, wondering why he even wanted to know, because he could not really care less who Carradine lunched with. It was just that Roscoe's reaction had made him curious.

'Mr Anger.'

'Oh, right . . . good mates, are they?'

'Served in Merseyside together.' Roscoe peered at Henry as he juggled this bit of information in his brain and could not stop from letting his face do the talking. So Carradine and Anger were old mates. Carradine had started his career in Liverpool, later transferring to Lancashire. That had been a good few years ago. Anger had served in Merseyside too, before his own, more recent, transfer across the border to the head of the SIO team. Shit. Old buddies. Anger promises he'll look after Carradine, get him a job on the SIO team and instead gets lumbered with Henry Christie whom he cannot seem to offload. Henry was in the way of Anger doing Carradine a good turn. That explained Carradine's behaviour and attitude towards Henry.

He allowed himself a short, mirthless laugh, and gave Roscoe a knowing look.

'Anything new I need to know about?' Henry inquired, bringing the whole thing back to a more professional footing. 'DNA back? Firearms?' She shook her head to both. 'Chase 'em up, will you?' Henry veered away and left the MIR, now understanding that he had obstructed a promised move. A rather wicked grin appeared on his face. Knowing that made him even more resolved to stick in there and show the bastards.

'Don't get me wrong, Ted, but I quite enjoyed that.' Cromer made a snipping gesture with the first two fingers of his right hand. Both men erupted in laughter.

'Which bit – getting hold of Tom's knob?'

'No – snipping off that little bit of foreskin.'

'He screamed a bit, though.'

'Yeah – but at least he told us where to find Spinksy.'

'Should've told us when we first asked.'

'Should've,' agreed Cromer.

'There *was* a lot of blood wasn't there . . . ? I mean, for such a small cut.'

'Gallons . . . wouldn't stop flowing.'

'Bet it's gonna sting.'

They were walking side by side across the moor-top golf course at Whitworth, a cold, damp, windswept course which had wonderful sweeping views away towards Rochdale and Manchester beyond. They had seen Spinks's Bentley in the car park, so they knew he was here and the information passed so painfully by Tom through screams, gasps and penile blood flow was correct. He had told them that Spinks was at Whitworth Golf Club with his girlfriend, but if he wasn't, he would be shagging her at his house.

Cromer and Jackman warned Tom not to contact Spinks, otherwise they would return and cut his dick off. He had promised them he would comply with that reasonable request as he dabbed at his bleeding genitalia with one of the salon's towels.

Even though the day was pleasant, the wind was whipping around the moors. The sheep and cattle which roamed unchecked over the course, leaving their droppings and hoof prints all over the tees and greens, looked cold and miserable.

There were few players on the course. The pair easily spotted Spinks and his lady on the eighth, approaching the green, very concentrated on their game. They did not clock the two men until both balls were on the green and within putting distance of the hole. They were laughing and joking with each other in an intimate way.

Cromer and Jackman took up a position on the edge of the green, side by side, hands clasped around their backs, watching as though they were golf aficionados.

Spinks was lining up for a long putt, head down, taking a few practice swings. It was his girlfriend who saw the deadly duo first.

'Johnny,' she said, looking worriedly past Spinks.

'Shh, I'm gonna hole this, babe.'

'Johnny.' Her voice became a little more urgent.

His head swivelled impatiently towards her, about to deliver short shrift for interrupting his concentration. He saw her expression, stood upright from his unplayed shot and turned in the direction of her stare.

Cromer gave him a friendly wave. 'Go on, it's OK, play your shot,' he called pleasantly. 'Don't let us interrupt you.'

The steamy basement underneath the bar reeked of beer, cigarettes and rotting vegetables. But at that moment, the only thing Ramon's sense of smell could distinguish was that of his own blood . . . and that was difficult enough as his nose had been virtually obliterated, broken by an iron bar, smashed to a pulp. Both his eyes were blackened and swollen, huge now, puffed-up and closing a little more all the time. Not that he could see much anyway because his left eyeball had burst, was oozing blood and puss down his cheek. Below his flattened and bloody nose, his mouth was a mess. Lips split wide open, teeth missing or loose, although before the teeth had gone he had bitten part way through his tongue. His lower jaw was hanging loose, too. Again, a blow from the iron bar, rather like a double-handed tennis shot which, whilst breaking the jaw just below the joint, had sent powerful shock waves coursing through his cranium – almost, only almost, knocking him unconscious.

His head lolled forwards into his chest and nothing seemed to make sense any more. Pain seared through his torso following the beating he had received. His fingers had been broken one at a time, snapped back like twigs, making Ramon howl with screams he never knew he could voice. His kneecaps had also been the focus of a lot of attention from the iron bar, both having been smashed.

Snot and blood bubbled out of his distorted nose.

But the screaming was over. Although his body was in the most extreme agony, he did not have the reserves to even moan anymore. Every last bit of juice had been beaten out of him remorselessly.

All he wanted now was release. He either wanted to be allowed to die, or to be taken to a hospital and pumped full of morphine.

His head was yanked upright.

'Can you hear me, Ramon?' came the whisper in his ear.

Blood dribbled out of his mouth. He did not have the strength to respond.

'Can you hear me?'

From somewhere, a muffled gasp escaped from his broken lips.

'Tell us the truth, my friend. Tell us the names of the people you conspired with, the people you allowed to steal our property. Just tell us.'

His head was held upright.

'Tell us the truth. You betrayed us, didn't you? You sold us out, didn't you?'

'No,' he managed to say.

'Liar.' His head was dropped, chin bouncing, the pain from the broken jaw arcing through his head like a million volts of electricity.

Lopez stood upright. He was stripped naked to the waist, sweat glistening on his pale, muscular body. 'He's a tough one,' he said to Mendoza, wiping himself down with a towel, 'which is why we recruited him in the first place.' Mendoza was sitting astride a chair, leaning on it, watching the proceedings in a detached way. 'One of his good traits,' Lopez said.

'He's admitted nothing,' Mendoza observed. He lit a cigarillo, blew lazy smoke rings.

'I never expected him to,' Lopez explained.

Mendoza regarded his second in command suspiciously for a long moment. A nerve twitched on Lopez's face. Then he gave a nod, stood up and said, 'Kill him – and then if we have to go on killing to get it back, so be it.'

He walked out of the basement, leaving Lopez and Ramon alone.

'With pleasure,' Lopez said under his breath. He picked up a 9mm pistol from the top of a nearby beer keg and placed the muzzle against Ramon's temple. Something in the injured man made him stir, made him realize what was about to happen. He raised his head and twisted agonizingly to look through his blood-encrusted eyes at Lopez.

'What?' Lopez said. He leaned forwards so he was close to Ramon's face.

'You,' the victim said, once, and managed to gob into Lopez's face, a horrible, thick mixture of liquids. Lopez recoiled, wiping his face angrily. Then, without further hesitation, he shoved the gun into Ramon's left ear and pulled the trigger twice in quick succession, blowing away the

160

opposite side of Ramon's face as the bullets spun out of his skull.

Spinks never made the putt. If he had not been interrupted he would probably have knocked the ball into the hole, which would have made it a par on the eighth. Instead, when he saw the two men by the green and his brain registered who they were, he ran.

Unfortunately for Spinks, his lavish lifestyle did not include fitness training. Consequently he was overweight – not grossly so by any stretch of the imagination – but enough to ensure he did not have the speed or the stamina to outrun the inter-lopers.

Jackman's lifestyle, as Cromer's did, consisted of regular exercise. They trained daily at an exclusive gym in the heart of Manchester, meeting at six thirty a.m. for a three-quarter-hour's workout, including aerobic and strength training. Each man was extremely fit, as they knew they had to be in their line of work. It kept them one step ahead of their competi-tors, who, more often than not, were about as fit as . . . well, Spinks.

Spinks panicked. He threw down his putter and legged it.

Jackman, the faster of the pair, got to him as he leapt into the first bunker. For fun, he rugby tackled Spinks, driving into him like a steamroller, forcing all the breath out of him and landing on him in the sand, pushing Spinks's face down into the neatly raked surface and making him eat a mouthful of it.

The girlfriend watched the proceedings in complete silence.

Cromer dealt with her. A few quiet words and she slotted her putter into her golf bag and walked away without even a backward glance.

Jackman dragged the disarrayed Spinks to his feet and, whilst holding him up by the scruff of the neck, brushed him down.

'You fucking twats . . . !' Spinks started to yell, gasping for breath.

Jackman punched him hard in the lower belly and let go of the collar at the same time, letting Spinks double over on to his knees, every bit of air expelled from him.

When he had almost recovered, Jackman hit him twice more

then he and Cromer led him towards the clubhouse car park, meek and mild, not an ounce of fight left in him.

'That's a good fella,' Cromer cooed patronizingly as they eased him into the back seat of his Bentley. 'Let's have a nice ride.'

Henry seemed to have inherited the inspector's office at Rawtenstall police station. He knew it was only a temporary state of affairs but even so it was useful to have a little bolt hole where he could retreat to and get his mind around things, not just in relation to the murder investigation.

Inwardly he seethed about Anger and Carradine. Old buddies, one looking out for the other. Promising things and then having the temerity to flounce around, sneering at Henry, going out for lunch, then returning together and asking him how things were progressing.

Henry could have punched Anger. He didn't, remaining cool, calm and bubbling.

'Twats,' he muttered in the confines of the inspector's office, then repeated the word for emphasis.

He sat back in the swivel chair again, staring out through the narrow window, watching the public go about their day-to-day business.

'Right,' he said eventually. 'Brain in gear, please.'

SIOs do not exclusively run one investigation at a time. Quite often they are required to steer two or three murders at once, which can be difficult and stressful. At the moment, Henry was fortunate in having only the one, but he still had a watching brief to perform over the fatal accident at Blackpool. In truth he had let that slip a little, knowing that the DS to whom he had entrusted it was more than capable of cracking it without Henry's assistance.

However, Henry needed to keep in touch.

Using an internal phone he called Rik Dean on spec and amazingly managed to get in touch.

'Anything happening?' he asked after the pleasantries.

'Roy Costain has definitely gone to ground,' Dean informed him. 'We've had one or two sightings – he's managed to evade us so far, but he's definitely in town.'

'Have the family helped at all?'

'Bunch of shits – no they haven't. Very obstructive, nothing coming from them at all. I put an FLO in with them, but they're not having it. Still reckon they're going to sue the cops.'

'Not surprising. They don't know right from wrong,' Henry said wearily. 'I definitely need to come and see Troy again. I said I would, but I got side-tracked.'

'Actually I haven't seen Troy for a day or two.'

'Right, OK,' Henry said, winding up the conversation. 'If I get a chance I'll be over later.'

Henry hung up.

Next job was to chase up the DNA results and the firearms analysis. The former should be done by now, the latter, he knew, could take longer. He got on the phone to Jane Roscoe in the MIR down the corridor to ask just exactly what had been done.

'Seen that ad on telly?' Tony Cromer asked Spinks. They were in the Bentley, Cromer at the wheel, Spinks in the rear. Jackman was following behind as they drove away from Whitworth down into the Rossendale Valley. Spinks sat hunched over, hurt and frightened. He knew better than to attempt anything with Cromer. Instead he responded miserably.

'What ad would that be?'

'Oh, God, it's for some car or other. Anyway, this guy sees an advertising hoarding for this car . . . I think it's a Peugeot or something . . . then he looks at his own car, which is a pile of shit . . . gets in his car and starts bouncing it off walls, y'know, ramming it, reversing it, scraping it, until eventually it kinda takes on the shape of the Peugeot in the hoarding . . . do you know which one I mean, now?' He glanced over his shoulder.

'Can't say I do . . . anyway, why're you telling me this? What interest is it to me? I want to know what's going on, what're you two goons playing at?'

Henry was back in the MIR chatting to one of the detectives on the squad who was reporting in about the status of the actions he had been allocated. Roscoe and Carradine were huddled together at a desk, ostensibly discussing MIR management issues, though Henry believed they were gossiping about him. Not good. He definitely was becoming paranoid.

'OK, good stuff,' Henry said to the DC. He looked up as the support-unit sergeant came into the room, dressed in her search overalls and looking like a cat with a mouse. 'Hello, Hannah,' Henry said, noticing she had a small, clear plastic bag in her hand and a video cassette in the other.

'Can I have a word?' she said. Roscoe and Carradine's eyes turned to her as they stopped their little scrum down. 'Think I might've found something.'

They drove into an old mill yard in Stacksteads, a township situated on the long stretch of road in the valley bottom between Bacup and Rawtenstall.

Once there had been many mills in the area, now most had been demolished; those remaining were either derelict or had been converted into factory units. None produced cotton any more.

This particular mill had a long, proud history, but it was now deserted and falling to pieces. Rufus Sweetman had bought it at a knock-down price with the intention of converting it into classy apartments. It stood by the trickle of the River Irwell and may have had some development potential, but Sweetman had owned it for three years and had done nothing with it.

The yard at the rear of the mill was bounded on three sides by twenty-foot-high stone walls and on the fourth side by the mill itself. The entrance to it was by way of a gap in the walls which had once been a proper gate.

Cromer drove the Bentley into the yard, stopping in the middle, gawking up at the multi-storey mill which in its day had produced millions of yards of cotton material. Behind, Jackman parked up the second car at the entrance to the yard.

'Ahh, some history here,' Cromer said. He shook his head sadly. 'All gone now. Everything produced by chinks and wogs these days . . . sad . . . what do you say, Spinksy?'

Spinks sat upright and tight in the back seat, mouth clamped shut, a premonition of horror to come shuddering through his veins. He could not speak.

Cromer patted the steering wheel. 'This is a lovely bus, y'know? Really smooth. Can't quite hear the clock ticking, though . . . ahh, no wonder, it's digital!' He laughed at his joke, twisted his head and looked over his shoulder at his captive with an evil smile.

There was complete silence between the men, the only sound being the gentle, very muted rumble of the huge powerful engine under the bonnet.

'What's going on?' Spinks squeaked, his mouth a dry cave.

'Someone's taken something that doesn't belong to them.'

'Like what?'

'Something that belongs to me boss.'

'Like what?' Spinks asked desperately.

'Like a lot . . . I mean a lot . . . of drugs.'

With that, Cromer snapped the automatic gearbox into drive. He rammed his foot down on the accelerator. The heavy car surged forward like a sports car half its weight, the front end lifting regally as power transferred to the wheels. Cromer held on tight, bracing himself.

Spinks let out a noise somewhere between a gasp and a scream as he saw the mill-yard wall getting closer and closer as the car sped towards it.

'Jesus fucking . . . !' he uttered. Something inside him did not believe that Cromer would do it. No one, no one, in their right mind would, whatever the reason, drive such a beautiful piece of machinery head first into a three-foot-thick stone wall. Surely.

Cromer did.

The car, still accelerating, hit the wall with a sickening thud, throwing Spinks out of his seat, sending him sprawling through the gap between the front seats. Before he could recover himself, Cromer selected reverse and the wheels were skidding as the car began a journey towards the opposite wall.

'You idiot!' screamed Spinks.

The Bentley connected.

Then Cromer was in drive again, but instead of going for another straight-on hit, he went for forty-five degrees, slamming the car into the wall so as to destroy the front offside headlights.

Then back in reverse.

'This is my fucking car, you prick!' Spinks shrieked.

To no effect.

Smack! The car hurtled into the wall behind again.

'Jesus, this is fun!' Cromer yelled with a whoop. 'It'll be a Peugeot when I've finished with it.'

'You bastard!'

Cromer found drive again, but anger, fear, horror, self-preservation all combined in Spinks and he went for Cromer's neck and head. He reached over the seat and his right forearm went under Cromer's chin whilst his fingers went to gouge out Cromer's eyes.

A grim smile came across Cromer's distorted face. He twisted his head downwards and tried to evade Spinks's probing fingers, trying to protect his eyes. The arm across his windpipe he could endure for a few moments, but he needed his vision. He pushed his right foot down and the car sped on, taking a swerving, tyre-squealing course across the mill yard until it rammed into the opposite wall again, smashing the radiator grille. The impact threw both men forward and Spinks lost his grip for a millisecond, just long enough for Cromer to twist and turn away from his attacker, shoulder open the driver's door and roll out of the car.

He hauled open the rear door and snarled at Spinks. 'Out.'

Spinks launched himself at Cromer, leaping out, arms like a pincer, going for the waist.

Cromer sidestepped easily. Spinks crashed to the ground, hurt, humiliated.

There was nothing clinical about what Cromer did next.

He knew it was childish, but even so he took great pleasure in it. With the highly curious eyes of both detective inspector foes on him, Henry ushered the support-unit sergeant out of the MIR, down the corridor into the inspector's office. As he left the MIR, he could not resist a supercilious glance in Roscoe's direction. Nor could he hold back a smirk at Carradine. He almost gave them both the swivel finger, but that would have been one step too far.

Hannah laid out the two items on the desk. 'It's a good job you made us search the scene again,' she said gratefully. 'We were all for packing up.' Henry nodded as he listened, his

166

heart hammering. 'We did the whole area around the scene and found this about twenty-five feet away from where the body was found.' She pointed to the clear plastic bag with a waterproof seal on it – a Lancashire Constabulary evidence bag. Inside it was a piece of crumpled paper which Henry recognized immediately as a sales receipt. 'It's for petrol.' Hannah's eyes caught Henry's. 'And for a petrol can,' she added wonderfully. Henry uttered a short guffaw and raised his eyebrows. 'It's for the purchase of petrol and a petrol can at a twenty-four-hour garage on Bury Road, timed and dated. I took the liberty of calling into the garage on the way back here and found they videoed the forecourt and the shop continuously with two cameras, giving a split screen. This is the video tape which covers the relevant period relating to the sales receipt . . . paid for in cash, by the way. One of the lads is taking a statement from the garage owner and we're trying to track down the cashier who was on duty at the time.'

'Have you viewed the tape?'

She shook her head.

'OK, let's get both items booked into the system. Get the sales receipt off to fingerprints immediately – get a motorcyclist to do it – and then let's you and me sit down and watch a video together . . . well done, by the way.'

'Thanks . . . but down to you, Henry.'

He blushed.

'But then again,' she added, 'it might be nothing.'

It would have been totally unprofessional of Henry to have kept the discovery of the tape to himself. Whilst it irked him, he invited his office managers into the refs room at the station and commandeered the TV and video for the first screening. Time and date were stamped on the bottom of the screen, so it was simple enough to fast forward to the right spot on the tape to link it in with the receipt.

The split screen was very grainy, hazy and in black and white. A cheap system, but better than nothing at all. As he reached the right place on the tape, he slowed it down to normal speed, waiting with anticipation.

The left half of the screen was the forecourt, the right the interior of the shop.

A car drove on and stopped at a pump. A man got out, filled the car. Not the one they were interested in, but even so Henry was slightly disappointed because it was impossible to read the registered number of the vehicle. He frowned. Make and model, yes. Colour would have to be guessed at. But number, no.

The man approached the cashier's window and then disappeared out of shot, before reappearing a few moments later, getting in his car and driving away.

'The shop's locked at midnight, apparently,' Hannah said. 'Everyone pays at the window up to eight a.m.'

'And the camera picks people up on the forecourt, but not at the payment window,' Carradine said. 'Not well sited,' he added.

Then, on the periphery of the screen, another car drove on to the forecourt, but did not stop at the pumps. Other than a shot of the wheels as it crossed the far side of the forecourt, there was nothing.

'Wonder if this is the one?' Roscoe asked.

The time stamp on the screen said three fifty-five a.m.

The detectives waited. The split screens stayed empty.

Henry mussed his face with his hands, impatient.

A man walked into shot on the right side of the screen, walking down the aisle in the shop, reaching up to a shelf for something, then walking back holding a petrol can.

'The cashier,' Henry said.

He disappeared off screen, probably taking up his position behind the counter.

A figure of a man then appeared on the left half of the screen, walking towards the pumps, his back to the camera, holding the petrol can.

'This is the guy who bought the can,' Henry said.

All four cops hunched closer to the screen, watching as the man went to a pump and filled up the can, all the while keeping his back to the lens.

'He knows he's being filmed,' Roscoe said.

Unknowingly, all four of them were holding their breaths, collectively waiting for the man to turn and walk back to the window.

The figure on the screen stood up, slotted the petrol-pump

nozzle on to its holder and screwed the cap on the can. He picked up the can and then walked away from the camera, across the forecourt, and out of shot.

'Cheeky bastard. He paid for it before he served himself.'

They continued to watch the screen for a few moments before Henry fast-forwarded it, but there was nothing else to see.

'Shit,' breathed Carradine. 'Doesn't give us much.'

'Gives us something,' Henry said. 'If this is our man, and there's a good likelihood it is, we've got height, build, clothing, gait . . . good stuff . . . breakthrough. Let's get it copied,' he said to Carradine and Roscoe, 'then I want it sent to technical support to see if they can do anything with the images. I know we only get the bottom edge of a car, but we need to put a make to it, if possible . . . OK, back on your heads,' he said, pushing himself out of his seat, ejecting the video from the player and handing it to Roscoe.

'Well done,' he said to Hannah. 'My gut feeling is that we've just had our first glimpse of a murderer.'

The support-unit sergeant left the room feeling very pleased with herself.

Roscoe looked at Henry as though he were pathetic. 'Another of your conquests, Henry? She looked all gooey-eyed . . . is it the overalls that do it for you?'

Henry exited without comment.

Roads and tracks of varying quality criss-cross the bleak moorland which rises between Bacup and Todmorden, a town nestling just within the boundary of West Yorkshire. Other than the A road which straps across the gap between the two towns, these other roads are not ones on which a Bentley, which when new cost somewhere in the region of £140,000, should be driven. However, the Bentley driven by Tony Cromer was the exception. He purposely picked rough tracks, bouncing the battered luxury car over and into pot-holes and ditches, bottoming it, tearing the ultra-expensive exhaust from its mountings. He spent a good ten minutes enjoying a kind of off-road experience. Eventually he met up with Teddy Bear Jackman, who was waiting patiently in their own car near to the small, hilltop hamlet of Sharneyford.

169

Cromer pulled in, climbed out and stood back to admire his handiwork.

The Bentley had been trashed, but he was impressed by the way in which it kept going. It was undoubtedly a fantastic car and it hurt Cromer to have had to do what he had to do. But business was business.

He walked around to the boot, which he had to force open.

Inside, curled up in a foetal ball, was the equally battered Spinks, who had also just enjoyed an off-road experience. He peered up with eyes surrounded by a face pulped and disfigured and broken by Cromer's merciless beating. He cowered and whined, terrified.

'Got good suspension, your motor.'

Spinks nodded, then coughed blood.

'Well? Change of heart?'

'I don't know anything,' he said weakly.

Cromer nodded. He tossed the Bentley keys into the boot, then leaned in close. 'You have any thoughts about a follow-up, a return match, and you're dead – understand?'

Spinks nodded.

Cromer slammed down the boot and climbed into the waiting car, next to his colleague. 'One down, nine to go.'

It was the end of a long day. Some progress had been made – such as the video from the petrol station. The cashier had been located and was being interviewed, later to be visited by the e-fit expert. It was a good lead and there would be some good actions from it. In the morning Henry fully expected the DNA results to be through, one way or the other, and maybe something from the firearms people at Huntingdon.

But now he was shattered. The nine o'clock debrief had gone well and everyone involved was still very much up for it. The following day's actions had all been allocated and Henry decided to skip a morning briefing so everyone could get working early.

After the debrief, Henry spent half an hour making up the policy log and then, confident he was hitting all bases, he got ready to hit the trail home. The thought of an hour in the car did not fill him with glee, but his bed was calling, and cancelling the morning briefing meant he could laze in it until eight a.m. A lie in!

He stepped out of the police station at nine forty-five p.m.

The evening was cool and fresh, in contrast to his body, which was stale and sweaty. His car was in the small yard at the back of the station and he walked round to it.

His mobile phone rang.

'Henry – it's me, Tara.'

The voice and name smote a wave of horror through him. Tara Wickson.

'Hi,' he said, trying to disguise the note of hysteria in his voice, vividly recalling the other night at the Imperial Hotel in Blackpool. A memory he had tried to bury over the last few days.

Thirteen

The first time Henry Christie had ever seen Tara Wickson he had been very impressed by her looks and had briefly imagined that she might have been 'interested' in him. A male ego thing. Then he had got involved with her and her family and their sordid, lawless affairs, and he had ended up covering for her. Not just a minor thing, but murder, and now it was coming back to haunt him. He had done something which, at the time, he had believed was the right thing to do. Now he regretted it, but was stuck with it because if he told the truth, his life as he knew it would be over. Anger, Roscoe and Lancashire Constabulary would descend on him like a pack of vultures. He would be torn to shreds and dumped.

It all came back to Tara, though. She was on a major guilt trip now. Henry should have been ultra-cool about it, used his interpersonal skills, kept his distance and dealt with it.

171

But instead he did a very stupid thing.

He slept with her.

Their discussion at the Imperial Hotel had gone round in circles, getting nowhere fast. Eventually Henry had looked at his watch and told her he needed to go. She looked disappointed, but nodded. She sighed and held Henry's eye.

He felt something stir in him.

'Just walk me to my room, will you?'

'OK.'

Should have said no.

They rode the lift in silence, side by side, arm in arm. On the second floor she turned left and he followed her down the corridor as though he was in a trance. She stopped outside her room and faced him.

'I did what I did because I thought it was right and proper,' he reiterated his argument. 'In the eyes of the law I have done wrong. I've perverted the course of justice, big time. If it comes out, I'll lose everything,' he concluded simply.

'I know,' she whispered. 'I'm just having difficulty dealing with it. There's no one else I can talk to about it, not even a professional counsellor. They have rules about clients revealing stuff about committing crimes that harm others, stuff like that . . . a counsellor would be duty bound to tell the authorities. I can't talk to my boyfriend or my daughter, or my mum . . . there's just you, Henry. Just you and me. We know the secret.'

He nodded, understandingly.

'And I am grateful for what you did, even if I am having trouble with it.'

'Yeah, yeah.'

There was a silent moment. She was standing in front of Henry, less than a foot away. Their eyes played over each other's faces. Henry could smell her sweet aroma, could see the detail in her face, the fine hairs on her cheeks. Her skin looked wonderful, despite the tiredness in her eyes. Henry felt himself struggle for breath. She had kept the beret on, tilted to cover the head injury she'd received all those weeks ago. Slowly she removed it and turned slightly for him to see.

'Healing nicely,' he commented. It had been a hell of a

blow, splitting her head open. She had looked more than a mess.

'I owe you a lot . . . my freedom for one thing, but I feel weak and helpless and on the verge of blowing it,' she admitted. 'And I just need someone who knows what I've been through to hold me tight, reassure me, and I can't think of anyone else but you.' She edged an inch closer to him and laid a hand on his chest, looked pleadingly up at him with eyes blue, moist, sparkling. Henry's throat tightened. He had once imagined holding her, making love to her, but it had been just that: imagination. Sex with no strings. This was now very different, almost like blackmail, but the feelings were overpowering him and he could not resist sliding his arms around her, one around her shoulders, one to the small of her back, pulling her slim, taut body towards him, feeling her contours moulding themselves against his. Suddenly his blood surged, torrenting through his veins. She ground her hips into him; her head went back as a small gasp escaped from her lips. Then his mouth crushed down on to hers.

And now she was calling him again.

'Henry, I need to speak to you . . . please,' Tara said over the phone.

'Look, Tara, I'm sorry but I haven't got time. I'm really busy.'

'I know you are—'

Henry ended the call with one press of the thumb and felt more like a bastard than ever. He expected an immediate re-call, staring at the display on the phone. It never came.

He veered away from his car and strode across the road to the pub on the corner opposite the station. He was urgently in need of a pint of Stella Artois.

'I thought you said you'd fixed it? I thought you said you'd sorted it . . . well, it's plainly obvious that hasn't happened, has it?'

Lynch stood there white-faced as he was dressed down by the top boss of the drug-dealing organization for which he worked.

'You told me you'd dumped that body in Greater Manchester.'

'I thought I had. In fact, I was sure I had. I misjudged.'

'This could cause us problems.'

'I know, I fucking know.'

'Have they identified him yet?'

Lynch shook his head.

'Only a matter of time,' the boss said. 'Only a matter of time before they start crawling round us . . . and as if we haven't got enough shit to deal with.'

Lynch hung his head and mumbled, 'Our tracks're covered.'

'Son, they better fucking had be.'

Lynch expelled an unsteady breath.

'And what about your chum, PC Bignall? How much does he know? How far can he drop us in it?'

'He won't say owt.'

The boss eyed Lynch. 'His colleagues'll be all over him like a rash when he wakes up. They'll very much be wanting to know how the hell he managed to get shot, won't they? He'll be weak and vulnerable and I'll lay you a pound to a pinch of shit, he'll blab. Do we need that? Do we fuck!'

'What're you suggesting?'

'Finish what you should've done in the first place.'

'Kill him, you mean?'

The boss did not respond, but he did not need to. His look said it all.

'Kill a cop?'

Silence.

'You're saying I kill a cop?'

'I'm saying he'll be one less thing to think about.'

The pint of Stella was ice-cold. Beads of condensation dripped down the outside of the glass. It tasted wonderful. Ice-cold in Rawtenstall, he mused. He took several large gulps and within seconds half of it had disappeared down his throat. Then he checked himself. He could easily have sunk it all, but then he would have wanted another because he would not really have appreciated the first. One, though, was all he was going to have. The length of the journey home saw to that. He moved away from the bar and found an empty table, surveying the pub as his mind churned.

He was annoyed with himself. He had been given a very meaty murder, one with which he could re-establish his reputation as long as he concentrated on it, did all the right things and got a result. The necessity was concentration. A job like this demanded 110 per cent and already he was failing in that department. His personal life was cutting that back to about 70 per cent.

Shit. Another misjudgement. Firstly in that he had covered up a crime and now because he had slept with Tara. Somewhere in his brain was a self-destruct button marked, 'Press Me – It'll Be All Right.' His teeth ground together. It was bad enough having to deal with Tara's guilt not having had sex with her; now it was a million times more difficult. And on top of that was his own guilt. Once again Kate had been betrayed. He had been desperately trying to change, keep a lid on his behaviour, but as the saying went, 'A bastard never changes his spots.' He could not help but want to have sex with other women.

About three-quarters of the pint had gone when his phone rang again. The words 'Number Withheld' on the display made his heart sink. He almost pressed the 'C' button, but reluctantly he answered.

'Henry Christie,' he said cringingly.

'Henry – John Gornall, Forensic Submissions.'

'John – hi.' Henry instinctively checked his watch, but did not make any comment. 'What's happening?'

'I stayed on because ballistics said they'd get back to us today and I was curious. Couldn't wait until tomorrow.'

'They got back to you, then?'

'Yep.' He sounded pleased. Henry waited. 'It's only a phone call from them, remember, but the paperwork will follow.'

'Fine.'

'About the bullet we dug out of that stolen car in Blackpool?'

'Yeah.' Henry tried not to come across as disheartened. He was expecting something about two bullets dug out of a burned corpse's back.

'Interesting stuff . . . the bullet we found in the back seat of that car was fired from a gun used in a building society robbery in Manchester about six months ago.'

'Oh, that is interesting.'

'The scientist at Huntingdon said it was recently fired, too . . . so it hasn't been in the car all that long.'

'Is it linked to any arrest?'

'They don't have that information but there are some case number references to a job in GMP, so it shouldn't be too difficult to get that info.'

'Go on.'

'The bullets were thirty-eights.'

'Right, good.'

'And the guy down in Huntingdon has also been working on the slugs found in the back of the victim in Deeply Vale.'

'Has he something on them, then?'

'Oh yes . . . the gun used in the robbery is the same one which fired the bullet into the car . . . is the same gun which fired bullets into the back of our unknown victim.'

Henry took a nanosecond or two to digest this. 'The bullet in the stolen car, and the bullets in the back of our dead man, come from the same gun. Is that what you are saying, John?'

'Yes.'

'And the gun was used in a robbery in GMP six months ago?'

'Yes.'

Henry sank the remainder of the drink as soon as he finished this call. He looked up at the big-screen TV hanging down in one corner of the bar, showing *Sky News*. The scrolling headlines made Henry reach for his phone again.

North Manchester General Hospital, once known as Crumpsall Hospital, is huge and old. It is a complex warren of corridors and Lynch found that he could wander unchallenged. It helped, he assumed, because he had his ID pinned to his jacket and anyone who displayed any sort of ID was deemed to be kosher.

Lynch knew the hospital well, had been there on numerous occasions for various matters over the years and knew exactly where he was going.

He walked swiftly, businesslike, and found the ward he was looking for, not too far away from the outpatient department.

176

It was late in the day and staff were sparse on the ground. Excellent.

At the entrance to the ward, he paused and peered down into it. On the right was an office, beyond that was the first of two private side wards, then, further on, the public ward.

He knew Bignall's exact location. The problem was getting to him without being spotted. He assumed the night-shift staff were in the office, a fact confirmed by a laugh and the door opening. A nurse stepped out, said something to one of her colleagues in the office, turned and walked into the ward.

Lynch dropped back into the shadow of the corridor. He watched the nurse stroll down the ward, checking on patients, sharing jokes, smiling, being professional. His eyes narrowed as he waited for his moment.

Henry tabbed through the phone book in his mobile until he found Karl Donaldson's number and pressed the call button. The connection was made more or less immediately and he heard the unmistakable tones of Karl's American drawl.

'Hi, pal.' Donaldson sounded weary and far away.

'Karl – how's it going? I'm really sorry about calling you at this time of night. I heard about the death of the lorry driver, but I've been so busy tied up with my own life, I just forgot to phone. It was really bad news.'

'Yeah, pal, thanks. I thought it could've been the opening to the Spaniard, but it didn't happen. One o' those things, I guess.' He pronounced 'things' as 'thangs'.

'Philosophical.'

'That's life, baby. I hear you've been landed with a big, nasty murder.'

'Yeah, gangland thing, I reckon. Not made too much progress yet, but I think things'll begin to move tomorrow. But what's your way forward, re the Spaniard?'

'Just doin' some shakin' down.'

In the background Henry heard music and laughter.

'Where the hell are you?'

'España, babe . . . out where the sun shines three hundred and twenty days each year.'

* * *

The nurse completed her round of the ward and returned to the office, failing to notice the figure of Lynch in the darkness, lurking silently. He waited, then stepped across the corridor and into the mouth of the ward. The door to the office was on the right. He crept close, listening hard. A patient on the ward coughed horribly. Lynch could make out the murmur of voices in the office. He crept nearer. The top half of the door was clear glass. He took a chance, sidled up and peered in with one eye – quickly – before flattening himself against the wall. Two nurses were in the office, sitting, talking.

He bent down and crawled past the door, rising back to his full height as he passed. The next door on the right was the private room in which Bignall was ensconced.

A troublesome thought entered Lynch's head as he reached for the handle. One of those thoughts in which something worries you, but you cannot put your finger on exactly what. He turned the handle and opened the door slightly. His eyes searched the dark room. The dark room! The private room which the nurse had not checked on her round. Why not?

The empty room.

The bed was made up, neat and tidy, bedclothes pulled tight, awaiting the next patient.

Because Bignall was not there.

Karl Donaldson tugged at the unbuttoned collar of his short-sleeved shirt and blew down the front of it, cooling his chest. He was sweating, feeling lines of moisture dribbling down his body, pooling in uncomfortable places.

Although it was almost midnight, Spanish time, the evening heat on the Costa Blanca remained oppressive. He took a sip from his chilled mineral water – memories of overindulgence still lingering – and continued to gaze down the road from the terrace of the restaurant at which he sat. From there he could see the arched entrance leading into the Ciudad Quesada, that being a sprawling estate of villas which had spread rapidly over the last few years to accommodate some of the massive investment in property in the area. It was about five kilometres inland from Torrevieja and Donaldson knew that his informant lived in a huge house on the estate.

Donaldson was more desperate than ever to nail Mendoza.

The man was at the very top of Donaldson's hit list. The American realized that his interest in Mendoza was becoming unhealthy to the point of obsession, but he remained determined to bring him down and his whole organization along the way. Donaldson could trace it all back to the death of Zeke, the undercover FBI agent whom Mendoza had cold-bloodedly had murdered, Zeke the agent that Donaldson had been controlling. Donaldson had taken it personally and, one way or another, Mendoza would soon be history.

He had already partly revenged Zeke's death. Verner, the man who had actually put the bullets into Zeke's brain, had been eliminated, taken out by Donaldson . . . and now all that remained was to do the same to Mendoza.

It had come to that.

Donaldson's nostrils flared at the thought of the man. He could picture the bullet blowing out his brains.

Then he sniffed.

But that would not happen, as much as he dreamed about it.

Donaldson actually wanted to destroy the Spaniard by legitimate means if at all possible, to see him go through the legal process, to watch his face as he was sentenced to life behind bars.

Which is where the informant came in. The man had appeared from nowhere and offered up his services, something that occasionally happens, and gift horses should not be put down too quickly.

He was high up in Mendoza's organization, fulfilling the role of business manager. It was his job to explore new openings, to seek out and explore new markets, to crush rivals if necessary and develop more profit for the boss man. He had been forging new connections in England in the last few years.

The informant was no angel. A couple of years earlier he had ordered a hit on a Manchester criminal, the kill being carried out by Verner. It had been whilst the body of the criminal was being disposed of that Verner had been surprised by two surveillance cops whom he had also murdered and buried. So the informant was very much implicated in the deaths of two cops, a fact which troubled Donaldson, but one which did not prevent him from going for the bigger picture: Mendoza.

Maybe when Mendoza had tumbled he would try to deal with the informant, but in the meantime he needed him.

'Do you require anything more?'

'*Si .. agua mineral, por favor.*'

The waiter nodded and trundled back to the bar.

What the hell am I doing here? Donaldson demanded of himself.

He had jumped on a plane to Alicante on a whim. No particular plan in mind, more just a determination to get to grips with the informant, wring the guy's neck and say, 'What the fuck is going on? Why give me false information about the truck full of immigrants? How did someone else come to stop the truck and get away with the drugs? That cannot have been an accident.' The questions tumbled through his mind.

In fact he had a million questions to ask, but wasn't really sure whether turning up out of the blue on the guy's doorstep would lead to any direct answers. All previous meetings had been in neutral territory – Holland, France – never in Spain itself and certainly never near Mendoza.

But desperation makes a man do foolish things.

The water came. It tasted good.

It was time to contact Mr Lopez.

Even before he knocked he could tell there was no one in. The flat was in darkness – only to be expected at this time of day – but there was something about the place which said to Lynch, *Empty*.

He put his shoulder to the front door, eased a bit of weight into it. It did not move. Standing back, he raised his foot and slammed it just under the Yale lock. The door moved. Twice more he flat-footed it and on the second blow the flimsy door broke and clattered open.

Lynch stepped into the darkened hallway, standing there, listening to the quiet.

Experience told him the place was devoid of life. His senses were not picking up the vibes emitted by human presence.

He went into the living room and switched on the light. He did not do this cautiously because he had nothing to fear.

The room was empty. As he looked round it, his mouth evolved into a sneer underneath his nose. Tatty second-hand furniture, a portable TV, fast-food wrappers tossed around, the stale reek of beer, cigarettes and chips. The room of a financially stretched middle-aged man who had made too many wrong decisions in life. Wrong wife. Wrong mortgage. Wrong everything . . . but a man ripe for the picking. A desperate man who needed money, whatever the source.

It looked as though he had not been back from the hospital.

So, a man on the run, maybe. A man who had made another bad decision. A man deep in trouble.

A man who would definitely die.

'This is dangerous. This is not how we make contact. This is out of order.' Lopez hissed the words down the phone into Donaldson's ear. 'I cannot speak.'

'I need to see you,' the American insisted.

'No.'

'Yes.'

'I cannot.'

'Yes you can,' Donaldson said. 'You wouldn't want Señor Mendoza to find out about our little relationship, would you?'

Heavy silence.

'This is outrageous,' Lopez said angrily.

'You bet your ass,' growled Donaldson.

'Where are you?'

Donaldson told him.

'Here? In Spain? You fool. Have you lost your head?'

'Meet me in an hour,' Donaldson said.

Lopez apologized profusely as he returned to the interior of the restaurant in Torrevieja. The business had closed for custom that night and now three people sat at a table in the centre of the room, picking at a range of tapas.

Mendoza was one of the three. He scowled at Lopez. 'Who the hell was that?'

'No one, no one,' Lopez said, trying to display an air of nonchalance. He took the spare seat at the table, unable to maintain eye contact with Mendoza. His boss sniffed, annoyed, and turned his attention to the other two men seated with him.

One was an old Italian, white-haired, deeply lined face, his rugged, weather-beaten skin burned almost black by the Sicilian sunshine. He had hard, grit-grey eyes and a jaw set firm. He was not a big man, but his presence could be felt at all times. He exuded power and danger.

The other was a much younger man, his grandson. Maybe twenty-two years old, fresh-faced, but had obviously inherited the tough eyes of his older blood relative and just a little bit of his aura. That was something he would grow into, rather like an outsized sweater that would one day fit him perfectly.

The older man sat back and sipped the red wine, his face screwing up at the harsh taste. 'How long have we been working together?' he asked Mendoza.

'A long time.'

'We have done good business over the years.'

Mendoza nodded. 'Very good.' Lopez watched him closely, saw he was very nervous, as he should be. A visit from these men was a rare occurrence.

'But lately things have not been good for you.'

Mendoza shrugged. 'Nature of the business.'

The old man shook his head. 'No, no, no. There is no such thing as the nature of the business, my friend, it is the nature of the man.'

Mendoza's eyes hooded over defensively.

'First there was the issue of the money owed to you by the man in England. He failed to pay his debt and because of that, you failed to pay your debt to us.'

'But I dealt with him,' Mendoza blurted. 'And the debt has been transferred to his brother.'

The old man shook his head again. 'A debt which now rests with a man who is in prison awaiting trial for murder. What are the chances of recovery?' he asked cynically.

Mendoza reddened, squirmed on his seat, said nothing.

'And then the issue of our operative, Mr Verner . . . a man who was rather good at killing. He was on loan to you and he, too, is now dead.'

Mendoza started to say something. His mouth opened and closed soundlessly. His eyes looked as though he was being hunted.

'Someone, somewhere, knew he was about to deal with an

issue for us and, as I understand it, they were lying in wait for his appearance and they killed him.'

'But not before he had carried out his task,' Mendoza argued weakly.

The old man held out his hands, palms forward, a calming gesture. 'The issue is, Carlos, that he was ambushed. That someone knew where he would be at a certain time and place. He was not killed by accident or coincidence . . . do you see what I'm getting at? Do you visualize the picture I am attempting to paint?'

Suddenly Mendoza's mouth dried up as a fear crept up on him, the like of which he had never experienced in his whole existence. Not even looking down the barrel of a gun in a back street in Madrid had invoked such terror. Not even being kidnapped and tortured by a rival gang. But looking and listening to this old man and his grandson was churning his insides, shredding his guts.

'And now, somehow, you lose what, four million pounds worth of goods and twenty illegal immigrants. Fortunately those people paid up front,' the old man said with a dismissive wave, 'but we have financed the drugs and now – poof!' His hands made an exploding gesture. 'Someone has relieved you of them.' He stopped speaking abruptly. His face became expressionless, but his eyes, which bored into Mendoza's, were like tungsten. 'We had faith in you, but something has gone seriously wrong. Maybe you're too enmeshed in it to see what is happening? I don't know, but your organization is, as I imagine your bowels are at this moment, loose.'

'I already know that and I have taken action to plug the holes,' he said, not realizing that his choice of words would have been comical in other circumstances.

'Good.' The old man's eyes moved slowly to Lopez, who felt a shiver of apprehension slide down his spine. Then his attention returned to Mendoza. 'Good, because we are losing faith with you and there will be no more business, no more loans, no more support, unless you make amends very quickly.'

'What do you mean?'

'Pay back your debt in full, otherwise this business relationship is terminated.'

'You can't do that!' The palms of Mendoza's hands slammed down on the table, the action jerking a reaction in the old man's grandson. Throughout the conversation he had remained silent, did not appear to be taking much heed, but always there was a brooding, sunken-eyed presence. His face rose and his eyes locked into Mendoza's, who saw the look and slowly withdrew his hands from the table. Chastened without a word being said, such was the young man's power. 'You know I cannot pay the whole debt.'

'Then what can you offer?'

'I will recover the drugs, then they will go through the original channels of distribution and then the money will start to filter back.'

The old man nodded sagely as he mulled this through.

'Not enough.'

Mendoza was exasperated. 'What then?'

'You own four building sites on which the houses are almost complete . . . as a good-will gesture, they must be signed over to us.'

Mendoza's mouth popped open. There was something like forty million pounds worth of property – potentially – on them, once sales picked up. He felt his insides crumble.

The old man raised his glass of wine. 'My lawyer will meet with yours first thing to arrange the necessities . . . and one more thing.' Mendoza waited for another bombshell. 'Clean up your organization – quickly.'

Fourteen

Henry knew that at some stage in the game, the chief constable would turn up and poke his nose into things which did not concern him – such as this investigation. Obviously and ultimately, everything that went on in that organization called Lancashire Constabulary concerned the chief, but even so, he could have done quite happily without the man's appearance – especially on the day on which the victim was finally identified through DNA.

The temporary DCI – as DI Carradine continually and snidely referred to him, just to wind him up – arrived at Rawtenstall police station at seven thirty-five a.m. the following morning. He'd had a poor night's sleep; thoughts of Tara Wickson, images of bullets being gouged out of dead bodies, tumbling through his brain all night long; thoughts of his latest infidelity, too. Bastard, he called himself many times throughout the night. Prime bastard. That's me. Henry, the changed man. Hardly. Exhausted, he eventually dropped into a fitful sleep at three a.m., awoken by the alarm at six thirty.

Kate had rolled close to him during the night and he could not disguise the huge erection he had woken up displaying. She reached for him, but guilt made him extract himself from her gentle grip, saying he needed a wee.

He did not return to bed, but showered quickly, got dressed and was ready to roll at six fifty.

The morning briefing went well, a buzz of excitement rippling through the assembled detectives at the new information. Lines of enquiry were opening up for people and they eagerly grabbed new actions to follow up.

As they parted, the chief was revealed at the back of the room. Short, squat, rounded, putting on weight, Robert Fanshaw-Bayley grinned at and approached Henry.

They had known each other for a long time. 'FB', as he was commonly known, had been a detective in Lancashire for most of his service, rising steadily but not spectacularly through the ranks. He had been an assistant chief constable before transferring to Her Majesty's Inspectorate of Constabulary for a short time before returning as Lancashire's chief only a matter of weeks before.

Henry had worked for FB in various capacities throughout the years and had usually been ruthlessly used by the higher-ranking officer. The two men could not be said to have been in love with each other, but they had a grudging mutual respect and Henry could get away with saying things to FB that not even a deputy chief constable would dare say. FB had most recently used Henry in the Tara Wickson debacle, but on the other hand had secured Henry's return to work and a position on the SIO team. FB had said Henry would actually be working directly to him on a 'special job', but nothing had transpired about that. Henry put it down as bullshit.

Henry did not know whether to be pleased or worried about FB's unannounced appearance. He squinted thoughtfully at FB as he got nearer.

'How goes it?' FB asked. 'Solved it yet? That's what you're paid for, y'know. How many days is it now? Four? Three days and then murder inquiries go to rat shit, don't they?' He fired the questions at Henry like his mouth was a Gatling gun.

Henry decided to come back with cheek. 'You should know, boss. Not many of your inquiries got solved within six weeks, as I recall.' It wasn't true. FB had headed numerous major investigations and every one had been solved sooner or later.

'Touché,' he said magnanimously. 'Time to talk?' Henry nodded. FB touched him on the shoulder. 'Let's hit the caff on the main drag, then.' Henry walked ahead of FB out of the MIR, just catching sight of Dave Anger coming in through the door at the far end of the room. It was only a brief glimpse, but enough to give Henry the satisfaction of seeing Anger halt quickly and his face go like millstone grit.

The café FB referred to was near the bus station. It served the most outstanding latte Henry had ever tasted. Not that he knew what a true latte should taste like, but, whatever, it was quite wonderful.

'Making progress then – at last,' FB said, adding the last two words sardonically. Henry nodded, a moustache of coffee foam on his top lip. 'It was a good briefing, Henry. Everyone still seems to be well up for it.'

'They seem to be a good bunch.' Henry wiped his lip.

'Rossendale lads.' FB winked.

'Used to be a punishment posting.'

'Still is.' FB had ordered a double espresso which he sipped, then winced.

'I hope – fingers crossed – that the DNA will be back today. I just can't see how anyone with two slugs in his back wouldn't be on record. This is the bit we're struggling with, not identifying the guy. No one coming forward to claim a missing relative. Nothing's come from the media shots at all.'

'That's the way it goes. I remember the handless corpse job in the late '70s,' FB reminisced. 'A definite gangland killing. No ID, then suddenly a bird walks into a police station and says it's her boyfriend. Just like that. Kicked off a massive international job.'

'I remember it well,' Henry said. As a PC in uniform way back then he had been fascinated by the case, which involved the international drugs trade, millions of pounds, unpaid debts, loose women, fast cars. It had been one hell of a story.

'Something'll turn up, is what I'm saying,' FB said. 'So . . . how's things with you?'

'OK,' Henry said hesitantly.

'Dave Anger making life uncomfortable?'

'You know, then?'

'I hear things. Don't worry about him . . . things'll level out, I'm sure . . . especially when you pull this one out of the bag.'

'Yeah, sure.'

'How're other things?'

'Can't wait for the Wickson inquest,' Henry lied.

'I'm sure that'll be fine, too.'

Henry wasn't so sure, but he said nothing about his doubts. 'I hear you're down to investigate that cock-up at Lancaster Crown, that GMP job that went shit-shape.'

'Mm.' FB looked along his nose at Henry. 'Partly why I've come to see you.' Henry waited. 'I'm putting a small team together to look at the allegations. I'd like you to head it.'

The revelation took Henry aback. 'I'd relish it,' he admitted, feeling himself swell at little, 'but I'd be struggling at the moment. This job's taking all my time. I don't see much slack ahead, not enough for a job like that, anyway.'

'Whatever, I'll be wanting you to head the inquiry team,' FB said as though he hadn't heard Henry's position. 'You'll have to make the time – one way or the other.'

Henry found his teeth were grinding, something they did quite often in FB's company. His swell had also deflated. 'OK,' he said unsurely.

'You need to be up and ready first thing next week – that's when I'll be in a position to get going fully. That OK?'

'Have to be, won't it?'

FB smiled and downed the last dregs of espresso. Henry finished the latte and they set off back for the nick. As they walked side by side along Bacup Road, Henry towering over the rotund figure of the chief, Henry's mobile rang.

'What the hell is that ring tone?' FB demanded.

'"Jumpin' Jack Flash".'

'Is it a work phone?'

'Yep.' Henry extracted it from his jacket pocket.

'In that case get something more appropriate.'

'What? Scooby Doo?' The phone went to his ear. 'Henry Christie . . . yep . . . yep . . . email me now . . . Good . . . thanks.' He ended the call and bunched his fists triumphantly. 'Forensic submissions, the little darlings. The DNA has come up trumps. Positive ID.'

Two other people up and about early that morning were Teddy Bear Jackman and Tony Cromer. They were at their local gym by six thirty a.m., working out for an intense half hour before hitting the road at seven fifteen a.m. They wanted to make a call on someone. A surprise call.

Rafiq Ali was an Asian gentleman who owned a dozen corner shop convenience stores in the Bolton area, all opening from six in the morning to midnight. They were all profitable businesses in their own right, but not as profitable as the drug empire he ran on the same lines – small and local – nor the prostitution business in which he specialized in providing young, very beautiful Asian girls and boys to clients with big wallets and small consciences.

Rufus Sweetman had paid Ali little attention over the years because their markets were in different areas. Ali concentrated on Asian kids, where the drug addiction rate was phenomenal, whereas Sweetman – who was an out and out racist anyway – dealt mainly with the white population. Sweetman had a feeling, though, that Ali was expanding his turf and that an early visit by his two negotiators and influencers would not go amiss.

Ali lived in luxury in a row of terraced houses in Bolton which he had converted into one huge abode. Jackman and Cromer knew he wasn't to be found there that morning. They had been told he had been gambling in Manchester and had holed up for the night in one of Manchester's top hotels. It was there they headed that morning.

Their idea was to pin him down in his suite, but as they drove into the underground car park below the hotel, they spotted Ali walking quickly across the concrete towards his motor, a Porsche.

'Wonder if some bastard tipped him off,' Jackman mused.

'Who cares – he's ours,' said Cromer.

Always ready and adaptable, accepting change as it came their way, they went for him.

Actually the first inkling that Ali got that something was amiss was the revving engine, the squeal of tyres and the approach of a car travelling far too fast for the circumstances.

Ali reacted immediately. He made a mad rush towards his sports car.

But then he had a moment of hesitation.

Was his car the best place to be? Or should he turn and leg it back to the lift? Or the stairs? Or maybe he should play hide and seek amongst the parked vehicles? Try to get up on to the street and disappear on foot?

His early-morning brain did its best to prioritize these options, but unfortunately they all got horribly clogged up, mangled and twisted. In the end the analysis led him to paralysis. He dropped his arms uselessly and stood there as the car screeched to a halt in front of him. Jackman and Cromer piled out of the car, unable to believe their good fortune.

Ali raised his hands and braced himself for the inevitable punch.

Find out how they lived, find out how they died. So very, very true, thought Henry once again, as he, Jane Roscoe and the chief constable raked through everything that was suddenly pouring in about Keith Arthur Snell. And there was a lot of it.

It would have been interesting to have worked their detailed way forwards from Snell's birth in 1978 to the present day, but that was something the intelligence cell could pull together. What Henry needed was a pen picture of the man, his known associates, any next of kin and how he had lived his life most recently.

Henry had already pinned up an A4 photo of the dead man on the wall of the MIR, blown up from a fairly recent mugshot, adjacent to the CSI shots from the crime scene. Henry, Roscoe and FB – whose detective instincts had been revitalized and who would not piss off in spite of Henry's subtle suggestions – had read and reread everything that had been sent through to them from the intelligence department. The SIO – Henry – now wanted to pull it together, to get the snapshot of Snell.

'OK, so what've we got?' Henry said, wanting to move on this. 'Keith Snell, twenty-six years old, born Cheetham Hill 1978. In and out of various institutions all his life. From a broken home, no family to speak of, no one particularly interested in him. Been thieving since he was eight, string of convictions for shoplifting and burglary. In and out of youth offender institutes, then prison since twenty-one. Chuck in lots of fines, probation orders, community service orders.'

'Pretty much a pain in the arse,' FB offered. 'Not bright, not Mr Big, probably not a full shilling.'

'Yeah, you're right,' Henry agreed. He looked down at his scribbled notes. 'Moved into drugs in his mid-teens. Cannabis busts, coke, then becomes a registered heroin addict by the age of nineteen.'

'So he's part of the Manchester drugs scene in some way, shape or form,' Roscoe said. 'Even if he's only one of its victims.'

Henry nodded, glancing through the long list of Snell's previous convictions from PNC. 'These all start off pretty tame . . . smacks of crime being committed to pay for drugs – shoplifting, snatch thefts . . .'

'But it escalates,' FB pointed out, 'probably as his addiction intensifies.'

'Yep. Snatch thefts lead to street robbery . . . more and more desperate,' Roscoe said. 'Then on to armed robbery.'

The details of the offences downloaded from the PNC were sketchy. In order to fill in the blanks, a visit to Greater Manchester Police was necessary.

'What are we looking at here?' Henry asked, although he had reached his own conclusion.

'Drug debts,' FB suggested. Roscoe nodded.

Henry nodded. 'Could be. The thick plottens,' he added

and took a pause. 'OK, we need a place of abode, next of kin, known associates . . . I feel a cross-border visit coming on and a good long look in GMP's intelligence files.'

FB murmured something inaudibly and thoughtfully. He was reading through the details of all the arrests of Snell. Then he spoke up. 'He was arrested about a week ago and lodged in the cells at the Arena police station . . . according to this he wasn't charged with anything . . . Interesting . . .' He glanced at Henry, a gleam in his eye. 'You know it's my policy for high-ranking officers, including myself, to get out and about with the plebs . . . sorry, operational staff.' He grinned at Roscoe. 'So, on that basis I think I might just come along to Manchester with you, just to see how things are at the pointy end these days.'

Henry frowned. 'Who said I was going to Manchester?'

'I did.'

The gigantic claw-like grab descended from the sky. Its talons settled almost gently around the body of the Porsche. There was the briefest of pauses – a moment when it seemed as though this was just a huge joke – and then, with a powerful jerk, the claw tightened its grip and sank its talons into the gleaming bodywork of the £70,000 car.

'Jesus, you fucking idiots,' wailed Rafiq Ali. But he was helpless and anyway, Jackman and Cromer just laughed as the grab took good hold and the crane lifted the sports car high into the air. Ali's bloodshot eyes rose with it, disbelief changing to devastation. 'Bastards.'

'I thought you were a Muslim?' Cromer said. 'Shouldn't you say "Allah!"'

'Fuck you!' Ali spat, his eyes still transfixed by the upward journey of his beautiful thoroughbred. 'I'll kill you for this.'

'Oooh!' Cromer said. 'These top crims are really sensitive about their cars, aren't they?'

'You guys are dead,' Ali snarled, but there was nothing he could personally do at this moment. His hands were pinned behind him, tied at the wrists with plastic handcuffs, the figures of Cromer and Jackman on either side, making him power-less.

The Porsche swung overhead. The crane operator gleefully

following the instructions given to him. Through an arc of 180 degrees it travelled, then came to a halt swaying gently in the air as though pushed by the breeze. The operator looked down for the nod.

Which was given to him by Cromer.

The four claws opened simultaneously. The Porsche dropped from the sky – right into the open, expectant jaws of the vehicle crusher below. For a few moments nothing happened. There was silence across the scrapyard. Then a motor started up, a powerful, throbbing one, building up the pressure in the massive pistons which were used to force the crusher shut.

The jaws wrapped around the Porsche, slowly, ponderously, starting to crush the car with a horrible crumpling sound.

'You fuckers!' wailed Ali. 'My car.'

Teddy Bear Jackman punched Ali very hard in the lower gut – one of his favourite blows. His fat, bunched fist rammed expertly into the soft underbelly of the gangster, doubling him up and sending him to his knees, then on to his face. For good measure, Jackman kicked him in the head, then bent down and dragged him back up to his feet, where he managed to retain a staggering balance. Jackman then took hold of Ali's elbow and steered him across the scrapyard towards a tower of scrap vehicle shells, stacked precariously on top of each other. Cromer followed, petrol can in hand.

Two huge tractor tyres, one on top of the other, lay by the foot of the dead car tower.

'Climb in there.' Jackman pushed Ali towards the tyres. The Asian looked quizzical. 'In,' Jackman explained. 'Leg over, get in, yeah?'

Puzzled, still reeling from the punch and blow to the head, Ali clambered over the tyres and dropped into the rubber circle.

'Stand up.'

'Look, guys, what the shit's going on, man?'

'You have something belonging to our boss,' Cromer declared confidently.

'Like what?'

'Cocaine. Lots of it. You robbed it from him on Birch Services.'

'I did hell. You are wrong there.'

'Here – stick this over your head,' Cromer said.

'What . . . why . . . ?'

Jackman looped a worn motorcycle tyre over Ali's head and shoulders. The tyre settled around him, pulling his arms tight into his side. Jackman quickly dropped a further two similar tyres around him, straightjacketing him

Ali's eyes were wide with fear. 'What're you going to do?'

'They used to do this in South Africa, didn't they – to the blacks . . . ? Jeez, I can't remember what they call it,' Jackman said, annoyed he could not bring it to mind.

Ali began to struggle like a wild man, started to scream.

Cromer stood up on the tractor tyres and splashed petrol over their captive. Ali ducked, tried to avoid it, but could not. Within moments he was well doused, fumes starting to rise.

'Four-star, this,' Cromer said. 'You can't just get it anywhere, these days.'

'You wouldn't,' Ali dared them.

Cromer gave him a wan smile. He reached into his pocket and pulled out a box of matches, lit one, held it in the air. The breeze extinguished it almost immediately. Cromer shook his head. 'I still can't remember what they called it.'

'Murder, I think,' Jackman suggested with a titter.

Cromer laughed.

Ali sank to his knees, trapped by the tyres, soaked by the petrol. 'I don't know anything,' he sobbed. 'I don't fucking know.'

Cromer lit another match, again allowing it to blow out in the breeze.

Jackman's mobile rang. He fumbled in his pockets for it.

'Best be careful with that,' Cromer warned him. 'They don't let you use them on petrol station forecourts, you know. Risk of sparks, apparently.'

Jackman shrugged and answered it anyway.

Cromer shuffled another match out of the box. He held its red tip to the striking side of the box, waited for Jackman to finish the call, which, after a few muffled responses, he did, then looked at his partner.

'OK,' Cromer said to Ali. 'I let those last two matches go out on purpose. This one, I won't, so, care to start talking, Ali Bongo, old mate?'

193

Devastated by terror, Ali was now speechless. All he could do was kneel there and shake his head and cry.

'They burn people when they're dead where you come from, don't they? Then float them down the Ganges,' Cromer said, laughing harshly. 'Oops, but I forget . . . you come from Bradford, don't you? Anyway, the best we can do for you is set you on fire while you're still alive, then maybe dump your body in the River Irwell. Not exactly the holy river, but it'll have to do.'

'We need to go,' Jackman hissed quietly to Cromer. 'Boss needs us to make it to Manchester airport.'

Cromer nodded. To Ali, he said, 'One last chance, pal.'

Ali raised his head, then shook it, no sound coming from his mouth.

'OK then.' Cromer lit the match. It flared up. He flicked it across to Ali, who screamed as it tumbled towards him. Then it touched him and went out with a damp *Phtt* noise.

'Ever tried to light diesel with a match?' shrugged Cromer. 'Virtually fucking impossible. C'mon, pal,' he said to Jackman.

The obscene screams from Rafiq Ali which accompanied their departure only served to make the partners in crime howl with hysterical laughter.

Fifteen

Henry Christie had worked in, been in, many CID offices over the years. No matter where they were, there were always certain similarities between them as, after all, an office is an office: desks, chairs, computers, paperwork, baskets, coffee cups and mugs.

But yet, each office has its own tangible atmosphere, its own way of speaking, telling you how well the people in it were doing their work, how they interacted, whether they

194

achieved or not. It did not depend on tidiness. Even the most untidy offices could be places where the staff delivered a consistently high quality of work. Nor did it depend on the age of the furniture, or whether there were posters on the walls declaring how fantastic it was to have a positive attitude. The people made the atmosphere, whether they were sitting at their desks or not. And Henry thought he could tell when he was entering a good CID office . . . or not.

Sitting in the CID office of the Arena police station just on the outskirts of Manchester city centre, he was trying to get a feel for this particular room and its denizens. But he could not quite get a handle on it.

It seemed tidy enough, the few people in the large, wide-open room had their heads down, beavering away; a coffee machine gurgled in the corner, a nice aroma filtering through the air. Yet something unsettled him slightly, making a knitting pattern of his furrowed brow. He felt strangely uncomfortable. As his eyes criss-crossed the room, they paused briefly on what was obviously a home-produced poster which said simply, *Invincibles!* Nothing else, just that word in striking red letters. His eyes moved on.

He exhaled, looked out of the window. Not far away was the Manchester Arena, where he had recently been to see the Rolling Stones on their world tour. Behind that was Victoria railway station and beyond that was the city itself, Deansgate, the Arndale Centre, etc. In the other direction was Manchester Prison, formerly Strangeways, and wonderfully, nearby, was Boddington's Brewery, which made one of the few bitter beers Henry could drink to excess. He was more of a lager man.

He and FB had travelled together to Manchester. During their journey from Rawtenstall, the chief had revealed why he did not want to miss the opportunity.

'The nick we're going to . . . ?' he began.

Henry nodded. He was driving.

'It's the one where the detective superintendent is based who I'm – we're – going to be investigating. The one involved in the cock-up trial at Lancaster.'

'I thought there'd be an ulterior motive. It wasn't just that you'd been missing the cut and thrust of being a detective at the sharp end, was it?'

'That as well . . . a bit . . . but it just seemed to be a good chance to get a sneak preview of the bastards, when they're not expecting us. Always an eye-opener to drop in on folk when they've just got off the toilet, if you know what I mean.'

Henry knew. Good tactic.

'The whole Sweetman investigation was conducted from there.'

'Supposing he isn't in?'

FB shrugged. 'In that case, I'll just have a nosy round with you.'

'I take it that you have a bit of a plan in your head.'

'Oh yes.' FB tapped his slightly bulbous nose, which Henry thought was getting slowly fatter and redder . . . probably because of the wine. 'I speak to the superintendent whilst you chat to the troops – ostensibly about Keith Snell – but if you can also manage to drop a few innocent but loaded questions about Sweetman and get some reactions, that would be good.'

Henry did not respond to this half-baked approach. He had no great desire to get involved in the Sweetman job until the Snell murder was out of the way. The fact that the two inquiries had some common ground only muddied the water for him. He would have liked to keep them separate and he hoped there was no true connection, but he also knew he would have to keep his antenna tuned in for any.

And now, after what seemed like the millionth journey during his life down the M61, he was sitting in a CID office whilst FB was chinwagging with the detective superintendent (who *was* in). He speculated on a few things while waiting, his mind butterflying over the walls in his mind.

Keith Snell – low life – murdered. Why?

Tara Wickson, lovely, lovely, lovely body . . . even sat there, Henry could still feel her fingers. He crossed his legs.

Kate Christie, ex-wife, to whom he wanted to remain faithful; he seemed to have a button in his brain more destructive than the US president's nuclear one.

And Karl Donaldson – what the hell was he up to, buggering off to Spain?

Henry shook his head and ran his hand over his short-cropped hair. Waited, watched, thought, worried.

His mobile phone blurted out that Stones riff, the one that

had annoyed FB. The one he would therefore be keeping. The display told him it was from Karl Donaldson's home number. Ahh, he thought, the coincidence of life.

'Hi, Karl, back already?'

There was a faltering silence on the line, then, 'No, Henry, it's me, Karen.'

'Karen . . . hi,' he said warily, responding to the tone of voice of Karl Donaldson's wife. She sounded upset. Henry knew her well. She had once been a police officer in Lancashire, where Donaldson had met her. They had fallen in love, married, had kids, all that palaver. Karen had transferred to the Metropolitan Police and now headed their training centre at Hendon. Once, Henry had severely disliked her, but now they were good friends. 'What's the matter?'

'It's Karl,' she said.

Immediately, Henry's insides went empty. This sounded like bad news. 'What about him?'

'I just haven't heard from him. Do you know where he is?'

'I spoke to him last night . . . he said he was in Spain . . .'

'Spain?' she exclaimed. 'What do you mean, Spain?'

'Spain . . . y'know, the country, Spain. He said he was there regarding you know who.' Henry did not want to say the name Mendoza, but also felt rather silly saying, 'You know who.' He stood up and crossed to the window, feeling he would be less likely to be overheard there.

'He told me he was going to see you,' Karen said accusingly.

'Oh.'

'So do you know where he really is?' she demanded, obviously thinking Henry was trying to pull the wool over her eyes.

'No. I spoke to him on the phone last night and he said he was in Spain. Are you saying he hasn't told you?'

'No,' she whispered.

'Have you spoken to anyone at the Legat in the American Embassy?'

'Yes. Nobody knows where he is.'

Henry felt a kind of creeping-crawling sensation cover his skin, contracting it tight. Could it be that Karl was on a non-authorized job? And what was worse, had it gone wrong somehow? He coughed mentally in order to make his next words sound upbeat. 'I wouldn't be worried, Karen. He's probably trying to find a phone charger right now.'

'But he always phones. He always tells me where he is, where he's going. But not this time. I thought something was wrong with him. He hasn't been acting normal, really distracted, really not with it. His mind somewhere else. Jesus . . . do you think he's having an affair?'

'Nope,' Henry said without hesitation.

'Then what? They have public phones in Spain, don't they? It's not like a third-world country.' She was gradually losing it, becoming hysterical.

'I'm sure everything's fine . . . now, come on, Karen' – he didn't dare call her 'love' because she was a superintendent – 'he'll be fine.'

'But what if he's got into trouble? No one knows where he is,' she said.

'He'll be fine,' Henry said firmly. 'This is Karl Donaldson you're talking about.'

'I know, I know,' she cried. 'It's just that . . . I'm at my wits' end, OK?'

'Karen, look, I'm in Manchester at the moment on a job. Just keep annoying the embassy and get them to talk to you. You know what they're like . . . secret squirrels and all that. If you need someone to talk to, Kate's at home today, give her a ring. I'll get back to you when I can. I'm sure he'll be fine . . . no one gets the better of Karl, the good-looking bastard.' That ending brought a little laugh from Karen.

'Right, right,' she said, pulling herself together. 'I'll speak to you later.' She hung up, leaving Henry with a dead phone in his mitt. He slowly folded it over and dropped it back into his pocket, thinking that if there was one thing Donaldson did, it was keep in contact with Karen – unlike Henry, who was poor at calling in to Kate. Donaldson was smitten with Karen and, because of this, the lack of contact made Henry suspicious.

Turning away from the window, Henry saw FB and two detectives he did not know enter the office. The three of them made their way towards him.

Henry – the cop from the sticks – took this brief chance to size up the two Manchester detectives.

To say they were spick 'n' span was an understatement. Both were impeccably dressed, class suits, matching ties and hankies folded into breast pockets. Their creases were as sharp as knife blades, their brogues shiny and creaking as they walked confidently and cockily, rolling their shoulders. Both put the rather shabbily dressed FB to shame – FB the hick cop from a hick force with his hick running mate, Henry.

These two Manchester City detectives were the epitome of the big city jack. Sharp, sassy, cocksure and very arrogant.

For a moment Henry felt a shade underdressed in his Burton's off-the-rack.

'I'd like you to meet DCI Henry Christie,' FB was saying. The older of the two jacks reached forward and gave Henry's right paw a quick tug. 'This is Superintendent Easton.'

'Pleased to meet you,' Henry said. The skin of Easton's hand was smooth and dry. Henry could smell aftershave on him.

'Henry's here for two reasons,' said FB. 'He's investigating the murder of a guy called . . . ?' FB's brow furrowed. 'What's he called, Henry?'

'Keith Snell.'

'That's it . . . one of your local denizens. His body was found just over the border in Lancs a few days ago . . . you probably heard about it. The one who was shot and burned? Just got the ID through.'

'Yeah,' said Easton. 'Name doesn't ring a bell, though.' Easton scratched his head. Henry caught the nervous gesture and instinctively knew Easton was lying. 'OK.' Easton turned to the other detective, a younger man, standing on the balls of his feet, rocking. He tossed a thumb in his direction. 'Phil here will give you a hand with that. He can be your SPOC.'

Henry squinted. 'SPOC?'

The younger detective guffawed. He reached out a hand and shook with Henry, giving Henry's hand a squeeze too much. 'Single Point of Contact,' he said patronizingly.

Only a minor thing, but one-up for the big city jacks.

'Phil's a DS in the office,' Easton said. 'He knows most of the local crims.'

'Yeah, not a bright bunch, I have to say,' said Phil. 'The gene pool around these parts isn't very deep.'

'You know Keith Snell then?'

'Yeah – a little.'

'Good, that'll be helpful. We really need to fill in his background.'

Easton turned to FB. 'You said Henry was here for two reasons.'

FB nodded. 'He'll be helping me with the Sweetman inquiry.'

'Right.' The faces of both detectives darkened considerably. As expected, this would be a very touchy area and Henry had a bit of sympathy for them. It's not nice being investigated.

'But I'm sure there'll be nothing to worry about,' FB said brightly. 'I intend to be in and out.' He tapped his nose conspiratorially. 'And everything we do will be transparent . . . so could you and me have a little sit down now,' he said to Easton, 'and I'll tell you what I need to know.'

'Sure,' Easton said magnanimously. He and FB left the office. Henry and his SPOC – as Henry had now and forever christened the man in his mind – regarded each other.

'Come down to my office. Let's have a brew and a chat, see what I can do for you.' He led Henry out of the main CID room, down a short corridor and into his cubbyhole of an office, just about big enough for a desk, two chairs and a filing cabinet. 'It's not much, but I call it hovel,' laughed SPOC. 'Grab a seat.' They sat on opposite sides of the desk. 'What can I do for you, Mr Christie?'

'I want to know about Keith Snell.'

'Bloody murdered, eh? Fancy that . . . one less for our books, I suppose.' SPOC paused, ruminating. 'Can't say I know too much about Snell, actually. A fairly regular customer, but no one I came across often. One of the run-of-the-mill volume offenders and addicts who cause havoc with our crime figures. His antics were getting more and more violent, though, the more addicted he became.'

'Gravitated to armed robbery, I believe?'

'Singularly unsuccessfully.' SPOC shook his head sadly.

'Family?'

Another shake of the head. 'The state was Snell's family. Care home after care home, followed by the Benefits Agency and various prisons.'

'Associates? Girlfriends?'

'Knocked around with the group of people you'd expect him to knock around with. Not sure he had a girl.'

'I'd like to see everything you have on him, all the intel please.'

'OK,' SPOC said brightly. 'Can you give me an hour?'

Henry blinked, refraining from saying, *A fucking hour?* Instead he nodded and thought, *The one-upmanship of the SPOC who also happens to be a BCJ – Big City Jack.*

Terminal 2, Manchester Airport. Heaving with holiday traffic, so much so that the figures of Teddy Bear Jackman and Tony Cromer did not fit in. Chalk and cheese. But even so, nobody really paid them much heed, all being busy with disorderly families, suitcases and flight delays.

They had parked on the short-stay multi-storey and moseyed as casually as possible down to the arrivals hall. Being early, they split up for a while. Jackman strolled to a café and ordered a cappuccino, baulking at the expense of it at the till. Cromer browsed through WH Smith's, looking through the true-crime section in the books. He liked to read fact as opposed to fiction, but though he leafed through a couple of enticing books, he did not buy. Instead he joined his partner with a pot of tea.

'The prices here are criminal,' Jackman moaned.

Cromer nodded. 'Think there's much surveillance here?'

'Shitloads.'

'Not a good place for us, really.'

'Naah – but a plane's got to land somewhere, so we're stuck with it.'

'Not keen on spending too much time here.'

'Me neither.'

Both were slightly spooked being in an environment where they could get caught on camera. Their natural instinct was to hide their faces, pull up their collars and look mean, but to do that here, to act furtively in any way, would be to draw attention to themselves. And the police round here were armed with big guns. Something to bear in mind, especially in this day and age when, because of the threat of terrorism, they were not averse to using their weapons.

'What does all this mean?' Jackman asked.

'That . . . er . . . lots of people are going on holiday or coming back from holiday,' Cromer ventured.

'No, y'prat. Why we're here. Who we're picking up.'

Cromer shrugged. 'It's obviously time for the big players to get involved. I think some major shit is about to happen. Someone, somewhere, has deeply upset Rufus, and I honestly don't think it's one of the big Manchester bosses. If it was, he'd have had a name by now. I'm sure of that.'

'Think so?'

'Poz.' He leaned nearer to Jackman. 'Wanna know what I think?'

'Your mind always intrigues me.'

'I think me and you are wasting our time doing what we're doing. I don't think any one of them we'll be visiting knows anything. I think that somewhere out there' – he made a wide, sweeping gesture with his arm – 'is someone muscling in on us and who is lookin' to make a very big name for himself, or herself. You never know in this day and age. And know what? I don't think anyone knows who it is.' He grinned. 'Those are my thoughts.'

'Thanks for sharing them with me. I must say, you do an awful lot of thinking.'

Cromer tapped his head. 'I think, therefore I fucking am.'

They looked up at the nearby arrivals screen and stood up simultaneously as they saw that the flight they were due to meet had landed.

It was a very thin file. Not that he expected it to be as fat as a Bible, but he had thought there would be more.

'Thanks.' Henry looked at his watch. An hour and fifteen.

'Not much, but that's all we have on Snell.'

'It's a great start.'

'You're welcome. I need to get out and about, but here's my mobile number if you need it.' He handed a business card to Henry, then left him with the file. Picking it up between finger and thumb, he weighed it. There wasn't much at all, but having said that, whilst Snell may have been a regular offender, he was nothing more than cannon fodder. He was easy to arrest and no doubt the young, keen officers tested their wings on him. He was not important, just an irritant, just a loser . . . and yet something gnawed at Henry.

He leafed through the few pages of the intelligence file, scratching his head as he did so, feeling more uncomfortable as he read it. For someone who was so prolific an offender, there was a dearth of Intel on him. Henry sat back and thought about the many criminals he knew who were similar to Snell.

Always being locked up.

Always in the eyes of the law.

Always visible on the streets and in the dives.

Always knocking around with other crims and low lifes.

Always generating some sort of Intel.

And then graduating up to more serious offences – rather like a flasher moving up to be a rapist – they were always of interest to the day-to-day cops who policed the front line.

There was very little about Snell's promotion to armed robber.

Henry now scratched his chin thoughtfully. The information he had so far been able to get on Snell was factual stuff from PNC. The crimes he had committed, where and when he had received convictions. There had been a lot of stuff recorded. Henry would have expected the local Intel to match it in some way. It didn't.

'Mm,' he said, thinking he had only said it in his brain, but realized he had actually spoken out loud. He thought about asking his SPOC about this imbalance, but only for a moment. He pushed himself up and went to the office door, peering down the corridor.

Henry loved field intelligence officers. In the old days they were called collators, but things had moved on in the '90s and the twenty-first century as the whole of the police service moved into intelligence-led policing. The old-style collator disappeared to be replaced by full-blooded intelligence units. The beauty was, though, that people who would have been collators in the old days had become FIOs and they were a wonderful source of information. They knew everything about everybody, made it their business to poke their noses into criminals' businesses.

Henry found the Intel unit on the third floor of the building and collared the detective sergeant, a grizzled old lag by the name of Ball, who reminded Henry of Shrek.

'Glad to help,' he said when Henry introduced himself and told him the nature of his enquiry. 'An inevitable death, I suppose,' Ball said, referring to Snell.

'What do you mean?'

'Marked for it. You know . . . the circle of a low life . . . eventually I think he would have overdosed and killed himself anyway . . . but two bullets in the back and being set on fire . . . musta really upset someone.'

'Any idea who?' Henry asked hopefully.

'Take your pick. Low-level drug barons are ten-a-penny in this neck of the woods.'

'What do you know about him, then?'

'Into heroin and anything else he could lay his hands on. Petty thieving to pay for his habit . . . God knows how he got into guns. Probably thought it would make stealing easier.'

'Never does.'

'No.' Ball looked thoughtful, then down at the file Henry had in his hand. 'You've got his file, I see. I copied it a few days before for Phil, the DS upstairs.'

'My SPOC? Did you now?' Henry waved the file. 'Seems a bit thin on the ground.' The corners of Ball's mouth turned down and so did his large ears. To Henry, Ball looked as though he had seen too many scrum-downs in his time. Ball took the file and flicked through it, his face perplexed and not a little fearful.

'Strange . . . looks like the edited version,' he said. 'He hasn't given you everything here.'

'Can you give me everything?' Henry asked, trying to make the question sound unimportant, though he had seen the look in Ball's eyes which asked the question: why the trimmed-down file?

'I don't see why not . . .' He breathed out through his nose, torn a little. 'There was nothing contentious in the file, as far as I know.'

'Phil said he knew Snell quite well,' Henry said, fibbing, but wanting to test the water.

'Yeah, he did. Always locking him up – on a whim usually. In fact Snell was in custody last week . . . we always get an 'in custody' shot from the computer system. Locked up on suspicion of armed robbery, but not charged. Given police bail, I recall.' Ball had walked across to a filing cabinet, was rifling through files, his hand emerging with one about half an inch thick. 'Here we are . . . Keith Snell . . . no longer of this parish, nor this world. I'll have to deal with it appropriately.'

Henry took the file from him. 'It's essential I have this copied fully.'

Ball nodded. 'No probs. I'll do it here and now.' He pointed to the photocopier in the corner.

Henry liked Ball more and more. He took the file back from Henry and placed it on the machine. Without looking at its contents, Henry could tell it was more like he had anticipated. Lots of bits of stuff which would provide useful leads for the inquiry team back in Rawtenstall. Nuggets of gold which, Henry was certain, would lead to the killer.

As Ball handed the copied file back over, he said, 'Between you and me, I think Phil used Snell as a source . . . unofficial, like.' He shrugged as if to say, *Do with that what you will.*

Henry thanked him and ten minutes later he was in the canteen, the file in front of him, skim-reading, picking up salient points, facts. The address of Snell's current girlfriend, his best friend, his associates . . . including one which made Henry gasp.

Closing the file, he knew he had two things to do urgently.

First he had to see Snell's girlfriend. She was vital, if not as a witness, then at least as someone who could point the murder team in the right direction regarding Snell's family and friends.

Second, he wanted to get back into Lancashire. Someone who lived there was someone he desperately needed to see.

There were some delays with passengers disembarking from the Alicante flight, something connected with a baggage-handler dispute. Jackman and Cromer waited patiently under the meeting point, discussing life, death and the universe as they so often did. They thought of themselves as philosophers and because of this, their favourite movie was *Pulp Fiction*, which they often revisited together.

Eventually passengers emerged.

Cromer edged his way to the barrier at the end of the customs run and unfolded an A4 piece of paper on which he had scrawled *Sweetman*, because he had never yet met or seen any of the two men he had been detailed to collect.

The SPOC eyed the file with apprehension, which he tried to cover with a show of bravado. Henry watched his eyes, his reaction to the fact that it had quadrupled in size. SPOC's Adam's apple rose and fell a few times. Henry said nothing about wandering down to the Intel unit and chatting to the FIO, nor did he challenge SPOC on the obvious lies he had spun to Henry. That would come later, Henry was positive on that point, even though he was inclined to grab SPOC's finely tailored lapels and bang him back against a wall. There had to be a good reason for the deception, but Henry knew this was not the time or place to go for it. At the moment Henry was still on the back foot, trying to get a handle on things, and he needed to be on an even keel before lurching forwards. He wanted it to be cold and sweet, like all good revenge should be.

'You've been more than helpful, Phil.'

'Pleasure.' His voice sounded strained.

'I'm sure you'll be hearing more from the murder team, and me, in the very near future. Your local knowledge will be crucial to this, I reckon.'

SPOC nodded. 'Happy to help.'

'I'll bet the trail leads back here,' Henry said.

'Meaning?'

'It'll be a Manchester crim who killed Snell,' Henry speculated.

'Oh yeah, yeah,' said SPOC.

Henry held out a hand. SPOC took it, they shook. This time there was a difference from the time when they had shaken earlier. SPOC's hand had become damp and lettuce-like, a far cry from the cool skin he had felt before. Henry kept looking into SPOC's eyes, but they did not waver from his scrutiny. They still had the same smugness and arrogance in them.

'See you again.'

'And you.'

Henry gave him a wide smile, whilst behind his own eyes he wondered what the hell was going on.

'Starving,' FB moaned dreadfully, holding his generous stomach. 'My belly thinks my throat's been cut.'

Wishful thinking, Henry thought. 'Why don't we grab a burger at the Arena? There's a McDonald's in the foyer. It's only just round the corner, walking distance.'

'Well, I don't really do fast food,' the chief said, 'but I'll make an exception this time. I'm ravenous.'

They trotted out of the police station, crossed the road and headed towards Manchester Arena.

Just before they turned the corner out of sight of the station, Henry glanced back, his eyes rising quickly to the third floor, where he glimpsed two people at the window he had stood at whilst taking the frantic mobile call from Karen Donaldson. He recognized the two as Detective Superintendent Easton and SPOC.

'We need to talk,' he said urgently once they were out of sight.

Easton turned to the detective sergeant, his face grim and worried.

'Country bumpkins my backside,' Easton said. 'We should never, ever have taken on that pillock, Snell. You said he'd be trustworthy.'

'Thought he would be.'

'Proved wrong, weren't you?' Easton growled. 'We may be in trouble here . . . Snell just complicates matters so much. It wouldn't be so bad if it'd just been the inquiry, but Snell as well. It would have helped if he'd been dumped in Greater Manchester, wouldn't it?'

'It would,' the sergeant said, chastened.

'So what are you going to do about it?'

'Think of something.'

'Mmm, like I said,' Easton muttered, 'as if we haven't got enough shit to deal with.'

At McDonald's there were hordes of young kids knocking about, early arrivals for a later concert by Busted, the in-vogue band of the moment. Henry's youngest daughter had been hassling him to get tickets for the concert, but Henry had left it too late and they had sold out when he rang. She still had not completely forgiven him yet . . . might never do so.

The expression fixed on FB's face was something to behold. His discomfort and distaste were both clearly visible from the way in which his mouth was twisted down at both corners as he manoeuvred his way through the kids, hissing through his teeth.

They found a couple of spare chairs and pulled them up to a messed-up table full of discarded food wrappers and plastic cups. They stripped their burgers as though they were uncovering the crown jewels, as opposed to greasy burgers on sloppy sesame buns.

'How did you get on?' Henry was first to put a question in.

FB bit hesitantly into his purchase, found it tasted better than anticipated, chomping happily as he replied. 'Told Easton what my plan was, told him we'd be here next week, told him we'd be thorough but fair, told him not to worry.'

Henry raised his eyebrows and bit into his own burger.

'But I was lying,' said FB coldly. He eyed Henry and cocked his own eyebrows. 'I wanted to get a feel of things, the lie of the land, lull him a bit.' Henry saw a glint in FB's eyes, a bit like a hawk homing in on a rat. 'And first thing I want to do is reopen the investigation into Jackson Hazell's death, the guy Sweetman is supposed to have murdered.'

'Good.' Henry slurped his Fanta Orange. 'Because I'm certainly not impressed by what I've seen so far, and how I've been treated. I got given a doctored Intel report on Keith Snell.'

'Doctored?'

'Sexed-down, you might say.'

'Explain.'

'My SPOC went to the Intel unit for me to dig out Snell's file – allegedly. When I looked through it, something didn't seem to gel. We have more Intel on town-centre drunks than they had on Snell, who was a high-volume offender. When I got a chance I snuck down to see an FIO who rooted out Snell's file for me – which is this.' He pointed to the paperwork on the messy table. 'No comparison to what I was given original-ly. Apparently Mr SPOC was digging around in Snell's file a few days ago. Don't exactly know when, but from the sounds of it, it was after his body had been found but before he was identified, i.e. today. Coincidence?' Henry finished. His face showed grave doubt.

'Why doctor an Intel file?'

Henry shook his head, swigged his juice. 'Who knows? I can only speculate at this stage, but I feel queasy about it.'

'What's your next move?'

'I thought you were the chief?'

'And you're one of the fuckin' Indians – don't forget that.'

'OK – two things. Firstly I'd like to go round and grab Snell's current bit of stuff. She doesn't live that far from here. I'd like to break the news to her that her loved one's dead – if she doesn't already know, that is. Then I want to pin some tough questions on her, but not round here. Somewhere where I feel safe and secure, because I think we need to start thinking safety first from now.' He held up a hand. 'Not that I want to be over-dramatic, you understand.'

'No, I agree,' FB said.

'And then I want to get to Blackpool. There's someone there I need to talk to urgently . . . so,' he went on hesitantly, 'if you've got the time, I'd like to do both this evening and then I want an emergency briefing at eight tomorrow because I think things are going to go skywards from now on.'

'Well, you're driving, Henry, so I'm in your capable hands.'

Sweetman and Mendoza embraced, kissed cheeks, but there was no warmth in the greeting, even when they held each other at arm's length and regarded each other with smiles. They were the brittle expressions of two men under pressure, two men who did not totally trust each other, but needed each other.

Lopez stood back, just behind his boss, whilst Grant, Sweetman's solicitor, assumed a similar position at Sweetman's shoulder. Jackman and Cromer hovered by the door of the hotel suite, watching the meet with unease.

Informalities over, Mendoza said, 'You and I need to speak – privately.'

'Urgently,' Sweetman agreed. He glanced at his three employees and jerked his thumb. Mendoza nodded at Lopez, who acknowledged the implicit order to leave with a smart click of his heels and an OTT nod of his own. The four men withdrew, leaving the main men to their business.

'Do you wish to freshen up from the flight?' Sweetman asked cordially. 'Best hotel in Manchester, this – Jacuzzi, power shower – your choice.'

'A two-hour flight is nothing.' Mendoza gestured to the tray of food and drinks on the table. 'This will suffice. We need to get talking. I feel that time is running out and we need to act quickly.'

Grant and Lopez moved together out of the room and along the corridor, trotting down the stairs to the hotel bar. They remained silent, aware of the presence of Jackman and Cromer, who were following them. Once in the bar, Grant bought a bottle of red wine and the two of them retreated to a table in the corner. Passing Jackman and Cromer, Grant said, 'You need to keep on your toes, boys . . . those two guys upstairs need good protection.' He winked, clicked his tongue, then walked on before either could respond.

The expressions on the faces of Grant and Lopez remained impassive, serious, non-committal. They spoke only a few sentences, their eyes constantly on guard for Jackman and Cromer. They did not have to wait long, actually, before the professional instincts of the two men kicked in and they quit the bar.

'At last,' gasped Grant.

Lopez took a long swig of his wine, wiped his mouth and smiled. 'Much better than the shit grown by Mendoza,' he said.

'Things are moving on,' Grant said.

'*Si.*'

'The question is, my friend, how do we manage everything from now on?'

Lopez shrugged. 'We will find a way.' He touched his glass on to Grant's, making a nice, ringing chink. 'One thing for sure is that our two glorious bosses are now in very deep . . . what? Shite, you say in the north of England.'

'Exactly – shite.'

'And our time is about to come.'

'I don't know.' Sweetman paced the suite. 'My best men have been out investigating in the only way they know how, and they have uncovered nothing. No one knows anything.'

'Soon the drugs will begin to seep into the market, then we might start getting names,' Mendoza said. 'But,' he went on dourly, 'that is no good for you.' His words hung in the air. 'That will be too late and it will be impossible to recover the drugs, even though you may be able to exact some revenge.'

'We need to help each other, here,' Sweetman said.

'Up to a point.' Mendoza's words held danger. There were no circumstances in which he would ever truly reveal his own financial predicament. 'I am the wholesaler, you are the retailer, we are in business and we need to support each other to achieve profitability. That is how we survive. I want you to recover the drugs, truly I do. Because if you don't, you are a dead man.'

Henry Christie and Robert Fanshaw-Bayley concluded their McDonald's delicacies with a large coffee each, which both found good and strong and which gave them each an injection of energy. They threaded their way out through the increasing mass of kids at the Arena and walked back to the police station to collect the car.

They chatted almost amiably.

'What's it like being chief constable, then?'

'Not so bad, really. Lot of dealing with bullshit politicians; the people from the Home Office are a particular set of twats, and I seem to be sitting on a hundred national working groups, never seem to get enough time in force, but I'm going to change that. I'm going to pull out of some of the groups, particularly those dealing with sexism and racism, because they bore the crap out of me. Equality this, equality that – fuck!'

Henry chuckled. He knew FB was a racist and a sexist deep down, but had the wonderful ability to disguise both traits when necessary, though he had recently been taken to an employment tribunal from a sexism case going back over seven years. He had emerged unscathed, poohing of roses.

211

'Do you really miss being a hands-on jack?'

'Sometimes, but I do get the odd occasion when I can get a grip again, such as this investigation, so I haven't lost it completely.'

Settling back into the front seats of Henry's Mondeo, they set off, driving out under the raised barrier of the police-station car park. Both men glanced up at the building.

'Shenanigans,' Henry said.

FB nodded. 'Shenanigans.'

Sixteen

The estate had one of the worst reputations for violence and intimidation in the country. Situated less than two miles from Manchester city centre, it was a warren of alleyways, a 1970s dream become a nightmare as employment plummeted, minority ethnic populations increased and the trade in drugs went right off the Richter scale – and the cops lost control.

'Shit,' FB said nervously, his wary eyes taking it all in: the deprivation, the dilapidation, the suspicion and anger on the faces of everyone on the street. 'You can cut the tension with a knife.'

Henry gripped the wheel tighter, the palms of his hands damp. He felt very vulnerable. The car might as well have had a big pointy finger hovering over it accompanied by the word 'Cops' in bright lights. He had heard horrific stories about this particular area, where, though it would be strenuously denied, the police often feared to tread unless en masse and tooled-up to the eyeballs.

'Makes Shoreside look like Palm Beach,' Henry observed, suddenly jamming his brakes on as a big, dreadlocked black guy walked purposefully in front of the car – then stopped in his tracks. The bonnet was only inches from the man's legs.

He glared defiantly at the two officers, rolling the whites of his eyes dramatically, daring them to do something.

On the roadside, others began to gather. Lots of teenagers, mostly black, some white faces in amongst them. There was a combination of laughter, sneers and jeers.

'You got a radio?' FB said through the side of his mouth.

'Uh-uh,' Henry replied.

'My arse is twitching, half-crown, thrupenny bit.'

Henry wound his window down, slowly poked his head out and spoke to the man obstructing the highway. 'Can you tell me where Sumpter Close is, please?' He tried to keep the nervousness out of his voice, tried to inflect a certain jollity into the tone. The black man shrugged. 'Please,' Henry added.

The man shook his head, dreadlocks swinging like a maypole.

Another moment of pure, unadulterated tension passed. Then, slowly, the man moved to one side.

Once, during the riots of the early 1980s. Henry had been on duty in Toxteth, Merseyside, part of a mutual-aid contingent from Lancashire supporting their colleagues in Liverpool. He and a small number of other officers had become detached from the main crew and found that their return to safety had been cut off by a gang of stone-throwing, brick-lobbing individuals. The officers had been trapped for about twenty minutes, only a short time in the history of the world, but it had terrified Henry as petrol bombs, bricks and everything else rained down. Another few minutes and they would have succumbed. Henry often shivered at the thought of what might have happened. They were saved by the appearance of another police unit which scattered the rioters. He knew what it was like to be caught by people who wanted to see you dead and he could easily have seen it happening here on the streets of twenty-first-century Manchester. He would have been quite prepared to take drastic action if necessary, but it did not come to that. Not tonight. Maybe the populace was feeling relatively chilled that evening.

Henry drove smartly past with a smile and a wave of thanks.

The man grinned pleasantly.

'I take it back,' FB breathed. 'I'd rather be on a national working group supporting the rights of gays.'

Henry, too, puffed out a breath, his heart hammering.

'Is this a good idea?'

Henry did not reply. He drove on and eventually found the close he was looking for, fortunately stuck right on the outer perimeter of the estate, away from the core. He pulled up outside the address, looked round carefully. The close was fairly quiet, seemed safe enough.

'It's up on that landing, I reckon.' He peered up through the screen to a first-floor concrete run outside a row of council flats. 'You staying with the car?'

'Up to you,' FB pouted.

'Might as well . . . but then again, we'd be split up.'

FB shrugged. 'We're big boys.'

'Five minutes ago we were vulnerable boys.'

'True.'

'But I would like to come back to four wheels and an engine.'

'I'll stay here and car watch, then.'

Henry got out and walked toward the stairwell leading up to the first floor. Typical steps. Blood. Vomit. Needles. He stepped over the obstacles and emerged on to the landing. Number twelve he wanted. The door numbers rose one at a time, starting at eight. He glanced over the balcony and could see FB in the Mondeo, seat reclined, fingers clasped across his chest like some sort of Buddha. Henry gave him a short wave of acknowledgement. Nothing came back from the chief.

He arrived at twelve, stopped outside the door and inspected it. It had been forced open fairly recently. Wood was splintered around the lock and the door itself was insecure. This made him pause before carefully toeing the door open with the tip of his shoe. It swung open easily, revealing a vestibule, the inner door of which was ajar. He stepped inside, elbowed the inner door open wider and looked into the living room. It was in darkness. He reached to his right and, using his fingernail, flicked on the light switch. Like the steps he had just climbed, the living room was stereotypical of hundreds of similar council flats he had entered over the years. Cheap, stick-like furniture, a second-hand settee, huge TV with video and DVD player – and that unmistakable council-flat aroma: a combination of mustiness, dope and the toilet.

'Grace,' he called softly. 'Grace? Are you here?' His voice rose a little. 'Grace – it's the police. I've come to talk to you about Keith.'

His voice projected into an empty space. He set foot into the living room proper, his experienced eyes taking in everything. He moved through into the kitchen and this is where he stopped abruptly when he flicked that light on.

The kitchen looked as though a snow plough had been through it, destroying everything in its path. A kitchen table had been broken into matchsticks, two chairs smashed beyond repair. The kettle lay on the floor surrounded by the smashed remains of cups, plates and other crockery. And on the linoleum floor was a browny-red swatch of congealed blood. It was splashed all over the lower cupboards, flicked everywhere under two or three feet. There had been a terrific fight here and someone had been badly assaulted. To Henry, veteran of many crime scenes, it looked as though someone had had their head kicked in.

He took it all in, his mind already hypothesizing what had happened.

Behind him he heard a click.

He spun, then froze.

'Put your fucking hands up!' the man with the gun said.

Henry's arms rose slowly, because pointed directly at his chest was a handgun which he recognized as a Luger. It looked an old gun, probably sixty years old, but nevertheless he did as instructed. Old guns were just as capable of killing as new ones.

'I'm a cop,' Henry said. His eyes moved beyond the fixation on the weapon to the man holding it. He was smallish, squat, dressed from head to foot in a camouflage gear, a green balaclava pulled down over his face with two eyeholes and a mouth hole.

'What're you doing here?' the figure demanded. The gun did not waver, remained steady, pointing at Henry's breastbone.

'I've come to see Grace.'

'Why?' It was a sharp demand.

'That's between me and her.'

'Wrong answer.'

215

'It's the only one you're getting.'

'I'll shoot you . . . this gun is loaded and ready to fire.'

'I'm sure it is.'

'I don't mind killing a cop . . . they deserve it.'

'I don't,' Henry said. 'Look, can I put my arms down?'

'No you fucking can't.'

'Why are you here?' Henry asked.

'Hey – you haven't got this quite right, have you?' The man held the gun out further, his forefinger fitted around the trigger. 'I ask the questions around here, numbskull.'

'Numbskull? Now there's I word I haven't heard in a long time. You'd better ask your questions then, because my arms are getting well pissed off.'

'What are you doing here?'

'Looking for Grace. I have something to tell her about her boyfriend,' Henry said. He saw the man's shoulders rise. 'Something about Keith Snell.'

'Tell her what?'

'I need to know if Keith Snell is actually her boyfriend, for a start.' Henry coughed. His mouth was quickly drying up, probably something connected with having a dangerous-looking gun pointed at him, held by someone who looked like an overweight soldier. Someone who actually reminded Henry of the young man who rampaged through the sleepy town of Hungerford in the 1980s, similarly dressed, probably similarly obsessed, killing everybody in his path.

'You know her boyfriend is Keith.'

'Not for sure, I don't.'

'Liar!' The gun was thrust further forward. The hand holding it flexed, becoming tired. 'Anyway – what about Keith?'

'Do you know him?'

'Answer my question or I'll shoot you.'

'OK,' Henry relented. 'I'm investigating his murder.'

The gun wavered for the first time. 'His what?'

'You heard – murder. He got shot to death, probably by a gun similar to that one.' Henry nodded at the weapon.

'Well, I didn't fuckin' kill him – he's my mate.'

'In that case, I need to speak to you,' Henry said evenly. 'You might be able to help. Can I put my arms down?'

'Who are you and where are you from?'

'DCI Christie, from Lancashire Police.'

'Lancashire . . . he said he was going to Blackpool,' the man said, then pulled himself up. Had he said too much? 'You're not GMP then?'

Henry shook his head.

'ID?'

'I need to reach for it.'

The man nodded. 'Go for it. Slowly, like.'

Henry made big, deliberate moves. His left hand went to his left lapel, which he folded back to reveal the inside of his jacket; his right hand delved inside the inner pocket, emerging with his wallet, from which he extracted his warrant card and held it up for the camouflaged gunman to inspect . . . though Henry did not hold it too close, ensuring the gunman had to peer, using all his concentration to focus on the small lettering on the laminated card. This ensured he was distracted and allowed FB to step up close behind him, having crept in through the front door of the flat, then silently from room to room.

The two cops moved in unison at a quick nod of the head from FB.

FB's right arm folded around the gunman's throat, hard and crushing.

Henry sidestepped like a dancer, went for the guy's right arm, pirouetted back into him and snapped the forearm down on to his upcoming knee – twice. The grip on the gun was released immediately, the weapon clattering down on to the kitchen floor.

FB yanked back on the man's neck.

Henry smashed his elbow back as hard as he could into the masked face and, with a gurgling sound, Mr Camouflage dropped like a sack of turnips.

FB released his grip, allowing him to fall, then looked disdainfully at the lower-ranking officer, who stood there shaking visibly.

'You are a trouble magnet, Henry.'

Henry exhaled, expelling air from the far corners of his lungs.

'Thanks, boss,' he said.

Both officers stared down at the moaning figure at their feet. With some degree of satisfaction, Henry saw that where the man's nose had once protruded, pushed up against the inside of the balaclava, it was now flat and blood was seeping through the fabric. Henry rubbed his elbow thoughtfully, proud of how well aimed the blow had been.

'How long before a name emerges?' Mendoza put the question to Sweetman.

'Can't tell.'

'You need results quickly.'

'I know, I know.'

Mendoza considered this. He had no time to waste on this. He was desperate, but did not want Sweetman to pick up on this.

'Give my men another twenty-four hours,' Sweetman said. 'They can start now, start with the remaining people, the ones they have yet to visit.'

'How good are they?'

'More than good.'

'Maybe, maybe,' Mendoza said, considering this.

'I'll send them back out now.'

The Luger was not a replica as Henry had half-suspected, but a fully working, dangerous weapon. He had never actually handled a real Luger, but had known of them since he was a youngster. Not that he was seriously interested in guns as such, but he had made it his job as a kid to research the weapons used by his on-screen heroes. Hence he knew about James Bond's gun, Harry Palmer's gun, knew all about the six-shooters used by Rowdy Yates in *Rawhide* and that Napoleon Solo, the Man from Uncle, used a Luger.

The magazine was full. There was a bullet in the breech. Henry made the gun safe and put it down on the mantelpiece.

He looked at the man who was in army jungle fatigues, now holding his balaclava over a smashed and bloody nose.

'Got taken from a German officer during Operation Market Garden,' the man said, pulling the mask away from his nose so he could speak. 'Good weapon, the Luger.'

Henry raised his eyebrows.

He and FB had dragged the man into the living room and dropped him as hard as possible on to the floor in front of the settee. FB took up a position by the door. Henry stood towering over the pseudo-soldier.

'Got a licence for it?' he inquired, knowing it was impossible to get one these days.

The man put the mask back over his broken nose, said nothing.

'Thought not. Big trouble number one,' Henry said. The man's watery eyes blinked. 'Name?'

'Colin, Colin Carruthers,' he mumbled behind the material, which he then held away from his face and said proudly, 'They call me Colin the Commando.'

'Why's that?' Henry asked ironically.

'Why d'you fuckin' think?' He held out his arms wide, as if to say, *Look!*

Henry blinked as though he was just waking up. 'Oh, right. I get it!'

'Piss-taker,' said Carruthers angrily.

'OK – fundamentals. Date of birth, address, soldier,' Henry barked.

Carruthers spouted the details as though he was a private in a prisoner-of-war camp. Henry recalled that he had read Carruthers' name in Keith Snell's Intel file.

'What's all this about, Colin?' Henry said.

'Protection.'

'Protecting whom?'

'Grace, Keith . . .' Suddenly there was great fear in his eyes.

'From what?'

'Themselves.'

Henry paused, aware that he should now be speaking to Carruthers in an atmosphere more conducive to the one they were presently in. A police station.

'Why do they need protecting?' FB threw in.

Carruthers turned to look at the chief constable. 'In deep . . . both of them.'

'Were you protecting, or were you out to kill?' FB said.

'Maybe both, if necessary.'

FB gave Henry a look and a nod.

'I think we need to take this guy back to Lancs for a good long talk,' Henry said.

219

'I agree.'

'But what about Grace?'

'Come back for her,' said FB.

'Oi – I'm not under arrest,' said Carruthers. 'I need a doctor. You bastards assaulted me.' He made to scramble to his feet. Henry helped him – grabbed him, yanked him up, spun him round and frog-marched him to the living-room wall, where, expertly, he pulled out his cuffs (an old pair of the chain-linked variety) and clipped them swiftly on a pair of chubby wrists, ratcheting them tight enough to make him squeal a little.

'You are under arrest,' Henry corrected him, speaking in his ear.

'What for?'

Henry shrugged. 'All sorts of things . . . the gun . . . threatening me with it . . . no licence . . . but mainly on suspicion of murder.'

'Oh yeah, right.'

'Yeah – I always start close to home, then work away,' Henry said. 'And you can have a doctor for free. Are you a smackhead, too?'

'No, I'm fucking not.'

'Oh, OK. Probably could've got you a script on the house if you had been.'

'I need to make this very clear,' said Henry, shifting in the driver's seat of the Mondeo and looking over his shoulder to inspect his prisoner. The cuffs were now on Carruthers' lap, his hands bound in front of him instead of behind. He was holding a roll of kitchen towel, dabbing his dripping nose. 'If you so much as try anything remotely stupid, Colin, I will continue the work I started on your nose and then will move on to other, even more delicate parts of your body. You sit there like a good bloke and do not move or anything, OK?'

Carruthers nodded compliantly.

'Good.' Henry twisted forward, glanced at FB. 'Ready to roll?'

'Yep.' In the footwell between FB's feet lay the Luger and its ammunition, together with the other items they had found whilst searching the prisoner: a Bowie knife, a Kung Fu death

220

star, a cigarette lighter which became a flick knife and a double-barrelled Derringer pistol.

'Let's go.'

They had secured Grace's flat as best they could and Henry expected an early return to it by his detectives.

As he pulled off the estate, neither he nor FB saw the van parked some one hundred metres away, two men on board, sitting low in their seats, watching.

'You've got a bit of a tale to tell us, then, haven't you, Colin?' FB said, tilting his head backwards.

'I've got fuck all to tell the cops,' he responded.

'Not true, not true at all,' Henry said gently.

Tony Cromer and Teddy Bear Jackman received their briefing, much the same one as they had been given previously: go forth and cause grief and mayhem and get some answers; go and make blood flow, frighten people, hurt them, kill them if you have to – but come back with a name.

'Boss,' Cromer began, a pained expression in his voice and on his face, taking care to choose his words correctly. 'I know we've only really spoken to a couple of the major players, and quite a few of the riff-raff, but there's just nothing coming out of folk. Not a word, fuck all, just fuck all!'

'Maybe you're not trying hard enough,' Sweetman said.

Anyone else – anyone – and Cromer's new expression would have been one of deep annoyance, but for Sweetman he kept a straight face, one designed not to anger or inflame. He nodded. 'How long we got?'

'A day.'

Cromer did the sums. Eight more big boys to visit, three hours per person – if they could be located quickly – no rest for the wicked. 'We'd better get going then.'

'You will both be well rewarded,' Sweetman promised.

Colin Carruthers was not the type of person who could sit there and say nothing. He was no criminal in the darkest sense of the word, even though the offences he had committed in terms of the firearms and other offensive weapons were serious. Henry did not see them in the same way as offences committed by a tooled-up drug dealer. Colin was an army fantasist and hopefully a harmless one. Yes, he would have to have his weapons confiscated, but if he came up trumps for Henry then there was a good chance Henry could do a deal for him. But then again, Henry pondered as they hit the motorway out of Manchester, the fat little bastard had pointed a loaded gun at him. A sheen of nervous sweat suddenly covered Henry's whole outer skin at that thought. Colin the Commando would have to provide some very good information to get out of that one.

'Where we going?' the prisoner called out.

'Burnley.'

'Why Burnley, for God's sake?'

'That's where the custody office is.'

Carruthers withdrew for a few moments, thinking.

'You and Keith good mates?' Henry tossed to him.

'Hmph . . . were, stupid bastard. He always came to me when he was in trouble.'

'Did he come to you recently?'

'Yep.'

'When did you last see him?'

'Dunno . . . week ago?' Carruthers fell silent, then suddenly added, 'But you'd know that, wouldn't you?'

Henry adjusted the rear-view mirror so he could see Carruthers as he drove. 'Why would I know that?'

FB's mobile interrupted the flow of the conversation, exasperating Henry. He did not let it show.

Grant and Lopez sat together in the hotel bar, chuckling, smiling. Real bonhomie.

'They're floundering,' Grant said.

'*Si.*'

'Haven't got a clue.'

'No.'

'When do we make our move?'

'Twelve hours?'

'Twelve hours sounds good.'

They clinked glasses.

The call was from his staff officer, something about meeting the Police Authority, and the conversation seemed to go on forever, Henry getting more and more frustrated with FB. Finally it ended and just as Henry opened his mouth to resume the unofficial interview, his own phone blared out – 'Jumpin' Jack Flash'. FB eyed him as he answered it, although at seventy mph on a pitch-black motorway was not the best of circumstances in which to chit-chat.

'Henry? It's me, Karen Donaldson.'

'Hi – have you heard anything?' Henry got in first.

'No, nothing.'

'Oh, bloody hell. What does the Legat say?'

'That they've heard nothing either – and now it's official. He's officially missing.'

'Right, right . . . at least that's a good thing. Means they're taking it seriously. Putting some resources into it.'

'Maybe.' Karen sounded doubtful.

'He'll be fine, Karen. He's a top man. He'll just be doing something and won't want to break cover. You know what he's like.'

'Suppose he's been hurt – or worse. I keep calling him, just can't get through.' Henry could tell she was on the verge of tears. In the background the kids were crying.

'When I get off duty tonight, whatever time it happens to be, I'll call you. Is that all right?'

Her 'OK' was very numb-sounding.

'I promise,' he said, ending the call. 'Karen Donaldson,' he said to FB, who groaned. He had known Karen whilst she was an officer in Lancashire and had crossed swords with her on numerous occasions. They had little affection for each other, just as FB had no time for Karl Donaldson either. He had also been at loggerheads with him. Henry decided not to say anything about the nature of the call.

'OK, Colin . . . you were saying . . .'

The motorway traffic was light at that time of day. Henry had pretty much claimed the outer lane and no one, so far, had pushed to overtake. He glanced into his door mirrors and saw that a vehicle was fast approaching, headlights blazing. The lights were high up and subconsciously Henry put it down as a van, or similar. But it was coming up fast. Henry automatically checked his speedo. It was now hovering around eighty-five mph. He had increased his own speed without realizing.

Suddenly the van was tailgating.

'Tosser!' Henry uttered.

FB glanced over, frowning. Carruthers looked too.

Henry signalled to pull across into the middle lane, but before he could manoeuvre, the van moved into that lane. Henry sniffed and assumed that he was now going to be overtaken on the inside. He clung to the outer lane and waited, but the van did not shift, hung there on Henry's shoulder. He released some of the pressure on the gas pedal, losing speed slightly to encourage the van to pass.

It stuck where it was, reducing its speed too.

'What's this guy playing at?' Henry said aloud. There was the implication of a sigh in his voice. He pressed the accelerator and the Mondeo surged forward – as did the van, still in position like one of the Red Arrows. On the whole, Henry had little or no time for road rage. He always tried to see the foolhardy manoeuvres of other road users as 'interesting' but ultimately nothing to get wound up about. And he was basically a peace-loving individual who had no desire to get into pointless altercations with others. It was undignified.

The van driver was starting to annoy him, however. Henry's new intention was now to outspeed the van and put some distance between him and it.

The speedo touched ninety.

Still the van stayed where it was, as if attached by a rope, in Henry's slipstream.

'This fucker's annoying me,' FB said curtly.

'And me,' Carruthers piped up.

'Shut it,' both FB and Henry voiced unanimously. Carruthers cowered down, browbeaten.

At a hundred mph Henry expected to be pulling away from the van. But there it remained, lodged to his tail pipe.

Henry knew the Mondeo had little else to offer. It was not the fastest motor in the world.

'We need to have words,' FB said gruffly.

'Serious ones,' Henry agreed. He eased some pressure off the accelerator. Speed dropped and suddenly the two vehicles were alongside each other, moving parallel, speeds exactly the same.

FB glared across at the driver.

Henry clocked the actual make of the van now – a Citroën, black. He ducked his head, leaned over and peered across at the man at the wheel, who, for the first time, turned to face them, and for the first time they saw he was wearing a full-face clown mask.

'Shit!' breathed Carruthers.

Then, in what seemed like slow motion, the masked driver deliberately turned the van into the side of the Mondeo. Henry squirmed in his seat, attempting to sit upright and respond, but at the moment of impact he was still half-leaning over FB and that was the last thing he remembered as the Mondeo swerved and hit the central reservation barriers and sparks flew as Henry tried desperately to control it.

Seventeen

As sour as things had become for Mendoza, this did not prevent him from indulging in the pleasures of the flesh.

Following the dispatch of Teddy Bear and Cromer to execute their jobs of the night time, the two bosses were left with little to do other than wait for a result. Despite the two men being fellow felons, they had little in common with each other and would have struggled to conduct a sustained conversation about anything beyond criminal activities.

Neither was tired, both high from the adrenaline rush of stress, a stress which demanded a release. To alleviate this, Sweetman suggested they hit the city, let their hair down, relax, get laid.

Which is exactly what they did.

Accompanied by Grant and Lopez, they lurched out of the hotel and were immediately in the city centre. Within minutes they were inside one of the big nightclubs, spending a couple of hours drinking and talking to women. Sweetman fixed them both up with a couple of expensive girls, one being a dark one, with Mediterranean looks which the Manchester hood thought the Spanish one would appreciate. He did.

The two players gravitated back to Sweetman's quayside apartment, via a meal in Chinatown, where Mendoza and his appointed hooker took up residence in the guest bedroom. Grunts, cries and gasps drifted from the room for the next hour or so, whilst Sweetman paid his girl off and sent her packing. He knew he was not up to anything and when his head hit the pillow, he was out like a busted light.

Meanwhile, both second in commands returned to the city centre hotel, both accompanied by ladies of the night.

In the morning Grant and Lopez met for breakfast in the restaurant, both wrecked by the previous night's overindulgence in food, sex and drink.

It was nine a.m. when they ate.

'When shall we break the news?' Lopez asked. He was drinking black coffee.

'How about noon?' Grant suggested.

Lopez grinned. '*Si* . . . I like that very much. High Noon.'

A clown in a Citroën. That was all Henry Christie could see in the dark swirl of the unconscious mind. Blackness. A horrible scraping, tearing noise. A clown in a Citroën. Then nothing. Other than he now knew he was awake. Sensation flooded through him. His leg twitched. He coughed and opened his eyes like a doll. And then the headache hit him hard, an iron ball and chain swinging against his cranium.

'Oh thank God, thank God.'

His head rolled to one side and he blinked rapidly at Kate. He tried to say a word, wasn't sure what word. Any word would have done.

Kate looked ashen, desperately anxious. 'Henry . . . oh, thank God,' she cried. Tears streamed down her face, cascading like a mini waterfall. Henry tried to force a smile. Hell, this was all so confusing . . . a clown, a Citroën . . . a storming headache . . . like an axe in his head, splitting his brain in half.

He exhaled, found more pain across his body. Across his chest, his lungs were tight and sore, had spikes hammered into them.

Kate was half-on, half-off the bedside chair, holding herself up, looking down at him, tears still streaming.

What? he wanted to say. That was it, that was all, that was the word he was searching for. What? He still could not force it out.

Instead, in a haze of pain and puzzlement, he closed his eyes again. It was much easier and the last thing he heard was a cry of anguish from Kate.

'How do you feel now?'

'Sore . . . confused. My brain feels like it's in a mush,' Henry said.

'You suffered a severe blow to the head and your body got a sound battering, too.'

'Oh.' His eyes hurt as he squinted at the doctor, a drilling behind his eyeballs. The white coat made him look away. It was too much.

'As it happens, you're basically OK. X-rays show no skull damage, nor any damage to the rest of your body. You're just bruised. Your experience is rather like having thrown yourself into a spin-drier. Wearing your seat belt probably saved your life.'

'Seat belt?' Henry's face screwed up. 'Er . . . ?' he found himself at a loss. 'Have I been in an accident or something?'

He was in a side ward, did not even know which hospital. Alone now. Everyone had left for the moment; even the worried Kate had withdrawn. They would all be back soon, crowding him. A nurse had propped him up on soft pillows. He carefully laid his head back. The pain had been held at bay for the time being. Drugs. Good drugs. Warm, soft, fuzzy drugs, comforting him. He closed his eyes again, thanking the world for drugs. Apparently he was lucky to be alive. But why? What did that mean? Why was he so bloody lucky?

What the hell had happened?

Try as he might, nothing would come. He had no idea why he was lying in Bolton Royal Infirmary. And he was getting to the point where he needed to know, because it was driving him nuts.

*   *   *

227

They came at noon. Their faces were serious, grave even. He was sitting up now, a bed tray across his knees, trying to digest some food which did not really want to go down. He had been concentrating on drinking the fruit drink, all he felt capable of keeping inside.

A few moments passed before he actually recognized his visitors: Detective Superintendent Anger and DI Jane Roscoe. Anger's face stayed very serious, Jane's relaxed a little with relief. They pulled up chairs on either side of the bed.

'Welfare visit?' Henry said with a forced smile.

Anger merely raised his thick eyebrows impatiently. 'The consultant tells us you're fit enough to talk to now.'

'Yes, sure,' Henry said brightly.

'How're you feeling?' Roscoe asked.

The patient shrugged. 'OK, I guess. Battered, bruised and a mushy-pea head, but otherwise not too bad.'

'Good – can you tell us what happened then?' Anger blurted sharply.

'About what?' Henry said blankly. His brain was hurting.

'The accident.'

'What accident?' His mind was adrift again.

Anger sighed, seething, and opened his mouth to remonstrate. Jane Roscoe held up a calming hand to hold him back.

She spoke. 'What *do* you remember?' Her voice was gentle.

Henry shook his head slowly. 'Erm . . .' he began pathetically, but could not follow it up.

'Do you remember going to Manchester with the chief?'

'The chief constable? Why would I be going to Manchester with FB?' Henry said, rubbing his tired eyes, trying to concentrate. Then something came back to him. 'Yeah, I did, didn't I?' He paused, forcing his grey matter to get hold. 'I remember having a Big Mac with him, surrounded by a load of kids.'

'What else?' Roscoe probed.

'Nothing, nothing there.' He was getting frustrated with himself. He banged his fist on the bed tray, rattling the cutlery and crockery. 'Shit!'

'It's OK, Henry,' Roscoe said consolingly. 'It'll probably take time for it to all come back. Funny thing, memory.'

'Yeah, yeah,' he said dreamily.

Dave Anger was less understanding and his dislike of Henry surfaced like a bubble coming up from the slime in the bottom of a cesspit and popping on the surface. 'I think you're taking the piss, Henry.'

'Boss!' Roscoe said sharply.

Henry stared distastefully at him.

Anger shot a warning look at Roscoe. 'No,' he said, getting to his feet. 'This is all one big piss-take. Someone ducking and diving their responsibility, trying to wangle their way out of a messy situation.'

'Boss!' Roscoe said again.

'No – he's having this, the bloody bastard.' Anger rose to his full height, like a bear about to attack. Then he bent over close to Henry and pointed a thick, stubby, accusatory finger at him. He growled through clenched teeth. 'I want to know fucking everything, Henry. I want to know why there were two guns in the car and two knives and an Intel file, what's been going on, who the third person was and I want you to stop playing this bloody amnesia game with us. It's boring and very annoying.'

Henry felt himself draw back into his pillows and stare at Anger like a confused, frightened rabbit.

'Mr Anger!' Roscoe protested. She stood up, hands on hips, trying to reign him back. She looked pretty intimidating to Henry, but Anger was having none of it.

'No! There's questions that need answering and this bastard has those answers in that – allegedly – jumbled-up head of his.' He towered over Henry. 'You – start talking – *Now*!' he ordered Henry.

Henry shook his head despairingly, on the verge of tears. 'I can't fucking remember!' he insisted.

'I don't believe you. Look, you pathetic bastard, the chief constable's lying through there in a bloody coma and there's a dead guy lying stiff as a board in the mortuary who was in the back of your car. And we found guns, too – one was a Luger – and some ammo. You'd better start remembering, because there's some very big questions need answering.'

They came at noon. Their faces were serious, grave even.

Sweetman and Mendoza were hunched bleary-eyed at the

table in the dining room of Sweetman's apartment, picking over the crumbs of a very late breakfast.

Mendoza's prostitute had gone and they were alone.

Lopez and Grant came in. Their approach had been well rehearsed.

'Cromer and Teddy Bear unearthed anything yet?' Grant asked.

'Not so far as I know,' Sweetman said. They were the first words he had uttered that day. He swilled some fresh orange juice down his throat.

'They won't,' Grant said firmly.

Sweetman raised his eyes. He did not ask the *Why?* question, no need to.

'It's not one of them,' Grant said.

'One of who?'

'One of the people they've been sent to terrorize. It's not one of them.'

'How do you know?'

'Had a whisper from a good source, a reliable source, who doesn't want to be named.'

'Who?'

'Like I said . . .'

'OK, OK. So you've had a whisper . . . what's the whisper?'

'I've been given a name.'

Mendoza and Sweetman sat upright.

'Speak it,' Mendoza said.

Grant paused for effect, keeping his eyes away from Lopez. He cleared his throat, then spoke.

Anger's approach may not have been the most considered and appropriate (and he did get himself escorted from Henry's room by the consultant and a nurse) but it did have some positive effect on Henry. Things, images, began to tumble along his battered dendrites. Now he could see the gun. Napoleon Solo. A Luger. Now he could visualize a journey along the motorway, adjusting his rear-view mirror, looking in his side mirrors, seeing headlights. But all these things did not merge into coherence. It was like doing a jigsaw puzzle without the lid.

He had been driving a car which had crashed. That he knew because he had been told so, not because he remembered.

FB had been severely injured. Another man had died. What other man? Why had there been an accident? What had caused it? What had he done wrong? The lights in the mirrors were something to do with it.

Henry wracked his brain, banging his forehead with the balls of his hands.

It would not come.

Perhaps if he got up and went to see FB. That would be a good memory jogger.

He was no longer connected to anything. The blip-machines had been removed, the drips extracted from his veins. No longer tied down to any medical technology, he was a free man. He sat up, hung his legs over the side of the bed, aware that he was only wearing a rear-fastening hospital gown, loosely tied up the back – and that he was completely naked underneath.

His feet touched the cold floor. Gingerly he took his own weight, stood up and felt OK. The first time he had been up, all previous visits to the bathroom via bedpan alley. Two steps, then a wobble. Balance out of kilter slightly. One more step . . . whoa! Not good. He grabbed the bed and eased himself back into a sitting position.

For the moment, Henry Christie was going nowhere.

Eighteen

Karl Donaldson opened his eyes. Warm, tawny sun filtered through the latticed shutters, spreading a glow across the room. He sat up slowly, rubbed his caked-up eyes and breathed deeply, blinking to try and focus. He looked at his own body, saw he was naked, saw how battered it was and knew he was fortunate to be alive.

Slowly he got to his feet, steadied himself and padded across the cold marble floor to the shuttered window, which he opened.

The view made his lips purse in wonderment. A beautiful valley, a river snaking through the floor of it and far away in the distance the shimmer of the sea in the heat haze. Rays of sunshine flooded in, caressing his body like a warm massage as he stood there gazing down the mountainside. Then a thought occurred to him. Maybe he was dead, maybe this was heaven.

There was a soft tap on the door.

Donaldson turned slowly, his aching joints not allowing quick action.

The door opened to reveal a beautiful girl standing on the threshold, long golden hair cascading across her shoulders, a dark Mediterranean shade to her glowing skin, wide brown eyes, dark eyelashes. A simple dress covered her, but also accentuated her full figure, her breasts pushing up against the fabric.

Yes, I am dead, Donaldson thought. I have gone to heaven and this is my angel.

The clothes were rough, well worn, but clean and cared for. The girl carried them in front of her. She crossed to the bed and laid the items carefully on it, together with a pair of shoes she placed on the bedroom floor. Her eyes stayed low, looking away from Donaldson's nakedness, though they did occasionally flicker in his direction.

'I heard you moving,' she said, drawing back to the door, Donaldson watching her open-mouthed. 'There is a towel there' – she pointed to a rail – 'and the shower is down the hallway.' She smiled nervously.

She held up a finger, silencing Donaldson, who was about to speak. She shook her head. 'Get a shower, shave if you like, then come out on to the terrace. You'll find it.'

'Just one thing,' he said quickly.

She nodded impatiently.

'How long have I been here?'

'Two days.'

'Two days? What the hell has been going on?'

'You've been recovering,' she said. 'You had a fever, then you slept and now . . .' She shrugged.

'One more thing . . . are you Spanish?'

'No,' she smiled. 'English.' With that she closed the door, leaving him alone. He stretched, standing in the sun, feeling it warm his bones, but also feeling aches and pains inside him. He closed the shutters and walked back to the bed, reaching for the towel, which he wrapped around his waist.

The shower, down the hall as described, worked very well. It was hot and powerful and Donaldson revelled in it, soaping himself gently, allowing the heat of the water to permeate through his tired muscles, helping to ease their tension. As he showered, his mind worked back to everything that had happened to him. It was as these thoughts rearranged themselves into order, he started to panic.

'Give me an hour,' Lopez had said to Donaldson. The hour stretched forever as the big American sat in the restaurant in Ciudad Quesada, drinking café solo, hoping the huge quantities of caffeine would keep him alert and ready for the worst. He was beginning to think this little unauthorized jaunt might not be such a good idea after all. No one in the office knew where he was, he hadn't even told Karen, though at least Henry knew something. But because he was in Spain very unofficially, it also meant there was no chance of being armed and at that moment he was feeling very vulnerable indeed.

Midnight came, went. Diners filtered away from the restaurant, leaving him and a couple of other hangers-on to annoy the waiters who were clearly desperate to wind up for the night.

Donaldson had nowhere to go.

Even the other two stragglers asked for their bills, paid up and left.

A chill descended on the night. The waiters began stacking chairs. One sauntered hesitantly up to him and said, 'Señor?' with a shrug. 'We are closing now.'

Donaldson nodded. 'Si . . . la cuenta, por favor,' he said, much to the man's relief. It looked like Lopez was a no-show. He counted out his euros on to the saucer, was about to stand and leave when a large black Mercedes, with tinted windows and a driver, drew up outside.

Lopez climbed out and trotted up the restaurant steps, nodding at the waiters. He walked confidently across to

*Donaldson's table and sat down, beckoning a waiter. The man
scurried over, all tugging forelock and bowing and scraping.
It was plain to Donaldson that Lopez was well known to the
staff.*

*'Do you wish for anything more?' Lopez asked Donaldson.
'Espresso.'*

*Lopez barked the order, then turned and regarded
Donaldson.*

*In the records which Donaldson kept on Lopez, he was
known only under the codename 'Stingray'. Lopez did not
know this, but it seemed an appropriate name for him as his
lips reminded Donaldson of those of a stingray. It was a
horrible, pale mouth, pink and bloodless, shiver-inducing.
Donaldson did not like or trust him, but he was willing to
become bedfellows with anyone who gave him a chance of
nailing Mendoza.*

*Lopez had approached him in the first instance and had
provided good information initially, but never quite enough.
He realized that Lopez was playing his own game here, too.
Quite what it was could only be guessed at. Maybe he would
find out more tonight . . . and even as Donaldson considered
this, his instinct warned him: 'Be very careful here. This man
is an informant and he is meeting you out in the open on his
turf . . . what does that signal?' Though it had been
Donaldson's idea to meet here, he would have respected
Lopez's decision to meet somewhere more discreet.*

The American's whole being came on the alert.

Showered, shaved, fully clothed – although no garment actually fitted him properly, everything just too small because he
was a large, broad man – Donaldson took a deep breath and
wandered through the house, walking out of the kitchen and
emerging on to the terrace, which had the same view as his
bedroom, only without the frame. There was a large wooden
dining table, six chairs, a stone-built oven; beyond was a swimming pool.

The girl was sitting at the table, reading a novel. She placed
it down and raised her face to Donaldson, smiling with perfect
teeth. Donaldson squinted, shading his eyes from the beating
sun.

'Hi,' he said.

'Hello.'

He paused, blew out his cheeks, gave her a cautious sideways glance, smiled himself.

'How are you feeling?'

'Confused and very, very sore.'

'Are you hungry? You haven't eaten for days.'

'Now you come to mention it, I'm ravenous.' On cue, his stomach roared like a lion. Both laughed.

'I'll do something simple,' the girl said, standing up. She was backlit by the sun filtering through the thin cotton of her dress. Donaldson caught his breath, reminded of the famous early photos of Diana Spencer. It was clear that this girl knew, as Diana had, the effect she was having. She was fully aware he could see her body. She grinned coyly, moved past him, closer than she needed to. He trailed her into the kitchen. 'Scrambled eggs on toast?' she asked.

'Wonderful,' he responded.

She set about the task in the spacious, simple room. Slicing bread from what looked like a home-made loaf, cracking and whisking four big, brown eggs, adding sprinkles of herbs, cheese, salt, ground pepper and some creamy milk.

'I'm at a loss,' he admitted. 'I kinda know why I'm here, but the finer details escape me. It's been a bit of a haze.'

'You've been ill . . . anyway, my father will be back soon,' she told him. 'He's down in the orange grove . . . he'll tell you everything.'

'Right, good.' He watched her, busy at the range, turning the thick toast under the grill, stirring the eggs which began to harden, boiling a kettle. 'What's your name?'

'Maria.'

It had to be, he thought. 'Last name?'

'Elliot.'

'I'm Karl Donaldson.'

'Yes, I know.' She glanced over her shoulder at him. 'You work for the FBI.'

'That's a point,' he clicked his fingers. 'My things.'

'All washed – what was left of them. They were in a bit of a mess, but Dad found your wallet and it seems OK.'

'Good. I need to contact some people. Was there a mobile phone?'

'No.' She spooned out perfect scrambled eggs on to perfect toast. 'It's ready.'

With equally perfect coffee, Donaldson sat and consumed the plain but delicious meal at the table on the terrace. Each mouthful made him feel better and better, his energy flooding back.

Maria busied herself in the kitchen, taking sly glances at him.

When he finished eating, he sipped the coffee, gazing at the view.

The situation he had brought about put his defences up: Lopez in the open, talking to a stranger, and it did not feel right. Donaldson's eyes constantly roved, seeking danger.

'What's happening?'

'This is unacceptable,' Lopez said. 'You have caused me great problems. When you called me, I was with him.'

'You handled it OK.'

'Maybe, but whatever . . . I am no longer your informant. Our relationship is terminated.'

Even though Donaldson was half-expecting this, it still punched him like a fist in the solar plexus. Without Lopez, Mendoza would be far more difficult to bring down.

'I don't think so,' Donaldson said. 'You're in too deep.'

Lopez shook his head. 'It is over,' he said, as though ending an affair. 'I do not need it any more.'

Desperation made Donaldson say the next words. 'What would Mendoza think if he knew you and I talked?'

Lopez grimaced. 'Threat?'

'Yes.'

'Is this the way you treat informants if they begin to waver, if they wish to withdraw their services? Is this the way the FBI works?'

'It's the way I work.'

'I have given you all I am going to give.'

'Lopez . . . I'm . . . I need to get Mendoza and if you will not help me, then as far as I am concerned, you're back on the shit pile with him. I can't – or won't – protect you any more.'

The expression in the Spaniard's eyes almost froze Donaldson's arteries.

'I'm afraid, Karl, that I cannot afford for you to make threats like that. My own game plan is coming together now and I no longer need you. You were part of it once, but now it's time to cut free. Coming out to Spain was a miscalculation on your part.' He smiled the smile of a stingray.

Heavy rain suddenly began to fall on the street outside.

Donaldson shivered, heard a noise and turned quickly, plucked from his memories. A man walked out of the kitchen door and on to the terrace. Late fifties, he looked healthy and tanned, slim and fit. Donaldson stood up as the man thrust a hand at him.

'John Elliot,' he introduced himself.

'Karl Donaldson.'

'I think I may have just saved your life, Mr Donaldson.'

Two guys were behind Donaldson before he could react.

'They are armed, Karl, and they will shoot you in the back without hesitation should I nod my head, or should you do anything idiotic.'

The men dragged Donaldson to his feet and quickly searched him, then forced him back on to the chair. 'He's clean,' one said.

The men sat down at an empty table, maybe ten feet away. A manageable distance for a handgun – if that's what they were armed with.

Lopez relaxed.

'What's this about?' Donaldson asked, a wave of his hand indicating the new arrivals, but really meaning the whole situation.

Lopez looked pained. 'Ambition, greed, power, lust, money, women . . . you name it . . . conspiracy of the highest order.' He shrugged. 'All those things.'

'All in relation to you?'

'Yes . . . I either have them or crave them, I don't mind admitting that . . . and I have been conspiring to collect them all. It doesn't really matter that you now know, because soon you will be dead and my words will go with you to your grave – if you can call it a grave.'

237

Outside, the rain beat down heavily.

'Is this about you and Mendoza?' Donaldson guessed, *knowing it was a rhetorical and quite naff question, but he was working out how best to take on the two hoods sitting behind him.*

'Very much.' Lopez warmed to it, shifting excitedly in his chair. *'A bit like a Greek tragedy, only we are Spanish.'*

'So, a Spanish tragedy?'

Lopez laughed. Donaldson weighed up flight or fight options.

'I have been scheming for years,' Lopez admitted, *'because I want what he has and now the time has come for me to make my move. I can hold back no longer.'*

'Is this a wise conversation?' Donaldson gestured by tilting his head back towards the heavies behind him.

'They were brought up on the streets of Madrid, fighting and killing for their very existence. They are merely brainless hoodlums, working conscientiously for whoever pays them at the time – and at the moment I pay them.'

'Greed, lust, power, money . . . my, my, my . . . you have some things to tell me then?'

'Nothing that will surprise you, I suspect.'

'Try me.'

'You were just a pawn in the game, to coin a phrase.'

'Now to be dispensed with, I guess.'

'I have been planning long-term the fall of Carlos Mendoza . . . and you were simply one of the devices I used.' Donaldson could see the eyes in Lopez's head twinkling. *Power-crazed bastard,* he thought. *'It's been a long haul,'* the Spaniard sighed. *'Planning, negotiating, influencing . . . killing, even. It has taken time and guile to back Mendoza into this corner, one from which he will be unable to escape.'*

'I'm intrigued,' Donaldson said genuinely. *This was a story he wanted to hear before he worked out how to get free of this deadly situation – and take Lopez with him.*

John Elliot had a pleasant expression, as though he was always on the verge of breaking into a grin of self-satisfaction. He seemed content and at peace with the world around him. Sitting next to Donaldson at the table on the terrace, the

American found himself to be a little envious of the man who, it seemed, had everything he wanted out of life.

'I'm a retired cop, actually. Been here since the day of my retirement, just over seven years ago. This place was really run down and it's only in maybe the last eight, ten months that it's all come together. Been real graft.' Elliot sipped from his glass of freshly squeezed orange juice, a little misty-eyed at the memories.

'You seem to have it sorted.'

'Mm,' he agreed, 'but I couldn't have done it without the pension behind me. I'll never make any money from this place, unless I sell it, but that's not the point, is it?'

'Any regrets?' Donaldson asked.

'Maybe one . . . the wife couldn't stand it. The hard work and discomfort that renovating the place took. No shops within twenty miles. She upped and left four years ago. Haven't heard from her since. Not even sure if I'm divorced or what.'

Donaldson regarded Elliot. Perhaps he hadn't got everything.

'Maria decided to stay. I couldn't have pulled it together without her, but I think she's restless now, which is fair enough. I don't intend to hold her back if she wants to leave.' He sighed wistfully.

'How do you make money, if you don't mind me asking?'

'Pension – as I said. Olives and lemons. I write articles occasionally about British ex-pat life on the Costas and I paint a little. Started selling the odd canvas . . . it's not much. Maria teaches English as a foreign language down in Torrevieja, so we make ends meet.'

'Sounds a good life.'

'It has its ups and downs like any other.' Elliot finished his cold drink. 'So, Mr Donaldson, now you've had a potted history of my life, how did you end up half-drowned in a flooded river bed?' He turned to him, waited for an explanation.

Lopez had stepped on to an unstoppable train now as he shared his Machiavellian scheming.

Donaldson had witnessed this type of 'opening the flood-gates' from felons before. At times when they felt comfortable,

239

they would reveal all, hoping that the recipient would let them bask in the limelight and fuel their already outrageous egos. Lopez obviously felt he could blab to Donaldson, which he actually found very worrying. It was like the Bond villain explaining his master plan to the secret agent whilst Bond was pinned to the circular-saw table, because the villain knew that Bond was about to die a most horrible death.

For James Bond, substitute Karl Donaldson.

'Where should I begin?' Lopez said thoughtfully. 'Not at the beginning. That is too far back. All you need to know is that Mendoza worked his way up the crime ladder until he was doing business with the Cosa Nostra in Sicily. They loaned him money to carry out operations for them, he paid them back and both grew rich . . . a happy situation. I have known Mendoza for many years. We were gang members in Madrid as kids, running protection rackets, stealing, hurting people. I followed him up the tree until I was well placed in the' – Lopez shrugged here – 'thing that he calls his organization.'

Donaldson pretty much knew the history of Miguel Lopez, but he let the man talk uninterrupted.

'But I always wanted what he had, always believed I was the better man, and that is how my campaign started. Manoeuvring and manipulating him carefully and skilfully into positions where he was made to look, shall we say, less than competent? Situations in which the Mafia paymasters would start seeing him as a liability . . . without, of course, him suspecting I was the one responsible for doing it.' He grinned at his own brilliance. 'I was always the better brain.'

'I'm sure,' Donaldson said sincerely. 'Examples?'

'The loan he made to a gangster in the north of England. Marty Cragg . . . a loan which would never have the chance of being repaid . . . I made it happen. The loan was made with borrowed Mafia funds and in the end he was forced to kill Cragg and transfer the loan to his wiser brother, Roy. A man who now languishes in prison, unable to pay it back.' Lopez grinned, shook his head sadly.

Donaldson scowled, remembering the murder of Marty Cragg. It had taken place at the same time and place as the murder of Donaldson's undercover operative, Zeke. Both men *had bullets put into their heads underneath a motorway bridge in Lancashire.*

'I know what you are thinking. Was I there?' Lopez placed the palm of his hand against his chest. 'Am I correct?'

'Yep.' Donaldson swallowed.

Lopez held Donaldson's stare. 'I was there when Verner killed Marty Cragg and the FBI agent,' he confirmed.

Donaldson felt something surge through him.

'Mendoza ordered the killing. Verner did the deed. And the knock-on was that the Cosa Nostra was very unimpressed by the way in which Mendoza dealt with the whole situation. Killing a federal agent is frowned upon and they became very twitchy.'

'And you were there?'

'I was there.'

'OK.' Donaldson held himself back from launching himself across the table and strangling him, but he did weigh up the odds of success. 'Carry on.'

'Whilst all this was going on, I was ingratiating myself with our Sicilian colleagues, whilst subtly destroying Mendoza's reputation. Little by little. Then I gave you Verner on a plate. One of our best killers, killed himself by an unknown assassin . . . you, I guess, Karl.'

Donaldson's teeth ground loudly.

'What was the story with the illegal immigrants and the drugs?'

'The next big opportunity. Another Mafia-financed operation. Millions of pounds worth of cocaine and twenty illegal immigrants. At first I thought I would give them to you, then I changed my mind. I had something in place which I thought would be more effective.'

'Hence the phone call telling me the lorry had changed.'

'Hence that.'

'I really need to make contact with the outside world.' Donaldson said, sipping more coffee, freshly ground, tasting amazing, rich and slightly bitter. Donaldson looked at John Elliot. 'I think my mobile phone went down the river. Can I make a call from the house phone, please?'

'Under normal circumstances, you could,' the ex-pat said.

'However, the storm yanked down all the phone lines and we don't have a mobile phone between us.'

'Oh.'

'That doesn't mean to say we can't still help you.'

Trapped by his own foolhardiness and now he was going to pay the penalty. He was still listening hard to Lopez, hoping he would remember everything, but the other part of his mind was formulating his escape plan.

'I've been grooming people,' Lopez boasted, 'moving people into positions . . . when I was in Manchester two, three years ago, I met a man with ambition. He wanted to become a major dealer, or should I say, I contacted such a man. Very ambitious, very determined. I began to deal with him. He had a good organization.' Lopez chuckled at that thought. 'He was sure he could set up the necessary infrastructure – he and I have been building up his business and suddenly he was ready for the big one – which I put his way, although he and I have never met, nor does he know my true identity.'

'The drugs in the lorry?'

'They were Mendoza's drugs destined for another big Manchester dealer with whom there have been business ties for several years, a man called Sweetman. I let my ambitious man into the secret and suggested he might like to help himself.'

'Making Mendoza look a fool.'

Lopez nodded sagely. 'And also ensuring that my own man will come out of this . . . not well.'

Donaldson looked puzzled.

'My plan is now very simple, Karl,' Lopez explained. 'Very simple indeed. I am about to take over Mendoza's organization on my terms. A management buy-out, you might call it.'

The vehicle was a battered old Land Rover. It bounced along the deeply rutted track, throwing the two people about inside it like balls in a bagatelle.

Donaldson held on to the door frame as his backside jolted out of the seat.

Maria gripped the steering wheel, holding the black rim grimly.

Donaldson eyed her, a mock-worried expression on his face. She caught his look, smiled radiantly.

'How far before we get to a road?' he shouted over the din.

'This *is* a road,' she teased, then relented. 'Another mile.'

Donaldson worked it out, guessing that Elliot's farmhouse was about four miles away from a real road, up narrow, treacherous lanes. 'You do this journey often?'

'Four days a week.'

'Ahh – Torrevieja, teaching.'

'It's great for the bum,' she shouted, hitting a boulder and pitching the Land Rover sideways.

Lopez had finished, told Donaldson everything he wanted to say. He stretched. 'My men will now deal with you, Karl. Goodbye.' He stood up.

'This seems to go against your policy of killing federal agents.'

'Not policy, Karl, best practice . . . but having said that, no one will find your body, so no one will actually know if you are dead or alive. I'm sorry things did not work out for us, but you were simply an avenue I was exploring. It proved to be a dead end, not what I wanted from my perspective.'

Lopez clicked his fingers. As if on cue, there was a flash of lightning, followed almost immediately by a deep roar as thunder rent the atmosphere. The rain suddenly became torrential, beating down loudly on the roof of the restaurant. 'The storms from the mountains have joined us,' Lopez said. He coughed. 'My men will deal with you cleanly and effectively. I owe you that much.'

'You're very kind . . . but do you think you'll get away with this? My people know where I am, who I'm seeing.'

Lopez shrugged indifferently. 'I don't really care. That's a bridge I'll cross when I come to it.' He nodded to his men.

'Up!' a harsh voice ordered from behind Donaldson.

Donaldson glanced over his shoulder. Both of the heavies were on their feet, guns in hand, pointed at his back. They were big-calibre revolvers, unwieldy, but probably reliable and deadly at close range. Donaldson rose slowly, a cynical, defeated expression on his face.

'You think you'll take over from Mendoza?' he sneered.

Lopez nodded confidently. 'I have everything in place. It will be my inheritance. He would not have achieved anything had it not been for my business skills anyway. It's only right that I now assume control.'

'Somehow I doubt it,' Donaldson said. Lopez shrugged, but a dark line of puzzlement crossed his face. 'He's too smart.'

'Unlike you, my friend,' Lopez said, dismissing the comment. He pointed at him for the benefit of his men and said, 'Finish him,' in Spanish.

They did not do it in the restaurant. They should have done, but they didn't, and once Donaldson realized they were not going to blast him there and then, that they intended to drive him somewhere isolated, kill and dispose of him, he knew he had a chance. Their mistake.

He was in the back seat of a car, a big old Peugeot. Child locks were on and he was sitting directly behind the driver, one of the two guys from the restaurant. The other man was sitting in the front passenger seat, twisted round, his piece aimed lazily at Donaldson's body mass. His forefinger was on the trigger and the gun looked dangerous.

They were confident guys. They had done this before, that much was apparent. Probably to some dumb hood or another, maybe more than once. They kept quiet, speaking only when necessary, the one in the passenger seat keeping constant vigil on Donaldson.

The car headed out of Ciudad Quesada, then turned inland towards the weather. The wipers struggled against the volume of rain. The headlights, on main beam, hardly seemed to penetrate the darkness ahead. They left the main road and began to climb.

Donaldson considered going for the driver. He could lunge, arms going around the headrest, hands on either side of his neck, and snap the neck within four seconds. Too long. Four seconds was a lifetime in these situations. It would be long enough to see two big, nasty bullet holes in his chest.

He also thought about the pros and cons of going for the one with the gun. He was a fraction too far away. It could be done, but the angles were not favourable.

He would have to wait . . . and there was also the problem of the car. Where would it veer to? Peering out into the rain, feeling the car go higher up steep mountain roads, there was a good chance that if he did try something, they would end up over a precipice. Donaldson wanted to come out of this alive . . . so he waited.

The road became narrower, winding around hairpins, rising all the time against the atrocious weather.

He smirked, snorting a laugh down his nose.

'What you laughing at?' the guy in the passenger seat asked.

Donaldson regarded him with a chill. 'The way you're going to die,' he said. The man's face dropped. He shifted, then smirked.

'Don't you mean the way you are going to?'

'No.' Donaldson turned away and looked out of the window, seeing dark trees rising through the heavy rain, liking what he saw. The elements were on his side and also the fact that two street-hardened tough guys were contracted to kill him. To him, that put them down as amateurs.

Twenty minutes later they stopped.

'As Mr Lopez said, this will be quick. You will not suffer.'

'Please thank Mr Lopez for that.'

'You stay seated,' he was ordered.

The driver climbed out and went to Donaldson's door whilst the other guy covered him. Donaldson knew this would be the only chance he had – one in the car, the other outside.

The driver had his gun in his hand now, pointed at Donaldson through the window. He put a hand to the door, pulled it open a fraction of an inch.

'Out!' the guy in the passenger seat barked.

Donaldson sighed and nodded. He knew if he got out, acquiesced, and then gave them the chance to both be out, he was dead. But one in the car, one out, different story.

'How much not to kill me?' he pleaded.

'You haven't got enough, gringo,' sneered the guy.

'OK . . .' He placed his hand on the inner door rest and pushed the door. The guy on the outside, the one getting drenched and severely irritated by the delay, stepped away from the car. Donaldson paused again, letting him get wetter. 'I'm an FBI agent, you know. They'll come for you.'

'Let them.'

'Hey, you fuckers! Hurry up!' the wet one bawled.

'They won't give up. You should let me go.'

'Get out of the car.'

'I'm going.' He opened the door a little more. Rain dripped in. The sound of it hitting the car roof was incredible, like marbles being thrown down from the heavens by the million. He gazed up at the wet one. He was half-drowned by now, miserable, wanting to get on with this. Donaldson opened the door a fraction further. Rain cascaded in now, soaking his trouser leg. He needed to move before he too got weighed down by water.

He swung both legs out, but not too quickly, then stood in the rain.

Wet One backed off.

Donaldson bent back inside the car, feeling the rain hitting the back of his shirt. Surely it didn't rain in Spain like this. He looked at Dry One, opened his mouth to say something further and got the desired effect. Wet One strode across and rammed his gun into Donaldson's ribs.

'Get out now. Stop fucking around.'

Donaldson nodded and slowly stepped away from the door, then slammed it shut.

One inside the car, one outside.

Dry One turned to open his door and join his companion, a movement which necessitated him having to look away for a few seconds. Donaldson stood upright, seeing Wet One stepping backwards away from him, the gun now out of Donaldson's ribs and pointing towards the ground.

Donaldson's right arm arced, his body twisted. The edge of his hand sliced through the air, blurred by the rain, almost impossible to see.

He connected with the side of Wet One's neck with such force that the head sprung sideways as though he had been struck by the axe of an executioner. The blow sent him staggering to one side, knees sagging weakly. Donaldson's follow-up was violent and decisive, as he drove the base of his right hand upwards to the man's nose, smashing his septum up into the brain like the blade of a small knife. He fell hard, dead before he touched the ground – but as he dropped, Donaldson wrested his gun from him and turned to take on Dry One.

Dry One was only just standing up after getting out of the car. His gun swung upwards. He fired.

The flash and the sound in the rain was dull, making Donaldson think that the bullets in the gun were sub-standard. He returned fire, his finger squeezing the trigger back twice in quick succession – the double tap. But only the first shell left the muzzle, the second stayed where it was. A misfire. He pulled again. Another misfire. Defective or wet ammo – or empty . . . whatever.

Dry One fired again – and his gun worked.

That was enough for Donaldson. He spun and ran low toward the dark edge of the road, plunging head first into what lay beyond the light.

The Land Rover emerged on to the main road, Donaldson sighing happily at the smooth flatness of the tarmac after the pot-holed terrain of the country track. A sign indicated Torrevieja and Alicante to the left.

'Where should I drop you?'

'Airport?' he dared to suggest.

'OK,' Maria said brightly. 'It's about half an hour from here.' She pulled the Land Rover on to the road. 'You never really told us why you came to be where you were,' she said. 'You've been really vague with us.'

'It's best you don't know,' he said, tight-lipped. 'I told your father quite a lot, but kept the details sketchy. It's better that way.'

A headlong plunge into the darkness, no idea at all of what was waiting there for him. Which was the more stupid? That or facing a man with a gun? Twenty metres into the forest he wished he had chosen the latter, something he'd had more experience with, as suddenly he lost his footing and the ground underneath him just disappeared, becoming a perpendicular drop of shale, rock and protruding branches. It was as though he had stepped off the edge of a cliff, which, in essence, is exactly what he had done.

He could not recall much of the fall, just covering his head, rolling into a ball and hoping for the best, as he bounced down the incline, his breath being driven out of him each time

247

he smacked down. Then, just as suddenly as he had started the fall, it was over and he stopped rolling.

Breathless he lay there, panting, feeling the pain. The rain beat down on him, torrential and as hard as little stones.

'I'm alive,' he said to himself. He took a moment to work out whether anything had been broken. His feet moved, his knees could bend; he flexed his fingers, his hands and arms and rolled his neck. Everything seemed to be in order, though he felt like he had just been hammered in a street fight, beaten, maybe, but still in one piece. 'Now if I can just get up.' He groaned and moved at the same time, turning over on to all fours, his head lolling wearily between his arms. 'Jesus, Jesus!' he gasped, then slowly rose to his feet. 'Made it,' he said triumphantly. 'I can stand . . . that's good . . . I'm on my feet . . .'

Still the rain battered down. He looked round into the pitch black, unable to work out anything at all. He had no conception of where he could be. He had fallen down a steep, rugged hill and miraculously hit the bottom relatively unscathed. Didn't think anything was broken. Slowly his breath came back.

Then something made him cock his head to one side. A noise. A rumble. Something not part of the rain. He tensed up, fearing something, but not having any idea of what it was. The rumble grew louder. It had a sort of liquid sense to it.

That was his moment of realization.

He was standing in a river bed. A dry river bed. It had been raining in the mountains . . . he recalled somebody saying that. Heavy rain, persistent.

As a wall of water hit him at knee level and scythed away his legs, the words 'Flash flood!' formed on his lips.

John Elliot found him next morning as he patrolled the periphery of his land, inspecting the damage caused by the storms and the flood. It was the first time Elliot had known the river bed to flood since he had lived at the farm, even though there had been bad storms in the past. In some respects the sight of a washed-up body on the banks of the river did not totally surprise him, nor did it panic him. Thirty-three years as a cop had made him immune to death.

248

Finding him alive was a bonus, but not a straightforward one. After conveying the bedraggled, exhausted man to his home, he would have preferred to call the emergency services, but all phone lines were down and he did not possess a mobile phone and the access lane was impassable at that moment, far too muddy even for the Land Rover. He and Maria were effectively cut off from the rest of the world for a time.

He knew of a retired doctor who lived in the next valley, but it was a four-hour hike, so he decided to tend the man from the river himself. There was no way he could accurately tell whether the man was badly injured internally, but he trusted to luck.

Elliot was reminded of the old cowboy movies where the patient fought a fever and either died or recovered. Donaldson was feverish for a day, then slept a deep, exhausted sleep for a further day before awakening to that wonderful morning sunshine and the delicious sight of Maria Elliot in her thin clothes.

Donaldson thanked Maria for the lift back to the airport. She said little to him as he alighted from the Land Rover, but her eyes said a lot.

Donaldson waved her off reluctantly. She drove back to her world as he walked into the terminal building and re-entered his.

Nineteen

Forty-eight hours after almost going headlong on the ward floor, Henry was discharged from hospital and found himself at home. He was still scouring his brain for the memory of why he had been driving down the motorway with the chief constable, another man, a gun and some bullets. But being cooped up in the house drove him barmy very quickly.

He paced like a caged rat and to escape this he decided to go for a walk, both to get out of the house and to get his mind turning again.

On the second morning at home, still booked off sick from work, he was striding down the promenade at Blackpool, heading north towards Bispham . . . when he suddenly stopped because he had no recollection whatsoever of how he had actually got there.

He knew where he was and that he must have walked there from home, but for the life of him he could not recall putting his feet out of the front door and setting off. To get where he was, he estimated, would have taken him a good hour and a half, but that ninety minutes was just a void.

A sensation of panic rippled through him.

'This,' he said worriedly to himself, 'is very bad.' He was convinced that his mind had now completely gone kaput. The madness of Henry Christie. He quickly found a seat in a shelter and plonked himself down next to two old ladies who were openly displaying their underwear. He smiled at them, but it must have been more a frightening grimace and they cowered away from the sex-crazed murderous fiend who was obviously about to rape and kill them.

He sat with his head in his hands for a few minutes, breathing deeply and trying to regain some iota of control. 'Get a grip,' he instructed himself with a growl.

Gradually he became aware that someone was standing near to him. He raised his eyes to see a man, out of breath, maybe as old as he was, a few feet away, looking at him. The man's right arm was in a sling. He looked dreadful, unshaved, eyes sunken, skin grey and sagging.

'Can I help?' Henry asked, wondering if this was the start of a new life for him, one in which he played a major part in the care-in-the-community scene. The man looked slightly demented, hunted even.

'Thank God you stopped,' he said, panting. 'I thought you'd go on forever. I've been following you for ages.'

Henry's heart missed a beat. 'Why?' he snarled. 'Do I look like a nutter?'

'No, no, no,' the man said. 'No, I need to talk to you.'

Henry's next thought was that he was being picked up.

Maybe the gay scene was actually his next move. 'I'm a cop, you know,' he said, hoping to fend the man off for good.

'Yeah, I know,' the man said. 'You're an SIO.'

This brought Henry upright. At that moment, something else jarred in his tumble drier of a mind . . . something about a clown and a van. 'How do you know that?'

'Cos I'm a cop, too.'

Henry's mind was definitely hurting now. 'OK, so why have you been following me?'

'My name's Lawrence Bignall,' he said. 'I know who killed Keith Snell . . . and I need protection.'

It took a few moments for Henry to actually remember who Keith Snell was, then, as quick as a brick flying through a window, everything suddenly slotted back into place. And at that exact moment Henry remembered something else which was vitally important, making a connection that, until then, he had been grasping for unsuccessfully.

He stood up. Everything was now clear.

Lawrence Bignall showed Henry his shoulder, peeling back the dressing to reveal an ugly red wound seeping unhealthily.

'Keith Snell did that to me,' he said.

They were sitting in an interview room at Fleetwood police station, Henry having decided to go there because it was quiet, out of the way, and there was less likelihood of an interruption. They had flagged a taxi down on the promenade to take them.

Bignall looked fearfully at Henry. 'I checked myself out of the hospital before treatment was complete . . . I couldn't stay in. It was too dangerous.'

'Why?'

'A feeling. More than a feeling, actually . . . I just knew I was a liability to them . . . and the truth is, I am,' Bignall admitted. 'I got scared and they saw I was scared. I'm surprised he pushed me out at the hospital in the first place.'

'Hold it there,' Henry said. Bignall was far too ahead of himself now. Henry needed to reel him in, rewind right to the beginning, then press play. But even knowing that, Henry still could not resist asking, 'Who's they? And who is he?'

Bignall's face screwed up, and he hesitated. This was one

of those defining moments and both he and Henry knew that. The moment of no return.

'They are the "Invincibles",' he said, 'and he is Phil Lynch.'

A good sign. Henry recalled both in his recently revamped memory.

He remembered sitting in the CID office at the Arena police station in Manchester – seemed like a year ago – and seeing a poster with the word "Invincibles" on it . . . and then he had been introduced to his Single Point of Contact, his SPOC. A detective sergeant called Phil Lynch.

A curious sensation travelled all the way from Henry's heart to what is affectionately known as the 'ringpiece'. He kept a calm, outward exterior, although inside he was almost having a cardiac arrest at this information. When he said, 'Let's take it back to square one, shall we? Tell me in a logical, chronological sequence, then I can understand everything you are telling me,' he did manage to keep a straight face and not jump up and down with excitement.

Two hours later, Henry, Dave Anger and Jane Roscoe were with Bignall. Henry had realized immediately that he could not keep any of this to himself. It was far too big for one man to handle and although it stuck in his gullet to go to Anger, he did it because it was the right thing to do.

Following Bignall's revelations to Henry, he had actually decided to relocate the witness away from any police station. Even though Fleetwood was a pretty quiet backwater, the police family is a pretty small one and word travels fast. He wanted to keep a lid on what was happening, so he contacted Rik Dean, the DS at Blackpool, and ordered – yes, ordered – him to drop everything and pick him and Bignall up at Fleetwood cop shop. Henry did not explain anything to Dean and Dean did not ask. It was unusual enough for Henry to 'order' anyone to do anything – he usually worked by persuasion – so Dean instinctively knew something big was afoot. He kept his questions to himself.

'Take us to headquarters,' Henry said quietly, 'and don't tell anyone anything.'

'OK.' Dean only glanced the once at Henry's less than professional appearance – unshaven and in a tracksuit and trainers.

Henry hustled Bignall out of the police station into the back of Dean's waiting car.

'Any news on Roy Costain yet?' Henry asked Dean in a whisper.

Dean shook his head. Henry shrugged, certain that before the day was out the police would know, at the very least, where Roy was, if not have him in custody. He kept that little nugget from Dean, not wishing to divulge anything just yet.

As they headed out of the fishing town, Henry keyed Dave Anger's number into his mobile and called him.

When he said, 'It's Henry Christie,' Anger barked, 'You're supposed to be off sick and I'm in a meeting, trying to sort out the sorry mess you left behind, actually.'

'I need to see you urgently.'

'Yeah, right . . . your head still playing tricks with you? I'm surprised you can remember who I am.'

'Don't be an arsehole,' Henry found the courage to say, eliciting a couple of very raised eyebrows from Rik Dean at the wheel, and a silent whistle of respect.

'Who are you calling an . . . ?'

'Just shut it and listen, OK,' Henry interrupted firmly. 'This is urgent and I can't talk to you over the phone. I need to see you face to face.'

'About your transfer request, I hope.'

Henry was a pan of water just about on the boil. 'No, it's about the accident . . . and the other stuff . . . the gun, all that. Take this seriously, it's very urgent,' he reiterated.

'OK,' Anger relented unhappily. 'Are you coming to see me at HQ?'

'No . . .' Henry's mind scrambled for a location, suddenly deciding that HQ was not the best place for Bignall. 'The Holiday Inn Express at Bamber Bridge, the new one just built near to Sainsbury's, just off the M6.'

'Why there?'

'Just be there – forty-five minutes, tops,' Henry snapped and folded his phone. He glanced sideways at Rik Dean. 'OK, change of plan.'

'Whatever.'

'And after we've booked in, there's something I'd like you to do for me.'

'Whatever.'

The hotel, as Henry said, was newly built, the paint barely dry. It was situated close to junction twenty-nine, overlooking a very busy part of the A6. Henry's journey took less than thirty minutes, which gave him time to book two adjoining rooms and settle Bignall down before Anger appeared on the scene. He purposely said very little to Bignall, but remained at the window, watching the road for Anger. When he spotted Anger's car going through the traffic lights, two people on board, he called him and told him what room to come to.

'This better be spot on, Henry,' the superintendent said, 'or I'll have your guts, mate.'

Henry simply laughed and was still sniggering superciliously when his mobile rang again, the number calling withheld.

'That you, Henry?'

He recognized the voice at the other end instantly. 'Christ – is that you, too?'

'I'll refrain from saying no, it's not Christ, but I have risen from the dead, so I have a great deal in common with the Messiah.'

'What the hell happened to you?' Henry demanded. Up until last night he had been in regular contact with Karen, Karl Donaldson's wife, who was growing ever more desperate as nothing had been heard about Karl. She was increasingly fearing the worst, as had Henry.

'Long story . . . tell you sometime . . . but just thought I'd tell you I'm fine, Karen's fine, I'm in trouble at the Legat, but what the hell, and that I'm on my way to Manchester to sort out some Spanish business, hopefully. I hear you had a nasty accident, too.'

'Manchester?' Henry ruminated, not hearing the rest of what Donaldson had said after that word. 'Karl, there is one thing I do need to mention to you.' Henry was still by the hotel-room window, watching Anger park up, get out. Jane Roscoe was with him and he squirmed slightly when he saw her climb out of the car, wondering briefly if Anger was fettling her. 'Clown masks . . . black van . . . ring any bells?'

It was a cautious 'Yep, why?' from the American.

'I've been upsetting people in Manchester . . . result was I got forced off the motorway by a guy in a van . . . a guy wearing a clown mask and driving a black Citroën van.'

Donaldson did not respond for a few moments, making Henry think the connection had been lost. He hated mobile phones.

'You still there?'

'Yeah . . . Henry, I need to talk to you before I go snooping around with both barrels,' he said decisively. 'Where are you now?'

Henry told him. 'You?'

'M6 heading north, just before the M62 turn-off for Manchester. I'll keep going. Should be with you in about twenty minutes, traffic notwithstanding.'

There was a knock on the hotel-room door. Henry finished the call and opened the door, revealing Dave Anger and Jane Roscoe standing in the corridor, both their faces set with cynical expressions and their non-verbals indicating impatience verging on infuriation. This told Henry that neither of them was a very happy bunny.

He greeted them warmly, holding back an urge to act like the lunatic they clearly thought he was. 'Come in, please.' They edged past him and caught sight of the man sitting on the bed in the adjoining room.

Anger turned to Henry. 'Who the fuck's that?'

'A witness to a murder . . . Keith Snell's murder.'

Their faces changed dramatically, Henry saw with satisfaction.

To coin a phrase, Detective Superintendent Carl Easton was up to his neck in it, rather like standing in a midden.

The Sweetman trial had been bad enough and the fact that an outside force had been contracted to investigate was not great, but he had totally believed he could wriggle out of that one; what was now giving him more trouble than ever began when he received a phone call.

It came on a particular mobile phone, a number known only to a select few, so he answered it without hesitation. But the voice he heard and recognized within one or two syllables sent an icy spike down into his bowels.

The voice was calm and measured. It was Rufus Sweetman.

255

'Hello, Carl, my friend.'

'Who's this?' Easton demanded, reckoning he did not know.

'You know who it is.'

'How did you get this number?'

'Contacts,' Sweetman said smugly.

'What do you want?'

'My property back – that's all.'

'You got all your property back at court,' Easton reminded him. 'I gave it to you personally.'

'I think you know which property I mean . . . fell off the back of a lorry, so to speak.'

Easton gulped, fell silent.

'Penny dropped?' Sweetman inquired.

'No, don't know what you mean.' He clicked the tiny red button on his mobile and terminated the call. He spun round to Lynch and Hamlet, his two detective sergeants, and stared at them, shocked.

'Who was that?' Lynch said. They were in Easton's office at the Arena police station.

'We've nicked Rufus Sweetman's cocaine,' Easton announced.

Hamlet whistled. 'Way to go!'

Lynch said, 'Effin' hell.'

Easton raised his eyebrows. 'He wants it back . . .' He smiled. 'But he can't have it.' He had opened his mouth to say more when his mobile rang again. 'Sweetman,' he guessed, and answered it. 'Yep?'

'Put it this way,' Sweetman's voice said coldly. 'All we want is our goods returned . . . and if we don't get 'em, one cop will die every day from now on. An innocent cop, that is, not a bent bastard like you.'

Click. Phone dead.

That had been two days before and no cop had died – yet.

One uniformed PC from the city centre was lying in intensive care after being approached by a man who asked for directions and then shot him in the lower gut, below the line of his ballistic vest; another officer had been treated for shotgun wounds to the arm after being ambushed in an alley by a masked gunman. Sheer luck and body armour had saved him.

256

Although the two incidents had not been officially linked, Easton knew they were. He also knew that the effect of the shootings was to terrify all patrol officers, all of them wondering who would be next to take a bullet.

Easton knew he was sitting on a terrible secret, one he could only share with a few people.

Easton had been a corrupt cop for nearly all his service. He took bribes as a uniformed constable back in the '70s, then later accepted backhanders for turning a blind eye or falsifying evidence to suit the circumstances. It was way back then he had started dealing in drugs through his prisoners.

All the while though, he kept an eye on his career because he wanted to combine crime-fighting with corruption – the challenge of a lifetime. Along the way he had carefully nurtured other cops and several of his contemporaries had retired with hefty Spanish bank balances after a few years of working alongside Carl Easton. He had nicknamed his team the Invincibles, because no one had yet beaten them. No one was going to, either, Easton believed.

Also along the way he had destroyed the careers of many criminals, sometimes by fair means, often by foul. He loved sending people to prison, particularly when he had engineered their guilt.

His goal had always been to run two careers in parallel. The cop and the criminal. Ridding the streets of the real bad guys, whilst stepping into their business shoes when they were getting kitted out in prison uniform.

And one of the crims he had most desperately wanted to put away was Rufus Sweetman – a guy who had been operating right under Easton's nose for years on his city-centre patch. He had grown to hate Sweetman – the way he held a middle finger up at the law – and also to covet everything he owned: the apartment on the Quay, Ginny Jensen, the fabulous-looking girlfriend, the house in the Bahamas, the cars, the money.

Sweetman had gradually become an obsession. The man Easton most wanted to destroy.

And whilst this obsession had been simmering, Easton had chanced upon an amazing supplier of drugs. A man he never met, only ever spoke to occasionally by phone. Obviously a

Spaniard or an Italian, but someone who supplied Easton with cut-price drugs with which he cornered a market consisting of young professionals.

How the man knew of him in the first place, he did not know.

Just a phone call from nowhere, two years earlier. This followed by delicate negotiations, Easton drawn by the prospect of drugs which often undercut other wholesalers by 50 per cent. The business had grown using 'his staff' as he called them – the band of corrupt detectives and uniformed cops whose pockets he had lined with cash. Easton's principle was that each arrest, particularly of a professional person (and there were plenty) had potential. Some arrests led into massive drugs markets which produced hundreds of thousands of pounds worth of business.

And all the while, Sweetman hovered teasingly.

In the end Easton decided to bring him down in a way which would ensure that he was off the streets for a long, long time and would also bolster Easton's own standing within the force, maybe even secure promotion. He fitted Sweetman up for murder.

The only thing was, there was no murder.

So Easton 'engineered' one.

The brutal death of Jackson Hazell, the unfortunate man who had fallen out big-style with Sweetman over a drug debt (something widely known in the Manchester underworld, and therefore by the cops, too). He had been kicked to death in an alleyway off Deansgate by three men, one of whom, it was alleged, was Sweetman.

In fact the three men who killed Hazell were Carl Easton himself, Phil Lynch and Gus Hamlet, Easton's core team. They planted some forensic evidence in Sweetman's trash, even verballed Sweetman up; they coerced false statements out of people who owed Easton a favour, which placed Sweetman in the right place at the right time.

And, all things being equal, he should have been convicted.

But the phone calls changed all that, put everything else in doubt, and Sweetman got released.

On that day Easton's team were acting on information from the mystery drug supplier. If they were interested, he said enticingly, there was a mass consignment due into Manchester from the continent. It was theirs for the taking, if they had the bottle. It would set them up for life.

Easton, whilst still at Lancaster Crown Court, had set his team of police officers, led by the murderous Lynch, to pull the job at Birch Services on the M62.

But what they didn't know at that time was that the drugs belonged to Sweetman.

Now they had this knowledge, but it did not concern Easton too much. What did concern him was that cops were now targets of random attacks. At heart, Easton believed his first love was the service, despite his corruption, and he did not really enjoy seeing other officers hurt. That made him angry. It made him want to destroy Sweetman once and for all. At least if he did it, he would make sure that, if the body was found – which it would not be – it would be in Greater Manchester this time.

Dave Anger could not disguise the look of utter contempt as he regarded Lawrence Bignall, a corrupt cop for whom things had turned out very badly indeed. Bignall was on the edge of the bed in the hotel room. Anger and Henry were on the two chairs in the room. Roscoe leaned against the interconnecting door, arms folded, listening to Bignall chatter away. He was talking as if it was just a friendly discussion with mates over a drink, not a life-changing revelation which would have massive implications for the rest of his days.

He shrugged. 'Second divorce, second time of being taken to the cleaners, basically left penniless. Ended up in a shit-hole rented flat, no dosh, plenty of debts . . . I was ripe for the picking.' He said this as though that was OK. He eyed the detectives nervously. 'Sounded like easy money. Deliver this, deliver that, don't fucking ask questions. Fifty quid, hundred quid. Do it once and walk away, that's what I should've done. Do it twice or more and they have you over a barrel. You're fucked.'

'Who's they?'

'The Invincibles they call themselves, like I said. Carl Easton and his crew of jacks. Lynch, Hamlet, Rogerson, Spooner . . . all that lot. Been together for years. Some retire, others come on board . . . like Lynch. He was always unstable as a PC, but he was just the right sort. No conscience . . . They rule the city centre.'

'Tell me about Keith Snell,' Henry said.

'Nobbut a little shit. Snouted for Lynch. Then Lynch started usin' him for deliveries . . . trouble was he wasn't trustworthy. The little shit peeked and got greedy. Fatal error. Put cash in front of someone like that, it changes 'em. Makes 'em avaricious.' He paused for effect. 'Did a runner with twenty-five grand, stupid idiot.'

'And got killed for it.'

'Yep. Thing is, Lynch actually gave him a chance to give it back. Locked him up about, what, ten days ago? Gave him a chance to hand it over . . . yeah, honest . . . but he buggered off with it, scarpered to the big lights of Blackpool, which is where we found him.'

'How did you find him?' Henry wanted to know.

'Paid a visit to his bird . . .'

'Grace?'

'Yeah . . . she wouldn't tell us anything, so Lynch pasted her bad. Then we nearly caught him with Colin the Commando, but he legged it in a stolen car, even though Lynch took a pot shot at him. He gave Colin a smacking, too.'

Henry's eyes narrowed as he mulled over the words, recalling the bullet imbedded in the back seat of the stolen Ford Escort. 'Go on,' he urged, glancing at Anger, who was enthralled by all this.

'Then we got a call from a guy in Blackpool. Gave us where Snell was.'

'Who phoned you?'

'No idea . . . Lynch knows . . . anyway, we tootle into Blackpool and find him in some dive. He takes a pop at us with his shotgun and I get an armful. Lynch gets him in some backstreet somewhere. Then we drive him up to Deeply Vale and set him on fire. Well, Lynch did. I was bleeding to death in the car . . . and the rest is history.'

'Why Deeply Vale?' Anger said.

'Because he thought he was dumping him on GMP, so Easton could then control the subsequent investigation.'

Henry allowed himself an inner smile of congratulation as

he thought back to his ruminations at the murder scene, wondering why the body had been left there. There is always a reason why a body turns up where it does.

'Tell me about the guns,' Henry said. 'What's the history of the gun used to kill Snell?'

'It was his.'

'Whose?'

'Snell's.'

'Snell's gun?'

'Yeah. He'd used it on an armed robbery months ago, one he'd got locked up for, but never got charged with. The gun got took off him – and others that were found at his pad. They're in the property store at Arena, guess they'll be destroyed eventually. I just sneak them out of the store and return them as necessary.'

'How do you manage that?' Anger asked.

'Got a duplicate key to the store and safe.'

'Jesus!' Henry uttered. 'So he got killed with his own gun?'

'Yep, ironic innit?'

Anger was visiting the toilet. Henry and Roscoe were in the room adjoining the one Bignall was in. He was relaxed now that he had got a weight off his chest and he was feeling safe being looked after by trustworthy cops.

Roscoe eyed Henry with some reverence. 'You done good,' she admitted grudgingly.

'Just doing my job, ma'am.'

Roscoe shook her head. 'Is there anything more to uncover in the Tara Wickson dog's breakfast, or have I misjudged you?'

'You decide,' Henry said.

The toilet flushed and a damp-faced Anger came out, obviously having had a wash. He wiped the palms of his hands down his trouser legs, then looked expectantly at Henry and Roscoe, waiting for something. They looked expectantly back.

With a jerk of his head, he beckoned Henry to follow him to the far end of the room near the window, where he spoke in hushed tones. 'This is going to be a massive job. Big implications.'

'Yep,' Henry agreed.

'Needs a careful plan.'

'Yep.' Henry suddenly realized that Anger was drowning here, did not know what to do.

'So,' the superintendent said, 'what I propose is this: over to you, Henry. It's your baby, sort it whichever way you want. Hang back for a while, or wade in, whatever you feel is appropriate. Just plan it, justify it and I'll back you to the hilt.'

Henry's surprise could not be held back. 'Are you sure?'

'Absolutely . . . you've worked hard on this one, you got the break, you get the glory. If you need any authorizations, I'll sort them . . . how does that sound?'

He did not want to dance up and down with glee. Instead he said, 'Good.'

'It's a two-add-two job,' Henry admitted. 'I upset Lynch and his mob . . . ha, the Lynch mob,' he chuckled at his own wit, 'and someone forced me off the road. Coincidence . . . don't think so . . . but, the van was a black Citroën, don't know the number, and it was being driven by a guy in a clown mask. Ring any bells?' he asked for the second time.

Karl Donaldson did not need to consider. The vivid memories of the M62 robbery were still with him. 'Same crew,' the American said. 'Gotta be.'

'Or just a coincidence?'

'Nahh, screw that, definitely same crew,' Donaldson said. 'To bring you up to speed, my trustworthy source, Señor Lopez, set Easton up to steal the coke – part of his master plan to cut off Mendoza's legs. The drugs've been bought with borrowed Mafia money, just another nail in the big man's coffin. His plan is to somehow retrieve the coke and set up his own show. Mendoza has been dealing with Sweetman for a few years, apparently, and all the time Lopez has had his head together with a guy called Grant, one of Sweetman's top men, with a view to stepping in at some stage, getting rid of Mendoza and running the show.'

'How do you know all this?'

'Lopez blabbed, thinking I was on my deathbed.'

'Why didn't Lopez just kill him, or something? Isn't that what they usually do? Far easier than this bloody chess game.'

Donaldson shrugged, open-handed. 'Search me, but Easton

is involved somewhere along the line . . . just another pawn, I guess.'

'So Lopez and Grant want the drugs and want to get rid of Sweetman and Easton, too.'

'Yeah . . . I think the drugs are the key. It's a very big consignment and anyone who gets his hands on it will become very rich. He didn't say it, but the way I think Lopez will play it will be to reckon that Mendoza lost the drugs . . .' Donaldson was thinking hard. Then he had it. 'I know what it is,' he proclaimed. 'If you ask me, he's going to try and outsmart the Mafia too . . . that's it! He gets the drugs, sets up his own network, cuts the Mafia out by saying Mendoza never recovered the dope and voilà! He's rolling in it! What do you reckon? You're the hypothesis guy.'

'Could be, could be,' Henry said non-committally.

'You never get excited about anything,' Donaldson moaned.

'Don't you believe it. But what happens to Mendoza and Sweetman and all the others?'

'That could well be where the bullets in the head come in.'

Donaldson had arrived at the Holiday Inn Express at the same time as Bignall was being loaded into an unmarked police car and driven away to be extensively interviewed by Roscoe at a safe house. It was likely he would end up in Witness Protection, depending on how much they could squeeze out of him. Anger had also left with Roscoe, whilst Henry and Donaldson walked over to the newly constructed Walton Fox pub, next to the hotel. They were drinking coffee at a table outside, watching the busy A6 traffic.

'Do we need to run with this together?' Henry asked. 'One thing could lead to another here.'

'Yeah,' Donaldson said, 'I do.'

'There's one person I need to see before doing anything, though,' Henry said, telling Donaldson who it was. 'But I need a lift – I'm carless.'

They finished their drinks and strolled back to Donaldson's Jeep in the hotel car park. 'Y'know, pal . . . it was a good thing Snell's body was dumped in Lancashire, otherwise Easton could well have been able to cover it all up.'

Henry guffawed. 'Didn't I tell you?'

'Tell me what?'

263

'The body was in GMP.'

'Eh?'

'Yep – definitely GMP.' He stopped and regarded Donaldson. 'Only by a few feet, admittedly, but it was on their patch. I know the ins and outs of that place like the back of my hand. I stole it.'

'Why?'

'Cos I wanted a meaty murder to show that bastard Anger I could do a good job, that's why.'

'You son of a bitch.' Donaldson slapped Henry hard between the shoulder blades and they continued to walk to his car.

'I knew no one would know the difference – except that PC who was convinced it was on GMP, but I'm sure he won't really be too bothered.'

Donaldson laughed heartily as he clambered into the Jeep. Henry dropped in next to him. 'Now you need to tell me about your Spanish jaunt.'

Had he been Spiderman he would have been climbing the walls. However, he was not, but that did not prevent him from trying. He felt like they were closing in on him, inch by dreadful inch; that the ceiling was dropping, going to crush him.

Troy Costain rushed to the cell door and hammered on it, the inspection flap rattling metallically but staying firmly shut. Tears streamed from his eyes as he begged, 'Let me out, you bastards! You fuckin' twattin' bastards. I can't stand this. It's giving me a shedder. Please,' he screamed, hammering louder.

Suddenly an eye appeared at the peephole. Troy jumped backwards into the middle of the cell, where he stood shaking and sweating.

The cell door swung open to reveal the figure of Henry Christie, still clad in the tracksuit he had set off in that morning.

'Henry – thank God you've come,' Troy bawled, sinking to his knees. 'You know I can't stand being locked up. Get me out of here, please. I've done nothing. What's this shit? Conspiracy to murder? What the hell does that mean?'

Henry stepped into the cell. His face was hard and unforgiving. He took hold of Troy's chin and tilted his face up whilst he bent down so they were eye to eye. Henry spoke quietly.

'A friend of yours came to see you to ask for help, didn't he?'

'What?'

'He came in a stolen car, didn't he?'

'I don't know what the—'

Henry snapped Troy's head further back. 'Don't lie, Troy, don't ever lie, OK? Somehow that car ended up in Roy's hands and then he killed Renata . . .'

'What?' Troy interrupted. 'Is that what this is about? Conspiracy to murder?'

'No . . . that's not what this is about,' Henry almost whispered, his eyes wild with menace. 'Your friend was on the run, wasn't he? And somehow the people who were after him found out where he was, didn't they?'

Icy realization dawned slowly over Troy's face.

Henry smiled dangerously. 'Do you know what they did to your friend when they found him?'

Troy's head, held by Henry's hand, shook slowly.

'Killed him. Shot him. Murdered him. And do you know why? Because you told them where he was, didn't you?'

Troy was like a statue now. Henry released the hold on his head.

'Therefore you conspired to kill him.'

Henry let go of him and Troy rose shakily to his feet, moved back and sat down heavily on the bench bed. 'No, I didn't do it for that.'

'You must have known they would kill him,' Henry said harshly. 'I now want the telephone number you called to drop your mate right in this, and I want the name of the guy you spoke to . . . then, maybe, we can start talking about where we go from here. Understand, Troy? You are in the biggest trouble you have ever been in – ever.'

'My mobile phone is in my property. It's one of the last ten numbers in there. The guy's name was Phil – and that's all I know,' he wailed. 'Honest. Keith had twenty-five grand on him and he told me how he'd got hold of it when he was drugged up. I thought I'd be able to get a backhander for telling them where the cash was. I didn't mean to get him killed.'

'Troy – you are the scum of the earth,' Henry said with disgust. 'And while we're about it, you can tell me where Roy is . . .'

Henry left Troy in mental agony in the cell at Blackpool nick, booked out his mobile phone from the property bag in the custody office and tabbed through the numbers Troy had recently called. With the business card that Phil Lynch had given him, Henry soon found that the number Troy had called was indeed that of the corrupt SPOC. Matching the numbers sent a spurt of adrenaline through his system, as the case against Lynch was getting stronger and stronger. It would be a good springboard into the rest of the inquiry into Carl Easton's corrupt team of big city jacks. Henry returned the phone, then ran up to see Rik Dean in the CID office. He thanked him for picking Troy up and asked him to confiscate the mobile phone, which could provide valuable evidence in the murder investigation. He told Dean that, for the moment, Troy was going nowhere, and gave him the whereabouts of Roy Costain. It would be a nice arrest for Dean.

Henry dashed back out to Donaldson, who was waiting for him in the car park, and they drove to Henry's house.

Kate was all over Donaldson like a bad rash, so relieved to see him alive, and once this show of affection was over, Henry almost having to prise them apart, she prepared a quick meal for the both of them. They devoured it, Henry got changed and within twenty minutes they hit the road again, heading speedily across the county to Rawtenstall, Henry's mind now filled with the prospect of an arrest followed by a protracted investigation and lots of arrests. He was going to be busy for quite some time.

It was a closed briefing. Henry, Karl Donaldson, Jane Roscoe, Dave Anger and the ACC Operations, now acting chief in the absence of FB. Henry had decided not to invite Carradine, just to be awkward, but nobody seemed to notice. The show had been well and truly handed to Henry – who had now formally returned to work from sickness.

266

They met at Rawtenstall police station, hijacked the inspector's office once again, imported a few extra chairs into the cramped space and scrummed down behind closed doors.

'There is good evidence against Phil Lynch regarding the murder of Keith Snell.' Henry glanced at Roscoe. 'Although Lawrence Bignall is still being interviewed, he's put enough down on paper to put Lynch right in the frame. There are other circumstantial bits of evidence to support what he says and as far as I'm concerned, we've enough to arrest him now. But, at the same time as we arrest him, I want us to get into the safe in the property store at the Arena police station and seize the guns belonging to Snell.' He paused, taking a breath. 'Those actions will open floodgates, I guess. These could sweep us to the murder and attempted murder of Colin Carruthers, me and the chief. It will also open up links to the job on the M62 where twenty illegal immigrants died in the back of a truck, and from there on, a lot of international stuff – hence the presence of Karl, here, from the FBI.'

'How do you want to play it, then?'

'We need to get Lynch sewn up tight. I want everything done to the nth degree – forensics, house searches, clothing, all vehicles he's had access to gone over by CSI, and I want to find that damned Citroën van. We've already got a lot of this information from Bignall, so my view is we need to act on it quickly. Once Lynch is nailed to the wall, we can go for the others.'

Henry saw nods of agreement. It was a plan and he was open to suggestions, but none came.

'I take it this is OK with everybody?' A murmur of assent came back. He would have liked to see a little more enthusiasm, but there you go. 'Right, let's work out some of the logistics.'

Henry and Donaldson drove out towards Manchester in an unmarked police car. Jane Roscoe sat quietly in the back as Henry whisked them down the M66. Why he had let her tag along with him he wasn't certain. Maybe it was to further demonstrate to her that he was an OK guy.

'It has to be better to pick him up at his home address,' he was saying. 'That way we keep a lid on it. None of his mates need to find out until it's too late for them – hopefully. He lives alone, so there shouldn't be anyone there to blab. It would be nice to keep him under wraps for some time at least.'

The journey did not take long, Henry exiting the motorway at Bury, where Lynch lived on a newish estate in the Walshaw area. Henry had a good idea where it was, especially after refreshing his mind from an A-Z map book he found at Rawtenstall nick.

'Everybody happy?' Henry beamed sitting at the wheel. He was buzzing, but there was no response from the other two, though he knew they were keyed-up for action. Even Donaldson, who would have to remain on the sidelines whilst Henry and Roscoe did the work of making the arrest. 'Soon be there,' he promised, as though to kids.

Henry reached a road where he could not quite be sure whether he should turn off first or second left.

He got it wrong, but it was just as well.

As he flew past the road end he should have turned into, a car drew up to the junction.

'That's him,' Henry snapped, recognizing Lynch at the wheel. He held back the urge to duck down behind his steering wheel and kept going without swerving.

Donaldson eyeballed Lynch, getting a good, if quick, look at his face. 'I recognize him,' he said. 'He's the guy that gave me the hard stare from the back of the Citroën van on the motorway.'

'Nice one,' Henry said, watching Lynch in his rear-view mirror. He pulled out of the junction and turned right, going in the direction Henry had just driven from, towards Bury town centre. 'Need to turn this bus round.'

Following a vehicle on a one-on-one is tricky. To effectively surveil someone travelling on four wheels generally requires at least four cars and, if possible, a motorbike. Henry was kicking himself for failing to anticipate this situation, but then again, he thought reasonably, it's impossible to cover all bases with the limited resources available. But he had not expected to have to follow his target, and this made him twitch a little nervously. Judgement again? He took a breath . . . go with the situation, keep assessing it and do your best, he told himself, gripping the wheel firmly. Then pick the best opportunity to lift Lynch.

'Wonder where he's going?' Donaldson speculated.

Henry slotted in three cars behind, hoping to hell that Lynch was such a confident bastard that it would never occur to him he was being tailed. If he started to use anti-surveillance tactics, Henry would be stuffed at the first junction.

He led them into Bury town centre. Henry had problems staying with him here. Having to hang back all the time meant either missing lights or running them. Henry ran plenty, unscathed more by luck than skill, and stayed with Lynch, who wound through the town and dropped on to the A58, going in the direction of Heywood and Rochdale.

'Doesn't look like he's going to the office,' Henry said.

It was just after eight p.m., getting darker, making following even more of a problem. Henry often had to rely on recognizing the rear light cluster of Lynch's motor.

All three were now getting jittery.

So much for a plan.

As for Lynch, it never entered his head he was being followed. For a start he thought he had done the job on those simpletons from Lancashire. Even though the two cops in the car he had forced into the ARMCO barrier had survived, it had given the Invincibles the chance to regroup and put a better game plan together. Sure, the cops from Lancs would come back, but then the gates would be firmly closed and they would find nothing. The chief constable was hospitalized, the DCI was off sick and Carruthers was now really dead as opposed to just brain-dead. A good job, well done.

Now all that remained was to sort Rufus Sweetman and his cocaine – and that is what he was en route to pull off.

Easton had arranged a meet at a uniquely brilliant location, ostensibly to hand the consignment of drugs back and therefore stop the random shootings of innocent cops. But Lynch knew that no handing over would ever take place. Secretly everyone knew that there would only ever be one outcome, but because the stakes were so high, they were all prepared to take the risk.

Someone was going to die and Lynch was damn sure it would not be him.

He checked his rear-view mirror as he pulled on to the roundabout under the M66. Damn sure . . .

They travelled through the small town of Heywood, then bore right towards Middleton.

'All the best places,' Henry said.

'I don't like this,' Donaldson said.

'Nor me,' Roscoe chimed in. 'Something's happening.'

Henry knew what they meant. That inner voice of the experienced cop, wittering in your earhole. He was hearing it, too. Over his shoulder he said to Roscoe, 'Give Dave Anger a call, tell him where we're up to.'

She nodded.

Henry was now only one vehicle behind Lynch. Traffic was light on the road and maintaining invisibility was getting more problematical. 'He'll clock us soon, if he hasn't done already . . .' Then Lynch's brake lights came on and he turned off the main road. Henry could not follow. He had no choice but to drive on and stop after a further hundred metres.

'I know what's down there . . .' He looked quizzically at his American friend. 'It's the Big City.'

That was its affectionate nickname – the Big City. It was housed in a massive warehouse on the edge of an industrial estate on the outskirts of Heywood, not far from the noise of the M62 at Birch Services. And although it was known as the Big City, it was actually more like a small town. It consisted of a main street, shops on either side, with side streets and alleyways shooting off this main drag, some leading into small squares, others to dead ends. Most of the buildings were merely shells, constructed of plywood, held together by four by two, some were merely frontages like a Wild West film set. Some of the buildings had stairs in them, leading up to first-floor landings and windows, from which rioters could pelt police lines.

There had been many scenes of urban disorder in the Big City, but they were all stage-managed and no one really ended up hurt, because each riot was risk assessed under Health &

270

Safety regulations and it was rare for someone to get hit by a flying fridge these days.

The Big City could be found on the perimeter of an industrial estate and it was the public-order training facility owned by Greater Manchester Police. It was the cops themselves who affectionately referred to it as the Big City, but it was also known by other names, such as Dodge City, or sometimes Moss Side. It was a good place to play and learn, an excellent venue to practise tactics, where things could be made to be very real indeed. Even personnel carriers and the mounted branch could come along.

It was in the Big City that Easton had engineered his exchange meeting with Sweetman.

'It's as good a place as any. There'll be no one around. It may belong to the cops, but it won't be in use. It's private and there'll be no one to interrupt our business.' Sweetman took a lot of persuading, but finally went for it with the proviso that each man could only be accompanied by two others and that no one should be armed. The no-arms requirement was ridiculous, but at least it had to be asked for.

'All I want is the consignment back, then it's over between us. I'll drop the civil case against you, then it's quits, OK. You get out of my life, I leave you be. Business, not personal.'

Easton agreed, knowing there would be no deal. It was all or nothing, and despite the words and the promises, each man knew that.

'In my occasional forays into the uniformed branch, I've taken part in Regional public-order training exercises down there, when all the north-west forces get together and throw bricks at each other.'

'Me, too,' Roscoe piped up, shuddering distastefully. 'I wonder if that's where he's going – and why?'

'If memory serves me correct – and I have had a nasty bang on the head recently – there's not much else down there, just a big industrial estate. So' – he looked at Donaldson – 'what do you reckon? Only one way to tell – on the hoof.' He then twisted to Roscoe in the back. She was dressed in her normal work suit – nice jacket, nice skirt, heels on her shoes, not exactly appropriate dress for traipsing around an industrial estate on a dark evening. 'You stay in the car. Me and Karl'll go and have a snoop around. That OK?' He expected some resistance and maybe some complaint about sexist treatment, but it did not come. She was relieved to be staying in a warm car.

Henry reached for his personal radio.

'Take care,' Roscoe said. Henry gave her a quick sideways glance and caught her eye in a fleeting moment. Something moved inside him, and he knew something had moved within her too, but he tried to ignore it. He was not going down that road again. He gave her a nod and dived out of the car.

He and Donaldson began to walk quickly toward the road junction Lynch had turned down, their heads down, fastening their jackets against the chill of the night.

The street lighting was poor and there was no problem in keeping to the shadows, two dark figures progressing cautiously but swiftly, keeping out of any pools of illumination. It was almost like a country road, overgrown verges on either side of narrow footpaths. In the distance, away to their right, could be seen the orange glow of the lighting on the M62, and they could hear the dull hum of motorway traffic.

Ahead, the road they were hurrying down did a sharp left, but straight on was the entrance to the industrial estate. Henry recalled it well now. It was a very large estate, rambling and untidy, with lots of open space on it, lots of waste ground and some huge units, one of which was the Big City.

Behind them, a car turned off the main road, headlights ablaze. Donaldson immediately pushed Henry to one side and both men dropped low on their haunches into a sodden ditch which was part of the grass verge. They watched the car drive past slowly, three people on board. It stayed on the road, did not go into the estate.

'Make out any faces?' Henry whispered. He could see the whites on his friend's eyes in the available light.

'No . . . looks like a recce, though.'

Henry spoke into his PR, using the dedicated channel for the SIO team. 'Jane, you receiving?'

'Yeah – go ahead.'

'If you haven't done so already, move the car into a more discreet location, will you? We don't want to spook anyone.'

'Done it already.'

'Good stuff.'

Henry and Donaldson were about to rise from their damp position when another car turned in from the main road.

'Getting busy down here,' Henry commented.

The car that had only just cruised by them moments before reappeared from the opposite direction. Instinct made the pair of detectives drop even lower, their bellies almost on the grass. The cars drove slowly toward each other and when they were alongside each other, only a matter of feet from where they lay hidden, they stopped.

Words inaudible to either Henry or Donaldson were exchanged by the people in the cars. Neither man hardly dared to raise his head an inch, but the temptation to have a look-see was overwhelming.

After a brief conflab, the cars separated. The one which had just turned into the road drove straight on into the industrial estate. The other executed a three-point turn and followed.

The two men rose from their secret place when they were sure the cars had gone.

Henry got on to his radio again. 'Jane, call me an old fuddy-duddy, but I think it might be as well if we had some back-up here after all. It's hard to say what might or might not be happening, but I'd rather have it coming and not use it.'

'Yeah – what do you need?'

'Whatever we've got closest to hand. At the very least get an armed-response unit on the way and see if there's any support unit on in the Valley. You act as the RV point. Can you fix it?'

'Yep. I take it you don't want GMP telling.'

'No – just use our people, OK?'

'Roger, will do.'

'And we will maintain radio silence for a while now . . . we're just going on to the estate.'

Crouching and running from shadow to shadow, they set off towards the Big City.

They discovered Lynch's car parked up, unlocked, behind a block of industrial units some way from the Big City. One of the things Henry had always taken pleasure in doing was disabling cars belonging to criminals. He had often done it in his younger days just for fun. Now he took the opportunity to dive under the bonnet of Lynch's motor and yank the spark-plug leads out, whilst Donaldson kept nicks. He knew it wasn't a subtle thing to do, but it would be effective for a short time and might give Henry some advantage. Not knowing how things were going to pan out, he would be happy to gain any advantage. This done, the two detectives moved on, keeping to the building lines of the industrial units and using all cover available, their senses sharp, alert for anything. Both men were nervous, not having a clue what they were getting into.

They emerged from between two units and looked across a road to a huge, detached unit which seemed to go on forever. The bottom half of it was constructed of breeze block, the top half corrugated metal. It had no windows on the side they were looking at. 'This is it,' Henry said. 'The Big City. GMP have it on lease for God knows how many years. It's just like a little high street inside. I think there's even a Burton's shopfront. Lots of alleys, the works. What you're looking at is the gable end, in effect, because the front entrance is round that side.'

Donaldson just nodded. Henry had noticed he had gone extremely quiet, but put it down to tension and circumstance.

They legged it across the road, flattening themselves against the outside wall of the Big City. There was a lot of cover next to the building, several builders' skips, a couple of tractor units, an old van and piles of building materials, all typical of such an estate.

On a signal from Henry, they sidled up to the corner of the building where they crouched under the lee of a skip filled with what looked suspiciously like asbestos. They dropped to their hands and knees and, comically, peeked around the corner, one head above the other, so they could see down the front elevation. It stretched far and there was a big car park and a large porch on the front of the building.

Two cars were parked up. One being one of the two cars Henry and Donaldson had seen minutes before on the road.

Three people were getting out. Henry squinted in the growing darkness, trying to get a good look at them. 'I recognize one of them,' he hissed.

'Mendoza,' Donaldson gasped. 'The guy on his left is Lopez . . . the other will be Sweetman.'

'Father, son and holy ghost,' Henry said less than reverentially. Both men drew back out of sight.

'Struck gold here,' Donaldson said. 'This must be the return of the drug consignment . . . shit . . .'

'What?'

'Don't know about you, H, but I've never known something like this go smoothly for any of the parties. Tears are often shed.'

'I want to see what's going down.'

'Me, too.' Henry thought hard. 'There are several emergency exits dotted around the building, one on each wall, I think. Maybe we could get in through one of them to watch things.'

'Worth a try,' said Donaldson, then clutched his chest. Henry thought he was having a heart attack, but it was actually the American's mobile phone vibrating silently above his heart. 'Shit . . . let me get this.' He scurried away a few steps out of Henry's earshot.

It was rather like a badly built shopping mall, lit by massive, but not brilliant, lights suspended from the metal roof.

They met in the middle of the main street in the Big City.

Easton was flanked by Lynch and Hamlet, their breath visible in the chill air of the industrial unit. Three holdalls had been placed on a trestle table in front of them.

Sweetman, with Mendoza and Lopez at either shoulder and Grant behind them both, like a formation of fighter planes, walked slowly down the road, which had been named, appropriately enough, Ambush Alley by the cops in the public-order units which trained there regularly. Officially it was called simply 'Main Street'. The four stopped, twenty metres away from Easton and his crew.

'I thought we agreed only two assistants,' Easton said.

'He's my solicitor,' Sweetman said, thumbing a gesture at Grant. 'He's here just to oversee the legal niceties.'

'Not a good start to proceedings.'

Sweetman shrugged.

'Is that my property?' He pointed at the holdalls.

275

Easton said it was, then, 'Where do we go from here?'

'You all step back twenty paces, leave the bags where they are and we pick them up. When we've gone, the matter is over. It's that simple.'

'Nothing is that simple,' Easton said.

The seven men stared at each other.

Suddenly the tension was broken by a mobile phone announcing that a text message had just landed. It was Mendoza's and he instinctively pulled it out of his pocket and thumbed the 'read message' button. That was the thing about texts. They were impossible to ignore, even in the most stressful of situations. Mendoza glanced at the display and skim-read the message, his face growing darker with each word he read, as it confirmed something which he had been suspecting for a long time now.

All eyes were on him, but as he replaced the phone in his pocket, looked up and shrugged, everyone's attention returned to the task in hand. Mendoza's mind was on other things as he sidled up to Lopez and smiled broadly at his second in command. He placed an arm around his shoulder and said, 'Soon all our troubles will be over, amigo.' He nodded in the direction of the drugs. Lopez frowned at this out of character display from Mendoza, and he never got the opportunity to put his plan into action. On his signal, he had intended that he and Grant would draw their weapons and start shooting. Grant would take down Easton, Hamlet and Lynch. Lopez would take great pleasure in wasting Mendoza and Sweetman. Then he and Grant would be in business.

The plan never came to fruition.

Mendoza's left arm gripped Lopez's shoulders, and suddenly there was a short-barrelled revolver in his right hand, rising from the pocket into which he had just placed his mobile phone.

Easton was first to see the gun. He opened his mouth and screamed, 'Get down!' He and his two sergeants started to dive, but Mendoza's gun did not even consider them. 'Double-crossing bastard,' he screamed and placed the muzzle of the gun hard against Lopez's right temple and pulled the trigger twice. The two soft-nosed bullets blasted through his brain and virtually removed the left side of his head as they tumbled out on exit. Mendoza's left arm was covered in blood and fragments of grey brain. He let go of the already dead Lopez, threw himself to one side and scrambled for the protection of the shop frontages.

Easton, Lynch and Hamlet all had weapons in their hands now and opened fire at Sweetman, Mendoza and Grant.

Everything that happened from that moment on, until it was all over, lasted perhaps thirty seconds.

Lynch discharged the single barrel of his shotgun at Sweetman, catching him in the upper arm and neck, sending him spinning.

Mendoza fired haphazardly, missing everyone completely, as he dived through the front door of a florist's shop just at the moment Easton fired at him and caught him in the upper thigh. Mendoza screamed as he landed and dragged himself behind the wooden panelling of the pretend shop.

Lynch ran up to the squirming Sweetman, blood gushing out of his neck. He stood over the criminal and racked another shell into the breech of the shotgun – a gun which was once owned by Keith Snell – then blasted his face off, killing him instantly.

'Get the other guy!' Easton yelled, pointing to the open shop door where Mendoza had managed to crawl. Lynch stepped across the bodies of Lopez and Sweetman, racking his gun again.

'That's far enough,' a controlled voice shouted behind all three of the corrupt cops. They spun to see two masked men standing in combat stance not twenty feet away, each brandishing an MP5 machine pistol.

Lynch was the first to react. Teeth gritted, he swung round with the shotgun. One of the men loosed a burst of his MP5, almost cutting him in half.

Easton, outgunned, turned to run and was drilled with about a dozen bullets from the gun of the other man.

Grant and Hamlet remained frozen in time. Hamlet dropped his gun and held up his hands, but to no avail. Both masked men fired simultaneous bursts, lifting both Grant and Hamlet off their feet, spinning them like ballet dancers, before smashing them to the hard ground of Ambush Alley, the Big City.

Teddy Bear Jackman and Tony Cromer did not waste another moment, ditching their weapons, grabbing the three holdalls and running for the exit. They disappeared into the night.

The sound of gunfire was muted through the breezeblock walls of the building, however, it was unmistakable to Henry Christie and Karl Donaldson, who knew exactly what guns sounded like. They had worked their way to the back of the Big City building when they heard the first shot from inside. Neither hesitated, but gave up all pretence of finding another entrance and now hared round to the front entrance, Henry yelling down his PR to Roscoe that they were responding to the sound of gunfire.

By the time they reached the entrance, each man had tried to count how many shots had been fired. At first it had been easy, but when the rapid fire came, it was impossible.

The door was open.

With extreme caution they edged carefully into the warehouse, coming straight on to Ambush Alley. Despite seeing the bodies lying ahead, they moved tentatively towards them, always expecting the worst, both men having pinned their IDs on to the front of their jackets. Not that a badge would have stopped a bullet, but it was a degree of psychological protection.

Henry counted five bodies. One was twitching horribly. He bent down and looked into the man's face. It was Lynch. He was still alive . . . and then he was dead.

'Shit!' he said, then looked at Donaldson, who was hopping from one body to another.

'Can't find Mendoza,' he said. 'He must have done all this.'

'Don't think so. Not alone, anyway,' said Henry, assessing the different wounds to each person. He had seen a lot of gunshot wounds in his time and could tell immediately that this was not the work of one man. 'He might have been part of this, but he had help,' Henry speculated. 'This one's been shot by a shotgun, this one by a pistol, or something, these three have been ripped apart by machine guns.'

'I want Mendoza,' Donaldson said. 'Do not tell me he got away.'

Henry looked round. 'Someone in there,' he said, pointing to the florist's shop. He had seen a splash of blood at the door. With Donaldson he walked carefully to the shop, and as he got closer he could see a man's leg.

'That's him,' Donaldson said, staring down unemotionally at the man who had haunted him for so long, someone he had dearly wanted to see in this position. 'Looks like he's been shot in the leg from here. Bullet must have travelled up into his innards,' he guessed, seeing the vast amount of blood the Spaniard was lying in. He squatted down by the body and carefully lifted Mendoza's jacket, his hand slipping in and coming out with the mobile phone, which Donaldson then slid into his own pocket, without Henry seeing the surreptitious move.

It would not have done for the police to check the phone and find out that the last text message the Spaniard had received had come from Donaldson's mobile, now would it? Donaldson looked up at Henry, then back at Mendoza's body, a cruel smile coming to his face. 'What goes around comes around, eh?

Henry blew out his cheeks. 'Yeah.' He stepped back and looked along Ambush Alley. 'Well, we've got the florist. I wonder if there's an undertaker down here?'

Twenty

The inquest into the death of John Lloyd Wickson, husband of Tara Wickson, and others was convened four weeks later. The proceedings were held at Fleetwood Magistrate's Court. It was a warm day, very clear, with fine views across Morecambe Bay towards the twin nuclear reactors at Heysham and further north to the hills of the Lake District.

Henry parked his car in the police-station yard and walked round to the court buildings situated on the seafront at

Fleetwood. He paused and took in the view. It was not often this clear and he savoured the moment, wishing he was walking or fishing in the hills, instead of having to go through the agony of explaining Wickson's death to the coroner, as well as the associated deaths which were even more difficult to describe and all quite gruesome: The death of the hitman, Verner, who had also killed Wickson and then been assassinated by the unknown sniper. Also in there was the death of another man, Wickson's driver. This was the one that really worried him, because this was the death he had attributed to Verner when, in reality, Tara Wickson had pulled the trigger of the shotgun which had blasted the guy's head off. He had done this for what he thought were the best of reasons – the man, Jake Coulton, had raped Tara's daughter and it had been the anguish of that which had unhinged Tara's mind. On reflection he had acted hastily – to say the least – and now he was going to have to go public with the story he had made up to cover the killing.

To say that he was nervous was an understatement.

If Tara cracked under pressure, all hell would be unleashed.

Dave Anger and Jane Roscoe appeared round the corner, walking from the direction of the car park. Both had been deeply involved in the investigation and their input into the inquest would be vital and telling.

They acknowledged Henry with curt nods and walked past him into the court, leaving him gazing at the view. He could feel his right leg twitching and something building up inside him as powerful as a volcano.

'Henry!'

He had not noticed her approach. He jumped, looked round and saw Tara Wickson approaching, dressed demurely and appropriately in a black suit. She looked stunning, the skirt clinging to her thighs, stopping just above her knees, the heels on her shoes accentuating the shape of her slim legs. Henry's heart seemed to miss a beat as he thought back to the night he had slept with her. He forced the memory out of his mind and waited for her to get level with him.

He hadn't spoken to her since the night he had left Rawtenstall police station and rudely ended a phone call with her. Something he was not proud of, but she had him running scared. That said, she had not tried to recontact him since.

'Hello,' he said stiffly. 'How are you?'

She nodded thoughtfully. 'I'm OK,' she said at length. 'You?'

He shrugged and admitted, 'Worried.'

Her face softened. She reached out and touched his face with her fingertips, something she had done once before. Then it had led to sex. A warm sensation shot down his spine, in spite of himself.

'You needn't be,' she said, looking him squarely in the eye. 'When I phoned you and you hung up . . . It was just to say I'd got my head together, that I was fine, that you'd helped me put things into perspective. I was going to thank you.'

He blew out his cheeks as though he was trying to get a sound out of an imaginary trumpet.

'I'm a big girl now. I realized that Charlotte needs me out here, not in prison, and if I've got to tell a few lies, then so what? She's the bigger picture and Jake Coulton got what was coming to him.'

'I'll have that,' Henry said, feeling relief sluice through him.

'Just a pity we'll never be able to get it together after,' Tara said. 'I know you value your home life and I respect that. I won't be hounding you, or anything. I'll just be out of your life.' Henry saw tears form in her glistening eyes. 'But the love-making was wonderful.'

'It was,' he agreed.

'So, after the inquest, you won't be hearing from me again.' She touched his face. 'See you in court.' She spun on her heels and walked into the building without a backward glance.

Before Henry could feel any regret, he got a whack between the shoulder blades. He staggered and twisted round with an 'Umph!' of breath driven out of him.

'Thought I'd watch the start of proceedings,' FB said with a laugh. 'Come on, let's go and get some good seats.'

The chief constable, now fully recovered from the road accident and more obnoxious than ever, put his arm around Henry's shoulder like he was an old mate and pushed him toward the courtroom doors.